THE GRAVITY OF US SERIES

JUST BREATHE * JUST SURFACE * JUST MELT

KATHRYN KALEIGH

ALSO BY KATHRYN KALEIGH

The Gravity of Us Series

(Reading Order)

Just Breathe

Just Surface

Just Melt

Standalone Suspense

Out of Ashes

CONTEMPORARY

Alpine Falls (Maybe Yours) Series

(Reading Order)

Still Yours (Maybe)

Yours for Christmas (Maybe)

Forever Yours (Maybe)

(ALPINE FALLS)

Stranded in Alpine Falls

Belonging in Alpine Falls

The Spirit of Christmas in Alpine Falls

Christmas Wishes in Alpine Falls

Finding True North in Alpine Falls

A Ghost of Christmas Magic in Alpine Falls

Secrets and Second Chances

Honeymoon with a Stranger

Not Our Wedding

(SILVER PINES)

The Way Back to You

Back to Where We Began

When We Were Us

(ONCE UPON FOREVER)

My Forever Guy

Our Forever Love

Forever Vows

Finding Forever

Accidentally Forever

(TRUE NORTH)

Borrowed Until Monday

Still Mine

The Moon and the Stars at Christmas

Perfectly Mismatched

On the Way to Forever

A Merry Little Christmas

On the Way Home to Christmas

It was Always You

(UNBREAK MY HEART)

Begin Again

Love Again

Falling Again

(FOR THE LOVE OF THE FLIGHT)

Just Stay

Just Chance

Just Believe

Just Us

Just Once

Just Happened

Just Maybe

Just Pretend

Just Because

(MAGNETIC NORTH)

Second Chance Kisses

Second Chance Secrets

First Time Charm

Three Broken Rules

Second Chance Destiny

Unexpected Vows

(FALLING FOR CHRISTMAS)

The Heart of Christmas

The Magic of Christmas

In a One Horse Open Sleigh

A Secret Royal Christmas

An Old Fashioned Christmas

(CITY SKYLINE BILLIONAIRES)

Billionaire's Unexpected Landing

Billionaire's Accidental Girlfriend

Billionaire's Fallen Angel

Billionaire's Secret Crush

Billionaire's Barefoot Bride

(TRULY, MADLY, DEEPLY)

The Lady in the Red Dress

On the Edge of Chance

Sealed with a Kiss

Kiss Me at Midnight

The Heart Knows

(STOLEN ECHOES)

When Cupid's Arrow Strikes

Chasing Fireflies

A Chance Encounter

(EDGE OF THE HORIZON)

The Forever Equation

Pretend Boyfriend

All our Tomorrows

Kissing for Keeps

Out of the Blue

The Princess and the Playboy

(RED LIPSTICK KISSES)

Red Lipstick Kisses and Small Town Wishes

Stolen Dances and Big City Chances

Chance Connections and Upside Down Plans

A Christmas Kiss on the Twenty-Fifth

Believe in the Magic of Christmas

Vows of Inheritance Series

(Reading Order)

Vow to Protect

Vow to Redeem

ROMANTASY

(IN THE SPIRIT OF LOVE)

Spirits of the Heart

Out of Dreams and Ashes

Etched Upon the Heart

WESTERN ROMANCE

(LONE STAR HEARTS)

Wanted by a Texas Ranger

Saved by a Texas Ranger

(WHISKEY SPRINGS)

Finding Natalie

Promising Samantha

Falling for Allyson

Saving Savannah

Claiming Charlie

Rescuing Keira

Protecting Gabriella

Courting Isabella

TIME TRAVEL

(INTO THE MIST)

Written in the Wind

Scripted in the Stars

Destined in the Twilight

Promised in the Mist

Trapped in the Melody

(DRAGON'S BLOOD)

Dragon's Blood

Lavender Blue

Champagne Silver

Twilight Frost

Mountbatten Pink

(WHEN HEARTSTRINGS BECKON)

Rescued in Time

Meet me in 1879

(WHEN HEARTSTRINGS ECHO)

Messages Across Time

Falling Through to Forever

Once Upon a Winter's Spell

(BECKONED)

Before the Storm

Twist of Fate

When the Stars Align

Once Upon a Christmas

Once in a Blue Moon

A Wish Upon a Star

(BEGUILED)

When Lightning Strikes

Storm of Time

Midnight Storm

When the Moon Falls

Stormborn Angel

(SPELLED)

Time Tempest

The Heart Remembers

A Moment in Time

Moonlight Shadows

HISTORICAL

(TAPESTRY OF BLUE AND GRAY)

Shadows Beneath Magnolia Blooms

Secrets Among Southern Roses

(IT HAPPENED BY ACCIDENT)

Accidentally Alluring

Accidentally Married

(SOUTHERN BELLE CIVIL WAR)

Beyond Enemy Lines

Love Always

Hearts Under Siege

Hearts Under Fire

Away Down South in Dixie

The Reluctant Bride

Stay with Me

Jasmine Kisses

Magnolia Kisses

Gardenia Kisses

(THE QUINNS)

Wait for Me

Take Me Home

Keep Me Safe

FATED MATES

Riley's Mate

Aiden's Mate

Brayden's Mate

STANDALONE SUSPENSE

THE GRAVITY OF US SERIES

KATHRYN KALEIGH

HE WILL RISK IT ALL
TO PROTECT HER

Just

BREATHE

THE GRAVITY OF US SERIES

"Audrey?" Bradley asks.

I blink and realize he must have been talking to me.

"I'm sorry. I was thinking about something else." I do it all the time. My family is used to it and it doesn't bother them, but he's looking at me like something's wrong with me.

"I was just asking how much milk you like in your coffee."

"Oh," I say. "Enough so it doesn't taste like coffee. Or motor oil." Geez. I'm not fit to be around other people. Brianna and Lilah were right. I should have brought them.

Bradley gives me a little grin, then as he makes the coffee, I twist at my wedding ring.

He'd asked about my husband. People are going to ask. I'm going to have to tell them. There's no way around it.

Bradley hands me a cup of hot coffee. I take it from him and set it on counter.

"You asked what brought me to Whiskey Springs."

"Just making conversation. You don't have to answer."

"This house belonged to my husband's grandfather."

"Theodore Albright."

"Yes. And now it apparently belongs to me."

Bradley sets his mug down, too. Leans a hip against the kitchen island and studies me.

"Last I heard it belonged to a fellow named Thomas Albright. He sold it to you?"

"No. I inherited it."

He tilts his head to the side and looks at me. "I'm a little confused now."

"Thomas Albright was my husband."

"Was." I can see him putting things together. *Was. Inherited.*

"I know it's confusing because I didn't take his name."

"Not unusual."

Apparently somehow word about Thomas's accident had not traveled to Whiskey Springs.

"Thomas Albright was killed in an airplane crash two weeks ago." I straighten my shoulders and force myself to follow through with the words. "I'm his widow."

Audrey

Houston, Texas

I BECAME a widow on a stormy Tuesday evening.

I'd just locked up the art gallery on McKinney Street and pulled out of the parking garage when the sky opened up. Blinding rain hammers the roof of my Toyota Camry, loud and relentless, like the storm had been holding its breath until I left work.

My windshield wipers fight hard, but the downpour blurs everything—the road, the streetlights, the familiar city skyline. Sheets of water pour down the window.

Even through the strong new car scent, I smell the rain.

Clean and fresh. Washing away the dust of southern humidity.

Normally, I like the rain. It makes the world feel quieter, softer somehow. But not tonight.

I slow at the intersection, squinting through the blur of headlights and storm. Typical spring in Texas—clear skies one moment, flooded roads the next.

I dread the drive home. Even with a straight shot on Interstate 10, it's still a long drive out to Katy. It's a mystery to me and probably always will be just why Thomas wanted to buy a house out in the suburbs when I worked downtown and he spent most of his time at the airport north of town.

So every day, often even on weekends, I get in my car and head east toward downtown while he gets in his car and heads north toward the airport.

As an airplane pilot, he spends the night away from home at least once a week. In his defense, I guess he thought I would be safer out in the suburbs. But the drive...

I hadn't complained. Not when the three-story house, all stone and glass, with its manicured lawn was so pretty. And new. The new house with its brand new appliances. No one else has ever lived in it before us. Considering it was my first house after living in apartments, I'm pretty happy once I get inside.

The gallery had hosted an event tonight for two very different artists. One of them was known for realistic photographs and the other for abstract watercolors.

Two artists, more different in every way possible, couldn't have been paired together even if we'd tried. Concurrent hosting is new. Something suggested by the new CEO to increase profits.

My job was easy. My job was to make sure everyone else did their job. The hostess. The caterer. Other than that, I spent most of my time talking to guests.

When the first phone call from a number I don't recognize shows up on my dashboard screen, I let it go to voicemail. After an evening of talking to people, I just want time to decompress. That's how I typically use the drive home. I'd replay the evening. Catalog everything away in my head and make room for a glass of wine and a book.

Thomas is on an overnight trip tonight to Austin, so it's just me. I'm looking forward to getting out of my heels and cocktail dress, grabbing a glass of wine, and curling up on the sofa in front of the fireplace with a romance novel.

Thomas and I usually watch a movie or binge watch some series or another, but when I'm alone, I'm content to just spend the evening quietly reading. My go to evening activity before I met Thomas.

The second time my phone rings, I hit the button and send the caller straight to voicemail. I don't need a distraction from driving right now. Not in this thunderstorm.

As though to support my decision, a flash of lightning splits the sky just as I merge onto the interstate followed by an ear-splitting crash of thunder that makes the air tremble.

The third time my phone rings, I'm nearing the outer loop, still gripping the steering wheel, cringing as every car rushes past, sending an extra spray of water onto the windshield. A quick glance tells me it's the same number calling. A local number.

My family lives in Atlanta, so it's either a wrong number or work. This time of night, just after ten, I'm going with wrong number.

But it could be someone with a problem related to the art gallery and as the manager, I'm responsible. I press the answer button on my steering wheel.

"Hello."

"Ms. Albright?"

"This is Audrey." I didn't take Thomas's last name and it rather annoys me that people always assume that I did.

Not that there's anything wrong with a woman taking her husband's name. I just hadn't. And it seems like people shouldn't make assumptions.

"This is John with the FAA."

"The FAA." My stomach knots. "I think you meant to call Thomas's number."

He's quiet for a moment. "Are you driving?"

"Yes." Thunder crashes again and I grip the steering wheel with both hands. Despite the rain and diminished visibility, cars and big eighteen wheelers fly past me on either side.

I just want to be home.

"I hear the storm," he says. "Can I call you back?"

"Sure. But Thomas isn't available."

"It's okay," he says. "I'll call you back."

"Sure thing," I say and disconnect the line.

How had John from the FAA gotten my phone number and why is he calling Thomas late at night?

It probably has something to do with Thomas's return flight home tomorrow. Probably delayed. Thomas, like all pilots, has a lot of delayed flights. It comes with the territory.

Thomas and I haven't known each other all that long all in all. We'd worked together a short time on the annual staff in college, but he'd been a senior and I'd been a sophomore. Four years after he'd graduated and moved on, he'd walked into my art gallery. That was about a year ago.

Although he'd remembered me, I hadn't recognized him right away.

Six months later we were married.

Thomas always seemed to be in a hurry to do things. He'd been in a hurry to get married. In a hurry to buy a house. He just didn't have much sense of delayed gratification. I'd teased him about it, finding it a bit endearing.

And he was charming enough that he was able to convince me to go along with most things. With me being one of the least impulsive people I knew, he amused me. I rather liked that he pulled me out of my comfort zone on occasion.

I exit off the freeway and head toward my gated neighborhood.

Katy, oddly enough, typically has more traffic than downtown, but this time of night, the roads are pretty much empty.

I drive through the gate, make the five turns required to get to my house, then pull into the garage. Turn off the motor and open my door to the welcome quiet.

The storm still rages outside, but inside the garage, it's blissfully quiet.

It's usually not so bad going from one garage to the next. Even when it's brutally hot outside. Work to home. The rain, however, makes the drive tricky and tonight was one of the worst storms I've driven through.

But I made it.

I let myself inside and head straight upstairs to the bedroom to change clothes.

Just as I step out of my heels, my phone rings again. I pull it out of my purse and glare at the number.

It's the same number. John from the FAA.

"Hello John," I say. "Do you have my husband's phone number?"

"Yes," he says. "But it's you I need to talk to."

I sit down hard on the little bench in my closet as realization slams into me. Glancing over at Thomas's clothes, neatly hung and organized, I smell his cologne from where he'd gotten dressed earlier in the day.

Thomas always calls when he lands. I'd gotten so busy with the gallery event and then driving in the storm, I only now realized that I hadn't heard from him.

I glance at the time. He should have landed about three hours ago. Three hours.

I'd been so distracted, it hadn't even occurred to me until this minute that he hadn't checked in.

"Why? Has something happened?" I ask, remembering that I'm on the phone with John with the FAA. "He should be in Austin." I have an overwhelming urge to hang up and dial Thomas's phone number. "The storm..."

"Yes. The storm that's over Houston now came down from the west."

"So Thomas got delayed." That would explain things. He got delayed and he didn't call because he knew I had an important event tonight. But that didn't explain why John from the FAA was on the phone with me.

"He didn't get delayed."

I thought for a minute. Thomas had taken me flying plenty of times. He'd taught me some basics. Flight plans. Weather reports. He was careful.

"A detour then. They had to detour him to another airport." Despite my optimist words, there's a knot forming in the pit of my stomach.

"He radioed in with engine trouble."

"Engine trouble? Emergency landing then." Panic is in my voice now replacing the annoyance. My phone is on speaker, but I'm surprised the phone itself doesn't crack with my herculean grip.

"Audrey. We lost contact with your husband's plane about five pm."

CHAPTER
TWO

Audrey

Two mornings later, I wander downstairs, wearing sweatpants and a t-shirt, my hair pulled back in a messy ponytail, where my two sisters are in the kitchen.

"Who are these people?" I ask, mostly to myself. I don't expect an answer.

There are people in my house. I don't like people in my house.

I didn't invite them.

Neighbors from the looks of them.

People I've never even met.

Sitting on my sofa. Talking in hushed tones. Light chuckles. Furtive glances in my direction.

We stand behind the island looking out over toward my living room.

Lilah, the youngest, is cutting an apple pie into slices and placing them on plates. Not saying much of anything.

Brianna, a year younger than me, stands next to me, hands on her hips.

"That's Mark and Mary sitting together on the sofa. They live two houses down on the corner. Melissa is sitting on the hearth in front of the fireplace. Her husband Kevin is standing next to her. They live next to you on the other side. And the guy standing at the patio door looking out is Bert. He's the president of your Home Owner's Association."

I look at Brianna, my mouth open in awe. "How do you know this? Never mind." Brianna talks to everybody. She never meets a stranger. But even more important. "How do they even know about Thomas?"

"It was on the news," Lilah says, washing the knife.

"It was on the news?" I ask Brianna.

Their gazes land on me at once—startled, uncertain, as if I've just confessed something unthinkable.

"It's okay," Brianna says, pulling me into a hug. "You're okay."

Lilah puts the knife away and arranges the saucers of pie slices on a tray.

I groan when the doorbell rings. "Why so many people?"

"I'll get it," Brianna says. "Lilah. Give Audrey some pie."

"I'm not hungry," I say, but I sit down at the breakfast table, and take the fork Lilah hands me.

I'm still feeling groggy. Someone, Brianna I think, gave me something to help me sleep last night. I'd slept for... I glance at my watch... twelve hours. I never sleep that long.

After distributing the pie to my guests, which makes absolutely no sense to me, Lilah sits down next to me with her own piece of pie.

"It's good, huh?" Lilah asks as she takes a bite. Lilah never eats sweets. Things must be really bad for Lilah to eat pie.

"Yes." Surprisingly so. "Who made it?"

"HEB I think. I don't know who brought it."

Brianna comes back from answering the front door with a man wearing a suit in tow.

I glance at him out of the corner of my eye, then take another bite of pie. I have a good case of not caring. Learning that one's husband was killed in an airplane crash will do that to a person.

"This is Andrew Harrington," Brianna says, then lowers her voice. "Your attorney."

Alarmed, I look up at Andrew Harrington. "I have an attorney?"

He holds out a hand. "I'm Andrew," he says, kindly.

I set my fork down and put my hand in his.

"Is there someplace we can talk?" he asks. "In private."

"Lilah, get Mr. Harrington some pie, would you?" She

turns back to Andrew. "Give me ten minutes and I'll have everyone out of here."

Andrew sits down across from me and dutifully eats the slice of pie Lilah puts in front of him.

Brianna takes the empty tray back into the living room.

"Thank y'all so much for coming," she says in what I recognize as her sweetest voice. "But we're gonna need a bit of privacy now."

Five minutes later she has my five unwanted guests herded out the door.

"We can talk now," she tells Andrew as she sits down at the table.

With Lilah on one side of me and Brianna on the other, I brace myself to hear what the attorney I didn't know I had has to say.

THREE

Audrey

"I've gone over all the paperwork," Andrew Harrington, Attorney says, taking a pair of wire-rimmed glasses out of his pocket and putting them on.

With the pie cleared away, I sit with my hands in my lap, watching him with heavy eyes.

He seems like a kind man. He has kind eyes and his tone is soft and understanding. Even so, it doesn't do much to keep the lump in my throat at bay.

The single word *widow* keeps swirling through my head. I'm too young to be a widow.

"I'm sorry," Brianna says glancing over at me. "Would you repeat that?"

"Sorry," I say, under my breath. My sister somehow knew my attention had wandered.

"Sure," Andrew says, looking into my eyes.

"Thomas made me executor of your estate, so I consulted with your accountant. I can skip over some of the details for now, but let me just boil it down.

"I'm afraid you're going to have to sell the house."

I blink at him. "Okay." Last night when the thought of living out here in Katy by myself crossed my mind, I'd shut it down. It wasn't something I could wrap my head around. But here he was bringing it up.

"You're okay with that?" Andrew asks.

"She needs to think about it," Brianna says.

"No," I say. "I don't need to think about it. I'm okay with it."

"Good," Andrew says. "That's good."

"So she'll have money, right?" Brianna asks. "From the sale of the house and insurance. She'll have insurance to start over, right?"

Frowning, Andrew rubs a hand over his face and removes his reading glasses.

"I regret to tell you the insurance is already allocated," he says.

"Already allocated?" Brianna says. "For what?"

"Thomas had some debt. Some rather large debts and even larger obligations."

Brianna looks at me. "What kind of debts did Thomas have?"

"I don't know. I didn't know he had any debts." I look outside at the mimosa tree Thomas had planted. He'd been so proud of himself when he'd dug that hole all by himself and dropped the five-foot tall tree we'd hauled from Home Depot into it.

"What kind of debts?" I ask Andrew.

"He had some pretty significant credit card debt, another mortgage, and—"

"Wait." Brianna holds up a hand. "Another mortgage?"

Andrew glances at me. Sits up a little straighter. "He has a condo in downtown Houston."

"Since when?" I ask. Thomas had never told me about him having another condo. When we'd met, he'd lived in an apartment near the Galleria.

"We can come back to those details."

"No. The condo is a mistake. There's no condo." I feel a little dizzy. A little faint. If there was a condo, I should know about it.

"Five years. It's not a mistake."

I steel myself for the sudden realization that I hardly knew Thomas at all. "Tell me why. Why did Thomas have a condo he never told me about?"

Neither one of my sisters says anything as I wait for Andrew to tell us these things about my husband. Things I hadn't known. Things I should have known.

"The child," Andrew says. "Thomas has a child."

I squeeze my eyes closed and Brianna grips my hand.

Lilah watches us all closely, then turns on Andrew. "You came all the way out here just to tell her this?" I hear the anger in Lilah's voice.

"It's okay, Lilah," I say, looking at her.

"No. It's not okay." She pins her gaze on Andrew. "If you don't have something good to tell Audrey, you can go. Can't you see she's already devastated?"

"I'm so sorry," Andrew says. "But I do have good news."

All three of us just look at him. A gust of warm Texas wind flutters a branch of the mimosa tree against the window.

"His grandfather left him a cabin. It's just outside a small town in the Colorado mountains."

"Who does that go to?" Brianna asks with obvious ire in her tone.

"It's protected. According to the grandfather's will, in the event that something happens to Thomas, it specifically goes to Thomas's first wife."

"Am I his first wife?" I ask, my voice sounding small. I no longer trust anything I thought I knew about my marriage.

Thomas has a child. A child with someone else. He'd never told me about having a child.

"Yes," Andrew says. "You're his first wife."

"The cabin is free and clear of any debts." He clears his throat. "There's a stipend that comes with it."

"So I own a house in Colorado?"

"Yes. Sort of. It's in a trust. It's yours but you have to live in it. You have to live in the house for one year for it to be yours. As long as you live there, you get the stipend that comes with it. But you can never sell the house."

"Thomas said we'd go to Colorado one day. I thought he meant we'd go there for a vacation."

"Audrey can't just move off to Colorado," Brianna says. "She has a job here. A life. Family."

"The cabin is paid for?" Lilah asks.

"Free and clear. All expenses paid by an executor."

"It must be a dump," Brianna says. "She can't live in a dump."

"It's not a dump," Andrew says.

"You've seen it?" Lilah asks, pinning Andrew with her gaze.

"No. But I've seen photos."

"Who's the executor?" I ask.

"I am," Andrew says.

Brianna sits back and crosses her arms. "It sounds fishy to me."

"What town?" I ask. "What town in Colorado?"

"Whiskey Springs."

Whiskey Springs. I'll think about it. Maybe something will come to me. A conversation. A mention.

But I know it won't. Just like the child. Apparently Andrew was a vault when it came to his personal life.

"How much is the stipend?" Lilah asks.

"The stipend is one million dollars."

"In lieu of millions of dollars in insurance," Brianna says, through gritted teeth. "The wife gets stuck with a cabin in the middle of nowhere and a million dollars. It won't last anytime." She looks at me. "You should contest the will."

"He has a child," I say. I don't even know who's side I'm on at this point. I'm just numb. Trying to hold all this information in my groggy brain and process it.

"So? He should have told you."

"And he shouldn't have died," I say. What I don't say is I shouldn't be a widow. I should not be a widow at twenty-seven.

"Ladies," Andrew says. "I'm going to leave some papers for you to look over. I'd like to come back in a couple of days after you've had some time to absorb everything."

My sisters glare at him.

"Okay," I say. "I need time to think about everything. And right now I'm very tired."

"I understand. I hate to be the one to drop all this on you. But..." He pulls a stack of papers from the briefcase at his feet. "There's one thing I think I need to clarify."

"Okay."

"The stipend. There's enough money in the account to last all of your lifetimes put together and it's in an account that compounds daily." He leans forward, his gaze locked on mine. "The stipend will be deposited in your account the day you sign the papers. One million dollars. Every year. In perpetuity."

FOUR

Audrey

"She can't go," Brianna says.

"She can't not go," Lilah says.

The three of us sit in my living room on the big sectional with nothing but the flames from the fireplace for light. The contract papers are scattered in front of us on the coffee table. Already dog-eared and highlighted.

It's dark now. After Andrew had left, I'd gone upstairs to take a nap. It seems like I can't get enough sleep.

Without reading it, I left the paperwork with my sisters to examine. And they had. I'll read it all later. Tomorrow maybe.

They'd gone through everything line by line. Brianna worked for an attorney for a year so she'd felt qualified to go through the paperwork line by line. Then she and Lilah had discussed it while I slept.

They'd even sent it over to our Uncle Carl. Uncle Carl is an attorney.

After I'd gotten up, they'd had pizza delivered of which I'd eaten all of one slice.

Not content with me eating just one slice of pizza, Lilah had made popcorn and set it out. I grab a handful and nibble on it.

"Audrey doesn't know anything about the mountains."

"How much different can it be than Katy?" Lilah, obviously not a fan of Katy, wrinkles her nose and picks up a bowl of popcorn. She doesn't eat sweets, but she'll eat anything salty. All ninety-five pounds of her.

"Have you ever been in the mountains?"

"She'll be fine. It's not just a cabin. It's a big house and it has maid service."

"I don't trust it." Brianna sits back and crosses her arms.

"You do know I'm right here," I say.

They both turn and look at me. I honestly think they had forgotten I was sitting right here.

"Of course we do," Brianna says.

"Is that in the contract?" I ask. "The maid service?"

"Yes," Lilah says, her face brightening. "We pulled up pictures on the Internet. Do you want to see them?"

"Sure." I shrug. I'm curious. For a lot of reasons. Not the

least of which is why Lilah is suddenly fighting against Brianna for me to go to the cabin.

She links her phone to the big screen television—one of Thomas's prized possessions—on the wall over the fireplace and pulls up Google Earth. Types in the address.

"I see a lot of trees." Squinting, I lean forward. "And a rooftop. I can't tell anything about it."

"See," Brianna says. "It's blocked or something."

"It might be blocked," I say, munching on popcorn. "Some private residences are."

"You're both missing the point," Lilah says. "It's big. It's not just a cabin."

"Andrew said he has pictures. Did you ask him to send them over?"

They both look blankly at me. Then they look at each other.

I locate his business card on the coffee table and send him a text asking for pictures.

"Now," I say. "We just wait. He'll send..."

My phone vibrates.

"He must have been waiting."

"You have photos?" Lilah asks. "Put them up on the television."

I have three photographs. The first one is of the outside of the house.

"It looks like a lodge," Brianna says. "Two stories."

"Three if you count the attic." Lilac stands up to move

closer to the television. "Look how pretty it is. It looks a log cabin but with glass. Look at all the windows. "

"We don't know how old the photos are," Brianna says.

Lilah turns on her. "Since when did you become so negative?"

"Since my sister is thinking about moving to the other side of the world to live."

"It's not the other side of the world," I say, keeping my eyes on the photo. Taking in the what is supposed to be a cabin, but looks more like a lodge just as Brianna pointed out.

"Couldn't be much worse than Katy," Lilah grumbles.

I don't say anything, but I tend to agree with Lilah. Something about the place looks so peaceful.

"Thomas never said anything to you about it?" Lilah asks.

I shake my head and lower my gaze to my phone.

"Lilah," Brianna admonishes.

"It's okay. We have to talk about him eventually." I slide to the next photo.

The inside of the cabin looks surprisingly modern with lots of light. An open floorplan much like this house.

"Look at that view," Lilah says. "You can sit in your living room and look out at the mountains."

"If she goes," Brianna says.

"I wonder if it's furnished," I say.

"It is. Fully furnished."

"That might not be the same furniture it has now."

"Brianna. Stop it."

"It doesn't matter," I say. "I don't need a lot. And with the stipend if I don't like it, I can replace it." I slide to the next photo.

"Look at that fireplace," Lilah says. "I think that's real wood."

Brianna bites her tongue.

"I can learn how to light a real fire," I say, knowing what Brianna is thinking. "How hard can it be?"

No one says anything for long enough that I shift my gaze to Lilah, then Brianna.

"You lost," Lilah says to Brianna.

"I know."

"Lost what?"

"The bet. I bet that you would be. Brianna bet that you wouldn't. I won."

"I haven't decided yet."

"You can't not go," Lilah says.

"She can live with me," Brianna offers.

"In your one-bedroom apartment? No thank you."

"Our parents."

I'm already shaking my head. "I'm definitely not moving back to Atlanta."

"By the way," Brianna says. "Our parents will be here in the morning."

"They should have just driven," Lilah says. "They'd be here by now."

"It's too hard on them. They're too old."

"They didn't have to come," I say. But I knew they'd be here for the funeral.

"It'll be good," Brianna says. "They can help pack."

"So they're too old to drive, but not too old to help pack?"

Brianna shrugs.

"Again. No need. I'm going to pack up my personal things and let the rest go with the house." I look up at the photo on the television. "It looks like my next place has everything I need."

Lilah is right.

I'm going.

Moving to Katy hadn't been my idea, but I'd gone along with it.

And Thomas had left everything to a child I hadn't even known he had.

And he might not even have known about it or intended it, but he'd left me a cabin in the mountains. Along with a healthy stipend.

I'm not going to let this opportunity slip by me.

CHAPTER
FIVE

Bradley Winslow

I FILL a mug with hot coffee, black, and take it outside with me. My dog, Biscuit, follows along at my heels.

Biscuit is a solid black lab that just showed up at my door one day. He was just a puppy. Probably ran off or someone ran him off. That was a year ago. Even now he's still pretty much a gangly puppy.

Sitting in one of the two wooden chairs on my deck, I stretch out my long legs, crossing them at the ankles, and take my first sip. The first sip always reminds me of drinking motor oil. Not that I've ever actually tasted motor oil. But if I did, I have little doubt there would be a resemblance.

My breath sends up a plume of smoke into the icy air and I set the mug on the little side table next to me to shove my hands in my warm pockets.

Biscuit lies down at my feet and tucks his head beneath his front paws.

The view from my deck couldn't be more perfect.

The cabin is remote by any standards. Five miles from the little town of Whiskey Springs, nestled high in the mountains along a winding mountain road. Technically not the end of the road, but the end of the road for all intents and purposes. It's been years since anyone lived in the cabin higher in the mountains. About once a week, a couple of women drive up and do whatever they do to check on it.

The snow-capped peaks, high above the tree line makes a wall to my west giving me an early sunset. The magnificence of it makes the early loss of daylight more than worth it.

Sloping down from my cabin, is a blanket of blue wildflowers stopping at the edge of little bubbling stream. The stream is currently swollen with snow melt.

A little doe stops at the edge of the stream, twitches her ears, then bends her neck for a drink of water.

A sure sign of spring. Already June. A late spring this year.

It's going to be a mild summer. We're going to need a lot of firewood for the cabins. More than usual.

That won't be a problem. My brother Wyatt is already on it. I heard the crack of his axe drifting through the valley just yesterday. Wyatt is old school. We have equipment, but Wyatt likes to heave the axe. I don't know if it's to keep himself in shape or to get out frustrations or to feel connected to our grandpa who chopped everything by hand in his day. Probably a little of all of the above.

Wispy clouds are drawn to the mountain peaks as early morning mist rises from the spruce and aspen and pine trees.

Today I've got to do some work in the Bentley cabin. Some major updating actually. My family owns thirty-seven cabins in and around Whiskey Springs at last count. One of those cabins, this one, I claimed for myself. My two brothers each claimed one for themselves, too. The other thirty-four are for tourists. Our busiest seasons are summer, of course, and oddly enough Christmas. People flock to Whiskey Springs for the trails and quiet serenity in the summers and the town's holiday festivities in December.

Our grandpa was a descendant of one of the first settlers of Whiskey Springs and he'd turned out to be a real estate mogul in his own right.

Somewhere along the way, someone had started naming the cabins by whoever they were bought from. So the Bentley cabin was one my father purchased from the Bentley family.

On occasion we'll flip one of the cabins when one of the

tourists falls in love with it and wants to buy it. We don't have a problem with that. About once a year, my brothers and I will find a nice spot and build a cabin from the ground up. Another tradition started by Grandpa. That man had more energy than anybody these days. They don't make them like that anymore.

We usually name the new cabins after the first person who rents them out or we name them after a pet. Or whatever seems to fit.

Last year, I'd started calling one Aspen Grove because it sat right smack in the middle of grove of aspen trees and the name had stuck.

Picking up my mug, the coffee cooled enough now to drink, I look to the east.

Misty tendrils drift up from the trees in that direction, too.

But then I smell it. Chimney smoke. I didn't light a fire in my fireplace this morning. Not enough time to enjoy it. But I know chimney smoke when I smell it.

I stand up and walk to the edge of my deck, put my hands on the rough wooden railing and lean over to get a better look. Biscuit jumps up and goes with me, ready for any adventure.

I pull my phone out of my pocket and dial my brother Caleb's number.

"Hey," I say. "Heard any rumors about anyone staying up at the Albright place?"

"Good morning to you, too," Caleb says.

"Sorry if my level of morning chipperness isn't up to your standards. But have you?"

"No. But it's not our cabin, so I might not hear about it."

"If we bought it, we could keep an eye on it."

"If they would sell it, we would buy it. You just don't like anyone close by."

"Probably kids again. I'll head up in a bit and run them off."

"Want me to call the sheriff?"

"No need. I'm perfectly capable of running people off on my own."

"I have no doubt about that."

"See you at Mom and Dad's tonight to go over plans for this year's cabin?"

"Wouldn't miss it."

I disconnect the line and slide my phone back into my pocket. With the shift in the wind, I can definitely see smoke coming from the Albright chimney. Doesn't look like anything to be alarmed about. Just smoke from a fireplace. It has three of them.

Technically it's not a cabin. Technically it's a manor. A house more suited to Vail or one of the larger, more affluent towns. Unfortunately, it's been neglected and left to run down. Probably been a good ten years since anyone lived in it. A house has to be lived in or it dies. Strange but true fact. I've seen it one too many times. I've also watched houses come back to life with a good dose of updates and care.

Maybe it's time we make another run at the Albright

family about buying it. We can focus on the dangers of having squatters and campers in there.

Last time we checked, it was owned by a city fellow named Thomas Albright. He wouldn't even talk to us about selling. Seemed convinced that he'd be using it someday. And maybe he will. I hope so for the house's sake.

No reason to hurry. The trespassers aren't going anywhere anytime soon. If I've seen it once, I've seen it a hundred times.

"Ready to go to work, Biscuit?" I ask.

Biscuit stands up and barks once. I take that as a yes.

I gulp down the rest of my coffee/motor oil and go inside to get ready to head out to the Bentley cabin after a quick stop by the Albright place to suggest whoever is homesteading there find a legitimate cabin to rent.

We certainly have enough of them to choose from. If they can't afford one of the cabins—a lot of people can't— they can throw up a tent at one of our two campgrounds. Thirty dollars a night will get a person a tent and a spot to pitch it on. If they're nice, we'll even throw in a bundle of firewood. We cater to people from all walks of life.

Young people might start off in tents, then come back a few years later as gainfully employed adults with kids of their own.

Sometimes we have to play the long game.

CHAPTER
SIX

Audrey

THE OLD FELLOW down at the General Store in Whiskey Springs had thrown in a bundle of kindling to go along with everything else I'd bought. He'd been free with his suggestions, especially after he learned I was headed up to the Albright place.

He'd even helped me load the bundle of firewood on the floorboard in the front seat of my car. It had been the only place left to put anything after I'd packed in all the groceries.

Even though I'd seen pictures, all of three, I'd had absolutely no idea what to expect, but with my house in Katy up for sale, I'd brought a lot of my personal items with me. I brought about half my clothes and would have brought more, but my sister Brianna had convinced me to at least check out the house first. To see if it was livable. Before I had my books and kitchenware shipped.

I hadn't been worried. I'd believed in the photographs I'd seen. What I hadn't counted on was how welcoming the house felt. How much like home.

Now that I have the fire in the fireplace going, I don't want it to go out, so I shove another log in there and poke at them with the poker.

Our fireplace in Katy had been gas, so burning actual wood is a new experience. We hadn't had a fireplace of any kind in our house in Atlanta where we'd grown up. As such, a fireplace is one of my favorite things to have in a house.

Satisfied that my fire is going to hold for a bit, I dust off my hands and walk around the big open area that encompasses the living room, dining room, kitchen, and a little study. When I'd gotten here last night, I'd been too tired to do much more than collapse on the sofa and sleep.

I promised both my sisters I'd FaceTime them this morning so they could see for themselves that I was in a safe place and not a hovel. It was definitely the opposite of a hovel.

Not even being the oldest of three could get me out of that. They were all worried about me.

And maybe they had good reason to.

A twenty-seven-year-old widow is someone to worry about to begin and end with without adding on the strange house in the strange place.

The house in Katy hadn't been mine to keep even if I wanted to. Thomas had bought it with such a huge mortgage, there was no way I could have kept it even if it had been an option. And that didn't even include the HOA, the taxes, and maintenance.

I honestly hadn't even realized how high we'd been living. My little salary at the art gallery wouldn't even have touched the expenses.

And then there was his debt. His insurance went to pay off his debt. I hadn't known about that either.

But the kicker of it all had been finding out that my husband had a child with another woman. A secret baby. And he took care of them. He paid the mortgage on a condo for them in downtown Houston.

No one gave me any kind of explanation, but I have a theory. My theory is that Thomas wanted us to live in Katy to keep me as far away from his baby mama as possible. It must have driven him crazy that I worked in a gallery downtown. Not that he and the mother of his child would have known each other even if we'd talked.

If I was right, he planned on us never meeting and we never will. If she was at the funeral, I would have no way of knowing. There were a lot of people from his work I didn't know and she could easily have been one of those many people I hadn't recognized.

My sisters and parents had kept me close and guarded during the entire funeral and the wake that followed.

But there had been one bright spot in Thomas's estate. This mountain cabin just outside Whiskey Springs, Colorado.

Somehow it was protected from whatever financial disaster Thomas's life had been. Apparently, Thomas's grandfather had passed after Thomas had his illegitimate child. He must have known about it and made sure the cabin was protected.

The attorney had tried to explain it, but I hadn't even pretended to understand. All I knew was that this mountain cabin now belongs to me. All I have to do is live in it.

A cabin bigger than our house in Katy, so technically not a cabin. Technically a house. A house that's going to take a lot of upkeep.

My sister Brianna calls me first.

"Good morning," she says with her usual morning chipperness.

"Remember," I say, grumbling a bit. "It's an hour later for you."

"Have you had coffee?" she asks.

"I have."

"Good. Then show me around."

"Don't tell Lilah," I say. "I'm supposed to show her first."

"It's what she gets for being a sleepyhead. Just give me a tour already."

I flip the camera and start with the fire in the fireplace.

"It looks kind of big," Brianna says. "I hope it's not shooting flames out the chimney."

"Really? It looks good to me."

"If you burn the house down, you'll have to move back here."

"Duly noted. I'll let it die down some."

"The furniture looks okay," Brianna says. "Does it smell old?"

"Actually no. Someone's been keeping it freshened up. It smells a little bit like... cinnamon. And vanilla."

"It looks like it would smell like wood and old leather."

"It does. All of those things. It's hard to explain."

"Nice couch," she says.

"This big couch is comfortable for sleeping," I tell her.

"You slept on it. Why?"

"Too tired to do anything else."

"I see your luggage sitting there by the stairs. You have a lot to do. I should have come with you."

"You have work. And besides, I needed to do this."

I take her from the living room, past the heavy dining room table with six heavy wooden chairs, into the kitchen.

"Everything looks new in here." I run a hand over the cast iron burners on the gas stovetop. "Look at the size of this refrigerator." The whole thing, a side by side refrigerator and freezer is twice as big as a normal appliance.

I open the door where I have the things I'd bought yesterday at the General Store. A half-gallon of milk. A dozen eggs. Some fruit and vegetables. "I don't think it's ever been used."

"I'm surprised they didn't stock it for you."

"There's water," I say. "That was already here."

"That was nice of them."

I ignore the sarcasm in her tone. "I have to figure out how to use this coffee maker. I just made instant this morning."

"You made instant coffee when you have that fancy machine sitting on the cabinet."

"I have to learn how to use it. And yes. If you'd come with me, you would have figured it out already."

"Let's go upstairs. See your bedroom. Then I want to go out on the back deck."

"How do you know there's a deck?"

"I see it through the windows."

"Good eyes."

I take her up the wide sweeping stairs. "There are three bedrooms. Maybe four. I have to decide which one I'm going to take."

"Take the primary."

"When I figure out which one that is. They're all huge with huge bathrooms."

"It looks kind of like a lodge, doesn't it?"

"It kind of does. I wonder about the history of it."

"You'll find out if you go into town any. People like to talk."

"You'll definitely find out when you get here."

"I'll make it my mission."

I show her the three bedrooms. All with big walk in closets and ensuite bathrooms. I show her the views from all three.

"They all have great views," she says.

"I think that was by design."

"Which one are you leaning towards?"

"I don't know. I think—Oh." I look at my phone. "Lilah's calling. Let me talk to her. I promised."

"It's okay. We'll talk soon."

I switch over to Lilah's call. "Hey Lilah."

"Hey. Are you ready to give me a tour?"

"I'm upstairs so we'll start here."

I give my youngest sister a similar tour of the house in reverse.

I haven't even chosen my bedroom yet and already it's starting to feel like home.

As I talk to Lilah, I notice that one of the bedrooms has a fireplace in it.

And I decide right then and there. That one's mine.

"I'm taking this bedroom with the fireplace," I tell Lilah. "You and Brianna can fight over the other two bedrooms when you get here."

"I can't wait," Lilah says. "You should have let me come with you."

"I know. And it would have been a whole lot easier to have you and Brianna with me, but I needed to do it by myself."

It was going to take me a while to process everything that had happened since Thomas's plane crash. To figure out what my next step is.

I've taken the first one by coming here. Having a million dollars sitting in my account certainly made that first step easier.

I check it a couple of time a day to make sure it doesn't disappear. That they don't take it back.

I find it hard to believe that there's a trust that just gives me money. I get them giving me the house. But the money is going to take some getting used to.

Sometimes I want to talk to Thomas so badly it takes me to my knees.

But then I just imagine him flying in his airplane. I like to think of him flying, a place where he was happiest. It helps with the pain. Doesn't help much with the shock. But that will get better with time.

At least that's what they tell me.

"What's that noise?" Lilah asks. "Doorbell?"

I stand at the front windows and look out toward the circle drive at the front of the house. "There's someone here. A pickup truck."

"Find out who it is before you answer the door," Lilah says.

"Lilah. I'm going to go now. I have a visitor. Love you. Bye."

Blowing out a breath of frustration, I disconnect the line and slide my phone into the back pocket of my jeans.

It's a small town. People are going to be curious.

My sisters have to get used to it. As do I.

I square my shoulders and open the door.

SEVEN

Bradley

IT'S BEEN AWHILE since I've been to the Albright place. It's a big house. Only four bedrooms, but if memory serves, all the rooms are oversized giving it a spacious feel.

Getting out of my truck, I can't help but notice the smoke billowing out of the living room chimney. Someone has a big fire going. Maybe too big.

Being part of the volunteer fire department, I'm always on the lookout for people doing things that aren't in their best interests.

Someone left pots of colorful flowers on the front porch. Blue butterfly begonias. White petunias. Salmon-colored geraniums. All fluttering in the breeze. A bumblebee buzzing from one to the other. Maybe the Albrights decided to rent the place out. Or... maybe that city fellow decided to come up for the summer.

A young lady, mid to late twenties, answers the door.

First impression. Pretty. But her eyes are haunted. And she's thin as a rail.

A city girl. I can always spot them. Brown hair with intentional blonde streaks pulled back in a messy ponytail.

Not squatters. Not squatters or kids.

"Do you always open the door to strangers?" I ask.

"No... I..." Looking confused, she leans against the door, one hand still on the knob. "I thought..."

"It's okay," I say, easing my expression into a more welcoming smile. "I'm your neighbor. First house down the way. You might have noticed when you drove in."

"I didn't really pay much attention," she says, twisting the doorknob. "Sorry."

"It's okay. My place is kind of hidden back in the trees."

She nods. Then seems to realize she's not being neighborly. "Do you want to come in?"

"I don't want to interrupt."

"You're not interrupting." She looks past me now toward my truck. "You have a dog in your truck."

"Yeah. That's Biscuit."

"He can come in, too."

I open my mouth to tell her that Biscuit is the kind of dog a person should get to know before he comes for a visit, but something, that hauntedness in her eyes perhaps, changes my mind.

"Okay. I'll get him." As I walk back to the truck to get Biscuit, I consider that she looks like someone who could use the company of a dog.

Tail wagging and tongue hanging out, Biscuit jumps out of the truck and races up the porch stairs toward the door. I follow at a slower pace.

She kneels down and lets Biscuit lick her face while she pets him.

The smile on her face says it all.

"Do you two know each other?" I ask.

Standing up, she looks at me, confused again. "No. He's just so friendly."

"He was a stray when I got him," I explain. "I thought maybe he was yours."

"Oh. How long have you had him?" She steps back, giving us both space to come inside.

"About a year," I say, my gaze drawn to the blazing fire in the fireplace. "That's quite a fire you have going."

"Yeah." She runs a hand over her hair. "So I've been told."

"Do you have plenty of firewood?"

"I don't know. I just got here." She glances around. "I don't really know."

"Your husband?" I ask, knowing it's not really a question, but she's wearing a wedding ring, so it's sort of open-ended.

"No. I—"

Biscuit jumps onto the sofa in front of the fireplace, turns around three times, then lies down.

"Biscuit," I say, pointing to the floor.

"He's okay," she says. "I know your dog's name, but I don't know yours."

"Bradley Winslow. And you are..."

"Audrey Sinclair." She sits on the sofa next to Biscuit and scratches his head. I sit on the armchair next to them.

"What brings you to Whiskey Springs, Audrey Sinclair?"

"It's a long story," she says.

I don't have to know Audrey to know that she's not about to tell me that long story right now.

"Do you happen to know anything about coffee makers?" she asks.

"I might know a thing or two," I say, trying to hide my relief that we're done with the small talk. "How can I help?"

CHAPTER
EIGHT

Audrey

I took a page out of Brianna's playbook and used diversion to get my new neighbor's attention off of me and my reason for being here.

He had a good point about me opening the door for strangers. But he'd looked like a regular guy. Unlike me, he looks like he belongs here in Whiskey Springs. Jeans. Worn work boots. A blue and green flannel shirt rolled up at the wrists. A white t-shirt beneath it.

Standing up, he lifts his baseball cap, runs a hand through short dark brown hair and settles it back on his head.

And he has a dog.

What's not to like?

"Whoa," he says, looking from my three suitcases to me. "You need some help getting those upstairs?"

"I wouldn't turn it down. I got them this far."

"Let me just..." He picks up two of them. Carries them to the top of the stairs like they're weightless, then comes back down for the third.

"Anything else you need me to take up?"

"That's it for right now. Thanks."

"All you had to do was ask."

Obviously I hadn't actually had to ask.

As he fiddles with the fancy coffeemaker on my counter. I find a bag of coffee beans—not expired in the pantry and pull the carton of milk I'd bought in town, from the refrigerator.

"Do you know how it works?" I ask.

"My brother actually has one similar to it. So. Yeah."

"Oh. Okay." I take two mugs out of the cabinet. Then on second thought I wash them before handing them to him. Even though everything looks clean, I really don't know if it is.

To be on the safe side, I'll run everything through the dishwasher after he leaves.

By the time I get the mugs washed, the scent of freshly brewed coffee fills the air.

"It smells like a coffee shop in here," I say.

"I usually drink motor oil."

"What?"

"Nothing. I just don't usually take the time to make good coffee. And besides I don't have one of these fancy machines at my place."

I study Bradley Winslow. He's tall. About six feet. Dark hair. A little uneven on the ends that barely brush his collar.

I reflexively compare him to Thomas. Thomas always had a perfect haircut. Cut every two weeks whether he needed it or not.

Would Thomas have known how to work this coffee maker? I'm thinking not. I'm thinking he would have found his way downtown to the coffee shop. Probably would have gotten up early and come back with two cups of coffee.

And yet he was a pilot. He could have figured it out. If he wanted to.

"Audrey?" Bradley asks.

I blink and realize he must have been talking to me.

"I'm sorry. I was thinking about something else." I do it all the time. My family is used to it and it doesn't bother them, but he's looking at me like something's wrong with me.

"I was just asking how much milk you like in your coffee."

"Oh," I say. "Enough so it doesn't take like coffee. Or motor oil." Geez. I'm not fit to be around other people. Brianna and Lilah were right. I should have brought them.

Bradley gives me a little grin, then as he makes the coffee, I twist at my wedding ring.

He'd asked about my husband. People are going to ask. I'm going to have to tell them. There's no way around it.

Bradley hands me a cup of hot coffee. I take it from him and set it on counter.

"You asked what brought me to Whiskey Springs."

"Just making conversation. You don't have to answer."

"This house belonged to my husband's grandfather."

"Theodore Albright."

"Yes. And now it apparently belongs to me."

Bradley sets his mug down, too. Leans a hip against the kitchen island and studies me.

"Last I heard it belonged to a fellow named Thomas Albright. He sold it to you?"

"No. I inherited it."

He tilts his head to the side and looks at me. "I'm a little confused now."

"Thomas Albright was my husband."

"Was." I can see him putting things together. *Was. Inherited.*

"I know it's confusing because I didn't take his name.

"Not unusual."

Apparently somehow word about Thomas's accident had not traveled to Whiskey Springs.

"Thomas Albright was killed in an airplane crash two weeks ago." I straighten my shoulders and force myself to follow through with the words. "I'm his widow."

NINE

Bradley

I TAKE a sip of the coffee I'd just made and burn my tongue in the process.

I'm standing in the Albright kitchen talking to the widow of Thomas Albright. Granddaughter-in-law of Theodore Albright.

"Not only a long story," I say. "But a confusing one. And sad."

She smiles a little and takes a cautious sip of her coffee. "You have no idea."

"I'm sorry for your loss."

"Thank you. I never know how to respond when

someone says that." She slips onto one of the barstools and I walk around to sit next to her.

"I don't think you really have to respond."

"Good," she says. "That's good."

"And just for the record, I don't think you have to tell people either."

"It's a small town. People are going to want to know."

"Only because they're nosy and don't have a life of their own. No one needs to know why you're here." I know she's right, but I feel instinctively protective toward her.

"I guess they'll find out anyway."

"They will. People have a way of finding out things about other people. Human nature."

She picks up her coffee mug and stares into it. Now I understand why she'd drifted off a few minutes ago.

"So... are you just visiting or are you planning on living out here?"

"I was thinking I'd live here," she says, still looking into her coffee as though she would find answers there. "It's either that or go back to live with my parents in Atlanta or live with one of my sisters in Houston."

"Do you have children?"

"No." Biscuit wanders over and nudges her hand for a pet. "No pets either."

"So it's just you. Up here. Alone."

"I have neighbors," she says, looking up to meet my gaze, a little smile playing about her lips. That little smile doesn't do anything to take away the hauntedness from her eyes though.

"You have one neighbor and I'm a mile away. It's nothing like Atlanta or Houston."

"Maybe that's a good thing."

"Maybe. What do you do?"

"Right now? I don't do anything. I worked for an art gallery in Houston. But... I didn't want to go back to it."

"I'm sure you have your reasons."

"Yeah." She blows out a breath. "Actually. I'm planning to take my time. Figure out what I want to do next."

"Sounds like a good plan."

I take a business card out of my wallet and slide it over to her. "If you need anything at all. Call me. That's my cell phone number."

She picks up my card. "Timber Ridge Cabins and Timber Company. Vice President."

"Yes. Well. It's a family business, so I'm not sure how much clout is behind that title."

She looks at me with her shadowed green eyes. I'd been right. I definitely understand now why she has that haunted look about her. Widowed for just two weeks. Still trying to get the ground back beneath her feet.

"Maybe it doesn't have a lot of clout now," she says. "But it will one day. It's you and your three brothers?"

"Yes. And our parents."

She turns my card over, end over end. "You've always lived here in Whiskey Springs?"

"I moved away when I went to college, but it was expected that I'd come back and help with the family business."

She nods. "Do you like it?"

"Sure. I like it okay."

"Just okay? There's something else that you dream about doing?"

"No. I can't say that there is. Not work wise anyway."

There are plenty of things I think about. Like getting married and having a couple of kids. But that's not the kind of thing to walk in a stranger's—a widow at that—house and say.

"Good. If there is, you should go ahead and do it. Don't wait."

"Speaking of work," I say, standing up. "I've got quite a bit of work to do on the Bentley cabin."

She stands up, too. "Thanks for making the coffee."

"Sure thing. Call me. I'll come back and teach you how to use it."

"Okay. I'll do that."

I have a feeling she won't call me. But I'll come back by. Maybe in the morning. Show her how it's done.

I have a feeling Audrey Sinclair is going to need a lot of protecting out here. And that same feeling tells me I'm the man to protect her.

CHAPTER
TEN

Audrey

I TAKE my cup of coffee, as good as any designer coffee, and sit in front of my fireplace with the big flames. They're starting to die down now and I resist the temptation to toss another log in there.

There are only a few more logs left from my shopping trip at the General Store. I need to take a look around to see if there is any more firewood already here. I hadn't thought to look until Bradley had ask me how much I had.

Speaking of Bradley, I'd done exactly what I'd said I wasn't going to do. I'd given him my whole life history.

He knew everything now. He knew where my parents live. Where my sisters live. That I have sisters.

He knows that I'm a widow and that I now own the house. It might be in a trust, but according to my uncle, the house is mine and there is nothing anyone including the baby mama and child can ever do about it.

Just like there was nothing I could do about Thomas's life insurance going to them. It's how they had set it up. Thomas and his grandfather. Independently it seems. What wife would think to ask her new husband if his life insurance was going to her or to another woman and child?

So now Bradley Winslow knows all about me and all I know about him is that he lives down the road and works in his family business.

I'd gone from not talking about Thomas and the whole situation to spilling it all to Bradley.

It's not entirely my fault. I blame his eyes. Bradley's kind eyes. His dog didn't help. Apparently I'm a sucker for a guy with kind eyes especially if he has a dog.

I pull his card out of my pocket and read over it again. Then enter his number in my phone contacts.

Timber Ridge Cabins.

A quick google search sends me to their website. They own upwards of three dozen cabins in town and supply all the town's firewood from their tree farm. They also provide Christmas trees for Whiskey Springs and the surrounding area.

Apparently the Winslows are a big name in the area.

Great. Now everyone around here will not only know that I'm here, but also why.

I guess if I was going to spill my guts to someone, it was only natural that I'd spill them to the guy with the kind blue eyes and adorable dog, not to mention whose family owns half the town.

Maybe it was simply that he's a stranger to me.

Talking about Thomas to someone I don't know is different from talking to someone who knew him.

I pause with my mug halfway to my lips.

What had I been thinking?

I'm sitting in Thomas's grandfather's house. Bradley would have known Theodore Albright.

He just hadn't known about me. Thomas and I hadn't been married all that long and Thomas had never told me about this place, much less brought me here.

So even though Bradley is a complete stranger to me, he's not a complete stranger to the Albright family.

When I screw something up, I do it right.

I need to talk to the attorneys. To see if it's okay for me to talk about the inheritance.

Bradley didn't seem to know anything about it.

Maybe I'll just be smart and keep it to myself from here on out.

Bradley didn't seem like the kind of guy who would gossip, but still... He is a product of a small town.

After finishing my coffee, I take my mug back to the kitchen. Put it in the dishwasher along with Bradley's mug and all the other dishes I can fit in there and turn it on.

Turns out the house is well stocked. I don't even need to bring any of my own kitchenware. Everything here is nicer than anything I had anyway. That was saying something considering that Thomas bought designer everything.

Some of my things, however, are sentimental even if it's not as high quality. I'll have it sent up here, then sort through it and donate what I don't want to keep. Maybe donating things locally will help me make a place for myself here.

Sometimes it's the little things that make a big difference.

I've no more than walked out onto the back deck than Lilah calls me back.

Having protective sisters takes some getting used to, but there are worse things.

ELEVEN

Bradley

I STOP by the General Store to pick up some supplies before I head up to the Bentley cabin.

"Headed to the Bentley Place?" John ask as he rings up my box of screws and half a dozen two-by-fours.

"Oh yeah. I'm sure I'll be back with an order of things I'm going to need. Just basically going up to assess. Take care of the most dangerous."

"Going to need new appliances from what I hear."

"You heard right."

"Just let me know. I can order whatever you need. Get it for you at cost."

"I'm counting on it."

An older fellow comes in through the front door. John waves and goes back to work tying the two by fours with a line of twine.

"You don't have to tie that up," I say. "I've got it."

"It's no trouble. I saw your new neighbor yesterday. Audrey."

"Did you now?"

"Yep. You want some varnish while you're here?"

"Not sure which color. I'll come back for it."

"Yeah. She didn't have much to say. Had to drag it out of her that she was headed up to the Albright place."

I don't think John is fishing for information. I think he's just making conversation. As such people tell him things. Not sure how much of that information he spreads.

"Didn't tell you why she's here?"

"Nope."

I hand him my credit card.

"She was a closed book. Got to admire that these days. My granddaughter could probably find out everything about on that intertube in about half a minute."

I chuckle. John's close enough to be in the right ballpark.

"I don't use it much either," I say. "But Cade's put up a website for us."

"You don't say? Maybe I'll get him to set one up for me."

"Couldn't hurt."

"Yeah. A lot of people are driving into Boulder and a lot

more are ordering things and having them delivered. Seems like the world is changing. Getting too big for a little place like this.

"Not a chance." I tuck my credit card back into my wallet. "We need you here."

"One of the big chains was nosing around. If that happens, I'm out."

"I'm on the city council, John. They'll never get my vote."

"Unfortunately, there's other people on there besides you. People that want the big chains."

Hefting my lumber over my shoulder, I grab my box of nails. "We'll fight it if it happens. Until then, let's not buy trouble."

"Getting too old to fight," John says. "See you tomorrow."

"Probably," I say. "Oh. Can I get a bag of kindling? Put it on my tab?"

"What you buying kindling for? You know I bought it from you."

"It's a gift. And a show of good faith to make sure you keep the doors open."

John grumbles, but he grabs a bag of kindling and slips it into my paper sack.

"Don't forget to put it on my tab."

"Get out of here," John says. "I got work to do."

He won't put it on my tab. I already know.

But from what I've seen of Audrey's propensity to make super large fires in her fireplace, she's going to need it.

I'm just being neighborly.

It has nothing to do with her haunted green eyes in her elfin-like features.

Doesn't mean anything that I can't stop thinking about her.

TWELVE

Audrey

I SIT ON THE DECK, talking to Lilah, listening while she tells me about her plan. Lilah is an artist at heart who works at a bar to pay the bills.

"I'm saving my money," she tells me. "so I can buy art supplies and take two weeks off to come and visit you. I can paint while I'm there, right?"

"Of course you can, but Lilah?"

An acrobatic little chipmunk races along the wooden rails, hops onto a long-hanging maple tree limb with fresh spring buds, and vanishes.

"Just quit your job."

"I can't do that," she says. "The Millers need me. I've worked for them since I was in high school."

"And how old are you now?"

"Twenty-three."

I wait while she takes a minute to think about that.

"I know what you're saying," she says. "But I can't just move in on you."

"You're right," I say, watching a flock of black birds swoop down onto the ground below. Their sleek black feathers stand out in sharp contrast to the dewy spring grass and flowers in a blanket of light blue sweeping down the hillside. "So come up when you're ready. Take your two weeks and then we'll talk."

"Okay. But you said you needed some time. That we had to wait."

"When do you think you'll be ready?"

Lilah hesitates. "Two or three weeks. Maybe four. But I can come earlier if you want me to."

"Lilah. Stop worrying. Just come when you want to. I'm sure that by the time you're ready to come up here, I'll be more than ready to see you."

"Okay. So tell me about your neighbor."

"Just a run-of-the-mill neighbor. You know how I feel about neighbors."

"I don't think you like neighbors very much."

"Not really." Handsome blue-eyed ones might be okay.

"How did you put it? They think just because they live

nearby they have the right to just drop in anytime they want to."

"Something like that."

"You sound good," Lilah says. "I'm going to take a nap before I have to get ready for work. Call me if you need anything."

"I will. I think I'm going to take a nap, too."

"Good idea. I love you, Sis."

"Love you, too."

After I disconnect the line, I get up to go back inside. The back of the house is more impressive than the front of the house and that's saying a lot.

It's got so much glass, being inside is almost like being outside.

I'm a little excited to see snowfall on the deck, but that will be awhile. It's just now summer. According to all accounts, summer will bring cold nights and warm days, but snow is unlikely until September. Not impossible, but unlikely.

I'm wondering if I should wash the bedsheets before I take a nap as I go back inside.

I walk to the sink, fill a glass with water, then turn around to face the living room while I drink it.

That's when I see the vase of yellow daisies sitting on the kitchen island.

They were most definitely not there before.

They were not there when Bradley was here. He and I

had stood right here while he made coffee. There had been no flowers. No vase. No flowers.

Frozen in place, I glance about the room.

I don't see anything else out of the ordinary.

The flames have died down in the fireplace. That's about it.

Giving the flowers a wide berth, keeping one eye on them, I walk around to the front door. Check the locks.

Everything seems to be in order. I know no one went in the back door while I was outside. I would have seen them.

I stand at the large front window and watch the road. My house is at the end. Anyone coming this far is most definitely either coming to see me or is lost.

There's no dust like there had been earlier when Bradley drove off. Not even a light dusting in the air.

No sign that anyone was here.

But someone was here. Flowers don't just randomly appear out of nowhere.

Maybe Bradley had slipped back in and left the flowers while I was outside.

It would be a little bit strange, but...

Checking the door lock one more time, I go back to the kitchen island and slide the vase of flowers toward me.

Where would he even get flowers? Just happened to have a vase of flowers in his truck?

There's no card.

No indication of who they're from.

I send Bradley a text.

> Hi. This is Audrey. Your new neighbor. Did you see anyone head up this way as you were leaving?

He's going to think something's wrong with me, but I need to know. Mostly I need to know if he came back and left the flowers.

If he did, it's still strange, but it's a kind of strange I can grasp. The alternative... not so much.

BRADLEY

> No. I stopped by the General Store in town, then came straight here to the Bentley house. Didn't see anyone. Something wrong?

> No. Just thought I heard something. Sorry to bother.

BRADLEY

> Seriously. If you need something I can be right there.

> Thank you.

I examine the flowers. Dewy and fresh. Like they just came out of a flower shop. I take a photo of them and make a notation in my phone. If anything happens to me either one of my sisters can access my phone and maybe this photo will be a clue.

I'm imagining things.

Maybe they were here all along and they just somehow got slid over to the middle of the island.

Maybe it's the grief causing me to get confused. Grief,

especially the kind that comes with trauma, can do that. I'd looked it up.

Not sleepy anymore. Definitely too on edge to sleep, I head upstairs to check out my bedroom and unpack.

As I walk upstairs, it occurs to me that I should get a dog. A big dog like Bradley has. A dog like Biscuit would bark and scare intruders away.

If I knew Bradley a little better, I'd ask him about the flowers. It would be good to have corroboration on something like that.

Trying to put the mystery of the flowers behind me for now—surely there's a logical explanation—I walk through my bedroom of choice and into the closet.

I'm delighted to see that it has a washer and dryer right there in the closet. What better place to have a washing machine than in the closet?

Unfortunately, when I open the lid of the washing machine, it smells vile. The dryer has pockets of rust. There's no way I'm going to put my clothes in either one of them.

Now I have a reason to call Bradley. To find out where to get a new washer and dryer.

And... I look around the closet... the closets in this house have most definitely been neglected. Unlike the kitchen, they don't look like they've ever been updated.

There is so much that can be done in here. Fortunately, I have some experience. This is going to be fun. It's been awhile since I felt that little unexpected spurt of anticipation.

I need some paper and a tape measure. I have a pad of paper in my computer bag, but no tape measure. It's not something I usually carry around, but if I'd thought it through I would have brought one. There's always something to measure in a new place.

It would be better to start with a blank slate in here. I need to pull down all the old uneven shelves and rusty metal rods and then I need to paint the walls.

I need paint.

Once it's painted, I can measure and start creating my own custom closet.

My hands tucked in my warm oversized sweatshirt, I wander around to the other two large bedrooms. They have similar closet situations. Same with the smaller bedroom.

I designed our closets in Katy, but I did that on a budget. I don't have a budget on these.

Nothing I like better than a project.

As I walk back downstairs to make myself some hot tea, I feel a little bit less sad than I have since that rainy Tuesday night when Thomas's plane had gone down and not only that, I'm feeling more optimistic than I have for a long time.

All at the prospect of designing my own closets from the ground up.

THIRTEEN

Bradley

WITH A TWO-PAGE LIST of nothing but basic supplies I need to get even started on the Bentley cabin, I lock up and head out. Biscuit jumps into the passenger seat and off we go.

My gaze lands on the bag of kindling I'd impulsively bought for Audrey and I check my messages to see if she texted again.

Nothing new, but something spooked her. She doesn't strike me as the kind of girl who would text a man she just met without a good reason.

Since she lives less than a mile from my cabin—actually

I can cut through and walk to her cabin in fifteen minutes—it's a mile by road, I can just swing by and check on her.

It's what a good neighbor would do, especially now that I know what she's been through. Hell backwards. That's what it sounds like she's been through.

She hadn't said where she was actually from, and I'll google plane crashes when I get home, but she has a southern accent. I'm leaning toward Texas. Assuming I'm right and she's from Houston or even Atlanta, it took a lot of courage for her to come out here and by herself, too.

I can't even begin to speculate why she would have moved out here. Maybe she hadn't had a choice. Or maybe she wanted the adventure. Or maybe it was just what she told me. To take some time to figure out what she wanted to do next. I imagine that includes adjusting to being a single woman again.

Biscuit sits up and barks once as we turn into her circle drive.

Already the old house is starting to look like it has a little more life in it. Just knowing that someone is living here will do that.

I grab the bag of kindling and slide out of the truck, Biscuit right behind me.

Biscuit bounds up the steps in front of me. Audrey might deny it, but Biscuit seems to know her. Or maybe Biscuit just likes a pretty girl as much as I do. I can't blame him.

"Hi," she says, looking surprised. Her cheeks are flushed like maybe she just ran down the stairs to answer the door.

"Hi. I don't normally drop in on people like this, at least not twice a day, but your text message made me worry that you'd been a little spooked."

She takes a step back to give me and Biscuit space to come inside.

Biscuit looks like he's in love as she scratches his head.

"Biscuit," I say. "Have some dignity."

"He's okay. He reminds me of a dog I had when I was growing up."

"I see." It's sort of a connection. "So. Are you okay?"

"I was upstairs. Wishing for a tape measure."

"Ah. I missed it."

"Missed what?"

"I brought you kindling."

"Oh." There's that ghost of a smile again. "For the fireplace."

"Since you seem to enjoy the fires so much. But if I'd known, I would have brought you a tape measure. What are we measuring?"

"Closets." She takes the kindling. Sniffs it. Then searches my eyes. "I want to strip everything out of them. Everything. All the shelves and rods. Paint the walls. Maybe even new flooring. And design them from the ground up."

"Sounds like my kind of project."

"You do renovations?" She straightens and Biscuit run

over to jump on the sofa in what he seems to think is his spot in front of the fireplace.

"My family owns a fleet of cabins. I can do just about anything that needs doing."

"That's amazing. Can I hire you?"

"I don't see why not."

"Do we need to negotiate a rate? How does that work?"

"Why don't we see how it goes? Figure it out as we go?"

She looks skeptical. "I don't know. I don't like surprises."

"I won't do anything without being upfront about what it's going to cost."

"You'll tell me first?"

"Absolutely."

Giving me a little smile that almost reaches her eyes, she takes the bag of kindling over to the hearth and sets it next to the one remaining log.

"Looks like I should have brought you firewood."

"I didn't find any around here other than what I bought at the General Store."

"Nothing against John at the General Store. He's a good friend of mine. But please don't buy firewood from him."

"Why not?"

"Because he buys it from me and upsells it to tourists."

"Oh." Her eyes widen. "Then I should buy it from you."

"Something like that."

She still hasn't figured out that I'm not going to charge

her to work on anything and I'm not going to charge her for firewood.

"Want to show me what I'm going to be working on?"

"Sure. Do you want something to drink? Coffee?"

"Maybe in a minute. Before I forget, I need to show you how to work that coffee maker."

"Right. I'll be glad you did. I had instant coffee this morning."

"Tell me it isn't true."

"I'm afraid it's true."

"So that text you sent me earlier. What was that about?"

A shadow crosses her features and she cuts her eyes toward the kitchen.

"When you were here earlier, did you notice those yellow flowers? The ones in the vase?"

I follow her gaze. "No. I would have noticed them because they're my mother's favorite. Yellow daisies."

She winces. "So they weren't there? You're sure?"

"No. I'm certain of it. Why?"

"Because after you left, I went outside. I sat on the bench and talked to my sister for a few minutes. Then I came back in." She takes a deep breath. "I went to the sink for a glass of water. That's when I saw them."

"They just appeared?" A little shiver shoots down my spine.

"Yes."

"And your door was locked?"

"I'm from the city. I always lock my door. But I checked anyway."

"Do you mind if I..." I gesture toward the flowers.

"Please."

I turn the vase around, looking for anything suspicious. But they look like just ordinary flowers in an ordinary vase. Still. I don't like it.

"No idea how they got in here?"

"None. I wasn't sure what to do with them. I took a photo."

I nod. "Smart. Do you want me to take them away?"

"What are you thinking?"

"I'm thinking about taking them to the sheriff. See if he has any ideas."

"Seems a little extreme for some flowers, doesn't it?" But she bites her bottom lip nervously.

"Not when someone seemingly got them inside your house without your knowledge."

"Okay. You can take them. Maybe he can run fingerprints on them."

"Maybe." Something about them isn't sitting right with me. I'm not thinking fingerprints, but I am thinking maybe they're bugged or poisoned. "I think I'll have that coffee now after all."

"Good. Show me how."

"Where are all your mugs?" I ask, opening the cabinet where she'd found them earlier.

"I washed everything." She opens the dishwasher letting out a wisp of steam.

It seems I'm not the only one feeling a bit paranoid.

FOURTEEN

Audrey

"Want some advice?" Bradley asks, running a hand over one of the uneven wooden shelves in my closet.

"Of course." My hands are wrapped around the warm coffee mug. Making coffee with the fancy machine had actually been surprisingly simple. I made the coffee I'm currently holding under Bradley's watchful eye and it's as good as any designer coffee. Well. Almost.

"After we pull down all these shelves and get everything off the walls, I can add a layer of insulation then drywall on top of that."

"Drywall? You know how to do that?"

He looks at me with a raised eyebrow. "I have some experience."

"Okay." I take a sip of my coffee.

"It'll give it a clean modern appearance and with the added insulation, it'll stand the test of time."

The test of time. I take a deep breath. He guessed right that I'm planning to live here permanently. I have some plans and ideas, but all of them involve me living out my life right here in this house.

"It's big enough," he says, looking around. "You could divide it into two sections. His and hers. Once you start designing."

His and hers. I close my eyes a moment. Press my fingers against the area between my eyes. But I force myself to open them. "I don't think there's going to be a *his*."

Bradley whirls around. Sees the look on my face. "Ah Geez. I'm sorry. I wasn't thinking."

"It's okay." He's right though. It is a big closet. A REALLY big closet. And I don't have enough clothes to fill it. Brianna might. But I don't and I doubt I ever will. "I'll think about it."

"Nothing wrong with having a lot of space. And you've got plenty of time to design it." He looks away. "You said you have four other closets to do, too, right?"

"Right. You're thinking we can strip them all before we start designing."

"Makes sense. That way you have a little more time to plan out what you want to do. By the way, whoever thought to put the washer and dryer in the closer was brilliant."

"I agree completely. But." I wrinkle my nose. "They have to be replaced."

He walks over. Lifts the washer lid, makes a face as he closes it right back. "No question about that."

I bite my lip to keep from smiling. "Maybe I should have warned you."

"That would have been good of you." Just as I had done, he peeks into the dryer.

"Does anyone deliver up here?" I'm still trying not to smile.

"Not really. Not without a huge upcharge. Just go online. Order what you want from Home Depot in Boulder. I'll drive down and pick it up."

"So I'll pay you to deliver them."

"I won't charge you for that."

"Well. You should."

"I can tell you're from the city."

I look at him with one eyebrow raised, as he follows me from the closet.

"Okay," he says. "Here's what I'm thinking. You buy the supplies. I can get them for you at cost. Then you help me with the work. We'll call it even."

"I don't know anything about drywall. I can design the closet and put in the shelves using the Elfa system, but that's about it."

"Then I'll teach you."

"Why would you do that?"

"I have a lot of reasons."

"Name one."

"I'll name two. First. It sounds like it's going to be a fun project and I like fun projects. Two. I knew Theodore Albright. He was a good man. I like to think he'd do the same for whoever moved in here if he could."

"Fair enough."

I'm not sure why, but his being so kind makes me feel weepy. I have to turn away from him and get myself in check as we head downstairs.

"It's getting late," he says. "I need to get Biscuit home. Get him something to eat."

"Right. I don't think I have any dog food." But I put it on my mental list of things to order. If Bradley and Biscuit are going to be working here, I'm going to need food for both of them.

He stops at the counter and studies the yellow daisies.

"Do you feel safe staying here by yourself?" He turns and locks his light blue eyes on mine.

I'm not sure. "Yes. I refuse to be frightened away so easily."

He grabs up the vase. "Come on Biscuit. Let's give the lady some privacy."

I swallow hard with the realization that I don't want him to leave. It's crazy but I like having him here.

"I'll go online and see about ordering the washer and dryer."

"Just let me know when it's ready. Tomorrow isn't too soon."

"Okay."

He stops at the door. "Goes without saying. Lock the doors. Don't let anyone inside."

"I know."

"Promise?"

"I promise." I bite my lip. It's like talking to one of my sisters.

"And call me if anything feels off. Or if anyone even drives up here. Anything. Anytime. Middle of the night."

"I will." I bend down to scratch Biscuit's back and let him lick my face.

"Text me about the appliances. Is tomorrow night good to start on the closets?"

"Sure. Sooner than I expected, but yeah." I stand up and reach for the doorknob. "Thank you."

"Come on Biscuit. See you tomorrow, Audrey." He strides across the front porch and starts down the stairs. "Lock the door," he says over his shoulder.

Smiling, I close the door and lock it.

I stand at the closed door and listen to the truck as he drives off.

For just a little bit of time, while Bradley was here, I hadn't felt empty inside.

It's just being in a strange place. And he's being kind.

That was all.

It has nothing to do with his mesmerizing light blue eyes and charming smile.

FIFTEEN

Bradley

THE NEXT DAY, I get to the Bentley place early and go to work. Like parts of the Albright house, the closets at least, this cabin requires a lot of gutting before it can be updated.

The Bentley cabin is in a great location. Right on the river. I open up the windows and instead of turning on music, I work to the sound of the rushing river just outside.

I start in the bathroom because bathrooms are notoriously difficult. It doesn't take long for me to decide that everything has to go. I'd been thinking I could keep the toilet, but the bleach I'd left in there overnight didn't touch the rust stains.

Just as we get the toilet up, haul it out, and drop if off next to the road for trash pickup, my youngest brother Wyatt drives up in his black pickup truck that looks just like mine. We all drive them. Me. Wyatt. Caleb. Our dad. Ford F-150s in black. Workhorses. Good for pulling trailers. Hauling everything from firewood to appliances.

"Good timing," I say as he gets out of his truck.

He straightens his blue jeans jacket and takes off his sun glasses. "It's a gift."

"Wish I'd known you were coming," I say with a nod to the toilet.

"Looks like you're doing okay by yourself."

"Not really the point." I head back inside and he follows.

"I was out this way making a delivery and thought you might appreciate some help."

"Won't turn it down," I say, handing him a hammer as we step into the bathroom.

He gives the room a once over. "I see you went with my advice to gut it."

"Yeah. I was trying to avoid it."

"Something eating at you?"

I take off my baseball cap and look at my brother. "Maybe," I say. "Let's get this sink out of here."

"Heard you met the new owner of the Albright place," Wyatt says.

"Where did you hear that?" I stop what I'm doing and look up from the rusted pipes beneath the sink.

"The trees have eyes."

"Apparently." I go back to twisting the pipes loose.

"Did you turn off the water?"

"It's turned off outside."

"Is that what's eating you? I know you don't want neighbors and were hoping we could buy it."

"She doesn't bother me, but... Hand me that wrench."

"But."

I take the wrench from him. "But something odd happened up there."

"Odd as in?"

"Somebody got into her house and left a vase of flowers."

"What do you mean they got in? Why would someone do that?"

"The doors were locked. She was out back."

"Maybe the door wasn't locked."

"She claims they were and I'm inclined to believe her."

"We may have to rerun these pipes," Wyatt says.

"I figured as much. They've got some rust."

"How do you explain the flowers?"

"I can't. They're in my truck now. Gonna drop them by the sheriff's office after I leave here."

"Seems like a lot of work for some flowers."

"That's what she said. But do you remember that stalker that killed that girl over in Boulder?"

"Yeah. I remember."

"He left that girl gifts for months before he killed her."

"You think she's got a stalker?"

"I can't rule it out."

"How old is she?"

"I don't know. Our age."

"Ah."

"Ah what?" I add another pipe to our growing stack.

"Ah nothing. Just ah."

"She's my neighbor," I say. "I feel an obligation to look after her. Besides, she's fragile." Wyatt gives me a look of skepticism. "Her husband was killed in a plane crash two weeks ago."

"I read about that. Down in Texas."

"Yeah. He was flying out of Houston. I looked it up."

"That's rough."

"Yeah. Well. She somehow inherited the house. I think she's in over her head."

"How so?"

"I don't know. She's from the city."

"She'll be okay."

"You haven't seen her, Bro. She weighs about a hundred pounds and she's got these eyes that looked haunted."

"Like you said, it's fresh."

"Yeah. Well. The flowers are eating at me."

Biscuit comes running back in through the open door and deposits a squirrel at the bathroom door.

Wyatt and I look at each other.

"Where did he learn to do that?" Wyatt asks.

"Hell if I know."

"Must be a full moon."

"Maybe," I say. Whatever it is, it seems to have everything off-kilter. "You're welcome to it. Don't you eat squirrel?"

"I think he brought it to you."

Biscuit, sitting down with the squirrel in front of him, looks quite pleased with himself.

"I'll pass. Do you have time to take a cord of firewood up to the Albright place? Tomorrow would be soon enough."

"You need to tell me something?" Wyatt asks, rubbing Biscuit's head.

"No. I do not need to tell you anything. She's buying wood from the General Store and as much as I want John to stay in business, it doesn't seem right for her to pay him. Not after everything Theodore Albright did for us."

"Okay. I'll take care of it."

"Take care of that squirrel, too, would you?"

"And what are you doing?"

"I'm gonna figure out how to get this shower out of here."

Wyatt curses under his breath as he picks up the squirrel by the tail and hauls it out of here.

"Go on, Biscuit," I say. "You can at least go keep him company.

Biscuit barks once, then dutifully follows along after Wyatt.

That's when I get a text from Audrey.

"Ride down to Boulder with me?" I ask as Wyatt comes back inside.

"What's the catch?" he asks, looking at me with skepticism.

I hide a smile. "I'll buy you lunch."

CHAPTER

SIXTEEN

Audrey

THE NEXT MORNING the cleaning service shows up at my door.

The cleaning service consists of a fifty-something-year-old woman with a kind smile.

"Hi," she says when I open the door. "I'm Claire. I'm here to clean your house."

I may have promised Bradley not to open the door to anyone, but I'd been expecting someone to come by to clean the house.

"Come in," I say. I can't very well leave her standing outside with a bucket filled with cleaning supplies sitting at her feet and a mop in one hand. "I don't think there's much to clean though."

She picks up her bucket and walks right in. "It doesn't matter. I vacuum and mop once a week whether it needs it or not."

"Really? That's why everything looks so clean."

"I've been doing it for years. You must be Audrey Sinclair. I can come back if this is a bad time."

"It's a perfect time, actually. I'm doing some cleaning myself."

"What happened?" she asks, looking a bit alarmed at the stacks of dishes, pots, pans on every surface and open cabinets to go along with them.

"I pulled everything out of the kitchen cabinets so I can clean them and wash everything."

"You're not supposed to do that," she says, rushing into the kitchen. Claire is about five two and weighs less than I do. "Let me finish this up for you."

"I'm the one who started it," I say. "Besides, I find it rather therapeutic."

She puts her hands on her hips and looks me over. "Alright then. At least let me help you. What can I do?"

"I haven't wiped down the lower cabinets yet. I've got everything out though."

She pulls her hair back with a clip and pulls on a pair of blue rubber gloves. "I'm your girl. Don't worry. I'm good at this."

"Okay then. Can I get you something to drink?"

"No, hon. I'm good. Don't you worry about me. Just pretend I'm not here. Unless you want to talk. I can do that, too."

I can tell immediately that Claire is going to be as good as she claimed to be.

"I don't like you up there on those cabinets," she says as I climb back up. "You should let me do that."

"I'm okay. I don't mind the company though."

"Okay," she says. "At least I'm here to call the ambulance."

I smile and go back to wiping down the empty cabinets. They don't really need it, but whenever I move into a new place, I feel better knowing I've wiped everything down. Just in case there are spider webs or dust or anything sticky from the previous occupants.

"I sure wish I'd known you were doing this," she says. "I would have come on up to help you."

"You're fine, Claire. After I get everything wiped down, I'm going to box up what I don't need. Is there a place in town that takes donations? Or do you know anyone who might need stuff?"

"Are you sure you don't want to keep everything? For a while at least?"

"I'm sure. I've got stuff of my own coming. And I can't stand to live in clutter."

"I hear you. I've got three daughters that live in town.

Between them and their friends, I'm sure I can find someone who needs whatever you don't want to keep."

"That's great. Perfect. It might be next week before I get it all sorted and boxed up."

"I can come back anytime to help you. I'll give you my number. And you don't have to pay me. The agency pays me."

"The agency?" I dip my cleaning cloth in a bucket of cleaning water, rinse it, and squeeze it out.

"Yes. We call it the agency, but it's really just Mr. Fields. He handles everything for Mr. Albright's estate.

"Is there a lot to handle?" I wonder.

"Oh I don't know. I only met him once. I use an app to document my time. It won't let me log in unless I'm within so many feet of the house."

"That's interesting." I wonder if there are cameras. I'll have to find out how to detect for cameras and bugs and such.

"It's all high tech. But the pay's good. And I like the work."

I want to ask her about the flowers, but I don't want to let anyone else know about them just yet. Already Bradley knows and maybe the sheriff. I don't need it spreading all over town.

"Does anyone else come up here?" I ask. "to work?"

"There's a landscaping service, but they don't come inside the house."

Keys. Of course. It hadn't occurred to me until right now

that other people have keys for various things. Like Claire. Claire has a key. People would have keys to a vacant house, especially one that has people coming out regularly to keep it up.

That could easily explain how the flowers got inside.

I latch onto it as the best possible explanation.

And I make a mental note to get the locks changed.

Someone had probably brought the flowers out as a housewarming gift and since I'd been sitting out back, they hadn't known I was here.

In and out. They would have been in and out.

And I'd sent those flowers off with Bradley to take to the sheriff's office.

A classic case of overreacting.

I want to tell him right now, but I'll wait. I'll wait until he comes by later to start working on the closets.

With Claire here, this is taking half as long.

"Don't you worry," she says. "We'll have this knocked out in no time."

As much as I've enjoying my alone time, I'm happy to have Claire here to keep me company.

Having grown up with two sisters, I'm used to having someone else around. Even when I'd been married to Thomas, I'd either been at work or Thomas had been there or I'd been with one or the other of my sisters.

Besides, Claire is likeable. So far, everyone I've met in Whiskey Springs is likeable.

It's a pleasant surprise. Something I really hadn't expected when I'd packed up to drive out here.

I rinse my cloth in the water again. There was more dust in the cabinets than it looked like. It had been a good idea.

When I'd decided to move here, I really hadn't been thinking at all. I'd just reacted to the situation.

Finished with that section of the cabinets, I climb down, Claire watching me carefully, pull off my rubber gloves, and check my phone.

My washer and dryer are ready for pickup. I take a screenshot of the information and text it to Bradley.

My order is ready for pickup, but there's no hurry. The delivery fee isn't that much, but no delivery times are available until next week. Just let me know if you'd rather I schedule the delivery.

Having to wait until next week is the thing bothering me the most. I'd found clean sheets in the linen closet and put them on the bed last night, but I'd feel a whole lot better if I could do some laundry. Even the clean sheets smell stale as was to be expected.

By the time I grab a bottle of water and twist off the cap, I have a response.

BRADLEY

Let me finish up here and I'll head that way.

"You look happy about something," Claire says.

"Oh. I ordered a new washer and dryer. Bradley is driving down to Boulder to pick them up."

Claire sits back on her heels and grins. "Bradley Winslow?"

"Yes. He's my neighbor." Of course she knows that. I don't know why I'm telling her. "He's just being kind."

"Bradley Winslow is a hottie," she says, rinsing her cloth and going back to work. "If I was thirty years younger... I'd set my cap for him."

"You're not married, Claire?" I set my phone aside and dump my dirty water out in the sink.

"Never found the right person who interested me enough for all that. I'm good just staying to myself." She sounds a little wistful.

"Things might be less complicated that way," I say, staring into space. Definitely a lot less painful.

But if I hadn't taken a risk... if I hadn't married Thomas... then I wouldn't be here right now.

I miss Thomas, there's no denying that, but I'm liking my new house.

I'm thinking tomorrow I'll go into town and explore some. Everyone seems so friendly and welcoming, I think it would be good for me.

Maybe Claire is looking for a little encouragement. "It's never too late," I tell her. "I had a great aunt who got married at eighty-years-old."

"Oh my heavens. That's too bold for me. I'm afraid I missed my chance a long time ago."

"I understand." But I really don't. Sounds to me like she had a chance once, missed it, and now she doesn't want to try again.

Even though losing Thomas was... and is... painful, I hope that one day I have the strength and the boldness to let myself love again.

CHAPTER
SEVENTEEN

Bradley

"Be nice," I tell Wyatt as I drive past my house on the way to Audrey's.

"I'm always nice," Wyatt says, looking vexed.

"Right," I say.

We'd had to wait for an afternoon storm to pass before we loaded up the washer and dryer at Home Depot.

Even though the appliances were still packed in their boxes, I put a tarp over them to make sure they stay clean and dry for the drive.

As we round the big curve, Claire passes by in her old

blue Nissan Sentra that had seen better days. Wyatt and I both hold up a hand to wave.

"Guess this was Claire's day to work," Wyatt says.

"She's a hard worker. A good woman."

"Wonder why she never got married." Wyatt wonders.

"Probably because she never set foot out of Whiskey Springs."

"I heard she was seeing Harry Pritchard for a while."

"Good God, Wyatt. Don't spread rumors like that." Harry Pritchard was a confirmed bachelor, still kicking at a hundred and one years old. In his seventies and eighties, he'd walked around town being an asshole to everyone. He'd been a banker in his younger years and I had yet to meet a person who really liked him—old or young version.

"It's not a rumor if it's true."

"Maybe. But it's definitely gossip."

I pull around to the back of Audrey's house and back up to the side door. A larger entrance and where most of the deliveries go in. It also has a covered area where firewood is stored. An area currently empty.

"You know your way around the Albright house," Wyatt comments.

"See. Gossip."

"Just stating a fact.

"Be nice."

When Audrey opens the door and steps out, Wyatt turns to me.

"Just helping out the lonely widow, huh?"

"Shut up, Wyatt."

"Hey." He unsnaps his seatbelt. "No judgement from me. Maybe she has a sister."

"She actually has two of them."

"Things are looking up."

I shoot him a look and we slide out of the truck, Biscuit along with us.

Biscuit runs up to Audrey and makes a fool of himself.

"Smart dog," Wyatt says.

"Again. Be nice."

Wyatt unsnaps the latches holding the tarp down. "I won't say another word."

"Hey," I say walking up to Audrey.

"Hey."

"We passed Claire heading out. She work out okay for you?"

"She's great. A hard worker and a nice person."

"Been coming out here most of her life from what I understand."

"Really?"

"She started working for Theodore Albright when she was a teenager."

"So they were tight?"

"I guess so."

"Huh. That might explain some things."

"Like what?"

"Nothing. Probably nothing."

"I should probably go up and disconnect the old appliances first."

"It's already done."

"How did that happen?"

"Claire and I unhooked them, slid them out, and cleaned the floor under them."

I lift my cap and scratch my head. "How did you do that?"

"Claire had a handcart in her car." She holds up a hand. "I don't understand it either, but she knew how to use it."

"Okay. Well. Come on. I'll introduce you to my brother." We walk back toward the truck where Wyatt is letting down the tailgate. "This is Wyatt."

"I'm Audrey."

"I know."

Audrey glances at me then back to Wyatt. "Thank you for helping with this."

"Not a problem," Wyatt says.

"He doesn't talk much," I tell her, shooting my brother a look. He just gives me an innocent shrug.

"That's okay."

I climb into the bed of the truck and help Wyatt unload the washer, then the dryer.

"Do we need to unbox them first?" Wyatt asks.

"Probably. Audrey, do you have an old blanket?"

"I think so." Audrey goes into the house to look for a blanket to wrap around them while we cut the boxes open.

"Try to be nice," I tell Wyatt.

"I am being nice."

I scowl at him.

"She's a widow," he says. "And you met her first. I'm just biding my time. Waiting until I can meet her sisters."

"There's something seriously wrong with you," I say, but I'm smiling to myself.

I'm rather liking this unspoken brother code Wyatt and I have going on.

I'm biding my time, too, but only because Audrey is a new widow and I have to be respectful of that.

CHAPTER
EIGHTEEN

Audrey

I STAY out of the way while Bradley and his brother Wyatt bring my new washer and dryer into the house and somehow make hauling them upstairs look practically effortless.

I'm almost just as glad to see the old appliances go as I am to see the new ones come in. Well. Maybe not. I can't wait to start washing things.

They get everything hooked up and running without a hitch.

"What happened in the kitchen?" Bradley asks as they walk through.

"Just making room for my things."

"That's a lot of stuff," Wyatt says.

"I know. It was really packed in. Claire helped me wipe down all the cabinets. It might take me a while to sort through everything."

"I think I'd just throw it all out and start over," Wyatt says.

"Be nice," Bradley tells his brother.

"I considered doing that, but some of the stuff like the silverware is nicer than anything I own."

"Theodore Albright only bought the best."

Wyatt picks up a faded green electric can opener. "A bit dated, though."

"Do you want some help going through it?" Bradley asks.

"I think I need to go pick up my truck," Wyatt says, obviously not wanting to get caught up in the mess of sort through a bunch of stuff.

"No," I tell them both. "I'm just taking my time. Do you want to hold off on the closet?" I ask Bradley.

"I just need to run Wyatt back to his truck. I'll come back and we'll get started."

"Okay. But we really should probably wait until tomorrow. It's kinda late to start on a big project."

"She wants to wait," Wyatt tells Bradley.

"How is your day looking tomorrow?" Bradley asks.

"Good. I was thinking about going into town. Taking a look around. But no definite plans."

"How about I come by about eleven? Take you into town, show you around. We can get lunch. Then we can come back and get started on the first closet."

"Okay."

"Sounds good. Let me just find my dog and we'll get out of here."

"He's in his spot."

"He's going to ruin your couch. Come on, Biscuit."

Biscuit stands up, shakes out his hair, then leaps off the couch and races over to Bradley.

"See you in the morning then."

"Thanks again for the delivery service."

"Anytime."

I stand at the back door while they load up the old appliances into the truck then drive off around the house toward the road.

With a sigh, I go back inside, locking the door behind me.

It's getting late and I'm exhausted. I'd done more today than I had planned, but Claire was there helping so we'd worked hard. I actually did more today than I've done since Thomas's accident. I'm quite honestly exhausted.

Claire is coming back out in a couple of days to do her regular cleaning that she didn't get to do today—the vacuuming and mopping.

I go into the kitchen. Make myself a cheese and tomato sandwich, then sit down in front of the television to eat.

With darkness settling in, the house is full of shadows. I

love the large floor-to-ceiling windows with no shades in the daytime, but at night, not so much. They're just a wall of darkness. Someone could be outside looking in and I wouldn't even know it.

Fighting the chill that runs along my spine, I go around and check all the doors to make sure they're locked. I add having someone come out to install electric shades to my growing mental list of things to do.

Then just to avoid being downstairs where I can't see out, but anyone can see inside, I head upstairs and, just as I had done last night, lock my bedroom door.

While I'm at it, I'll install shades in the bedroom, too. Again, during the daytime, I love all the natural light and having the blurring of indoors with outdoors. But not so much at night.

Using the last of my firewood, I light a fire in the bedroom fireplace and climb into bed.

This is the life. A roaring fire in the bedroom. A good book to read.

Then comes the guilt.

Thomas had to die for me to be here. I feel guilty about liking it here so much.

When Brianna Facetimes me, relief washes over me.

"Hey," I say.

"Hey. Are you okay?"

"I think so. Why?"

"I just thought you would have called today."

"I got busy. The cleaning service came. Actually the cleaning service is one person. A lady named Claire. Anyway. We got all the cabinets in the kitchen wiped down."

"That sounds like a lot of work."

"It was. Oh. Hey. I want to show you something."

I slide out of bed, put on my slippers, and take my phone with me into the closet.

"Look. New washer and dryer."

"Impressive," Brianna says. I can tell she's having to force her excitement.

"I know. It's not very exciting. But I like it."

I go back and climb into bed.

"Who brought them?" she asks, obviously bored.

"Bradley went into Boulder and picked them up for me."

"Why not just have them delivered?"

"Because it would be next week before they could get here."

"That was nice of Bradley." Brianna looks a little less bored.

"It was. He has a brother named Wyatt. Wyatt doesn't have much to say."

"Strong but silent type?"

"I guess you could say that."

"Well. I'm about to head out. Having a drink with a friend."

"Heading out? I'm already in bed."

"I know and it's an hour earlier out there."

"Well. Have fun. I'm going to read a bit, then go to sleep."

We disconnect the line.

I lay back and stare at the ceiling.

Brianna would be bored out here. There's no night life. At least not that I know of. Or even care to know about.

Lilah. She might be okay because she can paint. She's like me in that way. We're introverts unlike our sister. Brianna needs a lot of stimulation to keep her happy.

I don't think she'd find that in Whiskey Springs.

I feel a little sad knowing that my dream of having my sisters come out here to live with me in this big old house is only going to remain a dream.

And I don't know. I might not always like it here. But for now it suits me.

Picking up the novel I'm reading, a fairy smut book that had me turning pages when I started it two weeks ago, but lately I've had trouble concentrating on, I get through about two paragraphs before I find my mind wandering to a ruggedly handsome man with light blue eyes who wants to help me with my closet project and take me to lunch tomorrow.

I close my eyes and try to force my thoughts somewhere else. Not on Thomas. That way lies sadness.

A wolf howls somewhere in the distance, its mournful cry echoing the way I feel right now.

Something is most definitely wrong with me.

I try not to think about Thomas too much and it seems wrong to think about Bradley.

Picking up my book, I force my thoughts to travel to and stay in a fictional world with a heartbreakingly handsome fairy whose love for a mortal woman knows no bounds.

CHAPTER
NINETEEN

Bradley

BEFORE I HEAD up to Audrey's to pick her up for lunch, I make a run down the hill into town.

It might be full on summer for a whole lot of the rest of the country, but here perched high in the Colorado mountains, it's still springtime. The river rushes with snowmelt. Trees stretch with tender new leaves. Baby elk dart through the underbrush like secrets not meant to be seen. Everything feels on the verge of something. The season. Me.

I drive past a bulldozer working on repairing a section of road damaged over the winter. Fortunately it wasn't bad enough to shut down the road, but the town is good about keeping repairs up on the roads so they don't become impassable.

I slide into a parking spot in front of the sheriff's office and take the yellow daisies inside with me.

"Bradley," Maggie, the receptionist says batting her eyes teasingly. "you know you shouldn't have."

"Actually I should have, but unfortunately, these are possible evidence."

No point in trying to hide anything from Maggie. Like Wyatt says, the trees have eyes... and ears.

"Evidence? What is the world coming to? Wait. You're serious? Has someone been hurt?"

"Not yet. And I hope it's nothing. I REALLY hope it's nothing. But I want to see what Sheriff Morgan thinks."

"Go on back, Dear. He's working at his desk."

"Got a minute?" I stop at Sheriff Morgan's door and give him time to look up.

He removes his reading glasses and smiles at me. "Come in Bradley. Have a seat."

Sheriff Morgan is only about ten years old than I am, but he looks a lot older. Gray hair. Wrinkles around his eyes. A perpetual frown that he constantly fights. Comes with the territory of being sheriff and even though Whiskey Springs is a peaceful town, he works hard to keep it that way.

He's actually been looking a lot better since he got married a couple of years ago.

"I hope those yellow daisies aren't going to cause me to lose any sleep."

"Yeah. I'm with you on that. I'm just being proactive and overly cautious." I set the vase of flowers on his desk.

Then I tell him what happened with the flowers.

"Did you know that Audrey was moving in?" I ask him.

"I knew it." A tall man in good shape, but by no means small, he leans back in his chair and laces his fingers behind his head. "A lot of people have keys to the Albright place."

"I didn't really consider that."

"It's not something we'd normally give much thought to around here."

"Do you think it's anything to worry about? I keep thinking about that girl in Boulder. The one who was stalked by that guy."

"Yeah. I know the one." He sits up. Looks at me with big brown eyes that I'd hate to be on the wrong side of. "I won't discount it and say it's nothing. I'd honestly be surprised if it turns out to be anything. But having said that, I'm going to hold onto these. We can always run prints. If something happens and we need to."

Something about the order of that way of thinking seems off to me. Maybe because I've met Audrey and I like her. "Seems like we should run prints now rather than after something happens."

"I'm not seeing just cause. Let me think on it. Do some asking around. See if there's been any other similar activity around."

"Okay," I say, biting back anything else I might want to say. I hadn't expected to feel worse leaving out of the sheriff's office than I had when I'd come in. But I do. "Thanks for taking your time to see me."

"Bradley," Sheriff Morgan says, stopping me at the door. I turn. "Keep your eyes open. I don't mean to put any extra responsibility on you, but you live closest to the Albright place. To Audrey."

"Right."

"If you see anything out of order, call me."

"Don't worry. I'll take care of it." With a nod, I head out the door. "See you later Maggie."

By the time I'm back in my truck, I've decided that I'd wasted my time going to see Sheriff Morgan.

I'd planned on watching out for her anyway. I don't need someone telling me to do that.

TWENTY

Audrey

WITHOUT A CLOSET TO stand and stare into, I kneel on the floor in front of my three open suitcases and try to figure out what to wear.

What does a person wear to lunch in Whiskey Springs?

Not a dress or a skirt. I rule that out fairly quickly.

Boots. Hiking boots would be preferable. But since I don't have any hiking boots—another thing for the shopping list—I go with my lace-up ankle boots. They're comfortable enough and it's not like we're going to be walking into town. We're going to be driving. Not hiking.

So now that I have my footwear picked out, I decide on

a pair on blue jeans. Then I consider a sweatshirt, but no, a sweatshirt is too sloppy for my first day in town.

Being seen with Bradley Winslow, I'll probably meet some people. And even if I don't meet people, people will see me and they'll talk. I don't want to be that sloppy widow who's living in the Albright house.

I narrow it down to a white button-down shirt like I would have worn to work or a sweater.

I lay my options out on the bed and get into the shower.

By the time I get dressed, I've decided on the button-down shirt. It's a classic and dresses up the jeans.

Dressed, I take my time drying out my hair, then use a hot brush to smooth it out even more.

I want to make a good impression and it has absolutely nothing to do with it being sort of like a date with Bradley.

Not a date. I've hired him to help me with my closets.

But...since he's not charging me for the work, though, that could possibly change things.

Still, I tell myself as I blend in some foundation and a swipe on little bit of eyeshadow.

It's not a date. It's just lunch. He's being kind to take his time to show me around town. He knows I'm new here and he's trying to make me feel welcome.

When the doorbell rings at ten fifteen, I nearly jump out of my skin.

Bradley isn't supposed to be here until eleven. Fortunately, I'd gone ahead and gotten ready early.

I smear on some lip gloss, then head downstairs.

I don't see Bradley's truck when I look out the window. Instead, I see the tail lights of a jeep driving off.

That's odd.

I watch out the window for several minutes, waiting to see if anything looks out of the ordinary.

Maybe the jeep had been lost. But someone had rang my doorbell.

I need to move changing the locks up on the priority list.

The locks for the doors and the shades for the windows. In fact, those both need to move ahead of the closets. I'll ask Bradley if he can recommend someone for either or both of those. I'd rather get a recommendation than just using google.

Not being from here, I'm not sure I trust someone I find on the Internet. Not without a recommendation.

I head back into the kitchen and use the thirty minutes or so I have before Bradley gets here to sort through some of the things I pulled out of the kitchen cabinets. It's turned into a full-time job.

When I hear Bradley's truck coming toward the house, I breathe a sigh of relief.

I've really got to stop being so jumpy.

It's going to be hard to live here when I'm so jumpy all the time.

After watching Bradley step out of his truck, I open the door.

"Where's Biscuit?" I ask.

"He's staying with Wyatt today. Taking him into a restaurant in town is frowned upon."

"Oh." I'd been looking forward to see the dog and hadn't even realized it.

"We can stop and pick him up after lunch."

"Okay."

"Were you expecting some packages?" he asks.

"I don't know. Maybe. Why?"

"Cause the mailman left you a stack of boxes."

I look to my right and sure enough, there's a stack of half a dozen boxes there. My handwriting. My boxes. Things I'd had Brianna put in the mail.

"They got here fast."

"Your stuff from Houston?"

"Yeah." I put a hand on the door frame to steady myself. "Someone rang the doorbell and... I've really got to work on not being so jumpy."

"I think it's natural living out here by yourself. In a strange place."

"I didn't know it was the mailman. I thought... I didn't know what to think."

"The mailman drives an old jeep," he says.

"So I gather."

"Can I bring these inside for you?"

"Please. That would be great."

After he hauls the boxes inside, he stands just inside the door and looks at me.

"Audrey," he says.

"Yes?" I swallow hard.

"I know it's not good to be jumpy all the time, but whatever you do..." He sweeps a strand of hair back off my face. "Don't stop being cautious. Okay?"

"Okay. I won't."

Right now he could have asked me just about anything and I probably would have agreed. My heart is pounding. My blood pumping through my veins.

"You ready to get some lunch?"

"Ready."

I hope he doesn't notice my hands are shaking just a little as I grab my purse and meet him back at the door.

It might not be a date, but it's my first outing into town.

As he opens the passenger door of his truck and waits while I climb inside, I admit to myself that it's close enough to a date to count in my book.

Maybe being a widow changes one's perspective. Or maybe it's just being out here by myself living in this big old house, but whatever it is, I have to remind myself to be careful.

I could get in over my head really quick with Bradley. Too quick.

TWENTY-ONE

Bradley

"That's my little cabin through the trees there." I point out as we pass by my place.

Squinting she leans forward.

"It's hard to see, I know."

"It's cute. Cozy," she says. "The kind of place I probably would have chosen for myself."

"You don't like the big house?" I ask, glancing over, but keeping my eyes on the road. The drive along the mountainside is precariously narrow in places. It's clear now, but when I'd headed into town earlier, there had been a layer of fog below the road. Not above, but below. Simply a testament to how high up in elevation we are.

"I like it." She takes a deep breath. "I have mixed feelings about it, I guess."

"Like what?"

"Like if I had my sisters here, I think it would be great. But with just me, it's a little unsettling. I don't think it's the size of the house though. I'm thinking I need to change the locks and see about installing some electric shades for the windows. Just for at night."

"You got spooked right off the bat with those flowers."

"Yeah." She takes a deep breath, lets it out slowly. "What did the sheriff say?"

I don't want to tell her he blew it off as nothing. Not when that might cause her to let her guard down.

"Typical. He's going to check around. See if there have been any other incidents."

"So nothing." She looks out the window. "It's probably nothing anyway. I'm sure a lot of people have keys. Maybe somebody was dropping off a housewarming gift and didn't know I was home."

A person dropping off a housewarming gift should let themselves be known. Not leave flowers with no name. "I know a guy who can change out the locks. I'll give you his phone number."

"Thank you."

"Sure. Happy to do it."

"I don't remember the road being so narrow."

"You had to come this way on your way in."

"It was late and I was too tired to pay much attention," she says with a tight little smile.

We turn right onto the main highway leading into town.

I want to take the veil of sadness off her. I know it's not possible. It's something only time can do. All I can do is hope to distract her just a little bit.

"Is a hamburger okay?" I ask. "The Hungry Biscuit has the best burgers and fries around."

"A hamburger sounds good."

"The Hungry Biscuit it is."

I pull into the crowded parking lot and find an open space around back.

"It's busy," she says.

"Known for the best burgers and fries in the state."

"In the state. That's a bold claim."

"I'm curious to see if you agree. I'll come around. Get the door."

"I'm curious, too."

I slide out of the truck and walk around to open her door.

I haven't dated anyone since Zoe. That was three years ago. She'd had her sights set on California from the beginning. I'd hoped she would change her mind, but she'd gotten out of here so fast it made a man's head spin.

I was now considered the most eligible and most confirmed bachelor of Whiskey Springs. It wasn't a distinction I'd asked for, but I couldn't deny the truth of it either.

With my family owning Timber Ridge Cabins and me being the oldest male in the family, there was nothing I could say to dispute it. It didn't even seem to matter that our company was going to be split equally into three parts after we inherited it.

Maybe being seen with Audrey would get the scheming women off my heels.

After I open the passenger door and Audrey slides to the ground, her feet wobble on the uneven rocky surface.

I steady her with a hand on her arm.

"It's a little difficult to walk on this," I say.

"I noticed."

I slide my hand down her arm and press my palm against hers, linking our fingers, as we step away from the truck. She doesn't pull away.

Together, we walk around toward the front door of The Hungry Biscuit.

A cheerful bell rings above the door as we step inside. The scent of grilled onions and fresh-baked bread—comfort food and memories—fills my senses. A couple of locals glance up from their booths, then go back to their burgers.

She pauses just inside the door and takes a look around.

"I love this place already," she says, her voice light. "Quirky name. Smells amazing. And... I've never been welcomed to lunch by a giant hamburger before."

She's referring to the human-sized cardboard hamburger just inside the door, cheerful and absurd in the best small-town way.

I grin. "They're proud of their burgers."

A waitress waves us to a corner booth, the kind with worn red vinyl and a window view of the mountains. Audrey slides in across from me, tucking her hair behind her ear.

"So," I say, picking up a menu. Handing it to her. Then taking one for myself. "You more of a cheeseburger-and-fries girl or... grilled chicken salad with dressing on the side?"

She raises an eyebrow. "That seems like a rather odd question."

I lean in, lowering my voice just enough to make her smile. "It means I'm trying to learn your deepest secrets. Starting with your burger order."

She laughs—a real, honest laugh that warms something in my chest and gives me hope.

"Well," she says, studying the menu with a mock-serious expression, "you'll be pleased to know I'm a cheeseburger and fries, extra pickles and tomato, kind of girl."

"Dangerous," I say, smiling. "I like it."

And for the first time in a long while, something feels easy. Like maybe this isn't just lunch. Like maybe it could be something more. Something more than I had even with Zoe. Even with Zoe, things had never felt quite right.

Audrey is different.

And so far she's not talking about going anywhere.

TWENTY-TWO

Audrey

Retro music with nostalgia drifts from hidden speakers. Eighties tunes, maybe, from what I can hear.

The Hungry Biscuit has gone all in on branding. Their logo—a cartoon hamburger with a wide grin and tiny arms—adorns everything in sight. It's stamped on the napkins, printed on the paper placemats, even printed on the back of the laminated menus.

On the walls, framed photos of customers through the decades hang beside retro ads proclaiming Hot 'n Flaky Since '62! There's a black-and-white mural of a hamburger wearing sunglasses and snow skiing down a mountainside. A string of mismatched café lights zigzags overhead, casting a soft glow on red vinyl booths and chrome-edged tables that look like they've been here since the last century.

Near the register, a display case houses hamburger-themed merchandise—mugs, bumper stickers, even T-shirts that read The Hungry Biscuit — Whiskey Springs Original Hamburgers.

"I'm getting the idea that the Hungry Biscuit started here in Whiskey Springs."

"It did. It's in all the small towns now. Alpine Falls. Silver Pines."

"Cute."

He looks comfortable sitting on the other side of the booth.

One arm relaxed across the back of his seat.

"So The Hungry Biscuit." I lean forward and look into Bradley's light blue eyes. "Is it hamburgers or biscuits?"

"Hamburgers."

"Then why biscuit?"

"Biscuit is a generic term like widget."

"Is that why you named your dog Biscuit?"

He grins. "Something like that."

I nod, trying to keep a straight face. "It must be a Colorado thing."

"You don't have biscuits in Texas?"

"We have biscuits. But a hamburger is a hamburger and a biscuit is a biscuit."

"Fair enough. Tell me something you say that we don't."

"That's easy. We say y'all."

"That's a universal southern thing."

A waitress stops at our table. "Hey Bradley." She looks at me. "Hi."

"Hi."

"Evie, this is Audrey."

"Hi Audrey." She puts a hand on her hip. "What can I get for the two of you?"

Bradley looks at me.

"I'll just have a coke."

"Same for me," Bradley says.

"Be right back," Evie says.

"That's one," Bradley says.

"What's one?"

"Coke. I would have asked for a soda."

"Right." I lean forward. "Do you know everyone in town?"

"I guess I do. Unless they're tourists or just passing through."

"Are there any tourists here now?"

"There are. See that family over there? The one with the two parents, a little boy and a little girl? Tourists."

I look over my shoulder. "Anyone else?"

"I don't think so."

"Do you all like tourists?"

"Tourists are our bread and butter. We wouldn't have much of a town without them, certainly not Timber Cabins."

"Makes sense. What about new people? People who aren't from around here?"

"We welcome new people with open arms. Not everyone is lucky enough to be born and raised here."

"That's promising."

"What about your life back in Houston? You don't think you'll miss it?"

"Sometimes, but..." I look over at the whimsical hamburger painted on the wall. "There were a lot of things that I didn't like."

"Such as?"

"I didn't like living in the suburbs. And I didn't care for my job either. I just couldn't find a way out of it."

"You worked at an art gallery, right?"

"Right."

The server drops off our cokes and I take a sip of the sparkling, bubbling soda.

"But you didn't like it?"

I shake my head. "I didn't dislike it. It just didn't feel like what I wanted to do with my life. You know?"

"I do know. What is it you want to do?"

"I haven't figured that out yet. You'd think that by the time someone is twenty-seven, they'd have figured out what they want to do when they grow up."

"Maybe." He shrugs. "Maybe you just needed to change perspective to find it."

"That's what I'm hoping."

"You'll figure it out," he says. "When it comes to you, you'll know."

TWENTY-THREE

Bradley

AFTER LUNCH, we walk down to the General Store.

"You should be able to get some of the things on your list here," he says.

"Maybe," she looks around at the rows and rows of everything from cans of paint to paintings for the wall.

"Do they have new door locks?"

"I think they do."

I lead her toward hardware to a section of door locks.

"He can order something else if you want something different."

"I've been looking online. I'm thinking something with a keypad and a camera."

"John won't have that, but he can get it for you."

"I can just order something online." She turns and looks at me with her meadow green eyes. "Do you think you could install new locks?"

"I don't see why not."

"When we get back, I'll show you what I'm thinking. You can tell me if it'll work on my door."

"I can make it work. But I'll look at it. Make sure it's compatible."

"Okay. I need shades for my windows."

"We'll definitely have to special order those. I'll help you measure and I can install those, too."

"Seriously?"

"Sure. It's not that hard."

"You're rather handy to have around."

"So I've been told."

"Really? Who else told you that?"

"Mostly little old ladies with blue hair."

She laughs out loud.

She needed to get out. To think about something other than what happened to Thomas.

"Okay. So we're making progress. What else do you need?"

"Hiking boots," she says.

"Hiking boots? I didn't expect you to say that."

"They aren't for the house."

"Funny girl, aren't you?"

She shrugs. "I've been told."

"Definitely funny. So we need to go across the street for hiking boots. Anything else in here?"

"I could use a black marker and some trash bags."

"John definitely has those."

A few minutes later, a paper sack in my hand with a marker and a roll of trash bags, we head across the street to the ladies' clothing shop.

"Are you sure they have hiking boots?" she asks as we step inside. "It looks more like a place to get something formal to wear."

"Hello Bradley," a young lady greets Bradley from behind the counter. "How can I help you?" She shifts her gaze over to me.

"We need some hiking boots," I say.

"Of course. Back left corner. Let me know if you need help."

"I will. Thanks Steph."

The back of the shop is literally a wall of shelves with two benches in front for sitting. Stacks of shoe boxes. Boots. High heels. Sneakers.

Audrey wanders to the hiking boot section.

"See anything you like?"

She picks up a basic lace-up hiking boot in black leather. "These look good."

"Try them on. What size do you wear?"

"A six."

I stretch up over her head and pull down a box.

She sits on one of the benches and slips off her own lace-up boots. City boots. I open up the box and pick up one of the boots. The laces are still wrapped up in tissue. I get the laces started, then hand the boot over.

She slides it on her foot and starts lacing it up.

"Ouch." She jerks her hand back. "I think I broke a fingernail."

"Not surprising with all the housework you've been doing. You really need to let Claire do that."

"I have to have something to do." She lightly touches her broken fingernail.

"I know. Let me do this." I slide onto the floor, kneeling in front of her, and get to work on lacing up her boots.

"Handy," she says, looking down at me.

"I know. I'm a sucker for a pretty girl."

Out of the corner of my eye, I watch the elusive smile tug at her lips.

I'm betting she's smiled more in the last two hours than she smiled in the last two weeks.

She sits quietly while I lace up one boot, then slide the other one on and lace it up, too.

"How do they feel?" I ask, after I have both of them securely laced up and tied. I hold out a hand to help her stand up.

"They feel good," she says.

"You might have to break them in," I say.

"Hiking maybe?"

"That can be arranged."

"You'd go hiking with me?"

"I can't very well let you go by yourself." She raises a brow. "Bears and mountain lions."

"Somehow that doesn't make me feel very safe."

"I never walk anywhere without my can of bear spray."

"And I feel safe again."

She grins at me and my heart melts.

She's a widow. She's a widow. She's a widow.

She's not available for me to be thinking about romantically.

I need to keep my head about me. And yet it's virtually impossible with her looking at me with her siren green eyes.

TWENTY-FOUR

Audrey

WEARING MY NEW HIKING BOOTS, I walk with Bradley, carrying a shopping bag with my old boots, down Main Street.

Whiskey Springs is a quintessential small town with three traffic lights. Two way traffic with parallel parking on either side of the street. Half a dozen or so people driving up and down the street. About twice that many more walking the sidewalks.

An older couple holds hands as they cross the street. The family we'd seen earlier at the Hungry Biscuit step into the ice cream parlor. Two teenage boys with backpacks punch each other playfully as they walk home from school.

Tall, snow-capped mountains rise behind the town, cradling it like protective giants frozen in time. Their jagged peaks pierce the sky, a stark contrast to the quiet charm nestled in the valley below where time slows and every breath carries the scent of pine and possibility.

The faint aroma of firewood smoke lingers in the crisp air and swirls with the rich scent of cappuccinos from the corner coffee shop. As we pass the ice cream parlor, the sugary sweetness wraps around us, warm and nostalgic despite the chill.

New spring growth stretching out on the spruce trees. Tender spring flowers flutter in the soft breeze. Blue butterfly begonias. Salmon-colored geraniums. Pink and white petunias.

My new home.

We leave the main sidewalk and walk along a path leading to the bubbling river. A wooden plank bridge arches over the river leading to a little sitting area on the other side.

Wooden benches. A community of painted bird houses.

"It's beautiful here," I say, sitting on one of the benches.

"It's beautiful all year around," Bradley says. "And at Christmas everything is lit up with twinkling, festive lights. There's nothing else like it."

"I'm looking forward to seeing it," I say. "I'm especially looking forward to winter. To the snow."

"Yeah. The first snowfall is magical."

"And after that?"

He stretches out his long legs. Crosses them at the ankles. "After that depends on a lot of factors. I don't want to say too much that would influence your decision."

"Sounds a bit ominous."

"It's beautiful. You're going to love it."

"You're not all that convincing. Will we get snowed in?"

"One of those factors. Each year is a little bit different from the last. But the short answer is not usually." He takes a breath. "Unless there's a blizzard."

"I hope you're not on one of the tourist committees."

He laughs. "I'm on the town council."

I look over at him. Nod slowly. His ruggedly good looks would easily compensate for anything negative he might say about Whiskey Springs. Not that he's being negative. He's just being realistic. And it's probably because I live here now. As such, I should know the real scoop.

"You don't want me to have any unrealistic expectations?"

"I wouldn't want that."

"And since I'm not a tourist, you can tell me the truth."

"I try to always tell the truth."

"That's a good quality to have." Closing my eyes, I take a deep breath, inhaling the scent of blue spruce trees all around us. Let it out slowly. The melodic trickling of the river soothes me.

"Have you spent much time in the mountains?" he asks.

"This is my first time."

"So you just got in your car and headed up here with no

idea of what to expect? No idea about whether you would like it here?”

“Pretty much.” I open my eyes and meet his gaze.

“I would think that would take a lot of bravery.” His eyes are kind. Understanding. And questioning.

“I’m not sure I would call it bravery,” I say. “Maybe more like a sort of desperation. I didn’t know what else to do.”

“That didn’t involve moving in with relatives.”

“Right.” I’d told him about that. “I told you about my husband and the plane crash.”

He nods. “I’m sorry,” he says softly.

I nod. “I wish that were the whole story.”

He waits. Doesn’t push. Just watches me like he’s actually listening.

“I found out afterward, from his attorney, that he had a child. With someone else. A child I didn’t know existed.”

His brow furrows, but he says nothing.

“He left everything—everything—to the child’s mother. Except this house.” I struggle to keep my tone even. To keep the bitterness and hurt out of my tone. I take a deep breath. Let it out slowly. “And a monthly stipend arranged through some kind of legal arrangement set up by Theodore Albright.”

“You must be furious.”

“I don’t know what I am. Angry, yes. Betrayed. Grieving. But it’s not... clean. It’s not like I can just hate him and move on.”

I glance away, blinking fast. "I didn't come here to fall apart. I came here because I already had."

The words hang between us.

I draw a deep ragged breath. "It sounds pathetic."

"It doesn't," he says gently. "It sounds like you're surviving something most people wouldn't know how to face."

I look away again, blinking back fresh tears. His kindness cuts deeper than I expect—like it's peeling away a layer I didn't realize was there.

Thinking back, I realize... Thomas wasn't a very good listener. Not really. He and I had something, yes. But right now, I'm not sure what that something even was.

Everything feels like it was built on a foundation of half-truths and silence.

I'd done the math. The child came before me—before we even met. And somehow, that makes the betrayal worse. Because it wasn't just about what he did. It was about what he hid. He married me without ever telling me. Lived every day beside me with that secret buried like a landmine between us.

I go quiet, the words catching in my throat now, too heavy to carry any further.

He doesn't try to fill the silence. He just sits there, close but not crowding me, his presence steady. Solid. Like he's offering something I didn't even know I needed.

After a moment, I exhale slowly and lean my head

against his shoulder. He doesn't flinch or shift or say a single thing.

He just lets me rest there.

And for the first time in what feels like forever, I don't feel like I'm drowning.

A few seconds pass. Then his arm slips around me—slowly, carefully—like he's making sure it's okay, even without asking.

I don't pull away. I don't want to.

I let myself lean into him just a little more. Not because I'm ready for anything. Just because right now... it feels safe.

And safe is more than I expected to find.

TWENTY-FIVE

Bradley

"You're good help," I say, handing Audrey a chunk of wood I pulled from the closet with a crowbar.

She's wearing a pair of my work gloves that are too two sizes too big for her and an oversized sweatshirt that she changed into after we got back here to her house.

"You seem surprised," she says, coming back from adding the chunk of wood to a big cardboard box we'd designated as debris.

"Well, you are a city girl," I say teasingly. After our moment near the river, I'm purposely trying to keep the mood light.

"Never underestimate a girl from the city," she says. "You never know what we'll be able to do."

"I stand corrected. How are the washer and dryer working out?"

"Great. Couldn't be happier."

Her phone chimes. "It's my sister. If I don't answer, she'll send out the National Guard."

"Go ahead. I need to take Biscuit out for a walk anyway."

"Okay." She walks off, answering her phone.

I take a look around. Most of the demolition work is done on this closet. Just one more closet to go and tomorrow I can start floating the sheetrock.

I find that Biscuit followed Audrey downstairs and is already out back with her making his rounds, so I make a detour by the refrigerator for a bottle of water.

Audrey has got quite the mess in here. Unopened boxes of her own things that she had sent up stacked along one wall.

A row of half-filled boxes of things labeled *donate, discard,* and *keep (maybe).*

Then there are the things she's still going through.

Maybe later, after we finish peeling the old out of the closets, she'll let me help her go through what looks like a lot of junk left here by Theodore.

People live somewhere long enough, they pack things in.

I understand Audrey wanting to start with a clean slate.

I did the same thing when I moved into my cabin. Except that it was on a much smaller scale and it wasn't packed with someone else's stuff.

But take the Bentley cabin. Gutting the bathroom to start from the ground up. It's a lot of work, but it'll be worth it when it's finished.

The cabin has good bones. Most of them built back in the last century do. They just need to be modernized up to this century. Then they're good to go.

While I drink my water, I watch Audrey pacing along her back deck. I haven't met her sisters, but it seems like they might be a bit overprotective. It's understandable after what she went through. And then the way she'd loaded up and come up here. By herself.

She said she didn't have a choice, but there's always a choice. She chose to come up here by herself over moving back in with her parents or moving in with her sisters.

She hadn't said anything about getting her own place, but I can only imagine that had something to do with her finances.

From what she told me, her husband left her in something of a bind. Apparently her work at the art gallery didn't pay enough for her to get her own place.

Biscuit paces along beside her, matching her step by step. She idly pets the top of his head as she walks.

She's a good person, Audrey Sinclair. I'm going to do what I can for her.

And hopefully give her the space to heal.

In the meantime, I have to remind myself not to push her into something she might regret later. I don't want her feeling guilty because of me.

TWENTY-SIX

Audrey

"MY GOODNESS GRACIOUS," Claire says when she steps into the kitchen. "How on earth did you get everything sorted and put up? When I left here two days ago, I didn't think you were ever going to dig your way out of all this stuff we pulled out of the cabinets."

"I had a little help," I say. A lot of help if I was being honest.

Bradley had been amazing. He had an amazing attitude about not keeping things that I knew I didn't need.

And then to make things even better, he'd loaded up the

boxes of donations in his truck and gotten it all out of here along with my empty boxes.

"It looks amazing," Claire says, running a hand along the uncluttered countertop.

"Everything's organized," I say, opening one of the overhead cabinets.

"You've got four plates on one shelf. Four glasses on another and nothing on the top shelf."

"I know. It's great. My mugs are over here." I open another cabinet to show her my three coffee mugs.

"I've never seen a kitchen so organized. Maybe in a magazine."

"It's so big. I have a place for everything."

"And everything in its place. Well," she says. "I came prepared to work. But it looks like I'll just be doing my normal vacuuming and cleaning."

"You're making me feel bad," I say.

"Don't feel bad. I really am impressed."

"I couldn't have done it without Bradley."

Claire's face lights up. "You could do a lot worse than Bradley Winslow."

"He's just being helpful."

"I know. I know. But that's as good a place to start as any."

I can't help the little smile that plays about my lips. "Don't you go starting any rumors," I say. "He's very kind."

Claire doesn't know the real reason why I'm here. She doesn't know that everything my husband and I had saved went toward his bills. That his life insurance went to a child he had with another woman. People I didn't even know about until the attorney told me after the accident.

That I'd come here because I needed a place to heal.

That I came here because I was broken.

Not to get into a relationship, no matter how kind... and hot... Bradley Winslow might be.

"He's never been married," she says.

I cut my eyes at her.

She holds up a hand. "I'm just 'saying. But I'm getting to work now. I've got a house to clean."

While Claire goes upstairs and vacuums, I got out back and bring in an armful of firewood from the stack Wyatt had dropped off yesterday. He'd brought a trailer full of chopped firewood and stacked it in a covered area behind the house. A cord, they'd called it. I called it a ton of firewood.

I lay the logs in the fireplace, add some kindling, and strike a match.

Within minutes, I have a healthy fire going. Everyone else would say it was too big, but I rather like a big fire.

Settling myself on the sofa, I open up a box, about the size of a shoe box, and face a task I've been putting off.

It's time to send thank you notes to people who sent flowers and brought food to my house after Thomas's accident. Mostly people who worked with Thomas. The people at Skye Travels were all so very kind. Even his boss, Noah Worthington and his wife Savannah had stopped by my house. They'd brought a lush green potted ivy and a home-made apple pie.

They'd asked if there was anything they could do. I honestly think they'd meant it. And they hadn't stayed more than a few minutes. I appreciated that.

Other than the Worthingtons, the names are a blur. I don't recognize any of the others. But they were there. And I have to thank them for being supportive.

TWENTY-SEVEN

Bradley

I'M right in the middle of floating the sheetrock at the Bentley cabin when I get a call from the Sheriff.

With the windows open, the sounds of the river drift in a cool breeze. It's one of those cool, cloudy days that make me feel sorry for people who live in places like Nevada and Texas.

Only in the Colorado mountains can we be full on summer and have a pleasant day with highs in the fifties.

There is nowhere else I'd rather live.

"Hello, Sheriff," I say, walking out of the cabin's bathroom that is currently undergoing a complete trans-formation.

"Hello Bradley. I just wanted to give you a quick update. I made some calls. There haven't been any reports of missing girls or even any cases of stalking in the neighboring counties, at least nothing out of the ordinary."

"So no active serial killers."

"I don't think Audrey has anything to worry about. Just someone with a key who did something they shouldn't have."

"Right." Like go inside her house and leave a vase a yellow daisies. Flowers with no name. No indication of who they came from.

Not a very nice thing to do.

"So rest your mind," he says. "I recommend she change the locks for her own peace of mind."

"Got new locks on order."

"Good. Good. Just wanted to tell you what I knew."

"Thanks for the update." I disconnect the line.

I'm still feeling unsettled about it all. No matter what the sheriff says, I still don't trust that Audrey is safe. I'm just being overprotective. That has to be it.

When I finish up here, I'll go by her place. See if those door locks came in yet. Maybe stop in town and pick up a pizza. If the door locks aren't in yet, we can start measuring for the blinds. There's plenty to do over at Audrey's place. Enough to keep us busy for days.

And one thing I'd learned last night is that she needs help.

I know it's the grief, but sometimes she'll just stop what she's doing and stare into space. It's as though her mind freezes and she can't make decisions.

I'd convinced her, and rightly so, that she doesn't need all that stuff Theodore left behind. A lot of it was from the last century. She kept some of his really high quality silverware and some china, but things like the old green can opener had to go.

Audrey had brought some nice things with her. Between what she kept of his and what she brought of hers, she has a nice setup in the kitchen.

The sooner I can get her closet rounded out, the sooner she can move her clothes into her closet and start feeling like she's got a permanent home there.

I'm being selfish about that. I want to make sure she feels like she belongs. I want her to belong. To stay.

By mid-afternoon, I'm ready to knock off here and head to Audrey's place. If Wyatt isn't busy, I'll ask him to come by tomorrow. Help me make some progress on the Bentley place. We're nearing peak tourist season and the longer I drag my feet on it, the longer it'll be before we can rent it out to someone and start recouping the money spent to buy and renovate it.

As much as I enjoy what I do, I have to keep in mind that we have a business.

I pack up my tools, haul them to the truck and, with

Biscuit in tow, climb up into the cab of the truck and head toward Audrey's place.

Too early to get a pizza. I can drive back in later and get something. Even better, take Audrey with me. It'll be good for her to get out of the house.

I pass by my own cabin without so much as a twinge.

Just as I'm pulling up to Audrey's, Claire is pulling out.

She waves at me and I can already hear the rumors getting started.

I don't care if people talk. I don't care what they say about me spending time over here. Really, Claire is the only one who's seen me here. But people have seen us in town together now.

That's more than enough to give the gossips plenty to talk about.

Audrey doesn't meet me at the door like she usually does.

When she does open the door a couple of minutes later, her eyes are red-rimmed like she's been crying.

TWENTY-EIGHT

Audrey

"Are you okay?" Bradley asks as I open the door.

"Yes," I say, pushing my hair back. "I hadn't realized it was so late."

"It's not late. I'm early."

"Hey Biscuit." I lean over and hug the dog, taking a moment of comfort in him, then step back giving them room to come inside. "Claire just left."

"I know. I passed her on the road. It smells good in here. Like vanilla and some kind of flowers. Daffodils maybe."

"Claire did that. I don't know what she did, but everything feels so clean."

"It's nice to get the house cleaned up. What's all that?" he asks with a nod toward the papers spread over the coffee table in front of the roaring fire in the fireplace. Writing these letters makes me sad. In an odd way, writing the thank you notes seems to finalize the end of my life with Thomas.

"Just some letters I have to write."

I go over and gather them up, putting them back in their Kraft-colored box.

"Don't put them away on my account."

"It's okay. I don't want to look at them anymore tonight."

I don't have to tell him they have something to do with Thomas. He knows. I know he knows.

"Anything I can help with?" he asks.

"Nothing you want to get involved in. Just letters I should have written already."

"I'm sure people understand."

I give him a sideways look. Then change the subject. "The doorknobs haven't come in yet."

"It's okay. We can finish up that last closet if you want to."

"Okay and then I guess we can start measuring for window shades."

"That's what I was thinking." He turns and looks toward the tall windows at the side of the house. Out at the magnificent view of the mountains. "It seems a waste to block those views."

"It's just for night time. And just until things settle down."

"Right."

I know better. I know that things will never settle down enough for me to feel safe enough to have bare windows at night.

"You look tired," he says. "We don't have to do any work at all if you don't want to."

I nod slowly. "What do you want to do?"

"We can open a bottle of wine. Sit in front of that impressive fire you have going."

"Don't make fun of my fire."

"Just admiring it."

"You can build the next one."

We sit side by side on the sofa with Biscuit in between us.

"Biscuit likes your fires."

"At least somebody does."

"I like your fires."

"But..."

"But when I was growing up, my dad would have my hide if I burned up all the firewood in one week."

"I guess that could be a problem."

"You don't have to worry about it. Wyatt can bring you more."

"So Wyatt's in charge of the firewood?"

"For the most part."

"It doesn't seem fair to the trees." She gets up, grabs a poker, and adjusts the logs.

"In our defense, we plant more trees than we cut down."

"And that keeps people in jobs."

"Exactly."

"I'm just doing my part." I put the poker down and sit back down next to Biscuit. Clasp my hands in my lap. Then reach over and scratch Biscuit's ears. "I'm not used to doing nothing."

"We're not doing nothing," he says.

"How do you figure that?" I ask, cutting my eyes in his direction.

"We're taking a mental health moment."

"A mental health moment. I like it."

"It's very important. And. We're monitoring the fire."

I've noticed that Bradley is quite good at justifying things when he wants to.

"Claire said something that struck me as a bit odd today."

"Yeah? What did Claire say?"

Bradley stretches out his legs and gets comfortable.

"She just said something about Theodore. She said he had a brother."

"Theodore? He didn't have any relatives. Just Thomas."

"Are you sure? She seemed pretty certain."

"I think we would have known about it if he did."

"Maybe." I lean back against the sofa and close my eyes.

After a moment, I open my eyes and look into Brandon's light blue eyes. "You don't think there will be any problem, do you?"

"With you being here? No. You're all legal. Signed, sealed, and delivered."

"I hope you're right." When she'd said it, it had sent a little chill through me. Like maybe something wasn't right. It had made me want to check my account again. To make sure the money was still there. But since I'd just checked it that morning before she got here, I didn't do it.

Claire could be wrong about that. And even if she wasn't wrong, like Bradley said, everything was sewn up, all legal like.

Bradley

EVEN THOUGH I'M a hard worker and I don't normally sit still like this either, with Audrey it doesn't seem like we're wasting time.

We make hot chocolate and sit in front of the fireplace.

Her impressive fires are starting to grow on me. Nice and cozy on this unseasonably cool evening.

"To new beginnings," I say, holding up my mug.

"To just breathing," she says, holding up her own mug.

The glow from the fire dances in her eyes, and for a second, I forget what I was going to say.

She leans back on the couch, one leg curled beneath her.

"What are you thinking?" she asks, her voice barely above a whisper.

I hesitate. Then tell the truth. "That I want to stay right here."

Audrey holds my gaze, and the air shifts. Warmer. Swirling with something unspoken. Her lips part slightly, like maybe she's thinking about what she wants to say next. Like maybe she doesn't quite know what to say.

Lowering her gaze, she takes a sip of her hot cocoa and I decide she's not going to say anything. We sit quietly, the fire crackling. Biscuit snoring softly.

"I used to think I had everything figured out," she says softly. "Career. Plans. All neat and tidy. And then life said, 'this isn't it.'"

I nod, understanding more than I want to admit.

"Turns out... slowing down isn't the same as giving up," I say.

She takes a deep breath and her siren green eyes lock onto mine. Eyes that I want to tumble into and never come out of.

"How did you get so wise?" she asks.

"I'm not wise." I take a sip of cocoa. "There was a time. When I was young. About the time I was graduating high school." A log falls, sending up a flurry of embers. "When I wanted to get out of Whiskey Springs. I wanted to see the world."

"What happened?"

"I saw the world."

A little smile plays about her lips. "That's rather vague."

"I spent four years at Purdue getting a degree in engineering."

"You have a degree in engineering?" she asks.

"Don't look so surprised. But. Yes. I do."

"And you came back here."

"After I worked a year at a factory as an engineer. Again. Slowed down. Didn't give up. My family is here. We have a thriving business. I realized I'd rather spend my days working for myself than earning money to make someone else wealthy."

"That makes a lot of sense."

"Here. When I make decisions, they impact something I'm building for my family. I'm building generational wealth."

Biscuit opens his eyes and points his ears forward. Audrey scratches them.

She nods slowly. "None of you are married yet. And no children?"

"I always figured I had plenty of time."

"You said that in the past tense."

Biscuit sits up. Looking toward nothing in particular.

But then...

A loud bang.

The sound jolts us both. A sharp, metallic clatter against the porch railing.

With a loud bark, Biscuit jumps off the sofa and heads toward the front door.

Audrey bolts upright. "What was that?"

Biscuit stands at the door, barking. Biscuit has several different barks and this is one I've never heard before. It's vicious and unforgiving.

I'm already moving, pulse thudding. I cross the room in three strides and press my forehead ahead against the window.

Lightning flashes, illuminating the porch for a heartbeat.

Nothing.

But my eyes catch something just beyond the edge of the steps. A shape—maybe a figure—there and gone in the flicker of light.

"Someone's out there," I say, voice low.

Audrey rises slowly, her mug of hot cocoa forgotten on the coffee table. "Are you sure?"

Another crack of thunder answers for me.

I unlock the front door, but only open it a sliver. Biscuit presses forward, growling now, ears rigid, her entire body tense.

Rain lashes the porch, and wind pushes against the door.

I don't see anyone.

But I feel it. Something is off. Like the storm brought more than just wind and rain.

"I'll check it out," I say, even though every instinct screams to keep the door shut.

Audrey's hand grips my arm. "Don't."

Her voice is soft. Frightened.

"It's okay," I say.

I hesitate, then pull the door open just enough to step outside.

The rain hits instantly. Cold, sharp needles against my skin. Biscuit stays behind, pacing at the threshold but unwilling to leave Audrey.

Lightning flashes again.

There's nothing on the steps, but when I glance to the right, toward the side of the porch, I spot it.

A small box. About the size of a bracelet box. Square. Black. Sitting dead center on the porch floor, obviously left there on purpose.

I glance around, heart hammering. Still no sign of anyone.

I reach for it, half-expecting it to be hot or maybe to explode, but it's just a box. I hold it away at arm's length, expecting something to jump out. A spider. A snake.

But inside, there is just a single note lying there. Just a note.

Rain dots the paper as I open it, the ink already smudging.

You shouldn't be here. You were never part of the plan.

I replace the note and slide the box into my pocket.

With one last glance around, I turn and go back inside, securing the door behind me.

"What is it?" Audrey asks, trembling. "What did you see?"

I look into her eyes, haunted again, and everything inside me screams at me not to tell her.

CHAPTER

THIRTY

Audrey

HE HESITATES. Just for a second. But I feel the shift.

Something clenches in my stomach, instinct maybe, or dread.

"Nothing," he says too quickly. "Just the wind knocking something over."

He won't meet my eyes. That tells me more than his words ever could.

Besides, there's nothing out there to knock over.

I nod anyway. Pretend to believe him. Pretend I don't see the tension in his shoulders or the way his hand stays tucked deep in his pocket like he's holding onto something that might vanish.

"It's getting worse out there," he adds, flipping the deadbolt. "Let's stay away from the windows."

I drift back to the hearth, settling near the warmth though it doesn't quite reach the chill inside me. Outside, the storm howls like something alive. The rain lashes the windows in bursts, each gust louder than the last.

"I didn't know it was going to rain."

"It's like that sometimes up here," he says distractedly, standing next to me in front of the fire.

"You don't think someone's out there, do you?" I ask quietly.

He doesn't answer. Doesn't even look at me. Just stares into the flames like the answers are buried in the embers.

A beat passes. Two.

"No," he says finally.

"What is it?" I ask, with a glance toward his pocket where he still has his hand.

With a sigh, he pulls his hand out of his pocket. He's holding a black box, cheap cardboard faded with rain splatter. Hands it to me.

"What is this?" I ask, looking from the box up to him.

"It was outside."

I instinctively hold it at arm's length.

"I opened it," he adds. "It's a note."

I set it down on the coffee table and drop onto the couch in front of it.

"Why is this happening?"

"Are you going to read it?"

"Did you read it?"

"When I opened it, I couldn't help but read it."

I nod. He's mistakenly worried about my privacy.

"What does it say?"

Getting the idea that I don't want to touch it, he opens the box and holds it up.

You shouldn't be here.
You were never part of the plan.

"What does that mean?" I ask, searching his light blue eyes.

"Hell if I know." He runs a hand along the back of his neck. "But I don't like it."

"Are they talking about me or you?" I wonder.

"Good question."

"With no answer."

"I don't think you should stay here. Until we figure this out."

A trill of panic runs through me. "What do you mean?"

"Someone just threatened you."

"Or you." But now I know what he really thinks. He thinks the threat is toward me, not him. "Why would someone threaten me? What did I do?"

"I don't know why. Maybe it has something to do with the inheritance."

"But... why?"

"I think you should pack a bag and come stay with me until we find out who's doing this."

I stop, my mug halfway to my lips. "I can't do that."

"I have an extra bedroom."

"No. It's not that. I can't let someone run me away from the house. I won't."

A crash of thunder splits the air overhead, but it sounds like it's moved off a little bit more than it was.

Why would someone come out in the middle of a thunderstorm to leave me a threatening note?

"Did you see anyone outside?"

"I thought I saw a shadow, but I can't be sure. I was pitch dark."

"What do we do? Do we call the sheriff?"

"We can, but... I think we're on our own on this one."

"He wouldn't help us with the flowers?"

Bradley shakes his head, his lips in a thin line.

I lean back against the couch and close my eyes.

"Was there anyone you think might have followed you here from Houston?" he asks, sitting next to me.

"No. Why would they?"

"I don't know. I'm just looking for some kind of explanation."

"I know." I lower my head, covering my face with my hands. "I'm not sure there is one."

"I think the storm is about out of here," he says. "Feel like riding into town? Get a pizza?"

"Seriously?" I ask.

"It's not like we can do anything here."

"You're right." I take a deep breath. "Okay."

Sitting here while someone drops threatening messages off at my front door isn't helping anything. I refuse to cower in fear.

CHAPTER
THIRTY-ONE

Bradley

The storm moves out as quickly as it moved in.

Audrey and I head outside to my truck to go into town to get a pizza.

And I need time to think about what we need to do next.

We both look around as we cross the porch. I don't see any tire tracks. No footprints.

Nothing in the faint glow of the fading sunlight. Nothing to indicate anyone was here.

"Everything smells so good," Audrey says, taking a deep breath. "The spruce trees. Just wow."

I open the passenger door and hold it while she climbs inside.

I don't like the thought of her being up here by herself. It's a beautiful place. Always has been. But that has nothing to do with it.

Under normal circumstances I would think that she's perfectly safe up here, barring a bear or a mountain lion or something nature-related.

It was bad enough that someone had left flowers in her house. That was ambiguous enough that it could be interpreted as several different things. Someone with a key who didn't know she was home as one of the most likely things.

But this note appearing on her porch in the middle of a thunderstorm. An obviously threatening note. That was something else entirely.

No ambiguity. Clearly a threat to her.

I can't make her leave. It's her home. I can't force her to stay with me or even in the lodge, something I haven't brought up yet. I can only appeal to her good sense and logic.

The storm left the air feeling fresh and clean. And like Audrey said, it smells good.

The road from my house up to hers is a dirt road that was never paved.

There's an area of the road just before my house on the way to town that I always consider to be exceptionally precarious. Between Audrey's house and mine.

It's only a few yards, but there are no guardrails. It's an

area that I avoid driving during any kind of inclement weather, especially when there's no visibility. It would be far too easy to slide off the edge of the road and there's nothing there but a bottomless slide into the canyon.

I always considered it fortunate that it's a direction I didn't have to travel from my cabin to get into town.

But now I'm wondering if there's a way to add guardrails. Since I'm more of a mechanical engineer than a civil engineer, I don't know the ins and outs of how someone would go about adding guardrails. What I do know, however, is where to find someone who does know.

Just on the other side of that particular area, there is a large curve just before my cabin.

"Is that Claire's car?" Audrey asks, leaning forward in her seat.

I slow down as we pass Claire's old blue Nissan Sentra sitting in a wide place in the dirt road. "It is Claire's car," I say, pulling up behind it. "She must've had car trouble."

"Is she in there?"

"Probably. Wait here. I'll go see."

I climb out of the truck and walk over to the driver's side of Claire's car. She isn't in there, but her purse is on the passenger seat and her cell phone is on the dash.

If she had to get out and walk why would she leave her phone here?

Scratching my head, I walk around the perimeter of the car, looking for her. I don't see any signs of her or any damage to her car.

Perplexed, I go back to my truck.

"Is she in there?"

"No. I don't see her."

I check my phone and just as I knew I wouldn't, I don't have any cell phone service right here. "Do you have any cell service?"

Audrey checks her phone. "No. This must be a dead zone."

"I'm going to drive down a ways. Call the sheriff."

"Should we look for her?"

"It's going to be dark in a few minutes. The sheriff needs to send out a search and rescue team."

"The whole time we were sitting in front of the fire, she was out here. We could have helped her."

"We couldn't have known."

As I drive the distance down to my house, I can't help but wonder about Claire and the black box with the threatening note.

Had she gotten out of her car and walked back to leave the box on Audrey's porch? Then maybe something happened to her on the way back to her car? I didn't want to think that about Claire, but I couldn't rule it out.

And right now, it was looking like the most likely possibility. The only possibility.

THIRTY-TWO

Audrey

"I FEEL guilty having dinner while Claire is out there."

I'm sitting across from Bradley at a little pizza parlor on Main Street.

The booths have worn blue leather seats. Blue and white checked painted table tops. Everything looks worn, but clean.

There's an outside seating area with heaters, but everyone is sitting inside. All but one of the tables is filled.

A man in a white apron stands in the kitchen, kneading pizza dough. A young woman chops vegetables while an older woman puts on toppings and slides the pizzas into a brick oven.

They make everything from scratch and it smells so good it makes me realize I'm hungrier than I thought I was.

"She could have gotten a ride with someone."

I shake my head. "You said she left her phone and her purse."

"That part I don't understand," Bradley admits. "But Claire can be a little scatterbrained sometimes."

"She does tend to get caught up in whatever she's doing. She didn't even bring her phone inside the house while she worked."

"The older generation isn't quite as attached to their phones as we are."

"I guess." I'm not so sure about that. My parents don't go anywhere without their phones. It obviously depends on the person.

"Are you sure there's nothing we can do?"

"Search and rescue is out there. Doing their thing. If they need volunteers, they'll send out messages calling for them."

I nod. He's right of course. The last thing search and research needs is someone like me getting out there and getting myself into trouble. Then I'd have to be rescued. A more likely than not situation.

I can navigate my way around the city of Houston, but out here, no a chance.

"I just feel bad."

"It's not your fault."

"She'd just left my house. I can't help but feel bad."

"That's because you're such a kind and caring person."

A young lady in jeans and a blue t-shirt that matches the rest of the motif stops at our booth. "Welcome to the pizzeria. Can I take your order?" Her hair is pulled back in a perky ponytail.

"I think we're still deciding," Bradley says, picking up a menu. "Can we get a couple of cokes?"

"Sure thing. Take your time."

"Do you want something stronger?" Bradley asks. "A beer?"

"Not right now. I want to keep a clear head. There's too much going on."

"I agree. What kind of pizza do you like?"

"Pepperoni and pineapple."

He doesn't even bat an eye. "Sounds good." He closes the menu. "They'll find her. I'm sure there's a logical explanation."

"Right." Just like there's a logical explanation for why someone left a threatening note on my porch.

Whatever is happening, it's left me feeling disconcerted.

"There's another option," Bradley says after the waitress comes back and he places our order.

"Please tell me what that would be."

He smiles a little. "You could stay at the Whiskey Springs Lodge. Just until we figure out who's doing this."

I shake my head. "Somebody's trying to run me off and I'm not going. Just because I'm not there for a few days won't make it stop."

He takes a deep breath. Lets it out slowly. Unfortunately you're probably right."

"I won't leave the house. The inheritance stipulates that I live in the house."

He looks perplexed. "For how long?"

"I'm not sure. Forever?"

"That sounds unusual. What happens if you leave?"

"I'm not leaving."

"I understand that." He leans forward. "Hypothetically. Let's say you live there until you're a hundred years old. What happens to the house then?"

"I didn't ask. Maybe it goes to my children."

"Seems likely," he says, sitting back, obviously deep in thought.

Our pizza arrives and our conversation veers away from the stipulations of my inheritance.

But now he has me worried.

I'm just glad he's here to help me navigate all this.

I could tell my sisters, but they already worry too much about me.

It's better that I don't tell them.

THIRTY-THREE

Bradley

"WE'RE STOPPING AT YOUR CABIN?" Audre asks as I pull into the parking space next to my cabin.

"I just need to grab a few things. Some dog food for Biscuit. A change of clothes."

"Why?" she asks, her brow furrowed.

I pause, my hand on the doorknob.

It's dark outside now, but the moon is bright, streaming down in little patches between the trees. There's no sign of the storm that passed through earlier.

"Because if you won't leave your house, then that doesn't give me much choice."

"I don't understand."

"I can't leave you there in your house by yourself."

She looks at me as though I've lost my mind. "Wait," she says. "You're going to stay at my house?"

"Yes." I suppose I should have asked her. "Are you okay with that?"

"I don't know."

"While you're thinking about it, do you want to come inside?"

"I think I'll just sit here."

I really don't like leaving her out here by herself. Not after Claire disappeared from her car. But. I don't want to push her too far.

"Lock the doors." I climb out of the car. I'd feel better if Biscuit was in the truck, at least, but we'd left him at Audrey's house while we went into town for pizza.

"I'll be okay," she insists.

"I won't be long."

I hurry. I grab a bag of Biscuit's dog food. His water bowl. A pair of pajamas I've never worn and a change of clothes. Stow them in an overnight bag.

I toss a toothbrush and a razor into my toiletries bag.

I'm in and out in five minutes.

And yet when I come out of the house and see Audrey sitting there, I feel unimaginable relief.

All my protective instincts are zeroed in on this girl.

"Back," I say tossing my things in the backseat.

"You really don't have to do this."

"I know." I put the truck in reverse.

"I can just go into my bedroom and lock the door at night. That's what I've been doing."

My foot on the break, I look over at her. "Since when?"

"Since someone left those flowers."

I pull out onto the road, headlights lighting the way on the dirt road through the trees. "You shouldn't have to do that in your own house."

She shrugs. I need new door locks."

"Yes. You do." But I wonder. I wonder if even that would make her feel safe in her own home, especially after tonight.

Claire's car is still parked where we left it and another truck, one I recognize as a rescue vehicle, parked behind it.

"They still haven't found her," Audrey points out the obvious.

I pull up in front of her house and kill the motor.

We both look around before we get out. Looking for shadows in the moonlight. Anything that looks out of place.

This is no way to live.

I don't know how to fix it. Not yet. But I will.

I don't have a choice.

THIRTY-FOUR

Audrey

BRADLEY and I stand on the back deck, watching Biscuit make his evening rounds. It's apparently a whole ritual. First the perimeter, nose to the ground like a tiny hound on a mission. Then, once he's satisfied everything smells the way it should, he finally takes care of business.

"He doesn't run away?" I ask.

He shakes his head. "He hasn't yet."

"If he did... if he chased something..." I don't finish the thought.

Bradley glances over, one eyebrow raised like he hears more in my voice than I meant to give away.

"He'd probably get a little lost," he says. "But I think he'd circle back. Eventually."

I nod, even though I'm not sure we're still talking about Biscuit.

The cool air slides between us. I rub my hands together, suddenly unsure what I'm doing out here. On this deck, in this town, standing next to a man who sees too much and says too little.

Still, I stay. Bradley draws me in without meaning to. Soft and steady like a tide I'm not sure I can fight.

He doesn't push. Just stands there with his hands in his pockets and keeps his eyes on Biscuit, who's now pawing at a spot in the grass like he's unearthing treasure.

"You cold?" he asks after a minute.

"A little." I'm actually shivering, but I'm not ready to go back inside.

He shrugs off his leather jacket and drops it over my shoulders. It smells like spruce and campfire. Solid. Warm from his body heat. I wrap it around me. Hesitating, then shrug my arms into the sleeves. It's big, the sleeves covering my hands.

"Thanks," I murmur.

He leans on the railing, quiet again. The kind of silence that doesn't demand to be filled. The kind of silence that is rare.

"I used to think I knew where I belonged," I say before I can stop myself. "Now... I'm not sure."

Bradley doesn't look at me. Just says, "Sometimes it

takes losing everything to figure out what home really means." His voice is steady.

I glance at him, but he still isn't looking at me. It makes it easier somehow to talk to him. Too easy.

Maybe that's why I'm able to keep going. Why the words just tumble out of my mouth. Words that I don't even really know where they come from. "I didn't just lose him. I lost who I was with him."

This time he turns and looks at me with those eyes that seem to see everything without asking anything. Our eyes hold, and I feel a magnetic tug. A soft kind of tug that hums deep in my heart. The kind that slips in past the constant ache of pain and emptiness that lives there.

And then Biscuit barks, breaking the spell as he races toward the porch.

Bradley grins. "His highness is finished."

I laugh. A real laugh. One that loosens one of those balls of stress knotted in my stomach.

Inside, the house feels warmer. Softer, even, with the quiet hum of the heater and the faint scent of cinnamon from whatever Claire had done earlier. Biscuit trots in like he lives there, makes two circles by the couch, then flops down in front of the fireplace, obviously choosing his bed for the night.

Bradley grabs his overnight bag from the foyer and glances upstairs, then back at me. "Which guest room do you want me in?" He asks it like it's the most natural thing in the world.

"The one next to mine is already made up," I say, gesturing toward the stairs. "Clean sheets."

He smiles, but there's a question in it. One he doesn't quite ask.

I turn to fill the kettle with water, needing something warm to calm my nerves. "You'll be comfortable. It's quiet up there."

"Quiet's good," he says, then walks away with slow, deliberate steps. At the bottom of the stairs, he pauses. "Thanks for letting me stay."

I glance over, the steam from the kettle curling between us. "You're welcome. It's not like you gave me much of a choice."

His eyes hold mine for a moment longer than they should. Then he nods and disappears up the stairs, his footsteps muffled on the carpeted landing.

I let out a breath I hadn't realized I was holding.

Behind me, Biscuit snores softly on the floor near the hearth. I pour two mugs of tea, then hesitate. One or two?

I set both on the coffee table anyway.

Just in case.

CHAPTER
THIRTY-FIVE

Bradley

I SET my toiletries bag on the bathroom counter. Like the closets in this house, the bathrooms could do with some updates. I probably wouldn't gut them like the Bentley cabin bathrooms, but definitely some updates.

A new sink. New countertop. New faucet.

I pull back the shower curtain. New tub and shower.

Okay. Maybe I would gut this bathroom, too, and start over.

But it's not my decision to make.

I splash some water on my face and brush my teeth.

Maybe I shouldn't have pushed myself in on Audrey like this.

My being worried about her doesn't give me the right to just take over her life.

She was right. I hadn't given her much of a choice.

I need to apologize to her.

I head back downstairs to see if she's still up.

She's sitting on the sofa, her feet pulled up beneath her, two mugs of hot tea on the coffee table.

The only light comes from the fireplace.

My heart warms. She made me tea.

But then I see her face.

She's holding her phone.

"What's wrong?" I ask, sitting next to her.

Her eyes look haunted again as she meets my gaze.

She glances down at her phone.

"Someone named Mr. Fields called me."

"Who's that?"

"I don't know. He runs an agency that hires the people who take care of the house. He's the one who pays Claire."

"What did he want?"

"They found her. They found Claire."

"Is she okay?" Her expression already tells me she isn't.

"I don't know. They're taking her into Denver to the hospital."

"What else did he say?"

She pulls her gaze away from mine. "Just that they found her. She was unconscious."

I pick up one of the mugs. Press it into her hands. "She'll be okay. They were able to find her. That's a good thing."

"I hope so." She holds the mug up to her chin, breathing in the steam. "Do you think the same person who left the note hurt her?"

"I don't know. Maybe she can tell us what happened when she wakes up."

"Right."

"Is this mine?" I nod toward the other mug of tea.

"If you want it."

"Thank you." I pick up the mug and take a sip of the hot tea.

"You're welcome." She looks at me a moment. "You've never heard of Mr. Fields?"

"No."

"I thought you knew everyone in town."

"I did, too."

"Claire told me she has an app. That she has to log in when she gets here and log out when she leaves. That there's an agency she works for."

"I'll see what I can find out about it. Tomorrow."

"Okay."

"It's been a busy day. Let's just relax for a moment and enjoy this fire."

"It's not a very good one," she says, keeping a straight face.

"I agree. We've got to get it up to your standards." I get up and step over Biscuit to add another log to it.

"Biscuit is definitely relaxed," she says.

"It's a gift."

A smile plays about her lips and she glances toward the windows. A wall of darkness that we can't see past.

"We'll measure those windows tomorrow," I say.

She looks at me, her eyes wide. "I know I didn't say it, but I'm glad you're here."

"Me too." I sit back down next to her.

My gaze locks onto hers and she doesn't look away.

My heart thuds in my chest.

She's right beside me, close enough that her shoulder almost brushes mine. But not quite.

I could shift. Just a little.

But I don't.

Her gaze holds mine. Something unsure and unspoken flickering behind her eyes.

The soft firelight casts golden shadows across her face, catching in her hair. She looks like something I might have dreamed of once. When I was younger and life was simpler.

"I should head up," she whispers, but she doesn't move.

"Yeah," I say, even though I don't want her to.

She sips her tea and we sit there a few moments longer. Not touching. Not speaking.

Just feeling.

Finally, she stands up with a slow reluctance. "Goodnight, Bradley."

"Goodnight," I say.

She seems like she wants to say more.

Instead, she just nods, her gaze lingering a moment longer before she turns toward the hallway.

I wait until I hear her door click shut before I breathe again.

Biscuit shifts a bit from his spot in front of the fire, utterly at peace.

I wish I could say the same about myself.

Audrey

I WAKE the next morning to bright sunlight streaming in through my slightly cracked window.

It's so quiet. So peaceful. I have to listen carefully to hear the faint sound of the river in the distance. Birds singing their morning song. The breeze rustling through the aspen trees.

My first thought is Bradley. Wondering if he's still here.

I stretch beneath the warm blankets as the cold morning breeze drifts in through the window along with the sunlight.

I quickly replay the events of yesterday, my thoughts slowing as I come to last night.

That moment when Bradley and I had sat next to each other on the sofa, Biscuit snoring at our feet, all of us enjoying the warmth of the fireplace.

Bradley's light blue eyes had latched onto mine and held. So much warmth and kindness there. So much understanding.

Too much understanding.

It's only been three weeks since I'd become a widow. I'm still trying to adjust.

Should be still trying to adjust.

I think finding out Thomas wasn't who I thought he was had dulled some of the shininess off our marriage. Thomas and I hadn't known each other all that long and we'd been married even less time.

He'd had a magnetic confidence that I had been drawn to from the beginning.

When he proposed, it had seemed like the natural next step. The right thing to do.

I had been a twenty-six-year-old chasing a future I thought I was supposed to want. He offered all the things I told myself mattered: security, stability, a neat and tidy version of forever.

And he was a pilot. That had dazzled me more than I care to admit. There was something romantic about that. In retrospect, I'd believed that being with him might come with a passport to adventure.

But it turns out, charm like that fades quickly. And the sky always looks bluer from the ground.

I pull myself out of the bed, putting my feet on the cold wooden floor.

As I hurry across the cold floor to the bathroom where I'd left my slippers, it suddenly occurs to me that I can actually afford to have heated floors installed.

I slide my feet into my slippers and turn on the shower to let the water heat up.

I could put in one of those free-standing bathtubs with a separate shower, the showers with more than one shower head. Overhead rain heads and soft sprayers.

I could even put a fireplace in the bathroom.

Not even do I have the money to do it, I have a handsome and attentive neighbor who seems like he's willing and able to do just about anything to the house I can dream up.

Standing in the hot shower, I let the water run down over my head, washing away some of the guilt I'd been feeling at enjoying spending time with Bradley.

Thomas had always worked a lot, spending most of his time at the airport and flying. After we'd gotten married, he'd stepped up his work game even more. We rarely did anything together as a couple. That was probably one of the many reasons I'd felt so isolated out in Katy.

I don't even know if he visited his child downtown. I worked downtown. Maybe he visited his child and baby momma when I was at home in Katy. I'll never know.

There were so many things I didn't know about him. It doesn't matter now.

My life with Thomas is something I can start putting behind me.

Thomas's grandfather, Theodore Albright, had set me up with this house. I wish I could have met him. He unknowingly changed my life and I'll forever be indebted to him for that.

I turn off the water and step out into the chilly air.

Definitely seriously considering heated floors and a gas fireplace in the bathroom.

Right after the new door locks and window shades. And, of course, the closets.

I kneel on the floor of the bedroom and dig through the clothes in my suitcases. At least everything is organized even if it is still in suitcases.

I decide on a pair of blue jeans and a long t-shirt with a sweatshirt over it. It seems cooler today and cloudy. A nice reprieve from the heat that is currently hanging over Houston.

A little preview of the winter to come. I probably shouldn't be looking forward to winter so much. Bradley seems to think it's a novelty that won't last. Being from here, he would know. But being from here, he might not know just how long I might enjoy the novelty of a winter that includes cold weather and snow.

After getting dressed I spend a little extra time blow drying my hair out straight and smooth, but I don't put on any makeup. Just in case Bradley is still here, I want to appear casual and nonchalant.

Not that I am.

His quiet, protective presence has me feeling alive again.

And now that I'm feeling it, I realize it's been a very, very long time, before Thomas's plane crash even, that I've felt this way.

As soon as I open my bedroom door, I already know he's not here. The house feels quiet and empty.

I find a note written on a sheet of legal paper on the kitchen island.

MEETING MY BROTHER TO GET SOME WORK AT
THE BENTLEY PLACE.
BE BACK LATER THIS AFTERNOON.
CALL ME IF YOU NEED ANYTHING.

HIS SIMPLE NOTE makes me smile to myself as I make myself a cup of coffee using the fancy coffee maker. I feel ridiculously giddy at the thought that he's coming back this afternoon.

I'm getting far too used to having Bradley around far too quickly.

He's a friend. It's okay to have a friend.

Even if that friend does have me thinking about what it might feel like to kiss him.

THIRTY-SEVEN

Bradley

"You've been spending a lot of time over at the widow's house," Wyatt says as we carry a new sink into the Bentley cabin.

"Audrey," I say. "Hold on. Turn it on its side. Going to be spending a lot more time over there, too."

"You don't say." Wyatt gives me a raised eyebrow look.

"Not like that." We carefully set the sink down and start unboxing it.

"Okay then. Why not? And how?"

"I guess you didn't hear about what happened last night."

"I guess I didn't. You going to tell me?"

I pull away the packing material and hand it to Bradley to carry out of the bathroom.

"Do you remember Claire?"

"Claire? I don't think so."

"Older than us. She cleans the Albright house."

"Okay. What happened to her?"

"She went missing right after she left Audrey's house. Left her car on the side of the road. Her phone still in the car. Search and research went out last night looking for her."

"So that what all that commotion was about." We shift the sink into place.

"How do you keep your head in the sand like that?"

"It's easy. I don't bother people and they don't bother me."

"Impressive. At any rate, they found her unconscious. She's in the hospital."

He sits back on his heels. "Besides the obvious tragedy, doesn't that sound a little odd to you?"

"That's not the worst of it. Somebody left a threatening note on Audrey's porch during the rainstorm."

"What kind of threatening note?"

"It said *You shouldn't be here. You were never part of the plan.*"

"What plan?" he asks.

"I don't know, Bro. Something that involves Audrey."

"Or you," he says.

"That's what Audrey said."

"What are you planning on doing?"

"The basics. New locks. Shades on the windows. And…" I measure the sink on either side. Make sure it's even. "I'm staying in the guest room until we find out who's threatening her."

"So you're moving in."

"I didn't say I was moving in. I said I was staying there until we figure out who's threatening her." I say the words slowly, like I would say them to a child.

He responds in kind, his words slow and deliberate. "So you're moving in."

Scowling at my brother, I pick up a wrench. Point it at him. "It's not like that."

He shrugs. "Whatever you say."

"Let's get this sink installed so we can get out of here. I've got to install new door locks on Audrey's doors."

Wyatt sits back on his heels and smirks at me.

THIRTY-EIGHT

Audrey

"What are you smiling about?" Brianna asks before I'd hardly done more than answer her FaceTime call.

"I'm not smiling," I say, biting my lip because that was exactly what I was doing.

"What are you doing?" Brianna asks.

"I'm building a fire." I'm on my knees in front of the fireplace getting a fire going.

"I rather figured that," she says. "You have smut on your face."

"Oh." I swipe at my cheek to get the smut off.

Brianna laughs out loud.

"What?" I squint at my own reflection in the smaller part of the screen.

"You look like Cinderella."

Smiling, I sit back on my heels. "Why aren't you at work?"

"I am at work." She pans her phone behind her at the shelves loaded with books.

"What job is this one?" I ask. Brianna is currently working at a temp agency and even though she's had lot of offers for full-time jobs, she likes the novelty of working at different offices. I think she also secretly likes the lower sense of responsibility that comes with being temporary.

"It's for a publishing company. I like it."

"You like everything as long as it's temporary."

She shrugs, but doesn't say one way or the other.

"I think our parents must have messed us up pretty bad."

"Why do you say that?" Brianna frowns into the phone.

"Well. You don't have a full-time job—"

"I work full-time."

"Yes. But not at any one particular place doing anything in particular."

"I'm an office assistant."

"Brianna." I take a breath. "Never mind."

"I get it. Go ahead. Finish what you're trying to say."

"I was just going to say that you work for a temp agency." *Because you decided not to go to law school.* "Lilah works as a bartender because she wants to be an artist. And I…" I wave a hand in no particular direction.

"I thought you liked working at the art gallery," Brianna says.

"I didn't hate it."

"But it wasn't your career of choice."

"No. It wasn't."

"Well. It's okay. Because now you don't have to work."

"I'm going to start looking for a job after I get the house together."

"Are you still working on the closets?"

"How did you know about the closets?" I poke at the fire, sending embers up the chimney.

"Lilah told me."

"Of course. Yes. I'm still working on the closets."

"You're never going to finish working on that house."

I sigh. "I know. But I am going to start looking for work."

"I wouldn't. You've got plenty of money. You can do whatever you want to do."

"Maybe whatever I want to do is to work. Don't give me that look. I need purpose."

"Hey. Who am I to judge?"

"Why are you calling me from work anyway?"

"I wanted to talk to you about Lilah."

"What's wrong with Lilah?"

"I think you need to talk to her."

CHAPTER
THIRTY-NINE

Bradley

I STOP BY MY HOUSE. Shower. Pack a fresh set of clothes for tomorrow. Wash a couple of dishes I'd left in the sink. All the while keeping an eye on Biscuit as he surveys his yard.

I have no doubt that Biscuit thinks the yard is his domain. It might as well be. He knows every crook and cranny better than I ever will.

I bring in the mail. Go through it, tossing ninety percent of it in the trash.

Since Wyatt's words are stuck in my head, I take my time. Doing the things I would normally do at my house when I get home from work.

I usually either go into town for something to eat or throw something in the oven. Maybe the microwave.

But I know I'm not doing that tonight. I'm heading over to Audrey's as soon as can justify it. I have to feel like I'm spending enough time here at my place that I don't feel like I'm living at Audrey's.

I can't stand the thought of Wyatt being right. Just because he's Wyatt. And he thinks he's smarter than he is.

Audrey said something that has me wondering. Something that I don't quite understand. It sort of just slid past me at the time, but I keep coming back to it.

She said she *can't* leave. That the inheritance stipulates she live in the house to keep it. I can't stop wondering what's so important that she has to stay in the house.

Still mulling that over, I grab a beer from my refrigerator and take it outside with me.

It's been a cold, dreary day all day. Now it's a cold, dreary evening.

Clouds are gathered around the mountain peaks. Probably snowing up there. The weather is definitely keeping the hikers on lower ground today, doubtless making the shop owners on Main Street happy.

As soon as I open the beer, sit down on a chair on my back deck, Biscuit sits down in front of me. Looks east toward Audrey's house. Then look back at me and barks once.

"There is no way you're that damn smart."

Biscuit barks again. Just one bark.

"Okay," I say. "It's not like we're doing anything here anyway, is it?"

Biscuit stands up and wags his tail.

I water a little rock garden next to my deck with what was almost a full bottle of beer.

"Come on Biscuit. Let's go toss everything into the truck and see what Audrey's up to."

Biscuit follows me inside and waits at the front door while I gather everything up.

I no more than get the truck door open than he's inside, ready to go.

Someone moved Claire's car. Good. That means I don't have to deal with it.

I'm actually not too interested in getting involved with anything that looks like foul play. And what happened to Claire definitely hints of foul play. Whether by her or by someone else, I don't have any way of knowing.

She doesn't seem like the kind of person that would leave threatening messages on someone's doorstep. But then I really don't know anything about her. She's not originally from Whiskey Springs. I don't know how long she's lived here, but some people always seem to hover on the outside, never really becoming part of the community. She's one of those people.

I pull up to the front of Audrey's house and cut the motor.

It didn't take much time for this to start feeling more like home than my own place.

Just goes to show. A home isn't just a house.

A home is a place where a person feels welcome and it's more like a home if someone lives there that we care about.

I've found that place here. With Audrey.

Unfortunately, due to the very circumstances that got her here, I can't tell her that. It's too soon.

She came to Whiskey Springs to heal. Not to get caught up in a romantic entanglement.

It's going to take all the willpower I have to keep that in the forefront of my mind.

She throws the door open before I'm more than halfway across the porch.

"I'm so glad you're here," she says. "I need to show you something."

FORTY

Audrey

AFTER I GET off the phone with Brianna, I leave a message for Lilah to call me back.

Since she works all hours of the night at a bar, she sleeps all hours of the day.

I don't see how she does it. Mornings are my best time of day. I like watching the wonder of the sunrise. The way the sky pinkens ever so slowly. How just looking away for a few minutes and the whole landscape changes.

How the sky is like nature's mandala, especially early in the morning. So far, since I've gotten here, I haven't gotten up early enough to truly appreciate the sunrise, but I will.

I spend the rest of my morning, after talking to my sister, playing around with closet designs using a pad of graph paper I found on the desk Theodore had used. The desk is tucked away beneath the stairs in a space that will make a cute little office area. I make a mental note to fix it up for myself to do whatever it is I decide to do for work.

I'm thinking maybe I'll try to work from home. If the winters are as bad as I have a feeling they're going to be, I don't want to be driving to work every day.

When the lead on the one pencil I have breaks, I go in search of another pencil.

Someone must have cleaned out the desk, taking Theodore's personal papers with them.

Not finding another pencil and not wanting to drive into town just to buy a pencil, for God's sake, I look through his desk drawers.

It feels a little invasive at first, but I remind myself that it's my desk now. The house and everything in it is mine.

When I go to open the top left hand drawer, an obvious place for pencils if you ask me, I find it locked.

There's no key anywhere to be found. Not in the ceramic tray on the top of the desk or any of the unlocked drawers.

After a moment's hesitation, I pick up a letter opener and work on manually using it for a key to unlock the drawer.

I am a woman on a mission. Finding a pencil or even a pencil sharpener doesn't sound like too much to ask.

Turns out the desk is old and the lock isn't very sophisticated.

I'm able to open it right up with the letter opener. Unfortunately there is no pencil inside. How could the man not have more than one pencil?

What I do find is something unexpected.

A folded envelope, yellowed at the edges, sealed with wax in an old-fashioned manner, but someone used the letter opener to slit the top of it open. No return address. Just the name Theodore Albright scrawled across the front in bold, slanted handwriting.

My pulse skips.

Time seems to slow down, moving in slow motion as I sit back in the old wooden office chair that creaks with age.

I shouldn't read it. I know I shouldn't. Could this have something to do with Theodore's brother Claire spoke of?

I let out a sigh and do it.

Inside is a single sheet of paper. No date. No signature. Just a few lines written in a hurried hand:

> *Theodore,*
> *We agreed to keep quiet while you were getting*
> *things in order. But time is running out, and you*
> *know he deserves better than being erased. I know*
> *you think she won't understand, but she's stronger*
> *than you give her credit for.*
> *You can't change what happened, but you can*
> *at least make it right.*

If this goes to probate without his name in the file, I won't stay silent. You know I kept the records.

—J

My breath catches.

I stare at the letter, my stomach twisting.

Who is being erased?

And make what right?

I glance over my shoulder even though I know I'm alone.

For now.

Oddly enough, the letter was the only thing in the locked desk drawer.

I'm still sitting at the desk, the letter laid out in front of me when Bradley drives up.

The relief I feel is unsettling in itself.

Bradley is staying with me for now but I can't count on him staying here for long.

After the novelty wears off... after time passes and we don't find out who's leaving the threatening notes, he'll go back to his own life. Want to sleep in his own bed.

It's understandable.

For the moment, however, I'm just happy to see him.

"I need to show you something," I say, throwing open the door.

CHAPTER
FORTY-ONE

Bradley

"I'm pretty sure I have a pencil in my truck," I tell Audrey as she explains why she went exploring in Theodore's desk.

We're sitting in front of the fireplace, with Biscuit on the floor in his new favorite place, and she's holding a yellowed folded envelope with an old wax seal.

"It's okay," she says. "It's not about the pencil... but I'll take it. Later. It's about what I found in the desk."

"I take it you found a letter."

She glances down at the letter in her hands. "Yeah. It was already open so I read it."

"I would have read it if you didn't. What does it say?"

She hands me the letter.

I carefully pull it out of the envelope and read it out loud.

"Theodore,

We agreed to keep quiet while you were getting things in order. But time is running out, and you know he deserves better than being erased. I know you think she won't understand, but she's stronger than you give her credit for.

You can't change what happened, but you can at least make it right.

If this goes to probate without his name in the file, I won't stay silent. You know I kept the records.

—J

I look at Audrey. "Who is J?"

"I don't know. Maybe he's the brother Claire mentioned."

"Maybe." He looks back up at me. "Theodore must have read this."

"Someone did."

"It's odd that it was locked away like that."

"Agreed. We might not ever know why." I hand the letter back over to her.

"I don't understand."

"I know. It's troubling." I run a hand along the back of my neck. "Someone questioned what Theodore did."

"I should show it to someone?"

"I don't think so. I think it would just stir up something that's already settled."

"The inheritance."

"It's all settled, right?"

"As far as I know."

"You do what you want. But my advice? Just put it away somewhere."

"Yeah. I think you're right," she says, looking at me with her meadow green eyes. "I'm just worried that it has something to do with that note someone left on my porch."

"Yeah. I'm thinking we just hold onto that, too, for now."

She gives me a skeptical look.

"It's a small town. I don't think the sheriff could do anything."

"It's the same way in the city. Not enough resources. Somebody almost has to get hurt before they'll do anything."

Reaching over, I put a hand on hers. "I won't let that happen. I'm going to stay right here until we find out who's doing this."

"What if we never find out?"

"You sound like Wyatt." I squeeze her hand. "We'll find out."

I know she doesn't believe me. I can see it in her face.

But what she doesn't know is that I don't care how long it takes. I'm staying right here until whoever is threatening her is held accountable.

"My sister is calling me back," she says, picking up her phone. "I need to take it."

"Sure. Do whatever you need to do."

"Hello," she says into the phone.

"Come on, Biscuit. Let's go take a walk."

Audrey glances over at me with a little smile.

"Is someone there with you?" her sister asks.

"I'll tell you later. Brianna is worried about you."

I step outside into the brisk evening air, Biscuit slipping out ahead of me.

The sun is just sliding down behind the mountains, leaving an early sunset behind. The scent of firewood smoke hovers in the air, settling among the trees.

A couple of chipmunks scamper along the top rail of the deck, then leap onto the limbs of a nearby spruce tree, making a ruckus in the limbs, sending delicate little needles falling to the ground.

I can't help but scan the perimeter, out to the tree line, into the trees, looking for something that doesn't belong. *Someone* who doesn't belong.

Knowing that someone was here leaves everything feeling unsettled and leaves me with a lot of unanswered questions.

Is someone out to harm Audrey? Or just hoping to frighten her away without any intent of harming her?

It's such an ambiguous situation, I don't know if we'll ever have answers.

Audrey and Wyatt are right about that. And what if we don't find out who threatened her and left flowers in her house?

What will I do then?

That remains to be seen. I pick up a twig and toss it. Biscuit surprises me by chasing it bringing it back.

"I didn't know you could do that," I tell him, tossing the twig out again. "Where did you learn these things?"

To my way of thinking, the situation is fluid. It can go so many different ways. Maybe I will have to move in here permanently. Or maybe it will resolve itself. Or maybe Audrey will tire of having me around and send me back to my place.

Right now, she's caught off guard and doesn't know what to think.

How long that will last remains to be seen.

"Hey." Audrey comes to the door.

"Hey. All done?"

"Yeah. She was on her way to work. Couldn't talk. I was thinking about making dinner. Want to help?"

"Sure."

Biscuit races toward the back door as though he understands English.

Following her inside, I lock the door behind us.

This is most definitely getting far too comfortable. Far too fast.

The odd thing about it is that I don't mind.

I don't mind even a little.

Being with Audrey like this feels right.

And if I'm getting used to it, who could blame me?

FORTY-TWO

Audrey

THE SCENT of garlic and oregano fills the kitchen, warm and mouthwatering. Bradley stands at the stove, stirring the simmering pot of spaghetti sauce like it's a sacred ritual. He has a wooden spoon in one hand, a crooked grin on his face, and a dish towel slung over one shoulder.

"This," he says, giving the sauce a slow swirl, "is exactly how I taught my brothers to make it. They were thirteen and fifteen, more interested in burning toast than learning how to properly make a sauce. But. Being the older brother I am, I insisted. I told them, 'One day you'll want to impress a girl, and this is how you'll do it.'"

He turns to look at me then, eyes catching the light just enough to make my stomach flutter.

"Did it work?" I ask, tearing lettuce into the wooden bowl in front of me. "Did they impress a girl?"

He chuckles, the sound low and easy. "Maybe. But I'm not going to guarantee it. Caleb tried adding ketchup once. I didn't speak to him for a week."

I laugh, but the sound caught in my throat. It was suddenly too easy to picture a younger Bradley, patient and bossy, showing his brothers how to stir just right. It was too easy to imagine him like this in other kitchens, with other women. Doing some impressing himself.

"Where was your mother?"

"Outside. In her garden. She taught us how to grow basil and oregano. But she was never much into being in the kitchen. This was after I'd spent the summer with my mother's mother in Boston."

Biscuit thumps his tail against the floor and gives a little huff, flopping beneath the table and rolling to his back, waiting for someone to notice how adorably neglected he is.

"You're spoiled, you know that, right?" I crouch for half a second to scratch him under the chin before turning back to the salad.

Bradley's voice softens behind me. "You ever teach anyone to cook?"

I hesitate, then smile faintly. "Kind of. When we were little, my sisters and I used to pretend we were on a cooking show with our father as the judge. We'd have bake-offs but my super competitive sister, Brianna, tried to sneak hot pepper into our cookie dough."

"Sounds chaotic," he says, his voice soft.

"It was." I look up.

"Maybe chaos is what makes family work."

He's watching me, spoon resting on the counter now. Our eyes lock and something shifts in the air. Something thick and humming and fragile.

He takes a step forward.

I don't breathe.

The world narrows to the space between us, to the way his gaze flicks to my lips and back again. I'm not sure who moved first, only that his hand brushed mine, warm and pleasantly calloused and grounding.

Then the sauce sizzles behind him, spitting onto the stop top with a hiss.

He blinks and turns, muttering a curse as he grabs the spoon again. The moment shattered.

I clear my throat and toss another handful of lettuce into the bowl, pretending I'm not shaking just a little.

"Your brothers seriously owe you," I say, trying for a teasing tone that I'm not feeling. "That sauce smells like it belongs in a five-star restaurant."

He stirs the sauce like he's done it a thousand times. Slow, confident, the wooden spoon scraping in a lazy circle, keeping his gaze on what he's doing. "It was never really about the recipe," he says, voice low, almost too soft to hear over the simmer.

Biscuit gets up and wanders back to his place in front of the fireplace like he belongs here.

I watch the way Bradley's shoulders move, the way his hands guide the spoon. He taught his younger brothers to cook. I've never known another man who did that. A legacy built from tomatoes, garlic, and quiet loyalty. He says it's not about the recipe, but I think it is. Or at least, what it stands for.

He still isn't looking at me.

Maybe it's a good thing. Because if he does, he'll see everything written across my face.

How much I wish I'd known this version of him back then and how much I wish things had been different and I had been part of his life when we were younger.

How much I want to believe it's not too late.

He might even see the hope simmering in my eyes. The hope that he and I can create something together. Now. That it's not too late for either of us.

I clear my throat and look away.

I shouldn't want this. Not yet. Maybe not ever again. But when he looks into my eyes I long for something.

Something I can't even identify yet. Something that swirls into those places deep in my heart that I thought were locked forever.

FORTY-THREE

Bradley

When I came back inside from walking Biscuit, Audrey has the table set with a single white tapered candle softly glowing. One salad in front of each of our plates.

"It's my first real meal here." She says with a little shrug before I manage to hide my surprise.

"It's nice," I say. "It's perfect."

Biscuit heads over to his spot in front of the fireplace and curls back up.

Apparently I didn't hide my surprise quickly enough.

"It's too much," she says, picking up the candle and blowing it out. "My head wasn't—"

I reach her in three long strides. Put my hands over hers. "I just wish I'd thought of it. And—"

I put a finger beneath her chin and nudge her face up until her eyes meet mine.

Her eyes are red-rimmed and brimming with tears.

"Oh, sweetheart." I pull her against me, wrapping her in my arms.

She hesitates a second, two, then wraps her arms around me, resting her cheek against my chest.

"You're trembling," I say, pressing my hand against the back of her head, holding her steady.

"I'm okay," she says, her voice muffled against me. "I'm sorry. I just— Everything was just—"

"It's okay." I make little soothing sounds, but she seems to tremble even more.

I just hold her. It's all I can do.

Making dinner with Audrey was so unexpectedly... nice. Normal even. And I've gone and ruined it. Now I've hurt her. She thinks the candles were too much.

But it's not that. It's that they were just so... right.

And I've been telling myself to take it easy. To go slow. That she's a grieving widow.

That I can't make assumptions with her.

She's not a typical woman. She's not someone I can allow myself to get close to.

She's vulnerable and grieving.

My job is to protect her.

Not to want to kiss her like I do.

After a couple of minutes, she stills and lifts her head.

"Can I take this?" I ask, taking the candle she's still holding.

She nods.

I light it and set it in the middle of the table.

"You don't have to…" She runs a hand through her hair, shoving it off her face.

"I want to. Here." I pull out a chair and hold it while she sits. "I'll just fix our plates."

She sits quietly while I stir the sauce, giving a little extra heat, before making our plates.

I'm at a loss as to how to proceed. All I know to do is to act like nothing has changed.

"Now we get to see if I still remember how to make my grandmother's recipe."

"It's been a while since you made it?" she asks.

"To be honest, I haven't made it since I taught my brothers."

She freezes, her fork halfway to her mouth.

"Surely you're kidding with me."

"I'm not."

"So you've never made this to impress a girl?"

"You're the first."

She tilts her head to the side and looks at me with an expression between disbelief and something else. Relief maybe? Hope?

"In case you're wondering," she says. "It works."

FORTY-FOUR

Audrey

"Do you want help with that fire?" I ask.

"It takes a knack to get it up to your standards, but I'll get it."

I'm sitting on the sofa, a glass of wine in hands, my feet tucked up beneath me.

Biscuit, sitting on the floor, and I watch as Bradley gets the fire going. It's actually a very nice, steady fire.

"I think it's okay," I say. "Looks very professional."

"Are you sure?" He sits back on his heels and looks at me over his shoulder. "I don't want you to be disappointed."

"I'm not disappointed."

"Okay." Getting up from where he knelt in front of the hearth, he sits on the couch next to me and picks up his glass of wine.

"Haven't we tried this before?" he asks.

"I think we did, actually." I look toward the wall of dark windows. "Maybe this time we won't have any unwelcome guests."

"Let's hope not."

"What other things did you teach your younger brothers about impressing girls?"

"There's not much." He stretches out his legs. "Besides cooking spaghetti, they had to know how to cook eggs."

"You taught them to cook eggs?"

"Sure."

"I thought cooking eggs was just something all guys knew how to do."

"They have to learn it somewhere."

"You learned from your grandmother."

"That's right. And my grandfather taught me how to build the perfect fire. I still miss them both terribly. Anyway, my brothers weren't interested in learning to build a well-laid fire. Our father had already taught us how to throw one together and they were good with that."

"That explains your well-laid fire."

"What about you? Did you teach your younger sisters anything?"

"Not really. Except I always helped them with their homework."

"Practical and important."

"Underappreciated."

"I think just about anything we try to teach our younger siblings goes underappreciated."

"You might be right. Maybe it's supposed to be that way." I think about my two younger sisters. Both of them so different from the other and both different from me.

"Most people don't suspect we're sisters," I say.

"Really? Maybe it's because we live in a small town, but everyone thinks my brothers and I look alike."

"I don't know. I've only met Wyatt, but he's more rugged looking than you are."

"Rugged is a good thing, right?"

"It can be. It's not better or worse. It's just different."

I don't tell him that I find him more attractive than his brother. There's nothing wrong with Wyatt. Wyatt is a good-looking man.

But there's something about Bradley and his kind light blue eyes that strikes me deep in my core. That makes me feel more alive than I've felt in longer than I can remember.

FORTY-FIVE

Bradley

"I HAVE to be up early in the morning to meet my brother. We're still working out at the Bentley place."

"That's Biscuit's cue to go outside," Audrey says. "And mine to head upstairs.

She takes our two wine glasses, only half empty, to the kitchen.

I round my dog up and take him outside into the brisk night air for his walk.

I try not to think too much about what it means that I'd had such a good time with Audrey. Making dinner. Sitting in front of the fire. Talking about our siblings and our childhoods.

Both of us being the oldest, we have a lot in common, she and I.

Even though I'm from a small town and she's from the big city, it doesn't seem to matter.

She seems to belong here just as sure as if she was from here.

If she stays, she won't be like Claire, someone who stays on the periphery of the town. She'll be a part of the town, weaving her way into the fabric.

I don't know how I know this. It's just a gut feeling I have about her.

Biscuit finishes his rounds and we head back inside.

A quick glance around tells me that Audrey has already headed upstairs.

Turning off the lights, I follow, heading up to my room. Biscuit chooses to lie down in from of the fireplace and stay downstairs. For now at least. He'll probably be up later.

I stop at Audrey's closed door and listen until I hear water running in the bathroom.

I would have liked to have said goodnight to her.

But maybe it's better this way.

If we'd come upstairs together, I probably would have done something stupid like kiss her.

That wouldn't be fair to her.

She hasn't had time to grieve. As much as I might want

her to be something more, she hasn't had time to be in a place to be more.

I put a hand on her doorknob. Turn it. Not to open it, but to see if she locked it. She'd told me that she sleeps in her room with the door locked. But it's not locked.

For whatever reason, she's left it unlocked.

I go into my own room, but I leave the door open. I need to be able to hear anything out of the ordinary. To hear if anyone breaks in. Comes upstairs.

Biscuit is still downstairs, so he's an extra layer of guard dog.

The incident with the candle at dinner was another indication of just how vulnerable Audrey is. She'd lit a candle for a candle light dinner. An innocent gesture. All it had taken was one surprised look from me to reduce her to a trembling wreck.

I can't do that to her. It's not fair.

She deserves time. She came here to take time to heal.

I can't take that away from her.

And yet I don't know how I can be here with her. In the same house and not want more.

How is it possible that she and I can spend time like this together without me wanting to hold her? To kiss her?

To make a life with her?

I have to give her time.

To see what happens next. To be here for her while giving her space.

I never said it would be easy.

It's anything but easy.

FORTY-SIX

Audrey

THE HOUSE FEELS lonely without Bradley and Biscuit.

As I sit out back sipping my first cup of hot coffee, wrapped in a wool blanket because I don't have a coat yet, I consider again getting a dog. Or maybe a cat.

I'm mostly a cat person and we had cats growing up, but a dog seems like the best choice. A dog like Biscuit can come outside with me and a dog is better at scaring off intruders than a cat would be.

It would take an awfully fierce cat to scare anyone off.

I hate it that my gaze is constantly drawn to scan the

perimeter of the area around me. That I can't sit quietly without looking around me, even over my shoulder.

Deciding it's not worth being outside and it's too cold anyway, I take my coffee and go back inside.

The fire in the fireplace died down overnight, making the house now seem cold and dismal. I hope this isn't what winter is going to be like.

I'll have to keep a fire going all the time just to stave off the dreariness. I sit at the breakfast table, the only spot with a little bit of sunshine coming in through the window and finish my coffee. Still watching outside for anything that looks out of place.

There's nothing I can do about that.

I've just finished washing my coffee mug and laying it aside to dry when Lilah FaceTimes me.

"Lilah. What's wrong?" Lilah is usually... always... still sound asleep this time of morning. Probably not even gone to bed by this time a lot of nights.

"I quit my job," she blurts.

"But why? I thought you liked your job."

She scrunches up her face. "Like might be a strong word. More like I tolerated it."

"Oh." This is news to me. But in all fairness, I've been a little self-focused lately.

"You don't look as chipper as you did last night," she says. "Are you sick? Why are you wearing a blanket?"

"Just cold. I'm still getting used to the climate."

"Hmm." She scowls. "It's at least a hundred degrees here."

"It's okay. Tell me why you quit your job."

"Quit might not be the right word exactly."

"Lilah. What's the right word?"

"Fired?"

"Oh my God. Lilah. What did you do?"

"I might have tossed a glass of beer into someone's face."

"Did he deserve it?"

"She. She definitely deserved it."

"What did she do?" I pull my feet up under me on the couch and adjust the blanket around my shoulders.

"It doesn't matter." She blows her shoulder length hair out of her eyes. "So I was thinking... maybe I could come up there. Visit you."

"And do some painting."

"Yes! But I don't want to interrupt your time alone."

I bite my lip to keep from laughing out loud. My time alone has been spent mostly with either Claire or Bradley. "Sure," I say. "I'd like you to come visit me."

Lilah's face brightens. "I was hoping you'd say that."

"You're already packed, aren't you?"

"How did you know?"

"Older sister super powers." Bradley would understand.

Speaking of Bradley, Lilah is going to need to know about the threat I got and not only that, she's going to need to know about Bradley and how he's staying here. To keep me safe.

"When are you leaving?" I ask.

She has the decency to look sheepish. "I just passed by your old exit."

"You're in Katy?"

"Yes. I hope that's okay."

She knew it was. She absolutely knew it was.

"And?"

She shrugs. How did I not notice she was driving?

"It's a little sister super power," she says, impishly.

"Right." And just for that, I'm going to make her wait to tell her what's going on up here.

My biggest concern is going to be keeping her out of trouble. After what happened to Claire, I'm going to have to convince her not to go anywhere alone, especially after dark.

It shouldn't be too much trouble. As long as she has paints and cavasses, she's good. Brianna might be a different story completely. Brianna does not like to stay home alone.

"Did you brings paints and supplies?"

"Of course. I might have forgotten my pajamas, though."

"That just so does not surprise me. Okay. Drive safely. And text me every time you stop."

"Yes, Mother. I'll do it." But she doesn't look the least bit put out.

This is an adventure for her just as it was for me.

She'll be here in a couple of days. I have to get her room ready. Wash the sheets. Clean and stock the bathroom.

I'm excited to see my sister and yet... I'm not ready to share my time with Bradley.

That's just irrational.

I sit for a minute. Thinking.

I have to tell Lilah what's happening. If for no other reason than for her own safety.

CHAPTER
FORTY-SEVEN

Bradley

"Are you headed back over to the widow's house?" Wyatt asks as we tool up after putting in several hours of work at the Bentley place.

"Audrey. Her name is Audrey."

"Okay. Are you headed back over to Audrey's house?"

"Yes. We still don't know who left threats on the front porch."

"That's a bit disturbing. Did the sheriff say anything?"

"You know he didn't. Might as well keep him out of the loop on something like this."

"You should run for sheriff."

"Not a chance. If any of us were going to run for sheriff, it would be Caleb."

"Caleb could do it."

"I don't know why he would want to."

"I don't either."

I look over at Wyatt. "You brought it up. Why don't you do it?"

"It's not really my thing."

"Something going on with you?" I open the door for Biscuit to hop inside the truck.

"I just think you'd make a good sheriff. I know you don't want to do it. My two cents. Take it or leave it." Wyatt kicks his back tire and, satisfied with it, opens the driver's door of his truck.

"Thanks for the vote of confidence. But I'd just as soon leave it."

"Audrey's sister coming up yet?"

"She has two of them. And you'll be the first to know."

"Sounds good."

"What's with you and Audrey's sisters?"

Wyatt laughs. "You're so easy to stir up. Have fun. And watch your back."

"You too."

I close the truck door and start up the motor.

Wyatt knows he can mess with me because he can tell I like Audrey.

Just as I'm about to pull out onto the road behind Wyatt, my phone rings.

It's the sheriff.

"Claire woke up," he blurts out in lieu of a greeting.

"Okay. That's good. How is she?" And more importantly has she said anything?

"She hasn't said anything yet."

"But she's conscious?"

"That's what they're saying. I haven't been down there." He takes a breath and I have a feeling I know the real reason he's calling. Sometimes I hate it when I'm right. "She doesn't have any family. Maybe you and Audrey should drive down there to see her?"

"To Boulder?"

"That's where they took her."

Damn it. Visiting Claire was not in my plans.

"I don't want to bother her. I'm thinking it's best to just wait until she gets home."

"Alright. I'm sure they'll figure out a way to get her home."

I'm not biting on that one. "I'm sure they will. I'll give Audrey the update."

I disconnect the line and head toward town.

On a whim, I stop by the pizza parlor and order a pizza to go.

I enjoy cooking with Audrey, but she and I should probably get some work done. Maybe change out her door locks, if the new ones came in, or measure for her window shades, or start floating sheetrock in her closet. She's got to be tired of living out of suitcases.

And then I have some bathroom renovations to bring up. She seems open to modernizing things, but we've got to actually get something finished at some point.

As I sit waiting for the pizza, I replay my conversation with the sheriff. How did he know that I was hanging out with Audrey?

I'd taken those flowers into his office, but I'd done that as a neighbor.

He's making the assumption that there's more to my relationship with her.

How could he possibly know?

How could he possibly know... and be right?

FORTY-EIGHT

Audrey

I'M SITTING in front of the fireplace, researching random career options when I hear Bradley's truck driving up.

I'd told Brianna that working is important for me. The problem is I don't really have a career. I have a degree in business, but working in business never really interested me. Kind of wish I'd realized that before I graduated. Still. Having the degree had gotten me the couple of jobs I'd had.

My fire is much bigger than I know is recommended, and just as he mentioned in a roundabout way, I'm going to run out of firewood sooner rather than later.

I close my iPad and get up, stretching.

I'd actually expected Bradley a couple of hours ago despite telling myself how irrational that expectation is.

Bradley doesn't actually live here. Bradley and I are not in a relationship.

He's just staying here until we find out who threatened me.

Then, once that's settled, he'll be on his way.

In the meantime, I get to live in a make believe world where Bradley lives here with me.

Meeting him at the door, I'm delighted to see that he brought pizza.

"Hello Biscuit." I rub the dog's head and he prances like an excited puppy.

"You brought pizza," I say, taking the box from Bradley.

"I was thinking we could work on something tonight."

"Sure. What do you want to work on?"

"Your wish is my command."

"That's a rather dangerous thing to say to a girl."

"What can I say? I live on the edge."

"You do, don't you? Did you say you're on the volunteer fire department?"

"I don't remember saying. But I am. They know they can call me whenever they need me. For whatever they need me for."

I wonder why they didn't call him the night Claire disappeared. But I don't ask.

"Speaking of," he says. "Claire woke up."

"What? Really? Did she say anything?"

"Not that I know of. She doesn't have any family."

"Oh. She has that guy who pays her. Mr. Fields? Did you find out who he is?"

"I didn't think to ask anyone yet. I was kind of giving Claire time to recover."

"Right." I take the pizza into the kitchen and open up the box.

"It's still hot," I say. "Want to eat while it's hot?"

"Sure."

I take down two plates and put two slices of pizza on each. Then on second thought, I add a third slice to Bradley's place and take them with me over to the fireplace.

"Want a beer?" I ask.

"Not right now. There might be power tools later."

"Right."

"Nice fire."

"I know. It's not your elegant fire. But the house was dreary."

"You're going to love winter."

"I'm getting the idea that you're being facetious about that."

"I might be."

The pizza has lots of gooey cheese. Just the way I like it.

I read the message that pops up on my phone. "My sister, Lilah."

"Is she okay?"

"Yes." I look into his eyes and in that moment I really

wish I'd found a way to tell Lilah no. That it's not a good time for her to visit. "She's stopping for the night."

He looks at me sideways. "Stopping as in driving?"

"Yes. She's on her way here."

"Oh." He's quite good at hiding his surprise about this and I don't see any disappointment. So now I feel silly worrying about her interrupted our time together. "That's unexpected, isn't it?"

"Quite. There was some kind of problem with her job. She's been thinking about quitting anyway."

"Are you happy about it?" he asks.

"It'll be good to see her," I say, evading the question.

"Wyatt will be happy," he murmurs.

"Wyatt? Why?"

"Nothing. We should probably get to work on her room then."

"That's what I was thinking."

CHAPTER
FORTY-NINE

Bradley

AFTER I SHOW Audrey how to apply the mesh tape, she proves to be an exceptional assistant. We get her closet taped up in no time.

"So what do you think?" I ask as I gather up the supplies to mix the powdered compound.

"About what?"

"Becoming a handyman's assistant?"

She gives me a sideways look. "Depends on the handyman."

"That's an interesting answer." I give her a grin as I turn

on the faucet to fill the plastic bucket. And one that I happen to like.

"Are you making me a job offer?" she asks, keeping her tone light, but not looking at me.

I turn off the water and sit on the edge of the bathtub.

"That depends. Are you available?"

She looks over at me, meeting my gaze now. "I'll consider it."

And then there's a sound. Faint. A soft creak from downstairs. Like a door easing open.

The wind?

Or something else?

We both freeze. Her eyes widen, not leaving mine.

Biscuit sits up from where he had been sleeping on the bathroom floor. A low grumble echoes from his throat.

"Stay here," I say, much calmer than I feel. "I'll go see what it was."

"I'm coming with you."

Biscuit stands up and darts out of the bathroom at a run.

"I guess we're all going," I say. "Stay behind me."

"Not a problem."

We leave the bathroom and start quietly down the hallway toward the stairs.

"Why is Biscuit being so quiet?"

"I don't know." But I do know that if someone hurts my dog, there will be serious hell to pay.

At the top of the stairs, we find Biscuit sitting quietly in front of the closed door.

I glance back at Audrey who looks as confused as I feel.

By the time we reach the bottom of the stairs, I'm regretting not setting her up with window shades already.

I hadn't realized it was already dark, but the windows with such lovely views during the day are no more than walls of darkness.

We can't see out, but others can easily see in.

With Audrey at my heels, I walk across to the door and put a hand on Biscuit's head. He shifts, standing, then sits back down.

I look out one window and Audrey looks out the one on the other side of the door.

"See anything?" I whisper.

"Nothing."

"Biscuit. Stay. I'm going out there to look."

Audrey holds Biscuit's collar, even though I don't think she can hold him unless he chooses to let her. He's much too strong and big.

I flip on the porch light and crack the door. Nothing there but the wind blowing lightly in the trees.

The porch creaks under my foot as I step out. The wind brushes against my face, cool and dry, and I scan the yard. Shadows dance across the grass. Just branches shifting, I think. Hope. I descend the steps slowly, listening.

Nothing moves.

No footsteps.

No voices.

Just the wind.

I take another step forward—and that's when I see it.

A small object rests on the edge of the porch. Something that wasn't there before.

I crouch down, heart thudding, and pick it up. A plain, cream-colored envelope. No name on the front. No stamp. The flap tucked closed, not sealed. I hesitate, then pull it open and slide out a single folded sheet of paper.

You were warned, Audrey.
Go now, while you can.

No signature. No explanation.

Behind me, I hear the door creak open. Audrey's voice is quiet. "What is it?"

I fold the note and tuck it into my pocket. "Nothing. Just trash. Probably blew in with the wind."

She steps onto the porch, barefoot. Her eyes search mine.

I hold her gaze, but I don't say more.

Not yet.

Because I don't know who left the note.

I don't know what *while you can* means.

But I do know one thing. Someone doesn't want her here.

And that turns the worry in my gut into something sharper. Something burning.

Anger.

She deserves to know the truth.

And I won't keep her in the dark.

Not when shadows are starting to gather.

"Let's go inside."

FIFTY

Audrey

BRADLEY and I sit together in front of the fireplace, turned toward each other. Biscuit takes his place in front of the fireplace.

"We need to talk about this," Bradley says.

"About what?" I search his eyes, but I don't like what I see there.

Anger.

Even though I know it's not directed toward me, I feel the heat of it.

"These threats."

"What was out there?" I ask. "You said it was just trash blowing up."

With a sigh, he reaches into his pocket and pulls out an envelope.

"I can't not tell you," he says, putting the note in my hand.

"Another one?"

"Yeah. This one looks more rushed. Less planned."

"It's just an envelope," I muse. "No elaborate presentation like the one in the black box."

I pull the letter out of the envelope.

You were warned, Audrey.
Go now, while you can.

"I guess we at least know who the threat is directed toward," I say, putting the note back in his hand.

"This has to stop. I'm going to make it stop."

"How?"

"I don't know yet. but it's gone too far."

"What are you going to do? Chase the wind?"

"Somebody wants us to find these notes. They're going to a lot of trouble to do it. And risk. Somebody is coming up here, risking us seeing them leave these notes."

"I know, but…"

"Security cameras. I'm driving into Boulder tomorrow and getting some cameras. We're going to have security cameras all over this place."

"That might work."

"It will," he says with determination and certainty. "We'll find out who's doing this and I'll put a stop to it."

"Okay." I take a deep, shuddering breath. "Okay. We'll put a stop to it."

"You still don't think we need to tell the sheriff?"

"I don't think it'll do any good."

"I haven't told Lilah what she's walking into yet."

"Hopefully we'll get it sorted out before much longer. But..." he looks into my eyes. "when she gets here, you have to tell her."

"I know."

"You have to tell her so she can watch for anything unusual. And I don't think either one of you need to go anywhere alone. Not until after we at least talk to Claire."

"When is that going to happen?"

"I wasn't going to do it, but tomorrow when I'm in Boulder getting security cameras, I'll stop in and see if she remembers anything."

"Okay. Do you want me to go with you?"

"You can if you want to. But... when is Lilah getting here?"

I glance at my phone. "Not sure. Possibly tomorrow."

"I'll leave Biscuit here with you tomorrow."

"Really? That sounds like a great idea."

"Now," he says. "We've got some walls to mud."

"Sounds like fun," I say.

"You have no idea."

He gets up. Holds out a hand. "Let's go do something fun."

Putting my hand in his, I get to my feet.

Anything I do with Bradley is fun.

Sitting in front of the fireplace. Cooking. Taping walls with mesh tape.

Even... almost... chasing the wind.

FIFTY-ONE

Bradley

I'D HARDLY LEFT Audrey's house and made it past my own before I was regretting leaving not only Biscuit, but also Audrey behind.

I came so close to stopping and turning around that I slowed to a crawl for a few minutes.

But Audrey wasn't up yet, first of all, and second, I want to get to Boulder and get back as soon as possible.

I want to get those security cameras and get them installed. Enough is enough.

And I need to talk to Claire. By going to the hospital

where she is, I'm running the risk of having to drive her back to Whiskey Springs. But if I do, then I just do.

If I can find out why she was unconscious on the side of the road, any inconvenience will be worth it.

As a compromise to myself, I call Wyatt and wake him up. Tell him what I'm doing.

"See," he says. "You'd be a good sheriff. Nobody else though about putting cameras up around the house and it's such a simple thing. I should have thought of it. The sheriff should have thought about it."

"I guess we were all hoping there was nothing to it. That it would blow over."

"Doesn't look like that's happening. Do you want me to ride down with you?"

"Actually, Audrey has strict instructions to call me if anything feels off. I left Biscuit with her—"

"You left Biscuit. Dude. I think you have it bad."

"No comment. But if she calls me, I'm going to need you on standby."

"Got it. I can do that. Just let me know. Been a while since I've gotten the chance to kick someone's ass."

"Well." I pull out onto the highway. "That sounds like a story to be heard over a beer."

"You might be right."

"Oh. And guess what? You'll be happy to know that her sister, Lilah is on her way up here."

"Get out."

"No. I'm serious. So it's possible you'll get to meet her."

"I hope you know I was funning with you."

"Well, I'm not funning. She really is on the way here."

"Huh."

"And now I see the cat's got your tongue."

"I'll probably meet her on my next firewood delivery."

"Probably."

"I still think you should run for sheriff."

"Don't change the subject."

"Okay. Well. Since I'm on standby, I might as well get up and make myself a cup of coffee."

"I'll call you when I get back. We'll install cameras."

"I'll be ready."

My drive into Boulder is uneventful. Boulder, however, is a busy little city. Almost too much traffic for their infrastructure. Just an observation. Not my bailiwick. Although, I'm beginning to think maybe I should have considered civil engineering. I seem to notice things that a civil engineer would notice.

I did some Internet searching last night, so I know right where to go to get the best cameras at the best deal. While I'm there at the hardwood store, I get Audrey a new fireplace poker set. It's halfway supposed to be a joke that makes her smile, but mostly something she really needs.

I noticed that hers is getting worn out. I've had to screw the handle back on twice.

After that, I do a couple more errands, then head to the hospital to see if I can talk to Claire.

Unfortunately the staff denies that she's there.

Back in my truck, I give the sheriff a call.

"I tried to see Claire. They told me she's not there."

"She's there. She must have opted out of visitors."

"Then maybe as sheriff, you should drive down here and talk to her yourself instead of sending someone else."

"Maybe I will."

"I meant to ask you if you know someone named Mr. Fields that Claire might work for."

"I don't, but I'll see what I can find out."

"Thanks. By the way, Audrey has gotten two threatening notes left on her doorstep."

"You're just now telling me this?"

"You didn't seem all that interested when I brought those flowers in for you to check on."

"Those were flowers. Not threatening notes. I'll drive up there and take a look around."

"Sounds good. Audrey's there by herself today."

"I'll go by there. Take a look."

"Thanks. I'm about to lose service. Later."

Damn it. I hate it when Wyatt puts stuff in my head. I would be a good sheriff. But I'm an engineer. A handyman. Not a lawman.

Traffic is bad through the canyon. Everybody thinks they have to drive around the sharp curves like they're driving on a race track.

Makes me appreciate the small town of Whiskey Springs all the more.

If not for getting the cameras, I would have called it a

wasted trip. The cameras, however, make it worthwhile. Faster than ordering and waiting on a delivery.

Wyatt has experience in installing cameras like this, so I'm really surprised he didn't think of it before I did.

At any rate, I'm going to put him to work helping me install them. They'll be up and running long before nightfall. Time to put an end to the nonsense.

FIFTY-TWO

Audrey

I'M IN MY BEDROOM, sketching out some possible designs for my closet, when I hear a vehicle coming down my road.

It doesn't sound like Bradley's truck and it isn't the mailman.

I go to the window and look out.

It's a police car. My heart slams in my chest.

My first thought is that something is wrong.

I flash back to the police officer that had come to my house after Thomas's accident. It hadn't mattered that the FAA had already called me. The officer coming by my house had been the final confirmation that my world had shattered.

But this isn't that.

No one would know how to get in touch with me here.

I reflexively glance at my phone. No calls or messages.

Taking a deep breath, I wait for the buzzing in my ears to quiet.

Instead of going downstairs, I stand at the window and watch the sheriff get out of his car. He doesn't come to the door, though. Instead, he walks around, looking.

When the officer's car door slams shut, Biscuit, who had been sleeping on the foot of my bed, jumps down from the bed and with a low growl in his throat, shoots out of the bedroom and gallops down the stairs.

The officer isn't very old. Thirties maybe. Tall and clean-shaven from what I can see from here.

Surely he knows I'm home. My car is parked next to the house. Hard to miss.

Maybe Bradley told him about the notes.

I call Bradley's number, but it goes straight to voicemail.

Well. I tried.

When the officer turns and sees me standing in the window, I sigh. There's no getting away from facing whatever this is.

I follow Biscuit downstairs and put a hand on his collar while I crack the door open.

"Audrey Sinclair?" the officer asks.

"Yes." I keep one hand on the doorknob and the other on Biscuit's collar. My heart is still beating too fast.

"I'm Sheriff Morgan. Hey Biscuit."

Biscuit barks once, obviously recognizing the sheriff. That alleviates a little of my anxiety.

Sheriff Morgan is a large man. Tall and stocky with an imposing frown on his features. He fills the doorway and is not a little intimidating. It doesn't help that he's wearing reflective sun glasses, hiding his eyes from me.

"How can I help you?"

"I heard you've been having some trouble around here."

"Right." Another layer of anxiety drops off. He's not here to tell me anything. He's here because of the threats. "Did Bradley talk to you?"

He drags off his sun glasses, making him look a little bit less intimidating. There's a kindness in his eyes that I hadn't been able to see behind the sun glasses. "Something about some notes?"

"Yes. Do you want to see them?"

"Might be helpful." Although his words are sarcastic, he sounds genuine.

I step back to let him inside. As the door widens, Biscuit bolts outside, jerking free of my hand.

"Biscuit!" I call out for him, but he's headed toward the trees.

I glance helplessly from the dog to the sheriff. We don't usually let Biscuit go out front. He should be okay and I don't think he'll run off, but if anything happens to

Bradley's dog on my watch...I don't even want to think about it.

"The notes are on the kitchen island."

"Go," he says. "I'll take a look at them."

"Okay. Thank you." Leaving the sheriff, I rush down the porch steps toward Biscuit.

I realize I must have forgotten to take him out for a walk because he's already digging a hole in the dirt.

By the time Biscuit and I are heading back toward the door, the sheriff is coming out the front door.

"Did you find them?" I ask, referring to the threatening letters.

"Yes." He taps his shirt pocket. "I'm just going to take them with me. Start an investigation."

"Okay," I say. "If that's what you need to do."

"It's the only way to find out who's doing it."

Biscuit rubs the sheriff's hand. Patting Biscuit on the head, the sheriff smiles at me. Somehow seeing him smile doesn't comfort me any. In fact, his smile seems forced, unnatural even. But I just met the sheriff, for all of half a second ago, so I'm in no place to judge him one way or another.

As I stand at the window, watching him drive off, I breathe a sigh of relief.

I can't explain it, but him showing up like this unannounced without Bradley here leaves me feeling unsettled.

Bradley

"Hand me that drill," Wyatt says, from his perch on a ladder balanced against one of the blue spruce trees out behind Audrey's house.

"You sure we have to put these cameras up here in the trees?" I ask, glancing around before putting my attention back on the iPad in my hands.

Wyatt glances down at me. "Would you rather people just see them when they drive up?"

"Good point. I should have gotten the camouflage ones."

"These are good quality. You did good."

"Turn it a little bit to the left."

Wyatt turns the camera.

"Good. Better."

"Let me see."

I pass the iPad up to Wyatt. He makes some minor adjustments to the camera position and hands the iPad back.

"You're really good at this," I say.

"It's why I get paid the big bucks."

"Too bad there aren't very many people in Whiskey Springs who need security cameras installed."

"More than you'd think, but I can't charge people like Audrey. I have to go into Boulder and other places outside of town to actually charge people a premium price."

"You should get with Caleb. Let him set up the business side of it for you. Do some advertisements."

"Nah. Word of mouth gets me plenty of work."

"Still. Caleb could set you up a price structure."

Wyatt climbs down the ladder. "You do realize Caleb has nothing on me, right?"

"Actually. No. I always think of Caleb as being the business brains out of the three of us."

"If Caleb's the business brains, what am I?"

"Same as me. The worker. But you're good with electronics and oddly enough, forestry. I'm better with renovations."

"I guess we all have our strengths."

"Where do you think the next one needs to go?"

"Need to cover that blind spot over on the side of the house."

"Have to attach it to the external wall."

"It won't be noticeable."

Audrey comes out the back door.

"How's it going?" she asks.

"Take a look so far," I say, showing her the iPad.

"That's rather impressive. I think we're about to break this game up. So I heard from Lilah. She stopped for the night, but she'll be here in the morning."

"Good. That gives us time to get these security cameras up. I'll feel a whole lot better once all this is in place."

"Me too."

"Wyatt. I've got cold beer in the fridge when you get through."

"You didn't offer me a beer," I tell her.

"Didn't know I had to." She turns and walks back inside.

Wyatt props the ladder against the side of the house. "She's sweet on you."

"Just showing her appreciation."

"Whatever you want to tell yourself."

"She's still grieving."

"Been what? Four weeks?"

"Hardly time to get past the initial shock," I say.

"Maybe." He climbs up the ladder. "Hand me one of those cameras."

I hand one of the cameras up to him.

"Everybody is different," he says. "There's no clock to punch on things like that."

"When did you get to be so smart?"

"Always being underestimated."

"The youngest son always has such a hard life."

"You have no idea."

"Tomorrow you get to meet Lilah."

"Tomorrow I will be working over at the Danbury cabin."

"What's wrong with the Danbury cabin?"

"Got to replace a dishwasher."

"You're just trying to avoid meeting the sister."

"I told you I was just funning."

"Chicken."

"Maybe. Let me see that iPad."

I hand the iPad up to him.

It's nice. Spending time like this with my brother. Getting to see him do what he does best. Flipping our roles so that I'm the helper and he's the expert.

"One more camera to install. Then I'm going to have that beer. Then I'm going to head out. Let you have some time with Audrey before her sister gets here."

"I keep telling you, it's not like that."

Wyatt looks down at me. "Then maybe it should be like that. Nothing changes if nothing changes."

I hate it when Wyatt is right.

"You think any more about running for sheriff?" he asks, back on the ground.

"Good God, Wyatt. How many times do I have to tell you? I'm not interested in running for sheriff."

FIFTY-FOUR

Audrey

SITTING on the sofa in front of what everyone calls my too big fire in the fireplace with Bradley and Wyatt reminds me of hanging out with my two sisters.

The two brothers tease each other mercilessly while supporting each other with no qualms whatsoever.

I sit with my iPad in my lap, watching the six cameras all on the screen at once. It's a good app. I can touch any one of the six camera to zoom in. Then just slide it back into place so I can see all six again. And they are all recording constantly.

Nobody is going to be sneaking up on us leaving threatening notes on the porch or anywhere else without being caught on camera.

"I'm heading out," Wyatt says. "Got an early day tomorrow."

"Thanks Wyatt," I say. "For installing the cameras. I can't tell you how much better I feel having them up."

"Bradley drove into the city and bought them. I just installed them."

"Then thanks to both of you."

"I'll walk you to the door," Bradley says.

Using my iPad, I watch them standing out on the porch, zooming in just to get used to handling the app. I don't have the volume turned on, so I don't know what they're saying. I don't want to know.

I do however study the two men. Both are handsome and they look like brothers even though Wyatt is more rugged looking.

Bradley, in my opinion is the handsome one. It baffles me how no one has scooped him up already. As far as I can tell neither one of them has a girlfriend, at least not right now.

I'm about as close to an unofficial girlfriend as Bradley can get. It would be hard for him to have a girlfriend while spending his nights over here with me.

Bradley comes back in and I use the camera to watch Wyatt get in his truck and leave the driveway.

"Wyatt ordered some cameras to put down the road so

we can see anyone driving up. He'll come back and install those when they come in."

"He's a good guy."

"Of course."

"I need to pay him for doing all this work."

"You'll do nothing of the sort. He did it as a favor to me. If you go offering him money, he'll be insulted."

"How could anyone be insulted by taking money for work for hire?"

"A favor," he says. "What can I make you for dinner?"

"I could just eat a salad."

"I don't see how you do it."

"What's that?" I join him in the kitchen, setting the iPad on the island so we can watch it while we make dinner.

"Have the willpower to eat healthy like you do."

"It's not easy. Not when you cook such good pasta."

"You like my pasta?" I grin, ridiculously pleased.

"LOVE your pasta."

"I think there's still some left over if you'd like it."

"Okay.

"Okay then. Pasta it is."

I smile and our gazes lock.

There is something so very comfortable about spending a simple evening at home with Bradley.

I don't know what to make of him. He's never tried to kiss me. I don't know if he even likes me romantically.

Taking a wooden bowl from the cabinet to make a salad, I admonish myself.

I shouldn't be thinking about Bradley like this.

As a newly widowed woman, it's not appropriate. I should *not* be thinking about him romantically.

Setting a pot of water to boil for noodles, he smiles over at me and my heart flutters like a teenager.

Just because I *shouldn't* be thinking about kissing him, does not mean I'm not thinking about it.

What girl wouldn't be thinking about kissing Bradley? Certainly not any girl he looks at with that twinkle in his eyes.

I'm hopeless. Just hopelessly hopeless when it comes to Bradley Winslow.

I'm not sure I'd change that particular truth even if I could.

FIFTY-FIVE

Bradley

AFTER DINNER, I sit on the edge of the hearth assembling the poker set I bought Audrey.

"You thought it was time to retire my fireplace tools?" she asks, glancing up from her iPad. She's been watching the camera images all evening.

"They were worn out when you got here."

"I know. I didn't do it. Still. It was kind of you to replace them. Thank you."

My phone chimes with a text message.

I lean over to where I'd left it on the sofa and look at it.

"Everything okay?" Audrey asks, seeing my expression.

"It's my dad. Claire is coming home tomorrow."

"How does your dad know this?"

"I have no idea." I set the phone down and go back to tending the fire. "Small town? Everybody knows everything about everybody."

She wrinkles her nose. "Does that mean we're going to see her tomorrow?"

I like the way she just tosses out that word *we* like it's the most natural thing in the world.

"I think so. I really want to know what happened."

Audrey looks up from her iPad. "I hope she can tell us."

"What do you mean?"

"She was unconscious. She might not know."

"She'll know." I have to believe that. I have to believe that we can at least find out if she had anything to do with the threatening letters.

"Claire didn't do it," Audrey says suddenly, looking at me.

"How do you know?"

"Because she was in the hospital when the second note was left."

"You're right. You're absolutely right."

"We still need to know what happened. If the same person that left the note tried to hurt her."

"We'll find out." I turn back around to poke at the fire some more. It's soothing, messing with the logs and watching the flames.

Audrey makes a sound that has me looking over my shoulder at her. "See something?"

She shakes her head. "I thought I did, but it's just the wind."

"You know those are recording, right?"

"I know."

I get up and go to sit next to her. Hold out a hand for the iPad. "How about we take a break from the surveillance?"

"Okay." She hands me the iPad and watches as I close the cover and set it aside.

I turn toward her. Take her hands in mine.

"It's going to be okay," I say. "We've got a good start to measuring the windows. We'll finish that up tomorrow and get some window shades ordered. I think we'll both feel better when we have the windows covered."

"I've started looking. I still haven't decided what kind to order. Lilah will be here tomorrow. She's good at that kind of thing."

"Good. We both have siblings that are good at different things."

"Thank you," she says. "For being here."

"You don't have to thank me. I'm in it now."

"You didn't know what you were getting in to."

I squeeze her hands. "It wouldn't have mattered. I'd do it all over again."

"You're a good man. Why don't you have a girlfriend?"

"Maybe I'm working on that."

"Is that so? How are you working on that when you're here all the time?"

"Two birds with one stone."

Biscuit lifts his head and his ears tilt forward.

I let go of Audrey's hands and pick up the iPad to check the app.

"See anything?" she asks, leaning close enough to see.

"Just shadows."

Biscuit puts his head back down.

"Must have been a false alarm."

"Must have." I'm not ready to lose my excuse for staying here, but I am ready to find out who's leaving threatening notes. And whoever's doing it is bold enough to do it with my truck sitting outside. Knowing that I'm here and Audrey's not alone.

That in itself is disconcerting.

She yawns.

"You're tired," I say. "I'll walk you up to your room."

"You just got the fire going. Seems a shame to waste it."

"Biscuit is enjoying it."

"Yes he is."

"Come on," I say, standing up. I pull her up. "I'll monitor the iPad and you take your book." I pick up the novel she left on the coffee table and hand it to her.

"Maybe we'll get a reprieve tonight."

"Maybe."

"Bradley?"

"Yes?" On impulse, I take her hand and lead her toward the stairs.

"What if he... or she... knows about the cameras and doesn't bring any more notes?"

"Then I guess we solved the problem."

"I wish I had your optimism."

"I just refuse to live in fear."

She doesn't say anything.

I can't even begin to imagine what she's been through this last month or so.

The fact that she's even here. Functioning. Says a lot about her level of strength.

Just one more thing I like about her.

Audrey is an incredibly strong woman.

We reach the top of the stairs and stop at her bedroom door.

"Wake me up if anything happens on the cameras," she says.

"Okay." Even though I agree, I don't plan on waking her. She's practically asleep on her feet even now. If she can sleep, she needs to sleep.

I kiss her on the forehead. "Get some rest. I'll be here in the morning when you get up."

"No work tomorrow?"

"I want to catch up on some things here."

"Okay," she says, walking into her bedroom, leaving the door open.

"Do you want this closed?" I ask.

"No. You can leave it open."

"Okay." As she heads into her bathroom, I continue down the hall to my room.

Even the possibility of someone leaving threatening notes isn't enough to dampen my optimism right now. Things are looking up.

FIFTY-SIX

Audrey

AFTER GETTING READY, I climb into my bed and with the lamp on, open up my book to read a page or two.

Before I can open the book, though, I get a text from Lilah.

LILAH

I'll should be there early in the morning.

How early is early?

LILAH

Depends on what time I wake up. I'm two hours away.

> Okay. Let me know when you leave so I can be up.

LILAH

> Good night.

I put my phone on charge and hold my book in my lap.

Instead of reading, though, I let myself replay my evening, specifically the way Bradley had kissed me on the forehead.

Definitely a show of affection. But maybe it was the way a brother would kiss a sister.

Not having any brothers, I don't really know.

It meant something, though, for me.

I'm letting myself get attached. No two ways about it. Not smart.

As soon as we catch the person leaving the threatening notes, Bradley will be leaving me here alone. As he should.

He's been such a perfect gentleman.

But I'm sure he has a life of his own. Maybe there's someone he wants to date. He's put his life on hold for me, a stranger in need.

I have to keep myself together. To remember that I came here for a couple of reasons. One because the house and money had been left to me. And second, to give myself the time and space to become accustomed to being a widow.

To figure out what it is I want to do next with my life. I've been too busy today to even think about finding a job.

And now Lilah is coming for a visit. Things will get even

busier. It would be rude of me to start a new job while she's here visiting.

The job thing will just have to wait.

With a sigh, I open up my book to the place I have bookmarked.

But there along with my bookmark is a note.

With a chill running down my spine, I toss the book, my bookmark, and the note away from me.

My heart is pounding so fast, I put a hand over my chest. Take deep calming breaths.

I call out to Bradley, but his name gets stuck in my throat.

I hadn't opened the book since last night.

Someone had found a way to leave a note in it. Bypassed the security cameras.

I slide off the bed, sliding my feet into my slippers, then pick up the note with two fingers.

My heart pounding in my throat, I walk down the hall toward Bradley's room, holding the letter at arm's length.

His door is wide open. I hadn't expected that, but I don't have time to process it.

The second he sees me, he's out of bed and across the room.

He's wearing a pair of sleep pants and a white t-shirt.

"Where did you get that?" he asks.

I try to speak, but I can't get the words out. "I..."

He takes the note with one hand and grabs my hand with his other.

Leads me over to sit on the edge of the bed.

"Did you read it?" he asks. I shake my head. "No. You didn't read it."

He unfolds the letter and reads it silently.

"What does it say?"

"It's typed this time. It says *Don't think Bradley can protect you. Put up as many cameras as you want. You'll be leaving soon. One way or another.*"

"Let me see," I say, holding out my hand for the note. Surely I misunderstood him.

He hands me the note and stands up while I read it. Running a hand through his hair, he paces to the door and back. "This is too much. That's a bold threat."

"It's clearly a threat," I say, still staring at the paper. "How did it get in my book?"

"Someone was in the house again. Just like the flowers. Someone has a key."

I try to think. Had I left the house open today at any point? Only when Wyatt and Bradley had been outside mounting security cameras. Obviously a waste of time. But I'd been inside the house the whole time or just outside on the porch. No one could have gotten past me.

"What do we do?" I ask.

"I don't know." He comes back and sits next to me on the bed.

"We have to do something."

"We'll think of something." He takes the note. Sets it aside. "Are you okay?"

"I don't know. I will be." I don't have a choice. "I'll go back to bed now." Even though I know there's no way I'm going to be able to sleep. Not now.

He doesn't say anything and I don't make any moves to get up.

I'm still trembling.

"You don't have to go," he says. "Just stay here until you've had a chance to calm down."

"Okay." But I don't know if I'll ever calm down. Not completely. Not now.

You'll be leaving soon. One way or another.

Don't think Bradley can protect you. Put up as many cameras as you want.

It's like the person who did this has a direct line into my life. It's like they know everything.

They know about Bradley. About the cameras.

And they want me away from here.

One way or another.

I shiver a little as I consider just what that means. Dead or alive. That's what it means.

Whoever is doing this will do whatever it takes to run me out of this house.

"Maybe I should just go," I say. "Back to Houston."

"No," Bradley says, firmly. "We won't let this person run you away. You're tougher than that."

"I don't know. This feels bigger."

"Audrey," he says, putting a hand lightly beneath my chin.

I lift my gaze and look into his light blue eyes.

"I'm going to keep you safe, okay?"

I nod. "I know."

"Come here." He wraps me in his arms, holding me close against him. Resting my cheek against his chest, I listen to his steady heartbeat.

He holds me like I matter. Like I'm not just someone he promised to protect, but someone he never wants to let go of.

My fingers curl in the fabric of his shirt before I realize I've moved them, and I feel the breath he takes. Deep and deliberate. Before his chin brushes the top of my head. The scent of him is warm cedar and something darker, like coffee and days spent outside. It lingers in the air between us, stealing any thought of pulling away.

Outside, the wind rustles through the trees. Inside, it's just the two of us and this moment I'm not sure either of us knows how to define, much less name.

I haven't been this close to a man since Thomas. That thought lands like a stone in my chest. Unexpected and heavier than I want it to be. I thought my heart was done with this, that it had curled in on itself for good. But here I am, breathing this man in, and some long-quiet part of me is waking.

He doesn't loosen his hold, and I don't want him to. Because if I tilt my head back right now, I'm afraid we might close the rest of the space between us.

And I'm not sure I'd stop him.

His heartbeat stays steady, but mine... My heartbeat is doing its own uneven dance.He shifts just enough to look down at me, his gaze searching, his hand trailing from my shoulder to my elbow. Not a caress exactly, but it leaves a warm trail behind.

"You're trembling," he says quietly.

"I'm okay." My voice is steady enough, though I'm not sure if I'm trying to convince him or myself.

He studies me for a moment longer, then tucks a loose strand of hair behind my ear. The brush of his fingers along my cheek makes my breath catch.

"You don't have to be," he says. "Not with me."

For one dizzying second, I think he's going to kiss me. My pulse spikes, and every sensible thought is gone, replaced by the scent of him, the way his eyes have softened, the faint roughness of his jaw just inches from mine.

But then his arms loosen, and he leans back just enough that cool air rushes between us. The loss is almost physical.

"Come on," he says, voice low but different now, as if he's just as aware of what almost happened. "Let's get you tucked in for the night."

I nod, my throat too tight for words, and follow him out of his room down the hallway to my own. My body still remembers the heat of him, and my heart... well, it hasn't quite decided what to think or do yet.

FIFTY-SEVEN

Bradley

I'M TREADING on dangerous ground with Audrey.

Every cell in my body is urging me to kiss her. It would be so easy. No natural. So... right.

And yet I know it's not. It would be complicated. And messy. And so... wrong.

After she climbs into bed, I pull the blanket up over her shoulders, careful not to let my fingers linger. She's warm, soft, looking up at me with those tired, trusting eyes.

"Don't go," she whispers.

The words hit harder than they should. I'm not sure if

she means tonight... or in general. Either way, I feel them resonating in my chest.

I sit on the edge of the bed. "I'm not going anywhere."

Her hand finds mine in the dark, her fingers curling just enough to keep me there.

I stay. Listening to her breathing slow. Watching the way the clouds shift and the moonlight brushes over her face.

And trying, unsuccessfully, not to imagine what it would be like if I was allowed to be hers.

"Good night, sweetheart." Leaning over, I kiss her on the cheek. So soft and warm.

"Good night," she murmurs.

Leaving the door open, I make it as far as the hallway before I stop.

Every step away from her feels wrong, like I'm leaving something unfinished. The quiet in the house presses in on me, heavy and restless. Leaving her alone feels dangerous and wrong.

I turn back.

Her eyes are closed when I near the bed, but I know she's awake—the way her breathing changes, the tiniest shift of her shoulders.

I walk around to the other side of the large bed, the floorboards creaking under my weight.

I climb onto the bed, the mattress dipping, settle in beneath the blankets, and draw her back against me. She fits like she's always belonged there, her spine warm against my chest, her hair brushing my jaw.Every cell in my body urges me to lower my mouth to her shoulder, to close the last bit of space between us. It would be so easy. So natural. So... right.

And yet, my head is telling me not to cross that line. Not yet. It's too soon.

She's been through too much, too recently.

So I just hold her, my arm wrapped around her waist, my thumb tracing a slow, steady pattern against her hip beneath her cotton pajamas. Her breathing evens out, and I match mine to hers, letting the rhythm tether me to her.

Her soft hair against my cheek smells like jasmine. Her skin smells like honeysuckle.

I can tell when she relaxes and drifts asleep.

So soft against me. Her round behind pressed against me.

There's no going back from this.

Audrey is the woman I've been searching for my whole life.

If I have to wait for her. To wait until she's ready to go to the next level, then that's what I'll do. I'll wait. I'll wait an eternity for her if I have to.

She makes me feel whole. In a way I've never felt like before.

I hadn't realized until this moment that she's the one I've been waiting for.

I'm not sure if I'm keeping her safe tonight... or if she's the one keeping me.

FIFTY-EIGHT

Audrey

I wake the next morning with sunlight across my face. I feel its warmth even before I open my eyes.

I don't even know what time it is. All I know is that I can't remember the last time I slept so soundly through the night.

Stretching beneath the sheets, I run a hand along the empty side of the bed and catch the scent of warm cedar and outdoors.

Bradley.

My mind flashes back to last night. To feeling safe and warm. And I can't remember the last time I felt so content.

Bradley hadn't left me alone. I don't how long he stayed, but I remember him being here. Holding me.

Keeping me safe.

He hadn't had to do that, but he had.

I'd been frightened by the note I'd found tucked in the pages of my book like an ominous bookmark.

The words had left no doubt about the seriousness of the threat. Whoever wrote it knew everything. Knew about Bradley keeping me safe. And most importantly, knew about the cameras.

So it had been all for naught. Since the person making the threats knew about the cameras, we'd put them up for nothing.

Even more terrifying, he had bypassed our whole system and put a threatening note right here in my book. Right beneath our noses.

Heading into the bathroom, I start thinking about those heated floors again. And the gas fireplace in the bathroom.

Bradley might not appreciate me adding things to my list of things house renovations.

As I stand in the shower, the hot water streaming over my head, I remember that Lilah is coming today. She'd stopped for the night just two hours from here.

I never thought of Lila being particularly practical, but waiting until morning to make the drive up into the mountains is just that. Smart and practical.

I'm quite impressed with her doing that. Had I

mentioned how hard the drive was at night? I don't remember, but she probably did her research either way.

I decide on a pair of jeans and a comfortable sweatshirt for the day. I've learned that it doesn't matter that it's summer. It's still cold here in the mountains above Whiskey Springs.

Even when the sun comes out, the wind has a chill to it.

I don't envy the people living in Houston. Not even a little bit. I'll take the cold any day.

Dressed, I head out and hear Biscuit let out a bark before he runs in my direction. He meets me at the bottom of the stairs. Wriggling all over and licking me, he acts like he hasn't seen me for days.

I scratch his head and laugh at him. "What's gotten into you?" I ask the dog.

He just turns and runs toward the kitchen where Bradley is standing at the stove.

"Good morning," he says, tossing a towel over his shoulder.

"Hi. What's gotten into Biscuit?" the dog trails along at my feet.

"I don't know. Maybe he's just happy to see you."

"Maybe. What are you doing?"

"I'm making you breakfast."

"Oh." I sit down on the nearest bar stool.

"Is that okay?"

"It is. It's wonderful. It's just..." I watch him flip an

omelet. "I don't know what I did to deserve so much kindness."

"I just want to make you happy," he says, coming around the kitchen island, leaning over, and kissing me on the forehead. "How did you sleep?"

"I can't remember the last time I slept so well."

"It's the clean mountain air," he says, going back to flipping the omelet.

I watch him a moment as I replay a memory of sleeping curled up against him.

"Yes," I say. "I'm sure that's it."

He grins. "So. Your sister will be here this morning." He makes a cup of coffee in the fancy machine and puts it in front of me.

"Yes." I glance out the window. The coffee is just the way I like it. "The roads should be clear, right?"

"I think so. Why don't I take off after breakfast? Give you time to get her settled?" He glances at the iPad open to the security camera app. "You're got the cameras and I have the app on my phone, too."

I swallow thickly, realizing I don't want him to go. Realizing I'd been expecting him to be here when Lilah got here.

I'd been looking forward to introducing them. Looking forward to Bradley getting to know my family, starting with Lilah and for them to get to know him.

"Okay," I say. "Sure. What about Claire? Claire is coming home today, right? We were going to go talk to her."

"I'll go. You'll have Lilah here."

"Right. I don't want to drag her into this, especially not right away."

"I wouldn't think so."

"You don't have to go out of your way to go talk to her though."

He scoops up an omelet, puts half of it in on one plate and sets it in front of me. Puts the other half on another plate for himself and sits down next to me. "I want to go talk to her. I need to. I need to know what happened that night. There's too much coincidence. I'd like to be able to make sense of it."

"So would I. This looks wonderful." I take a bite. "It is wonderful."

"I'm glad you like it."

"You know," I say. "I'm not sure you realize what you're doing here."

"What am I doing?"

"You're going to make it hard for me to let you go."

He doesn't say anything. He just grins.

FIFTY-NINE

Bradley

TRUE TO MY WORD, I clean up from making breakfast and head out.

Audrey and I didn't talk this morning about anything serious. She's focused on her sister's arrival. As she should be.

I left Biscuit with her again today. Not that I don't want to take him with me, but it's good for her to have him there. Biscuit is a good enough guard dog.

Relieved that the roads are clear, I drive past my house and keep going. I'll go by later and change out my clothes, but right now I have something I need to do.

Audrey and I didn't talk about the threatening note she found tucked in her book last night.

We didn't talk about sleeping with her curled in my arms.

And we didn't talk about how she'd actually laughed when she'd met Biscuit coming down the stairs. She hadn't even realized she was laughing. It had been spontaneous and real.

And it had warmed my heart.

She's healing.

And as she's healing, she and I are getting closer and closer.

She'd been onto something when she'd told me cooking for her would make it hard for her to let me go.

Maybe I hadn't done it consciously, but subconsciously, that was sort of the whole point.

I didn't want her to let me go.

She'd told me she couldn't move out of the house. That she has to live in the house in order for the inheritance to be valid.

I pull out onto the main highway and head toward Whiskey Springs.

So okay. I get that she wants to make sure she keeps the house.

I, on the other hand, have never lived anywhere that I found to be all that important. Probably the result of living in several of my family's cabins since I'd come back from Purdue.

It was convenient to live in a place while I was doing renovations there.

It had also made it easier for me let go of places. To see a house as just a place to live.

Some people think of their houses as an extension of themselves.

I think maybe my parents might be attached to their house. But I get that. They'd built it from the ground up right after they'd gotten married. It's their home. They had raised a family there. Three boys.

That's probably different. They have a lot of memories tied up there.

My brothers and I have a more transient mindset.

Long way around to say that if she wants to live in the Albright house, I have no problem living there with her. On the contrary. There are plenty of things she and I can do to make it better.

I'd planned on staying around today and doing some of those things, but then I'd remembered that her sister was coming in.

I don't want to make things complicated for her. For her to have to explain why I'm there.

I can only imagine that that would be awkward. Lilah expects to find her sister up here all alone, grieving for the sudden loss of a husband.

I can readily admit that I'd had something to do with that not happening quite so much.

Not my fault though. Not my fault that someone is

leaving Audrey threatening notes. If that someone, if anyone, so much as touches a hair on Audrey's head, God help them.

I might be a little bit crazy to think it, but I'm thinking I've found the girl I want to spend the rest of my life with.

And it just so happens that I don't care where we live.

If she wanted to move back to Houston, that might be a different story. I'd have to give that some serious thought. Serious, serious thought. But I don't see that happening. She seems to fit here.

She's making a home for herself. The threatening notes aren't helping, but otherwise, even with that going on, I think she likes it here.

I pull into a parking space downtown and park. Nothing is open yet, so I get out and walk around the little city park.

I'm looking forward to showing Audrey Whiskey Springs at Christmastime.

If Christmas was a town, it would be Whiskey Springs.

But right now, the trees have new growth on them. There are flowers popping up everywhere. Both the kind people plant in pots and the kind that spring up naturally along the edges of the path.

The river is swollen with snowmelt.

And endless cycle of winter, spring, and now summer. Fall is probably my favorite season. The leaves turn vibrant beautiful colors and flutter to the ground like silent raindrops.

I want to share all the seasons with Audrey.

Maybe I'm getting ahead of myself.

But I'm a Winslow and the Winslows go after what they want.

It's taken me a long time to find the woman that I want to go after.

And now that I've found her, I have to wait until she's ready. I don't mind.

Not even a little.

All in all, I think waiting is going to make us stronger and closer.

Maybe it's time I talk to her about how I'm feeling. I want to take the idea that I might be leaving out of her head.

Instead, I want her to be thinking about the possibility that I might be staying.

CHAPTER
SIXTY

Audrey

THE HOUSE ISN'T LIKE I was hoping it would be when my family started to come to visit.

I don't have the closets done or my office or all the little things that won't be obvious to anybody other than me. Like new door locks and window shades.

But when I see my sister's old car coming up the road, I realize none of that matters.

I meet her at the car and I can't hug her hard enough.

"You're crying," she says. "I knew we shouldn't have let you come up here by yourself."

"No," I say, wiping the tears away. "These are happy tears."

"Are you sure?"

"I'm positive."

"Okay then. Whoa." Audrey closes her car door and freezes. "There's a dog."

"That's Biscuit."

Biscuit is sitting several feet away. I'd told him to sit and stay. So he was doing just that. Sitting and staying.

Audrey glances from Biscuit to me, then keeps her gaze on the dog. "He's huge. Is he friendly? Does he bite?"

"I have to warn you. He licks. But he has such good manners. Biscuit. Come here."

Biscuits barks once, then runs over and, wriggling all over, standing next to me as though waiting for an introduction.

"This is Biscuit. Biscuit this is Lilah. My sister."

Lilah holds out a hand tentatively for Biscuit to sniff.

"I didn't know you were afraid of dogs," I say.

"I'm not. But that's more like a horse."

"Come on. Let's get you unloaded."

"Mom sent homemade cookies." Lilah reaches over and grabs a box from the passenger seat.

"When did Mom start baking?"

"I personally think they're homemade from HEB."

I shrug. "Close enough."

"I thought so, too."

"It looks like someone ate some of them."

"Someone might have. It was a long drive."

"I know. But I'm so glad you're here."

She pops the trunk and we drag out her luggage. She has paints and canvases on the back seat to get later.

"Did the dog come with the place?" she asks as Biscuit follows along beside me as we near the front porch.

"No," I say slowly. "I'm watching him for a neighbor." It's as close to the truth that I can get without telling her too much for right now.

She scrunches her face at me. "You hate neighbors."

"Hate is such a strong word. Anyway, it's different up here. Up here you have to have neighbors to survive."

"Sounds like you've moved to the wild west."

SHE HAS NO IDEA. "It sort of is like that."

"I confess," she says as we reach the front door. "I'm a little concerned."

"Don't be. You're going to love the house. It's huge." I open the door to the inviting scent of wood smoke and cedar.

Biscuit trots in along with us.

"Biscuit acts like he lives here."

I close the door and lock it behind us. "He's a friendly dog."

"It's bigger than I expected," Lilah says. "And you've got a fireplace. Real wood?"

She leaves her suitcase in the middle of the floor and heads straight to the fireplace.

"I'm going to paint it," she says.

Biscuit flops down beside her.

"You can paint anything you want. Do you want coffee?"

"What kind?" she asks skeptically.

"The good kind." While Lilah sits in front of the fireplace, I go into the kitchen and make two lattes.

It's good to have my sister here.

I'm glad I came up here by myself. I don't regret that.

It was something I needed to do.

But I'm glad Lilah is here now.

Now I just have to figure out how to tell her that I'm not wanted here.

Not wanted here by someone unknown to me.

Someone who sees fit to leave me threatening notes about just how much I'm not wanted.

CHAPTER
SIXTY-ONE

Bradley

A FEW MINUTES in the General Store has me deciding on a teddy bear with a helium balloon.

"I'm glad to see somebody using this helium thing. The wife assured me that people would want balloons," John says as he airs up the balloon.

"They will. People just don't know about it yet. You should put it on your website."

John turns and stares at me, scratching his cheek. "Website."

"Yes. Put it on your website. Front page. Maybe run a discount."

John ties the balloon on the teddy bear. "Don't have a website."

"John," I say. "You need to get a website. Everyone has them now."

John makes a sound that I can't decipher and probably don't want to. "You sound like my wife."

"You should really listen to her, you know."

"Got this helium thing, didn't I?"

"Maybe you should put some balloons in the front window."

"You're right. Should have thought of that. I'm getting too old for all this modern stuff."

I don't have the heart to tell him that helium balloons are hardly modern.

"You want to buy a general store?" he asks.

"Me? No way. And you aren't selling." I swipe my credit card. "Just have one of the grandkids make you a website and you'll be fine."

He grumbles as he hands me the bear and balloon.

"Tell Claire I said hello," he says.

I hadn't told him the bear and balloon was for Claire. It bothers me a little bit that he knows this. But it's Whiskey Springs and not only doesn't everyone know everything about everyone, it would be poor form for me to visit anyone just coming home from the hospital without some kind of gift. It's not hard to figure out.

"I will," I say, heading out the door. "And listen to your wife." I add over my shoulder.

I have it on good authority that Claire actually came home last night. I didn't want to tell Audrey because I didn't want to drive out to Claire's last night and with her sister coming in this morning, I didn't want her fretting over it.

So I drive out of town, down toward Glenwood Springs where I happen to know that Claire lives.

She lives in a double-wide trailer on the outskirts of town. The trailer is hidden down a little road behind a grove of spruce trees.

The yard is clean, if not well-manicured. Not surprising since Claire lives alone.

I pull up beside her car and park. I really hope this trip is worth it and that Claire can provide answers.

Claire answers the door wearing a long, threadbare robe, her hair looking like it hasn't seen a brush in days.

"Bradley," she says. "Come in. I wasn't expecting company."

"It's okay," I say. "I won't stay long." I hand her the bear and balloon. "I got this from the General Store. It's from Audrey," I add quickly so she doesn't get the wrong idea.

"Oh. How thoughtful. I didn't know John sold balloons."

"We should help him get the word out."

"We should," she agrees. "And I'll tell everyone. Not that I see that many people. Have a seat."

I sit on an old threadbare sofa with an old cat curled up sleeping on the other end.

"That's Blackie," she says sitting on the equally thread-bare recliner across from me. "He mostly sleeps a lot."

"It's okay. How are you feeling?"

"I'm so glad to be home. The Doc won't let me go back to work for another week though. I don't like putting Miss Audrey out like that."

"Audrey is okay. I promise she's not worried about you not being at work."

"Where are my manners, can I can you something to drink?"

"Thank you, but I can't stay."

"Are you sure? I can make coffee."

"I have some in the truck. I'm good."

"Okay. Well. I know you didn't drive all the way out here just to bring me this balloon."

"I need to know what happened that night. How did you end up unconscious on the side of the road?"

"It's the craziest thing. I'd just left Miss Audrey's, you know." I nod. "I'd slowed down for the narrows. And I saw these two kittens on the side of the road. I wasn't sure what they were at first. Thought they might be wild, but they looked like just regular kittens.

"I thought Blackie would love having some kittens around, so I pull over and get out. They take off. Of course. They run. But by then, I'm convinced they must be lost, so I follow them. I'm calling out to them, real sweet like. One of them stops and looks at me. That's when I know I'm doing the right thing. Poor little thing. All scared and hungry.

"Anyway. They take off again and I follow. It's dark and then..." She looks down and shakes her head. "I don't remember nothing after that. They said I slid down and hit my head. I don't know."

"I'm so sorry that happened to you."

"I'm just sorry I never got those kittens. For Blackie."

"I'll watch for them and if I see them, if they're tame enough, I'll bring them to you. How about that?"

"You are such a kind man. I told Audrey she needs to hold onto you. And I'll tell her again when I see her."

"Well. I appreciate that sentiment," I say. "And I especially appreciate you taking time to talk to me about what happened."

"It was no bother. None at all."

"So you didn't see anyone else? No other vehicles on the road?"

"Oh no. It was just me. Not very smart. I know."

"You have a kind heart. Do you need me to do anything before I head out?" I ask.

"I don't think so." Holding her bear and balloon, she follows me to the door.

"Keep your doors locked," I say.

"Will do."

She stands out on her little porch while I climb back into my truck. I give her a little wave and she goes back inside.

Dead end. Audrey was right. Audrey had already figured

out that Claire couldn't have left the second note, being in the hospital and all.

I didn't think Claire had left the notes, but I thought maybe she'd seen who did. But Claire hadn't seen any other vehicles. Even if she had, she probably wouldn't remember them. All she seemed to remember was chasing a couple of kittens she'd seen from the road.

I'll take a look around. See if I can find them. But they're mostly likely moved on to somewhere they can find food.

With that done, I head back toward town. I'll get some work done at the Bentley cabin while I wait to hear from Audrey.

CHAPTER
SIXTY-TWO

Audrey

FORTUNATELY, Lilah loves the view from her bedroom so much that she doesn't question why I put her at the end of the hall.

"Oh wow," she says, standing at the window. "I can see everything from here. The river. The mountains with their snow-capped peaks. Is that a meadow? I love it. I can't wait to start painting."

"I thought you would like it. You can help me design your closet if you want to."

"That's your department," she says. "I can paint a mural on the wall, though, if you want me to."

"Let me think about that. Maybe."

By the time I finish showing Lilah around and setting her up in her bedroom, it's time for lunch.

"Do you want to drive into town? They have a great pizza place."

"Can we just eat something here? Maybe tonight. I'm just so sick of driving." She hides a yawn behind her hand.

"Sure. I can make some sandwiches. Then you can take a nap."

"You're the perfect sister. Don't tell Brianna I said that."

"Brianna who?"

Lilah laughs and takes a seat at the bar. The same seat where I had sat while Bradley made breakfast.

While I get out bread and ham and cheese and a tomato, I don't see Lilah open up my iPad.

"Why do you have this?" she asks.

"Why do I have what?" I ask, turning around to find her staring at the screen on my iPad.

My stomach drops. I know exactly what she's asking me about. She's asking me about the security cameras.

"Do you not feel safe here?"

"We just put those up yesterday," I say. "Let me get these sandwiches made and I'll explain."

After I throw together a couple of ham and cheese sandwiches and grab a bag of chips, Lilah and I head out to sit on the back deck to have lunch.

"I can't believe how cool it is out here," she says.

"I know. I doesn't take long to get used to it either." I set the tray of food down and Lilah sets down the iPad, then opens it up.

I reflexively glance around the tree line as I take a seat.

"I'm getting a bad feeling about this," she says. "We should have come with you."

"Lilah. You didn't need to come with me. I'm okay. It's just..." I open the bag of chips and hand them over.

"It's just you feel you need surveillance on the house. You must have put these cameras up for a reason.

"Yes. It's just that. Let me start from the beginning."

I tell her about the yellow daisies. About the first note that was left in a box. Then the second note that was left in an envelope.

"Can I see them?" she asks. "The notes?"

"The sheriff took them for evidence. But I took photos." I open up my phone and show her the photos of the notes.

"Okay. Somebody wants your inheritance."

"That's what's I'm thinking. So yesterday Bradley and Wyatt installed these cameras."

"Neighbors."

"Yes."

"And?"

"Last night I found another note tucked in my book."

Lilah looks me with a blank expression. "How long's it been since you looked in the book?"

"Not sure. I was thinking I read the night before, but I can't swear to it."

"I'm hoping you didn't. If you did, that means someone

got past all this." She sweeps a hand over the camera images.

"I know." I bite my lip. "I have the note. It's upstairs. I'll show you later."

"Okay."

"But that's not all."

Lilah slides her plate aside. "There's more?"

"Nothing bad."

"Something good would be nice."

"The neighbor I told you about. Bradley."

"I remember."

"He's staying here until we get this figured out."

"Staying here?"

"Yes. In one of the other guest rooms." I don't look at her. I don't look at her because I'm remembering how Bradley had spent the night in my bed. A little different from staying in the guest room.

When Lilah doesn't say anything, I steal a glance at her.

She's grinning.

"What's funny?"

"Nothing," she says. "It's just I was picturing you up here all alone. I should have known something was up when you said a neighbor was helping you. You don't like neighbors."

"I like this one," I say in a low voice.

"When do I get to meet your knight in shining armor?"

"You want to meet him?"

Lilah looks at me sideways. "I'm thinking if he's living here, I'll should be meeting him."

"He's not living here."

"Okay." She shrugs. "Staying here."

"I guess tonight."

"Good. I don't like the thought of you being up here by yourself. I'm glad you've made a friend."

"Thank you," I say.

A blackbird lands on the deck and I toss it a chip.

"For what?" Lilah asks, watching the bird grab up the chip and take off with it.

"For not being judgmental."

"I am in no place to be judgmental."

"What have you done?"

"I told you. I got fired."

"And now you're here."

"Yes." She smooths back her hair, adjusting the scrunchy holding it back. "The lease on my apartment is up at the end of the month. I didn't renew it."

"Wait. Shouldn't you be home. Packing?"

"I haven't decided what I want to do just yet."

"Explain." I say it, sliding into my older sister mode. Something I haven't done since Thomas's accident.

She lifts an eyebrow, but she explains anyway.

"In some ways," she says, glancing around at the trees fluttering softly in the breeze. "I envy you."

"How could you possibly?"

"You get to start over. Somewhere new. You can be anybody you want to be."

"And yet I'm still me."

"Yes. Well. Maybe. It's sort of a choice, isn't it?"

I shrug. "Maybe."

"Imagine a world where you didn't tell anyone about your past."

"Are you wanting to reinvent yourself, Lilah?"

"I'm a twenty-three-year-old bartender. What do you think?" She tosses a potato chip toward a black bird. It picks it up and flies away with it.

"You're also an artist."

"Yeah. Well. It's not something I can exactly live off of." Her eyes look heavy and she yawns to prove it.

"Yet." I stack our empty plates. "Are you... wanting to move here?"

"I don't know." She raises her face to the warmth of the sun. "I guess I wanted to come out and see."

"And?"

She looks at me and smiles. "I probably shouldn't make a hasty decision."

"Probably not. I'll text Bradley. Let him know we're going out for pizza tonight. And you." I point at her. "You need a nap."

"I could just sleep right here."

"Up. You have a perfectly good bed to sleep on."

After herding my sister upstairs, I clean up the kitchen.

Not fifteen minutes later, Wyatt drives up with a load of firewood in the back of his truck. No trailer this time.

"Hey Wyatt. Is that for me?"

He steps out of the truck and pulls on his work gloves. "Bradley wanted me to top off your supply." He glances over at Lilah's car. "Your sister make it okay?"

"You could say that. She's upstairs taking a nap."

Was that a flash of disappointment that crossed his face? It happens so quickly I can't say for sure.

"Security cameras working out?"

"Yeah." I stuff my hands in my pockets. "I'm not so sure just how much good they're going to do."

"How so?" He leans against the truck door.

"Bradley didn't tell you?"

"Haven't talked to him today. What happened?" I see a fierceness in him now. I would not want to be on the other end of that expression.

"Another threat," I lower my voice, even though I have no reason. I already told Lilah. "Left it in the book I'm reading."

"Son of a bitch," he says. "Pardon my language. But there's no sense in that. If a man's got something to say, he should just say it."

"I agree. No need to apologize."

"I'm going to drive around. Unload this. Then get out of your hair."

"We're all going for pizza tonight. You want to come?"

"I can't. I've got a previous commitment."

"Okay. Next time then."

"Trust me. I'd much rather go for pizza." Back in his truck, he closes the door and tips his hat.

I smile as he drives around back.

Despite the obvious similarities between the two brothers, Wyatt is more wild-west. Maybe it's because Bradley graduated from Purdue. He's much more polished and could even pass for urban.

Not Wyatt. Wyatt is all small town.

Bradley is someone I could take to an art exhibit.

Wyatt is the guy to have on your side in a bar brawl.

They're as different as Lilah and I are.

SIXTY-THREE

Bradley

AFTER SPENDING the middle part of the day running new electrical wiring at the Bentley cabin, I stop by my place to shower and put on decent clothes.

Apparently, Audrey and I are taking Lilah into town for pizza tonight. Or maybe they're taking me.

Whichever way you want to spin it, the three of us are going.

I find it a little amusing that Audrey asked Wyatt to go. And even more amusing that my brother found an excuse not to go.

Wyatt talked big, but when it came right down to it, he chickened out.

My tough little brother is afraid to meet Audrey's sister.

Now that is funny as hell.

I get to Audrey's door and knock. I always knock. I'm a guest. One day... One day if things go the way I'm hoping, I'll live here, too, and I won't have to knock.

"Hi," Audrey says with a smile.

I'm so happy to see her smiling and not even realizing it, that I want to gather her in my arms and kiss her.

"Hi." Okay. Maybe I'm just looking for an excuse to kiss her. Any excuse will do.

"Come on in. My sister's still upstairs getting ready."

"It looks strange not having a fire going in the fireplace."

"I know. Speaking of. Your brother brought some more firewood. Are you trying to tell me something?"

"I just know how we like our fires."

She smiles and, biting her lip, catches me off-guard with a look that I can only describe as being a little bit flirty.

It's a cute look on her. One that has me spiraling down a road I honestly hadn't seen coming.

I'd been attracted to her from the moment I saw her. I knew I liked her.

I even knew I'd been thinking about maybe having a future with her.

But this... seeing her standing there, her hands in the

back pockets of jeans that might be a little bit more filled out than when I first met her...

This has me thinking just how done I am. Audrey is the one. I have no more doubt about that.

"Sorry to keep you waiting." A younger, more light-spirited version of Audrey comes bounding down the stairs.

Whereas Audrey is dark and sultry, Lilah is light and airy.

She's right. They don't really look like sisters unless you know. They have the same build. Same long hair. Audrey is brunette. Lilah is blonde.

Lilah has a ready smile.

"It's okay," Audrey says. "He just got here. Bradley. This is my sister Lilah."

Lilah holds out a hand. "It's nice to meet you."

"You too." As I shake her hand, all I can think is that my brother missed out by not coming tonight.

Lilah is perfect for him.

I turn to Audrey and take her hand. It might look like a proprietary move, but it's my way of telling Audrey that she's the one for me.

We climb in my truck, Audrey in the middle, and I can't say I don't like the arrangement.

While I drive, I listen as Audrey tells Lilah about things we see. The steep ravine area that's not safe to drive when it's cloudy up here. How the currently swollen river that follows the road for a while flows downhill into Whiskey Springs.

She points out my cabin as we pass by.

"That's Bradley's cabin," she tells Lilah.

"A neighbor," Lilah says with a knowing nod. "but not too close to be a bother."

I suspect they have some kind of inside joke between sisters. Whatever it is, it's amusing to listen to.

"Is that your phone ringing?" Audrey asks me as we turn onto Main Street.

"Yeah. I'll check it later." I focus on finding a place to park outside the pizza parlor. It's crowded tonight.

"Friday night," Lilah says.

"You're right," I say. "I hadn't even realized it."

"I hadn't either," Audrey says. "The days just blur together up here."

My phone rings again as we walk toward the restaurant doors.

"It's the sheriff," I say. "I should answer it."

"Go ahead," Audrey says. "We'll get a booth."

Music spills out the door along with the sounds of people talking.

"Something wrong, Sheriff?" I ask, answering the phone, walking away from the noise of the pizza parlor, the phone pressed to my ear.

"We've had a break in the case," he says.

"A break? What kind of break?"

"I arrested Claire. For trespassing. And making threats. Stalking."

"Claire? Claire didn't do it."

"She did it. She confessed. And we got her prints on the notes."

Audrey

I know something's wrong the minute Bradley walks into the crowded pizza parlor and sees us sitting in a booth across the room.

His smile is forced and he looks troubled.

"What's wrong?" I ask as he sits down next to me.

Bradley glances around. Makes sure no one is listening. "He made an arrest." He keeps his voice low. So low, even though he's sitting next to me, I have to lean close to hear him.

"Who?" I glance over at Lilah, wondering if she can hear us.

"Claire."

"Claire?" I look over at Lilah. "They arrested Claire." I tell her.

Lilah is shaking her head. She leans forward, her elbows on the blue and white checkered table. "Claire didn't do it."

"How do you know that?" Bradley asks her.

"It just doesn't add up." Lilah presses back against the booth and picks up a menu. "Sorry. I don't mean to overstep."

"How could Claire do it?" I ask Bradley.

"I don't know."

"I'll go talk to him tomorrow. But he said she confessed and her fingerprints were on the notes."

"That is so... unexpected."

"I know."

"Well. Maybe he knows something we don't."

"Maybe."

I'm beginning to think this was a bad idea. Coming to the pizza parlor. It's crowded and noisy.

But Lilah doesn't seem to be concerned about it. She watches everything. Takes in everything. I imagine she's seeing it with her artist's eyes.

"I hate we had to leave Biscuit home alone," I say.

"We'll get an alert on our phones if anyone approaches the house."

"I know. We just got one."

"Oh? I must have been on the phone. What was it?"

"Just a bird. Flying around the back patio."

"Oh. That reminds me. I was thinking we should put up motions lights around the house."

"You're adding to our list," I say, willing to let him add to a list that I've been making ridiculously long. Like heated bedroom floors and a gas fireplace in the bathroom.

"I don't think we're ever finish working on the house," he says, then tips back his bottle of beer for a swallow.

Something warms deep in my heart. Such simple words spoken nonchalantly. Words that mean so very much to me.

I glance over at Lilah, typing something on her phone now, then back to Bradley.

He looks over at me with an amused expression on his face. Lost in his light blue eyes, I search for something logical to say. Something that doesn't reveal just how much I'm feeling for him right now. "You don't think it was Claire either, do you?"

"I don't see how it could be."

"Take the note that was in my book. They can dust it for prints, too."

"I will. I'll do that."

I lean across the booth. "What do you think about this place?" I ask my sister.

"It's fun," she says. "I could get into it."

The server stops at our table. "What can I get for you all?"

We order a pizza to go with the beer that I probably won't drink.

"Lilah is thinking about moving up here. With me," I tell Bradley after the server walks away.

"Is that so?" He doesn't look at Lilah as he speaks. He looks at me. I see questions in his eyes.

Looking for answers to unspoken questions.

"It's a big house," I say softly, the words catching in my throat. I don't want him to move out.

Not because Lilah might be moving in and not because they may have caught the person leaving threatening notes.

Not for any reason.

"We still have lots of things we're working on," he says, finding my hand under the table and squeezing.

"Yes. We do." I don't know if he's talking about things to do around the house or things we're working on with us.

Maybe both.

But both the way he holds my hand under the table and his words give me hope that he's not thinking of moving back into his cabin.

I still haven't told him about the money I'm getting for staying there and I don't think he knows. He could know. It's a small town. All it would take is for one person to know and everyone would know.

I don't want to ask. I want to maintain the illusion for a little while longer that everything will continue to be the way it is. Only better.

Having both Bradley and Lilah living with me in the big house sounds like the perfect life to me.

I'm getting ahead of myself. I'm still supposed to be

grieving. Not planning my future. Certainly not a future with another man.

But, truly, who's to say that it wasn't part of a grand scheme?

Me getting married to Thomas. Thomas's accident. Me moving up here.

It's possible. Anything is possible.

CHAPTER
SIXTY-FIVE

Bradley

WHILE AUDREY and Lilah are in the restroom, I check the security camera app.

The pizza parlor is noisy and crowded. Wouldn't normally bother me. But right now I want to have quiet time with Audrey.

It hadn't taken me long to get used to our quiet evenings at home. Cooking. Working on projects around the house. Sitting in front of her ridiculously big fires in the fireplace.

Just as Audrey had said, the motion was simply a bird flying close to the house. I zoom in to see it more closely.

Looks like a black bird hopping around on the back deck searching for crumbs. After a moment or two, it takes off.

Maybe by some odd quirk, Claire was actually the one who left the notes.

I don't get it. But then I'm not the sheriff. The sheriff is supposed to know what he's doing.

Either way, maybe Audrey and I can take a breather from being threatened.

We will see.

I'm willing to give the sheriff the benefit of a doubt.

I'm not, however, willing to leave Audrey alone. Not yet.

It is, however, hard for me to think about leaving her alone at all. For any reason. Threat or no threat.

Maybe I'd started out staying there with her with the intent of protecting her.

And I still have that protective instinct.

But it's grown. Now I just want to be with her whether she needs protecting or not.

The three of us pile in the truck and drive back to Audrey's house without incident. I find myself thinking about Wyatt again. Wishing he had come with us.

"I see why you don't like to drive up here," Lilah says, peering out the passenger window down the side of the mountain as we cross the precipice between Bradley's cabin and my house.

"And this is with a full moon. Right, Bradley?"

"That's right. I have a call out to a friend who's a civil

engineer about looking into putting rails up. But... I doubt the county will find it cost beneficial."

Lilah looks at Audrey. "You could probably pay for it."

"It'll probably cost upwards of millions to do it," I say.

"I don't think that's in my budget," Audrey says.

"That's not in anyone's budget." I pull around to the front door and kill the motor.

Suspect arrested or not, I can't help but look all around us. Even with the full moon, I can see no more than shadows in the trees. Someone could be lurking there.

I'd never really been on alert like this. Whoever had left those notes at Audrey's doorstep had taken away some of the peacefulness and safety I'd always felt in going about my day. I don't know if I'll ever get that back.

I hope I will and I notice Audrey looking around too, as she slides out of the truck on my side.

Hand in hand, neither one of us saying anything, we walk around and I open the passenger door for Lilah.

Somehow Claire just didn't strike me as the kind of person who would even think to leave threatening notes on anyone's doorstep, much less do it. She struck me as a simple woman more interested in taking care of her cat than...

"Claire has a cat," I say.

Both girls look blankly at me.

"I don't think she has any friends or family. Someone needs to take care of the cat."

"Call the sheriff," Audrey says. "We can keep her cat here. As long as we need to."

"Let's get you two inside. I'll call him."

Biscuit is so giddy with excitement, you'd think we'd been gone for days.

Lilah is a bit wary of him, but she'll warm up. Everybody warms up to Biscuit.

While Audrey builds one of her huge fires in the fireplace, I take Biscuit and step out back to call Sheriff Morgan.

"She's been ranting on about that cat all evening," the sheriff says.

"I can take it. Keep it here until she gets out."

"Alright. Come by the station in the morning. We'll drive out and pick it up."

"Will you tell her so she won't worry? It's just the humane thing to do."

"I'll tell her."

We disconnect the call and I stand there a moment, watching the breeze flutter through the trees. I get the feeling that alleviating Claire's mind about her cat is low on Sheriff Morgan's priority list. I'd bet money he won't even tell her.

That's a shame. Maybe Wyatt was onto something when he suggested I run for sheriff. Not necessarily me, but anyone other than Sheriff Morgan. Someone with compassion.

Maybe a lack of compassion comes with the territory.

It's hard for me to say. I'd been away at Purdue when Sheriff Morgan had become sheriff and he wasn't from here. So I couldn't say one way or the other about him.

It's such a beautiful night with the light of the full moon beaming down.

It gives me hope. Hope that Audrey and I can slide into a normal life now.

It's time I tell her what I'm thinking.

We don't have to be in any hurry. She can take as long as she needs for grieving the man she was married to before. But I want her to know where I stand.

That I'm interested in more just being here to protect her.

I want a life with her.

And it's past time I talked to her about it. Let her know how I'm feeling.

CHAPTER
SIXTY-SIX

Audrey

"That's a big fire," Lilah says.

"So I've been told."

Lilah sits curled up the sofa, a faux fur blanket over her shoulders, her eyes heavy.

I kneel in front of the fireplace, working on getting a fire going.

Lilah looks toward the back door where Bradley is pacing back and forth while he talks to the sheriff about Claire's cat.

The thought of that poor cat being left alone breaks my heart and I can only imagine how distraught Claire must be at the thought of having no one to take care of her cat while she's in jail.

I can't shake the feeling that Claire was wrongfully arrested. But she did have access. She had access to the porch before she left that night and she had access to my book. She also has a key to the house.

There's probably an explanation for the second note, though I can't begin to fathom what it could be since she was in the hospital at the time someone left it on my front porch.

No one saw her in the hospital.

Bradley went to see her and the staff denied that she was there. Claire doesn't seem like the type of person to turn away a visitor.

It makes my head hurt to try and figure it out.

"Bradley likes you," Lilah says.

"What makes you say that?" I glance up toward the back where he's pacing back and forth.

"I can just tell," Lilah says smugly. "And you like him."

"It's too soon for me to be thinking about anyone that way," I say.

"When it happens, it happens," Lilah says sleepily. "Never knew there were any rules. Maybe back in the 1800s, but even then..." She shrugs. "Nobody cares."

"Maybe," I say.

"Don't let worrying about what somebody might think keep you from following your heart."

I poke at the logs, watching the embers flutter up the

chimney. I hear what my sister is saying. And I know she's right.

"I don't think he feels that way," I say, but she doesn't hear me.

The back door opens and Biscuit rushes over to lie next to me on a rug I put down for him. I found the rug in one of the guest rooms and he loves it if the number of hours he spends on it is any indication.

"Okay," Bradley says coming from outside and slipping off his jacket. "Tomorrow we're going to have a visitor."

"Who?" I ask, trying not to cringe. Now that Lilah is here, I really just want to spend some time with my sister. And Bradley, of course, but that goes without saying.

"Blackie."

I look at Lilah. She shrugs and adjusts the fur blanket around her shoulders.

"Claire's cat," Bradley explains. "I'm going out tomorrow to pick him up.

"Good. Bring his food and litter box, too." I stand up and dust my hands off on my jeans.

"I will. Can I talk to you for a minute?"

"Sure."

He's still holding his jacket.

"Let me get my jacket."

"It's okay," Lilah say, stirring. "I'm going up to bed."

"You don't have to go. I just got the fire going."

"It's okay," Lilah says. "I'm asleep on my feet. I'll catch tomorrow's fire."

"Okay." I bite my lip, trying not to smile. She says it like having a fire in the fireplace is an event. I guess it sort of is.

Bradley hangs his coat in the coat closet and comes over to sit next to me on the sofa as Lilah makes her way upstairs.

"Something wrong?" I ask, grabbing Lilah's blanket and wrapping it around me.

"No," he says. "Everything is right."

"Oh. Okay." I slowly let out the breath I didn't know I'd been holding.

"I've been thinking and since I know it's not good to think and not share, I thought I should let you know what I've been thinking about."

"Okay. Sounds serious."

"Maybe." He straightens and leans forward toward the fireplace, his elbows on his knees.

The fire crackles and shifts, sending sparks flying up the chimney.

He holds out a hand and I put mine in his. He wraps his fingers around mine.

"I know it's too soon. Too soon for me to be thinking like I am. Too soon for you."

I forget to breathe.

My thoughts tangle up and I can't think.

"I don't want to just be here to protect you. I want to do that, too, but I want more. I don't want to leave just because you don't need me here."

My eyes well with unshed tears. "I don't want you to

go." I can barely get the words out past the lump in my throat.

He stills. Looks at me.

"Ever," I breathe, the word no more than a whisper.

"It's not too soon?" he asks.

"No." A tear spills from my eyes, down my cheek.

He leans forward. Kisses the one tear away, then another that follows.

With my heart swelling, a little smile tugging at my lips, I look into his light blue eyes.

"It's you, my love," he says, shifting to face me. "It's always been you. Even before I met you, it was you."

I put my hands on his shoulders and clasp my hands behind his neck.

He puts his hands on either side of my face and lowers his head until our breath mingles.

He presses his lips against mine and I melt into him. The world goes quiet.

Home. That's the word that resonates through my head as his lips move over mine.

His kiss is warm, certain, and filled with the kind of promise you don't have to put into words.

I sink into him, my heart daring to believe again.

It's not just a kiss. It's a beginning.

A promise whispered between mingled breath and heartbeats.

Home. That's the word that resonates through me as I melt into him.

Biscuit sighs and rolls over in his sleep, the soft sound grounding me.

For the first time since I lost everything, I don't feel alone.

And as his forehead rests against mine, I know this is the beginning of the rest of my life.

The End.

AUTHOR OF JUST BREATHE

KATHRYN KALEIGH

Just SURFACE

THE GRAVITY OF US SERIES

"Would you like to see it?" I ask him. "The painting. Would you like to see it?"

"Sure."

"Well. You have to come over here."

He seems to come out of his daze and walk over to me.

He stops right in front of me, his eyes never leaving mine. "It's beautiful."

I smile. "You haven't even looked at it yet."

"I don't have to see it to know. I already know it's lovely."

I shrug and dab my paint brush into a mix of white and blue, making an even lighter blue. One that matches the color of his eyes.

I touch the paint lightly to the canvas, turning a dot of paint into the image of a pale blue wildflower.

"You make it look so easy," he says.

I glance up. He's watching me paint now.

"Do you paint?" I ask.

"No. But I appreciate art. And you have talent."

"You know art?"

"I spent a fair amount of time in the Museum of Fine Arts in Boston."

"I'm impressed." I dab more flowers onto the page, mostly because he seems to like them. "And surprised."

He looks back at me now, with a little smile on his lips. "You don't expect to meet anyone out here who appreciates art."

"I rarely meet anyone anywhere who appreciates art."

"I find that very sad."

"It is sad."

"You must be Wyatt," I say, adding some green paint to my brush.

"And you must be Lilah."

"Impressed and surprised once more."

"My brother is in love with your sister and your name has come up."

"I knew she was wrong," I say, stepping back to study my canvas.

"Who was wrong about what?"

"Audrey. She thinks Bradley is just here temporarily. To protect her."

"Sometimes it takes a minute to figure those things out."

"Sometimes," I say, meeting his gaze again.

"Sometimes not."

Something in those blue eyes tug at me and tell me we aren't talking about our siblings any more.

"What's that?" I ask. "Under your arm."

"What?" He seems to have forgotten he was holding something. He pulls it out and glances at it. "Security camera to keep you safe."

"Are you supposed to be installing it?" I glance past him. "Bradley's on his way out here with a ladder."

"Right. Yes." He doesn't look away. "Will you have dinner with me? Tonight?"

"Okay," I say, more than little amused.

"And tomorrow night?"

"I don't know. Aren't we supposed to see how tonight goes?"

"Who makes these rules?"

"I don't know."

"Wyatt," Bradley calls. "Where do you want me to put the ladder?"

"I have to go. I'll pick you up at six."

As he walks away to join his brother, I remember with a bit of annoyance at myself that it was only days ago that I vowed to myself to never date again.

CHAPTER
ONE

Lilah Sinclair
Houston, Texas

I WOULD HAVE BEEN BETTER off taking a job as a showgirl.

Not that I knew any dance moves.

And learning choreographed dance moves would defi-nitely have been more challenging than learning how to mix a Paper Plane cocktail and knowing the nuances of how that's different from the Last Word cocktail.

As a bartender, I'm not only required to know how to mix every possible drink, but also know a little bit of the history of each one. For example, the Last Word is a pre-

Prohibition cocktail that has suddenly become popular again.

People like it when their bartender can give them factual information. I only make it up about ten, maybe twenty percent of the time.

If I don't know how to mix a drink or some interesting fact about one, and I have time, my good friend Perplexity can help me out.

Fortunately, I have an excellent memory and I never have to look anything up more than once. So far. That, I am certain, is destined to change, simply because there are over ten thousand distinct mixed drinks.

Not to mention wines, beers, and spirits.

I work at two different bars. When I go in, I go all in. Besides, no point in not squeezing the most out of everything I'm learning about alcoholic drinks.

Tonight I'm at the Hobby Center. Only open when there is a Broadway event. Opening nights, like this, are my favorite. I love the elegance. The richness. The sophistication of it all.

With a tray of drinks in hand, I head off to deliver them to a group of well-dressed people who were standing in the far corner near the window when I left them.

I weave my way unobtrusively among the other patrons. Like moving furniture. No one notices the servers.

I find my group of three women and three men easily enough. Separately, they all look stunning, but together, they make an unforgettable picture. The men are wearing black-tie tuxedos and the ladies are wearing sparkly evening gowns. All in their twenties, about my age.

And yet they obviously come from a world I can only dream of being part of.

There was a time when I somehow thought I would

I have no misperceptions that I landed this particular job at the Hobby Center in downtown Houston based on my bartending skills.

They hired me because I make people look twice.

No one notices the servers. Until they do.

I'm not particularly tall. An average five six. One hundred fifteen pounds. Long, healthy blonde hair that I'm supposed to wear loose around my shoulders when I'm out on the floor.

My work uniform is a black form-fitting cocktail dress. Very tasteful with a high neck and long sleeves. I've been told I wear it well.

I've even been told that I have a rich girl look, whatever that means. I assume it means my figure. Maybe a combination of my figure and my straight hair with just a hint of curl on the ends.

It helps that I have a ready smile. I sometimes wonder where I got that.

The figure and hair I come by honest. Both my sisters have a similar build with similar hair. My oldest sister has more of a serious sultry look and the middle sister wears a perpetual vexed expression that men, for some reason, find sexy.

I definitely came out ahead with my ready smile, in my humble opinion.

This particular group ordered champagne. Their loss and no challenge for me.

Holding my tray on one arm, I hand out glasses of champagne with my free hand.

Moving furniture.

The women take their flutes without bothering to acknowledge me. The men give me quick glances, artfully designed to not make their girlfriends or wives jealous.

I don't care. This is just a job for me.

"Hey," the slightly plump girl with blonde streaks says to me just as I lower my tray and start turning to leave.

I look at her with a pleasant, questioning smile.

She doesn't look the least bit familiar to me and she shouldn't. I've worked here for three months and I've only recognized a repeat customer a couple of times.

Honestly, they would recognize me before I would recognize them.

"Can I bring you something else?" I ask politely.

"You look familiar. Lily? Layla?"

"Lilah," I correct, feeling an unease creep along my spine. We don't wear name tags and there's no reason for this young woman to recognize me.

"Yes. That's it."

As though I don't know my own name. But I keep my expression schooled in politeness. "Enjoy your evening," I say, starting to turn again.

"Didn't you date Trey?"

How could she possibly know this? "I think you have the wrong person." There's a time for honesty and there's a time for most definitely not admitting to something. This is the latter.

"No," she insists.

"Bernice," the man next to her says in a warning tone. "Let it go."

But Bernice does not appear inclined to let anything go.

"He told me about you."

"Enjoy your evening," I say again and this time I do turn around.

"He said you're a little too clingy for his taste."

Two steps away, I stop. My heart is beating like a jack-hammer. But I take deep breaths and count to ten.

The man murmurs something to her.

She's had too much to drink. It happens. There's no need for me to take offense. I don't even know this woman and she has no reason to know me despite knowing my name and that I dated Trey for all of five minutes.

But Bernice follows me. I *feel* her following me. *Hear* her heels clicking on the marble floor behind me.

Then I sense her breath as she walks up behind me.

"Trey told me that you're a good lay, but you'll never be more than that. Someone to just fuck when he feels like it. But he said he's not a garbage collector and you're just trash—"

I'll never really be able to explain what happened after that.

All I know is that I turn around, my fingers closing around the stem of a glass of red wine from the man standing nearest me and tossing it. I just toss it and the deep crimson liquid sails through the air. Right across Bernice's smug elegantly painted face.

Her gasp is sharp and wet, the wine dripping from her chin, running down her neck, and blooming in red blotches across her white silk blouse.

CHAPTER
TWO

Lilah

HALF AN HOUR LATER, I'm sitting in Natalie's office. Natalie is the boss. The big boss. Vice-President big boss. I normally would have to go through three other bosses to get to her kind of big boss. I don't think she was even here. I'm pretty sure they called her in. For this. For me.

My heart is still pounding faster than is natural, but I keep my gaze down.

I'm in a precarious situation and I know it.

Twenty minutes later, Natalie, in her perfect light blue trim business suit walks in and leans against her wooden desk.

"Please tell me you have a good explanation for what happened," she says. She stares at me, her lips pressed tightly together.

"I—" I clear my throat and try again. "I do."

But Natalie doesn't seem to hear me. "I know it wasn't an accident. It's on camera. Do you want to see the footage?"

I shake my head. I really, really, really do not want to relive the moment.

Less than one hour. It only took one hour for my life to be flipped upside down.

"Do you know the definition of assault?"

I look up at her then, searching her eyes for some semblance of compassion. Anything.

I see nothing but coldness.

"I've never been in trouble," I whisper. From the look on Natalie's face, nothing about me or my history matters right now.

I should have called my sister while I waited for Natalie. Brianna would know what to do.

But I don't know her phone number and, besides, my phone is in my locker. I memorized hundreds of drinks and I didn't bother to memorize my own sister's cell phone number.

Brianna can bail me out of jail. I'm going to jail.

I straighten in my chair and raise my chin. My uncle is an attorney. I can claim temporary insanity. Or permanent insanity. Whatever it takes.

Don't panic.

After making me sweat for what seems like an eternity, Natalie finally breaks the silence.

"Get your things out of your locker. Get out of here." She stands up straight. "Needless to say you're fired."

With disbelief, at being fired or not being hauled off to jail, I'm not sure, I stand up, feeling wobbly on my heels. I grasp the arm of the chair.

"You got lucky," Natalie says. "The girl's husband convinced her not to file charges."

"I don't even know her," I say as though that would work in my defense.

"All the more reason to not let her get to you. I suggest you find a different line of work."

I nod. I could not agree more.

I'm almost to the door when Natalie stops me.

"Lilah," she says.

"Yes?" I turn. I feel about two inches high and any kind word from Natalie. Any semblance of understanding. Would be a balm to my soul right now.

"Leave the dress."

I nod again and walk dazed back to the locker room.

I keep my eyes straight ahead. Fortunately I'm the only person back here. Everyone else is behind the bar or out on the floor working.

I never want to see any of these people again.

Grabbing my clothes out of my locker, I head to the

dressing room. My hands tremble as I slide the dress off over my head and put on a t-shirt in its place.

I manage to hold my emotions at bay as I scramble into my jeans. Slide my feet into my sneakers.

The woman, Bernice, could have pressed charges. I could have gone to jail.

If Trey said those things about me. About me being trash, then all I'd done is prove him right.

By the time I make it to my car, tucked away in the far corner of the parking lot, my hands are trembling so hard I can hardly wrap my fingers around my key fob. I close the door, and the quiet slams into me harder than any insult ever could.

In the darkness, I lean my forehead against the steering wheel. The scent of wine still lingers on my fingers. And then the tears come. Hot. Unstoppable. Until I'm shaking too hard to breathe.

CHAPTER

THREE

Lilah

"Drink this," Brianna shoves a mug of hot tea into my hands.

"I don't need tea," I say. "I need a whiskey."

I didn't call Brianna on the way home from work. She called me.

We have a circle of friends and family app on our phone that alerted her that I had left work early. I hadn't even considered that when I'd finally stopped crying long enough to drive out of the parking lot.

As such, she'd known something was wrong before I even answered the phone.

"I got fired," I'd told her.

"What happened?"

"I'll call you tomorrow. I just want to go home and go to bed."

Being the older sister that she is, she was waiting for me when I got home. I pretended to be annoyed, but the truth of it was I was happy to see her.

The first thing I'd done when I'd gotten home was to wash off my makeup. The streaks of dried mascara down my cheeks took a special solvent to get off.

And now Brianna wanted details. *I got fired* was not nearly enough to satisfy her.

"Drinking isn't going to solve anything. We need to figure out your next move."

Déjà vu. Almost unnaturally so.

It's been less than a month since Brianna and I'd had a similar conversation with our oldest sister Audrey.

Admittedly, Audrey's situation was a whole lot more dire than mine. Even though... if I'd gone to jail... my situation could have been pretty dire.

"You can't compare this to Audrey's situation," Brianna says, sitting on the arm of the couch, breathing in the steam from her own mug of tea.

"You're being a freaky mind-reader."

"Audrey's husband *died*. You getting fired doesn't even compare. You'll get another job."

"I don't want another job."

"Right. You do know you have to work, right? Our family is not independently wealthy."

I look up at her with something that tells her I think she's wrong.

"No," she says. "You cannot count Audrey's inheritance."

"Stop reading my mind!"

"It's hard to not read it when you just put your thoughts out there like that."

With a huff, I sip my hot tea. Even though I won't tell her, she's right. The hot tea is soothing.

Sliding next to me onto the old comfortable couch I'd gotten from my grandparents, she picks up a stack of index cards on my coffee table. It'd taken plain index cards and turned them into flashcards. The name of a drink on one side. The recipe on the other. Riffles through them.

"You spent so much time learning all these mixed drinks."

I shrug. "Yeah. Well." It stings. I can at least admit to myself that it stings. I could have been doing what I really love instead of memorizing drink recipes.

She hasn't even seen the cards on my nightstand. Different kinds of wines and what they go with.

"You're good at it, too."

"It's good brain exercise," I say.

"That's for sure." She puts my cards back down, slips off her shoes, and curls her feet beneath her.

"At least you still have your other job. Maybe you can pick up more hours there. You said they tip better anyway."

I'm already shaking my head. "No. I don't want anything to do with bartending."

"But..."

To make sure she understands just how much I mean it, I set my mug down and pick up the index cards. Well over four hundred of them. I take them over to the garbage can in my kitchen and dump them in.

"There," I say, wiping my hands together. "It's done."

"Maybe you should sleep on it."

"I'm going to sleep on it," I say. "But I won't change my mind."

"You might be overreacting."

I slide back into my spot on the couch and pick up my mug. "I almost got arrested. I don't think I'm overreacting."

Brianna just shrugs.

"It's not what I want to do anyway," I say.

"I know," Brianna says with genuine compassion. "But sometimes it's like that."

"You don't understand." I murmur.

"I've known you your entire life," Brianna says. "I think I have a general idea of what makes you tick."

"Then you know I'm not cut out to work in the service industry."

She looks at me sideways. "You say. And yet out of the three of us, you're the most cut out for it."

"Well then, we must all be pretty bad off."

Brianna leans back and closes her eyes. She has brunette hair like Audrey. Long enough to curl softly around her shoulders, but she keeps it pulled back, leaving just a couple of strands loose around her face.

In addition to her usual vexed countenance, she looks tired.

"You didn't have to come over here tonight. I'll be okay."

"You're lucky she didn't press charges."

"I know. Can she change her mind? Come back and press charges anyway?"

"Yes. She has a two-year statute of limitations."

"Oh. My. God." I cover my face with my hands. "I have to sit on pins and needles for two years hoping she doesn't decide to press charges?"

"Yes."

"What do I do?" I turn to my sister." You're a paralegal. You must know some way to resolve this."

"I do," she says. "You wait,"

I close my eyes. My life just became a living hell.

"But... you can get a good attorney. They have footage showing that she provoked you. She followed you across the room and provoked you."

"Slander," I say. "She slandered me."

"What did she say exactly?"

"I don't want to talk about it." I sit back and hide my

embarrassment behind my tea mug. How had Bernice known exactly what to say to me that would provoke me into a haze of anger?

Brianna gets up, goes to my kitchen, and comes back with a little notebook and a pen.

"What's this for?"

"Write it down. Write down everything you remember. Word for word. I know they have the video, but you need to put it down in your words. Include what you were feeling."

"I really don't want to relive it."

"Do it anyway. You asked what you could do. This is a way for you to preserve your memory. Don't look at me like that. I know you have a good memory, but two years is a long time. Memories fade."

"Fine." I set my mug aside and start writing. Once I start, I can't stop. The words just flow out of me onto the page.

Finished, I close the notebook. "What do I do with it?"

"Just keep it."

Great. A tangible reminder of what happened tonight.

The neighbors, a friendly couple in their thirties, pull into the lot, their headlights sweeping across the pavement before clicking off. They climb out of their car, their voices low and intimate, as they walk past, carrying the kind of easy warmth that only comes from years of being together.

"So you're quitting your other job?" Brianna asks.

"Yes."

"And then what? How are you going to pay your rent? What are you going to live off of?"

"I'll figure something out. Just not tonight."

"Like what?" Brianna challenges.

"I can go back to school. Get a master's degree."

"Good idea. I think that's a good idea. How much money do you have saved up?"

"Saved?" I look at her like she's lost her mind. "I can hardly pay my rent and my student loan payments."

"Lilah." Brianna gives me with that long-suffering look of hers.

"I can sell my paintings."

"Maybe. Didn't you try that once before?"

"Yes. But I didn't keep at it like I should have."

"You're back to the idea of being a starving artist."

"Maybe. Although I'm hoping to be something more than starving."

"Okay." Brianna takes a deep breath. Lets it out slowly. "I hate the idea, but you can come live with me."

"No. I don't think so." I pick up my mug of what is now lukewarm tea. "I have a better idea."

"That's not a good idea and you know it."

"You don't even know what my idea is."

"I know perfectly well what your idea is. You're thinking about going to live with Audrey."

I hate it when she does that. "Just until I figure things out."

"That's what they all say. I really think you need to reconsider."

"Fine," I say. "I'm going to sleep on it." I stand up. Stretch. "Right now would be good."

I want tonight to just go away. I want to wake up in the morning and find out it was all no more than a bad dream.

But unfortunately, my older sister has other ideas.

FOUR

Lilah

"Lilah," Brianna says. "I know how much you love your art. Your painting and sketching." She looks around at the half dozen pieces of art I have displayed on my walls.

They're some of my favorites. But I can sell them if I have to. Anything to keep from going back to being a bartender.

The thought of walking back into a bar and working with the public makes me feel sick to my stomach.

"I know. It's not a real job." I sit back down and pull a throw around me.

Brianna is talking about my art now and it's like catnip to my soul. So I stay.

"Only a few people make a living at it. You can do it in your spare time. Like you've been doing."

What she really means is like I haven't been doing. Despite my good intentions, by the time I get home from working, I'm so exhausted, all I can do is fall into bed, then get up and do it all over again.

"We should call Audrey," Brianna says.

"No. We should not call Audrey." I don't want anyone else to know what happened tonight. I don't want anyone to know that I almost got myself arrested. I've never been so embarrassed in my entire life.

"You're going to have to tell her eventually," Brianna says.

"Why?"

"Don't ask stupid questions."

"Okay. I'll tell her I got fired. But not tonight."

"Okay," Brianna says. "Maybe tomorrow you'll wake up and decide that you can go back to the job you still have."

"The woman knew I'd dated Trey."

"Trey? That ass hat?"

"Yes." Brianna never liked Trey and obviously that has not changed.

"What did she say?"

I shake my head. I can't say it out loud. I'll never say it out loud. I'd rather die than tell anyone what Bernice said.

"It doesn't matter. But I'm never going to date again."

Brianna gives me one of her rare smiles. "You'll date again. You'll forget all about Trey. All about this night. And you'll date again."

"I don't think so. I've got two years for this to hang over my head. I can't be with someone and then suddenly get arrested. What would be the point? Just more embarrassment."

"Lilah. It's not the end of the world. Everything will look better in the morning. Whatever happens, you've got family support. You know that."

"I know." I blink back tears that threaten to spill over. I'd cried so much sitting in my car, I don't know where I could possibly have more, but here they are, welling in my eyes.

Maybe it's a sign to do what I've been thinking about.

"Will you help me pack?" I blurt.

"What?"

"Will you help me pack up this place?" I straighten, gesturing around my little one-bedroom apartment. "I've been thinking about moving and now seems like a good time to do it. My lease is out. I'm running month-to-month."

"Okay. I've got the day off tomorrow." She runs a hand over the arm of my couch. "If you're moving in with me, we'll need to sell your furniture."

"I was thinking I could put it in storage."

"A complete waste of money. By the time you're ready

to move out and get your own place again, you'll want new furniture."

I run a hand over the old threadbare linen-weave couch. "Okay. I'll sell it."

I'll sell my furniture, but I don't know that I'm moving in with Brianna.

Brianna lives in Houston and apparently one person too many recognizes me in Houston.

It's time for me to get away from here.

I've overstayed my welcome.

CHAPTER
FIVE

Wyatt Winslow

I PROP A LOG ON A STUMP, lift my axe, and drop it down, splitting the log into two perfect pieces. The two pieces fall with a crash on either side of the stump.

I balance one of them on the stump and repeat the process.

We have commercial grade log splitters. Kindling splitters. Wood chippers. Everything a man could possibly need to make his own firewood without wielding an axe.

But, what can I say, I like chopping firewood by hand. There's something inherently satisfying about the process.

When I was no more than a boy, my grandfather on the

Winslow side taught me how to chop down trees, how to chop them into firewood, and how to lay a perfect fire.

My grandparents on our mother's side taught me to appreciate the arts. I'd spent two summers in Boston with them, rotating summers with my two older brothers.

My oldest brother, Bradley learned how to cook during his summer rotation. Since I didn't take to the kitchen, they took me to museums and art galleries.

I discovered I have a special affinity for the classics like Monet and van Gogh. Not something I would ever tell my brothers. They would never let me live it down.

My brothers and I, the Winslow boys, are known around the little town of Whiskey Springs, Colorado for being rugged, manly men. We own and operate our family business Timber Ridge Cabins and Timber Company.

As of last count, we have thirty-seven cabins. One of those cabins, I claimed for myself. My two brothers each claimed one for themselves, too. The other thirty-four are for tourists. We're always buying and selling cabins, though, so that number is fluid.

The cabin I'm living in right now, in fact, is a renovation project. Once I have it renovated, I'll be moving out and it'll go into the rental column. I'm taking my time on it, though, because I like the location. It sits right next to the rushing Whiskey Springs river and there's nothing like falling asleep with the sound of the river right outside my window.

Our busiest seasons are summer, of course, and oddly enough Christmas. People flock to Whiskey Springs for the trails and quiet serenity in the summers and the town's holiday festivities in December.

Our grandpa was a descendant of one of the first settlers of Whiskey Springs and he'd turned out to be a real estate mogul in his own right. He'd started the whole thing that got us where we are today.

I set the axe down as my brother drives up in his black Ford F-150 pickup truck. All three of us drive them, new ones, and our father drives an older model. Not only are they convenient for hauling everything from firewood to appliances, it makes us easy to recognize without putting billboards on the sides of our trucks. No one wants to drive around in a billboard.

Bradley gets out, his big gangly black lab named Biscuit climbing out with him and running in my direction.

Seeing me, Bradley follows along behind the dog.

Biscuit puts his feet up on either one of my shoulders and licks me in the face. He's big as a horse and sweet as a kitten.

"Yeah. I'm happy to see you, too."

"That dog has absolutely no manners."

"Wouldn't be Biscuit if he had any manners." I lift the dog's paws off my shoulders and drop them to the ground.

Wiggling all over, his tongue hanging out in unadulterated bliss, the dog runs circles around both of us.

"Wish I had some of that energy," Bradley says.

"You look troubled."

"Those cameras we installed around Audrey's house might have been for nothing."

"Why do you say that?" I pick up my fallen logs, stacking them off to the side. Bradley helps.

Bradley and I had spent most of yesterday installing a security system of cameras around Audrey's house. I learned to install security cameras by helping out a friend and turns out I'm pretty good at it. Gives me a little side hustle.

"Somebody left a note in her book."

"Her book?"

"Yeah. Some novel she's reading. Left it right there like a bookmark."

"We just put those cameras up yesterday. Maybe they left the note before that."

This is the third time someone left threatening notes for her. The first two were left on the front porch while Bradley and Audrey were inside. Dropped off right under their noses.

"Maybe." Bradley straightens. Looks off into the distance toward nothing in particular.

"But..."

"But I don't think so. She reads every night. She would have noticed."

"Maybe she missed a night."

"Yeah. Maybe. Anyway, her sister is coming in this morning. You want to grab some lunch?"

"I'm always up for some lunch. The Hungry Biscuit?"

"Sure. You drive."

"What's wrong with you? You always drive."

"Trouble sleeping. Worrying about those stupid notes."

I grab my jacket and throw it over my shoulder. "You should run for sheriff."

"Why would I do that?"

We climb into my truck and I start the motor.

"Why not? You'd do better than that yahoo we got in there now."

"And who would manage all the renovations we've got going on?"

I put the truck in reverse. "You talking about the Bentley cabin? That's almost finished."

"Hardly."

"Added something else?"

"Yeah. I decided to add on a back deck."

"You do know that I'm quite capable of doing that, right?"

"Figured you'd help out."

I turn onto the highway and we head toward Whiskey Springs.

Our parents live in the city limits of Whiskey Springs, but us three brothers live out in the secluded cabins.

Bradley lives further out than any of us. He lives up the mountain meaning near the end of a deserted dirt road. The only person who lives further up his road is Audrey living in the Albright place.

Audrey Sinclair, from Houston, had inherited the

Albright place after her husband was killed in a private plane crash a few weeks ago.

She'd no more than moved out here when she started getting threatening notes. All anonymous. Somebody claiming she doesn't belong in the house.

We pull up to the Hungry Biscuit, a growing local chain, claiming to have the best burgers and fries, a sentiment I don't disagree with, to find it crowded.

I park across the street and we walk over. Get in line.

"You got time to take a load of firewood out to Audrey's this afternoon?"

"I just took her firewood."

"I don't mean a cord. Just top her off. And while you're there see if three cameras are enough to line the road up to her place."

"Why didn't you just ask me to check about the cameras?"

"Two birds," he says sheepishly.

I study him while he gives his name to the hostess. We step back to wait outside.

The air is brisk, even for June. One thing I love about Whiskey Springs is that it rarely gets hot even in the heart of summer.

"I know what you're up to."

"Not up to anything," he says too quickly.

"You just want me to meet her sister. And. You haven't even met her yet."

"Hey." Bradley holds up his hands. "You told me you wanted to meet Audrey's sisters. Wasn't my idea."

"I think you should meet her first."

"Chicken. She's Audrey's sister. She can't help but be anything but hot."

"There's more to a girl than looking hot," I say with a grumble.

"Speaking of the devil," Bradley says. "There's Sheriff Morgan."

I look up just in time to see the sheriff step up to the hostess's stand.

"Ass hat," I mutter under my breath.

Bradley looks over at me. "What is it you dislike so much about him?"

"Just something about him. Can't explain it."

"Mr. Winslow."

"Our table's ready."

"Good.

Walking inside and following the hostess to our table, Bradley speaks to the sheriff. I pretend I don't see him standing there.

I don't know what it is. Something about him just rubs me the wrong way.

CHAPTER
SIX

Lilah

I wake up completely disoriented.

Soft sunlight spills across my face, but the air is unusually chilly. A different kind of chilly than the usual coolness from the air conditioner.

Then the pieces start to come together along with the sounds floating in through the window cracked just enough to let in some fresh air. Sounds of the river flowing easily within walking distance and birds singing their morning song in the limbs of the fragrant blue spruce trees damp with morning dew.

Needless to say, I'm not in my apartment in Houston

and I'm not in one of the dingy motels I'd spent the night in getting here.

I'm at my sister's new home. The Albright house just outside of Whiskey Springs. In the Rocky Mountains of Colorado.

The home she inherited from her late husband's grandfather.

The inheritance came with conditions. Significant conditions.

She has to live in the house and she can't sell it.

But. It also comes with perks.

Lots of perks.

All expenses paid. And she gets a substantial annual stipend gifted to her. One million dollars.

One million dollars at the beginning of every year. The first deposit hit her account the minute she sighed the papers.

Brianna had been the most skeptical of all. I had been the one who was most in favor of it.

It had been my opinion that Audrey had to do it. She had to move here. As far as I could see, she didn't really have a choice.

And now she has a new boyfriend.

The three of us had gone into town for pizza last night.

His name is Bradley Winslow. The oldest son of an influential family in town.

They own dozens of cabins around the town, mostly in the outlying areas. They also own a lucrative timber company, supplying firewood to the county. Apparently they plant as many trees as they cut down. It's admirable how they're protecting the environment while making a good living.

I can tell by the way Bradley looks at my sister that he likes her.

She's worried that it's too soon to be interested in anyone after losing her husband.

I tried to assure her that there are no rules.

Seeing the way they look at each other says everything to me.

If she wants to be with Bradley Winslow, then nobody says they shouldn't be together. Not in my book.

I stretch and think about my day stretching ahead. No bartending jobs to go to.

My sister, Brianna, is right. I have to have income to live. I know I'll have to look for a job. But for now... for today at least... I can take a deep breath and not worry about having to go to work.

I feel rested enough to unload my paints and canvases from the car. I certainly didn't feel like it yesterday. I've never driven this far and certainly not by myself. Driving across Houston from downtown to Katy doesn't count, even though no one can say it's not a long way.

It was a very very long drive from Houston to Whiskey Springs and I'm thinking I'm not going to do it again.

If I need to go back to Houston, I'll save up my money and get an airplane ticket.

Putting my feet on the cold floor, I hurry across to the bathroom.

Cold floors in June. Interesting.

I've never cared much for the heat that comes with living in Houston. Always just saw it as part of the way things were.

Born and bred in the south. It's just the way things are.

But now that I'm here, I'm seeing that there are other ways to live.

I dig my slippers out of my suitcase and slide a sweater on over my pajamas.

It's early, but I'm ready to locate the coffee machine and start my day.

The first day of my new life.

CHAPTER
SEVEN

Wyatt

"What the—?"

I roll over and look at the digital clock glowing brightly on my nightstand.

Seven thirty in the morning.

Who the hell is knocking on my door at seven thirty in the morning on a Saturday morning?

I slide out of bed, pull on a pair of jeans and a flannel shirt before making my bleary-eyed way out of the bedroom and across the living room to the door.

I open the door to find my brother Bradley standing there holding two coffee cups. He's grinning like a loon.

I take one of the coffee cups, slam the door in his face, and turn around.

It doesn't stop him. He just opens up the door and walks right in like he owns the place.

"You're welcome," Bradley says.

My only answer is to take a sip of coffee. "To what do I owe the pleasure of this early morning wake-up call?"

"Just wanted to repay the thanks the couple in the Smith cabin called and woke me up with."

"The Smith cabin. Nice couple. What did they want?"

"They just wanted to let us know how grateful they are that you came out on a Friday night and fixed their shower."

"Wasn't a problem," I say, flopping down on my couch. "Where's the dog?"

"I left Biscuit at Audrey's."

"So really. Why are you here so early?"

"Had to run into town and while I was there I bought coffee."

"Didn't have to do that."

"I owed it to you."

"For what?"

"For thinking you'd fabricated an excuse for not going out for pizza with us last night."

I run a hand through my hair and look at my brother. "Why would I do that?"

He sits on the arm of the couch and tips his coffee cup back for a sip. "Can't imagine why."

"So," I say. "What's the verdict?"

"You'll like her."

"The sister."

"Her name is Lilah."

"You like her," I say, still trying to get my brain to wake up and fighting the irritation at having my plans to sleep half the day away thwarted so rudely.

"I like her as Audrey's sister. Yes." Bradley stretches out his legs. "I think you'll like her."

"Not interested."

"Wait a minute." Bradley sits forward and looks at me. "When you met Audrey, you were all for meeting her sister."

"That was before you went and fell in love with Audrey."

Bradley looks at me like I've lost my mind.

"I don't know why you'd say that."

"You don't even know it. It's written all over your face."

He doesn't say anything for a minute. Someone on a motorcycle drives past. A guest staying at the cabin up the road.

"That has nothing to do with you and Lilah," he says finally.

"It actually has a lot to do with it."

"Please explain."

"It seems self-explanatory enough to me," I say, running a hand over my face. Now that I'm up, I need to shave. "If you and Audrey are going to get married—"

"I didn't say anything about getting married."

"Okay. If there is any possibility that you and Audrey MIGHT get married, I don't want to risk getting involved with the sister. It could make family gatherings... uncomfortable."

He swirls his coffee cup. "I see your point," he says. "And you could be right."

"I'm right."

"But there's also the possibility that you could like her."

"You know I don't do long-term commitments."

"You could change your mind," Bradley says.

"Right." I can see where he might think that, but there is no way in hell I'm going to change my mind.

It's just not going to happen.

"By the way," Bradley says. "The wireless cameras came in. They're out in the truck. Think you can go out to Audrey's house with me today and put them up?"

"I should have known you wanted something. You could have led with that."

"And where would the fun be in that?" Bradley asks.

Brothers. Can't live with them. Can't live without them.

EIGHT

Lilah

"Good morning," I say, finding Audrey in the kitchen, before I see that she's feeding that humongous horse of a dog they call Biscuit.

Seeing me, Biscuit runs over and puts his head beneath my hand. I take a step back. Wary of this giant dog. And yet he seems so friendly.

"He just wants you to pet him," Audrey says. "He won't hurt you."

"So you say."

"Biscuit." Audrey pats her leg. "Come here."

The dog goes back to Audrey and starts eating the food she puts down for him. "You want coffee?" she asks.

"Please. Where's Bradley?"

"Work. I guess." She gets two mugs down and starts making coffee. "He doesn't exactly actually live here."

"Not exactly." I take the cup of coffee she hands me. "This is good. Almost like designer."

"It is designer. Homemade designer."

"I'm a little surprised you know how to work that fancy machine."

She shrugs. "Bradley showed me. It's easy." She finishes making her own cup of coffee and looks at me. "Want to sit on the deck?"

"Okay. But it might be too cold."

"You get used to it. Besides. The sun is warm. It's a nice combination. Warm sun and cool breeze."

As she opens the back door, Biscuit runs out past us.

As we step outside behind him, Audrey hesitates, looking around.

"So," I say, sitting down on one of the chairs at the little outdoor table. "Bradley lives here, but he doesn't *live* here. Sounds a little confusing to me."

"He's staying here. To keep me safe."

"What's he doing?" I ask, nodding toward the dog walking around the perimeter of the yard, staying just on this side the tree line.

"He's just making his rounds. Making sure everything is as it should be."

"So he's like a guard dog."

"He's a very good guard dog. He hears things before we do."

I shiver involuntarily. "How do you stand it? Always being on alert?"

"Stubborn?"

"It's a new look for you," I say. "It's good." I warm my hands on the mug.

"I like it here."

"Hmm."

"Hmm what?"

"Nothing. I just wonder how much you liking it here has to do with Bradley."

"I liked it here before I met him," she says.

I narrow my eyes at her. "And that was all of what? Five minutes?"

"Maybe," she says with a little smile.

"It's good to see you smiling again."

"It's good to have something to smile about."

"How are you doing? With the whole Thomas thing?"

"I'm okay," she says, but the smile isn't there anymore. "There was so much all at once. Him dying in the plane crash. Finding out he had a child with someone else and he'd never even told me. His insurance going to the baby and the mother."

"It's a lot," I say, rather wishing I hadn't brought it up. "But you came out better than you would have with the insurance. Getting money in your account every year."

"That's true."

"Does Bradley know about that?"

"I didn't tell him."

I watch Biscuit dig a hole in the ground, sending dirt and foliage scattering, like he suddenly found the secret treasure he was searching for.

"I know it's not my business, but..." I say.

"But you're going to tell me anyway."

"I can wait. It's not important."

"Just tell me already."

"If you and Bradley do happen to get serious... Not saying you will. I know he's just *staying* here to protect you. But if you do get serious and he does move in for real, don't you think you should tell him?"

"Because it's like Thomas keeping secrets from me." She sits back and sighs. "I didn't think of it like that. I guess I'm still getting used to the idea of getting the money. I check my account every day to see if it's still there."

I smile. "It's not going anywhere."

And if my gut sense is right, neither is Bradley.

CHAPTER
NINE

Wyatt

As we planned ahead of time, Bradley drove ahead to check on Audrey.

If ever there was a man smitten, it's my dear heartsick brother.

I feel fortunate I have never had the misfortune to suffer such a state. He can't go two seconds without saying something about her and I feel certain she's front and center in his thoughts constantly.

While he drives on up to her house, the house I still think of and probably always will, as the Albright house, I stop a few yards out and pull over onto the side of the road and get out.

Pulling over is just a habit. Not a necessity out here. The one-lane dirt road ends at Audrey's house.

I grab one of the camouflage painted security camera boxes and, tucking it under my arm, leave the road to look for areas a person might do just what I'm doing. Get out of their vehicle and walk up to the house.

Whoever has been leaving the threatening notes on Audrey's doorstep needs to be stopped. Has to be stopped. Before they escalate into doing something more serious.

I walk along what looks like an elk trail, circling around toward the back of the house.

I hear the rushing water of the river before I see it.

Personally, I like the way my little cabin sits right on the riverbank. So far, it's never flooded, but that's always a possibility. Up here, the house is high enough, it's not going to flood. Not possible unless water starts running uphill.

I've been out here walking before. I don't even remember why. I do remember that the old man Albright was alive at the time.

Actually there's a trail, or used to be, from the Albright place to the cabin Bradley is currently living in. No one uses it. I guess it's easier to just drive.

It's as pretty up here as I remember. A clear view of the snow-capped mountains across the valley. A meadow sweeping down from the back deck of the house to the river.

This is the perfect elevation. Below tree line. High enough that trees flourish. Aspens. Maples. Fragrant blue spruce trees.

The meadow is dotted with blue and white flowers waving in the breeze. Little sparrows fluttering among them as well as bees buzzing from flower to flower.

When I see her, I stop in my tracks.

A slim, young lady. Light brown hair with streaks of blonde fluttering about her shoulders. She'd pulled it back, but the wind has tugged strands loose that she shoves back with her wrist.

She's wearing a light green printed full skirt that bellows in the breeze and a chunky emerald green wool sweater. A combination that works for her. A hat she seems to have forgotten she was wearing hangs down her back, tied at her neck in a bow.

She stands in front of a painter's easel, a paint brush in her left hand, and a wooden paint palette in her right hand.

I can't see what she's painting and frankly I don't care. She could be painting nothing but circles and I would find it beautiful.

Just as I've never seen anyone as beautiful as she is. Her features are delicate. Like I would imagine a fairy princess would look.

I don't know how long I stand there, just taking her in. I could look at her, simply look at her, for hours. Mesmerized. Just mesmerized.

She doesn't see me. She's completely focused on what she's painting.

Somewhere in the back of my mind, it registers with me that this is all the more reason to have security cameras out here.

I don't know who she is. Where she came from. What her name is.

All I know is that I have fallen utterly and completely head over heels in love.

CHAPTER
TEN

Lilah

THE WIND BLOWS SOFTLY TOSSING the hair I'd pulled back across my face. The hat I'd borrowed from Audrey slides off my head, hanging against my back, secured only by a bow around my neck.

My sister had been right. The warmth of the sun offsets the chilliness of the breeze coming off the river.

The water, rushing over boulders of all sizes, rumbles along the river, sending the occasional water spray in my direction. But the air is so dry, it dries almost immediately.

The paintbrush feels a little rusty in my hand at first,

but it only take a few streaks on the canvas to have me getting back in the groove.

The scent of the paints in my palette are better than the most expensive perfume. There's nothing I love more than the feel of a brush in my hands and the scent of fresh paint on a canvas.

I heard a truck pull up to the house. I'm not far. I'm not brave enough to venture out of earshot of the house. Hear Biscuit bark as Bradley gets out of his truck and gives him a treat.

I don't see the matching black truck stop a ways down the road. Not at first, anyway.

When I see the man standing at the edge of the forest, watching me, I sense no danger. None.

Even less when I spot his black truck, exactly like Bradley's parked not too far away.

It doesn't take much for me to put it all together. Maybe all those brain exercises, memorizing mixed drinks, was paying off.

This has to be Wyatt Winslow, Bradley's brother. He has a similar look, except that Wyatt looks more rugged, like he belongs outdoors.

I let him watch me paint. Mostly because I don't want to stop. I've been looking forward to getting out here, setting the artist trapped inside me free.

Finally, after what could have been two minutes, probably closer to five, I look up and meet his gaze.

He looks a little startled. As though he didn't expect me to see him standing there.

I would've had to be blind not to see him. Not so much because he stands out. On the contrary, he blends in with the terrain with his brown flannel shirt and jeans. He's wearing a baseball cap over short, dark hair.

I would've had to be blind not to see him simply because of the way he watches me. As though he's never seen an artist at work.

"Would you like to see it?" I ask him. "The painting. Would you like to see it?"

"Sure."

"Well. You have to come over here."

He seems to come out of his daze and walk over to me.

He stops right in front of me, his eyes never leaving mine. "It's beautiful."

I smile. "You haven't even looked at it yet."

"I don't have to see it to know. I already know it's lovely."

I shrug and dab my paint brush into a mix of white and blue, making an even lighter blue. One that matches the color of his eyes.

I touch the paint lightly to the canvas, turning a dot of paint into the image of a pale blue wildflower.

"You make it look so easy," he says.

I glance up. He's watching me paint now.

"Do you paint?" I ask.

"No. But I appreciate art. And you have talent."

"You know art?"

"I spent a fair amount of time in the Museum of Fine Arts in Boston."

"I'm impressed." I dab more flowers onto the page, mostly because he seems to like them. "And surprised."

He looks back at me now, with a little smile on his lips. "You don't expect to meet anyone out here who appreciates art."

"I rarely meet anyone anywhere who appreciates art."

"I find that very sad."

"It is sad."

"You must be Wyatt," I say, adding some green paint to my brush.

"And you must be Lilah."

"Impressed and surprised once more."

"My brother is in love with your sister and your name has come up."

"I knew she was wrong," I say, stepping back to study my canvas.

"Who was wrong about what?"

"Audrey. She thinks Bradley is just here temporarily. To protect her."

"Sometimes it takes a minute to figure those things out."

"Sometimes," I say, meeting his gaze again.

"Sometimes not."

Something in those blue eyes tug at me and tell me we aren't talking about our siblings any more.

"What's that?" I ask. "Under your arm."

"What?" He seems to have forgotten he was holding something. He pulls it out and glances at it. "Security camera to keep you safe."

"Are you supposed to be installing it?" I glance past him. "Bradley's on his way out here with a ladder."

"Right. Yes." He doesn't look away. "Will you have dinner with me? Tonight?"

"Okay," I say, more than little amused.

"And tomorrow night?"

"I don't know. Aren't we supposed to see how tonight goes?"

"Who makes these rules?"

"I don't know."

"Wyatt," Bradley calls. "Where do you want me to put the ladder?"

"I have to go. I'll pick you up at six."

As he walks away to join his brother, I remember with a bit of annoyance at myself that it was only days ago that I vowed to myself to never date again.

ELEVEN

Wyatt

"Wʏᴀᴛᴛ," Bradley says. "What's wrong with you?"

"Nothing." I tear my gaze away from Lilah and focus my attention on the hole I'm drilling in a maple tree.

"Watch what you're doing. You're going to fall off the ladder and break your fool neck."

"Hand me that camera," I say, purposely keeping my gaze off of Lilah. For two seconds. Just to show Bradley that I can.

With the camera installed, I look back over at Lilah. She's folding up her easel, getting ready to go inside. Disappointment slides through me, settling in my veins.

I climb down the ladder and watch her easily gather up her things and head back to the house.

"Maybe you could be a little more obvious," Bradley says.

"Maybe."

Once she's inside, I turn back to Bradley.

"You need to decide what you're going to do about Audrey."

"Why? Audrey is mine."

"No question there. You just need to decide what you're going to do."

"Why is that?"

"Because I'm going to marry Lilah."

"What's wrong with you? You met her two seconds ago."

"When you know, you know."

"Come on," Bradley says. "Where do we need to put the next camera?"

"On the road," I say. "To catch anyone driving up."

"I thought that's what we were going to do anyway."

"Never said it wasn't."

Biscuit comes running toward us at a gallop. He must have slipped out past Lilah.

He runs circles around us before sitting in front of Bradley to bark for a treat.

"Got him trained," I say.

"The treats were Audrey's idea."

"Biscuit isn't complaining. Put the ladder on this tree

over here. We'll shoot it right down the road. Catch them coming around the big curve."

Bradley props the ladder against the tree as instructed. "So when is the wedding?"

"We're not there yet." Pull the next camera out of its box. "She doesn't know about it yet."

"I see. She doesn't know that she's marrying you."

I climb up three rungs. Look down at him. "Well. No. We just met."

Bradley bursts out laughing. "Something is seriously wrong with you."

"Yeah. Well. At least I know what I want when I see it."

"Didn't say I don't know what I want. But." He hands me the drill. "As you oldest brother, I need to caution you about something."

"What's that?" I turn on the drill. Make a small hole in the tree.

"Girls don't like being told what they're going to do."

"Bro. Thanks for the brotherly advice. But I think I've got this."

"Okay." Bradley holds up his hands. "I did my job. I told you."

"They don't like to be left waiting either," I say under my breath.

"It's only been a couple of weeks," Bradley says.

"Seriously? It's creepy when you do that."

"I might be older than you are, but I'm not deaf."

I whistle as I attach the camera to the tree, pleased with

the way it blends in among the leaves. "You'll need to keep an eye on this one. Make sure the leaves don't obstruct the view."

And while I'm at it, maybe I'll download the app onto my phone so I can get alerts, too. Can't have too many of us watching after our girls.

Lilah

AFTER STOWING my paints supplies and easel away in my room, I wash the paint from my hands and take a peek into my closet.

My sister and Bradley had gutted it, pulling out any rods and shelves, then sheetrocking the walls. A blank slate, it smells like fresh paint.

Audrey's letting me have input on how I want to design it.

I like this old house. With updates, it's as good as new. I especially like all the windows, even though Audrey has ordered shades to cover them at night.

She doesn't feel safe having the windows uncovered in light of someone leaving threatening notes on the front porch.

I don't blame her. And now that I'm here, I have little doubt that whoever is trying run her off will be trying to run me off, too.

I'm not a threat though. Not like Audrey. The house is in Audrey's name and she's the one getting the inheritance trust money.

If I stay here, I'll need to find a way to pull my weight. I've got some ideas about how to sell my paintings online. Copies of them anyway. I'll sell the originals, too, but that's less likely to happen.

I have to be realistic. I'm thinking I can paint one new painting every day, then spent the rest of my work day posting things online.

I find my sister in her bedroom, bent over a pad of graph paper.

"Well," I say, sitting on her bed. "That was interesting."

"What? Your painting session?" She looks up.

"No. The painting was fine."

Audrey sets her pad of paper aside. "What was more interesting than painting?"

"Wyatt Winslow."

"You met Wyatt? Bradley said he was out looking for somewhere to... oh... You met Wyatt."

"Yes." I bite my lip to keep from smiling.

"Was he nice to you?"

I lay back on the bed and stare up at the ceiling. "Of course." I look over at my sister. "Why wouldn't he be?"

"Just asking." She picks up her graph paper. Studies it.

"I already figured out what to do with my closet."

"Already? How? You just got here."

"It's not that hard."

She blows out a breath. "I just want it to be perfect, you know?"

"Nothing's ever perfect. Just build it. Then if you don't like it, you can tear it out and start over. It's not like you don't have enough money."

"You're probably right."

She turns to a fresh page of graph paper. "How are we doing your closet?"

Shelves down one side. Two rows of hanging rods on the other. The top row all the way across. The bottom row only halfway across to leave room for dresses and skirts."

Audrey looks up at me. "It's so simple. What about drawers?"

"I've got a dresser in my room."

"You do, don't you?" She glances around. "I could get a dresser."

"You should get a dresser. Get something nice and sturdy. Good quality."

"I can see that."

"We can drive into Denver. Look around. We need new furniture."

"We. You've decided to move in?"

"I'm still thinking about it." I've already pretty much decided I am, but I'm not ready to tell her that. Not when I made that decision before I left Houston.

"So what did you think about Wyatt?"

"Wyatt is... not what I expected."

"More rugged than Bradley."

"Exactly. But..."

"But...?"

"I don't know. He's kind of sweet."

"Wyatt?"

"Are we talking about the same Wyatt?"

"I sure hope so." I lean up on one elbow. "Because we're going out tonight."

CHAPTER
THIRTEEN

Bradley

AFTER SUCCESSFULLY MOUNTING the security cameras out at Audrey's house, I stop by my parents' house to wash my truck.

By the time I get the truck washed, it's time for me to head back to my cabin. Take a shower and get dressed for my date with Lilah.

After taking a shower and shaving, I put on a pair of black dress pants, a white button-down shirt, and a leather jacket. With Lilah being from the city, I'm thinking she'll be impressed with the look. I even put on my good lace-up leather shoes.

I'm feeling a little bit overdressed, but I don't want her to think that just because I live in a small town I don't know how to clean myself up.

I leave early to give myself time to stop by the General Store to see if they happen to have any fresh flowers.

"What can I get for you?" John, the owner of the General Store asks as I walk toward the checkout counter.

The General Store has just about anything anyone could want. John carries everything from milk to t-shirts to firewood.

"Got any fresh flowers?" I ask.

"No. But it looks like I'm going to have to start carrying them. People keep asking me for them."

"That's too bad." Apparently he does not carry *everything* a person could want.

"You got a date?"

"Yes. I do, as a matter of fact."

"Let me guess. The Sinclair sister. The one that just got here."

"Does everyone know everything?"

"Pretty much. You're from here. You know everybody knows everybody else's business."

"How could you possibly know that?"

"I didn't. I heard she was coming into town and I guessed. Guessed right, too, didn't I?" He grins smugly.

"I guess you did. Think they have any flowers up at the lodge?"

"Nah. They don't have flowers either. Fresh flowers are

a big investment. I could have them delivered in, then go weeks without someone asking for flowers."

"Why doesn't someone put up a greenhouse? Keep flowers on hand all year round?"

John looks at me as though I've just said either the stupidest thing or the most brilliant thing he's ever heard.

Apparently the most brilliant. He points a finger at me. "That's what my wife needs. She's been needing something to occupy her time since she retired from teaching."

"Well then. There you go."

"Let me think on it. You up for building it?"

"Sure. I can build it. Now I just need a bouquet of flowers. For tonight."

"Hold on." He picks up his phone. Starts typing.

I lean against the counter and flip through the pages of a scenic calendar of the Rocky Mountains he has for sale.

He must have been texting because I hear a response come back.

"If you don't mind fresh picked flowers, the wife has some roses growing in our backyard. Says you're welcome to cut a dozen."

"Actually. If she has roses, all I need is one."

"Head on over there. Pick one out. I'll call you about that greenhouse."

"You're one of the good ones, John."

"Just don't tell the wife about the greenhouse yet. I want to talk to her first."

"I won't say a word."

I check my watch as I head out. I have just enough time to run over and get a rose from John's backyard, then drive up to the Albright house. If I hurry.

Maybe it will pay off in the long run. If John builds that greenhouse so we always have fresh flowers. But in the short term, I can't be late for my date.

CHAPTER

FOURTEEN

Lilah

"I KNEW it was too good to be true," I say coming downstairs.

"What's too good to be true?" Audrey asks from where she's sitting with Bradley in front of the fireplace with the roaring fire.

On second thought, I decide not to voice my disappointment in front of Wyatt's brother. "Nothing. Who's that?" There's a black cat sitting on the far end of the sectional, away from them.

"This is Blackie," Audrey says. "Bradley just brought him home from the vet in Boulder."

"Is he okay?"

"He was just getting checked out. The doc says he's in good health. Had to buy special senior cat food for him though."

I sit down next to the cat. He's a solid black cat with thick short hair.

"Hi Blackie," I say, sitting next to him. He takes a tentative step, then climbs into my lap.

"It's a good thing I'm wearing a black dress." Blackie puts his front feet on my shoulders and rubs his face against my chin.

"He likes her," Audrey says. "He acted afraid of us."

"It's because you two smell like dog." The dog in question is curled up in front of the fireplace sleeping. "Have they met?"

"Sort of," Audrey says glancing at Bradley.

"They acted like they didn't see each other."

"That's kind of odd." Blackie sits down in my lap and purrs. I glance at my watch.

It's four minutes until six. If Wyatt doesn't show up in four minutes, I'm going back upstairs and get ready for bed.

I'm not supposed to be dating anyway. Not after what happened with Trey. Not with the cloud of being arrested hanging over my head for the next two years.

It'd for the best if he didn't show up.

"How long is Blackie staying?" I ask.

"Until Claire gets out of jail."

I wince. "Right. But you don't think Claire's the one who left the notes."

"I know she's not. She couldn't possibly be. She was in the hospital when the second note was left."

"Why would she get arrested then?"

"That's what we can't figure out," Bradley says. "The sheriff says her prints were all over the notes."

"Maybe someone set her up." I rub Blackie under the chin and he purrs even louder.

Audrey and Bradley look at each other again. They're already acting like a couple. I'm both surprised and pleased at how my sister is doing.

I had expected her to still be grieving and I'm sure she has a lot going on in her head, but by all outward appearances, she appears to be doing remarkably well.

I haven't really talked to her about it, not seriously. And I don't want to open up any wounds she's healing on her own.

Sometimes things are best left alone.

Two minutes. Wyatt has two minutes to get here.

"Well," I say to the cat in my lap. "I'm going to head upstairs. Get ready for bed."

"Don't you have a date?" Audrey asks.

"He's not here." I shrug. "So I guess not."

"He'll be here," Bradley says. "If he says he'll be here, he'll be here."

"Maybe I misunderstood."

"I don't think so." Bradley glances at his watch.

That's when I hear the truck drive up and stop outside. One minute. Wyatt made it with one minute to spare.

"I'll get it," Bradley says. "You're occupied."

"Blackie. I'm pleased to meet you, too. But I have to get up now."

"Come on, Blackie." Audrey pulls Blackie out of my lap, but he won't let her hold him. When I stand up, Blackie sits down in my spot.

"I don't think she likes the smell of Biscuit."

"Maybe. She'll have to get used to it.

"Do I have cat hair on me?" I ask.

"No," Audrey says, sweeping a hand down my sleeves to be sure. "You're good."

"Okay." I give her a smile. "Time for me to go then."

"Have fun."

"Thanks," I say, turning around.

I blink.

The man standing next to Bradley looks like a completely different man from the man I'd seen by the river.

I blink again.

Wyatt Winslow is looking at me with a little sideways grin that I know deep in my gut is going to be my undoing.

He doesn't fit any molds that I carry in my head.

Not a city guy, too soft to work with his hands.

Not the lumberjack he'd looked like when I'd first seen him.

No. The Wyatt Winslow standing in my sister's living

room is someone entirely different. Someone I don't quite have a readymade spot for in my head.

"Hi," he says, taking a step forward.

"Hi. I didn't think—" I was going to say something about him not making it on time, but the words drift away, forgotten, when he pulls a single red, dewy rose from behind his back and holds it out to me.

We walk toward each other, both moving at the same time. I take the rose from his hand, pressing the rose's dewy softness against my cheek.

"It smells fresh. Like outside."

"It's fresh from the garden," he says.

"Really?" It looks like it's fresh from the garden. A little bit wild. Not like the perfect roses that come from the flower shops.

In that way, it reminds me of Wyatt.

Wyatt

Bradley and Audrey fade into the background the moment I see Lilah.

I honestly don't know if they're even in the same room with us.

All I can see is Lilah.

She's wearing a little black dress that skims her slim body in all the right places. Her blondish hair is swept over shoulder. Straight and smooth with just a hint of curl at the ends.

I don't know much about women's hairstyles, but it looks like maybe she spent some time on it.

Something glimmbers on her eyelids and her lips are glossy. A different, more polished look than she'd worn when I'd met her.

I'm instantly thankful I'd worn something worthy of being seen with her. And I log the information. Lilah is not the kind of girl a guy wears jeans on a date with. She's the kind of girl a guy would pull out the tux on special occasions. In fact, a tux would not have me overdressed tonight. I guess I unconsciously knew that when she wore a skirt outside to paint.

But it's her green eyes beneath dark lashes that pull me in and suck me right under.

I'm a man lost at sea. There's no finding my way back and I wouldn't want to if I could.

"I should probably put this in water," she says, her gaze locked onto mine.

"Probably." But neither one of us moves.

"I'll just bring it," she decides.

"Okay." I glance over to where Bradley and Audrey are sitting on the sofa pretending not to watch us. "Lock us out," I say to Bradley. "Ready?" I ask Lilah. "We have reservations."

"Ready."

I hold out an arm and after an instant of confusion, puts in her hand in the crook of my elbow.

Blackie hops down and follows us to the door.

"You can't go with us, Blackie," she says, releasing my

arm to pick up the cat and hand him over to Bradley. "We'll be back."

"Your cat?" I ask.

"Not mine. Someone named Claire."

"Right. *That* cat."

Outside, I open the passenger door for her. She looks up, then back to me. "This might be difficult."

"Let me help you," I say.

"Okay." She puts a hand on the inside door arm, but I simply scoop her up in my arms, bridal style, and lift her up.

"Oh," she says as I place her gently on the seat.

"All good?"

"Yes." The word comes out a little breathlessly. With a smile, I close her door.

Obviously she's never had a man lift her into a truck before.

It seems, I muse, as I walk around the truck to the driver's side. I have quite a few advantages in my favor already.

With a girl like Lilah, I'm going to need every advantage I can get.

In the driver's seat, I look over at her. She's already buckled in. I buckle my own seatbelt.

"Ready?"

She nods. "You said we have reservations?"

"Yes. At the Whiskey Springs Lodge. They have the nicest restaurant in town."

"It must be to need reservations."

"Reservations aren't really necessary, but I wanted to make sure they weren't having any kind of event tonight."

"And if they did?" she asks.

"I'd figure something else out."

"It's good to be resourceful." She toys with the rose in her hands and looks straight ahead as I turn the truck around and head down the hill.

"We have cameras all along this road now," I say. "If anyone comes up to the house, you'll know."

"Audrey is worried about that."

"You're not?"

She shrugs. "I don't know what to think yet."

I drive around the big curve just before what I call the narrows. Everyone calls it something different.

"I do know that I don't like this road." Holding onto her seat, she looks down.

"No one does."

"They should fix it."

"I think Bradley's looking into it."

"Audrey told me you're a lumberjack."

"Did she now? It's just one of the things I do for my family's business."

"You have cabins and provide firewood."

"That's right. But I'm thinking of branching out and doing something different."

"Like what?"

"I'm thinking about building a greenhouse and opening a flower shop."

Good God. As soon as the words are out of my mouth, I wonder what the hell made me tell her that.

I'd suggested the idea to John at the General Store and it had somehow stuck in my head.

A flower shop. I don't anything about flowers.

The most I know about flowers is that you bring a girl a rose on a first date and if you like her, you turn it into a regular habit.

"Wow. That sounds… daunting," she says. "I don't know anything about flowers."

"Neither do I."

SIXTEEN

Lilah

Even over the new car scent of the truck, I can tell that Wyatt smells like old leather and spruce trees. Outdoors. He smells like outdoors, but freshly showered beneath it.

Obviously knowing his way, he drives along the backroads with nothing to light his way except for the truck's headlights and the soft glow of the full moon.

At the highway, he turns left, then turns left again before long.

According to the sign, we're approaching the Whiskey Springs Lodge.

"Wait," I say, shifting to look at him. "You don't know

anything about flowers, but you're thinking about opening a flower shop."

"Yes. There isn't one in town. I had to get that rose out of someone's backyard."

"Their backyard?" I ask skeptically, running a hand along the thorns.

"I had their permission. John, the guy who owns the General Store, didn't have any flowers, but he had some in his backyard."

"That's one of the strangest things I've ever heard. But it's nice." I run my hands along the stem, avoiding the thorns.

"That's why it doesn't have a ribbon or anything."

"It doesn't need it." I look at him, studying him beneath my lashes. "You sound like me."

"How so?"

"I knew nothing about mixed drinks, but I took a job as a bartender at an upscale bar."

"How did you manage?"

"I studied. I learned everything there is to know about liquor and wine and beer."

"Impressive."

"Yeah. Turns out it was all for nothing."

"Maybe not. You could open a bar."

"No thank you. Not a chance."

"And you don't know anything about flowers?"

"I like them," I say.

"But you could learn them."

"A person can learn about anything they want to."

"I like your optimism."

We turn a curve and the lodge comes into view.

It's a two story lodge with what looks like an attic serving as a third story.

"It's not what I expected," I say. "It's grand."

"They actually talked about calling it the Grand Lodge, but it didn't stick."

"It's very impressive. It looks like it's made out of real logs."

"It was. It's over a hundred and fifty years old."

"Looks like it's been kept up well. And there are a lot of cars here. It's a good thing you made a reservation."

"It's rather unusual. People usually come in on the train to stay here." He finds a spot and parks the truck.

"Maybe they're just having dinner."

"Maybe. Wait there. I'll come around."

I wait while he comes around to open my door, wondering if maybe I can just slide out.

My dress is too slim for me to step up with any dignity at all. Not that I minded being picked up and placed on the seat. Not that I minded that even a little.

He opens the door and smiles at me.

"Can I help you out of the truck, milady?"

My cheeks flush at the unexpected endearment. No one has every called me that before. "I think it might be the only dignified way for me to get out."

"Then I have a job to do," he says.

He scoops me up like I weigh no more than a child and set me down on my feet.

My heart racing, my hands are still resting on his shoulders, his hands are on my waist, and our gazes are locked onto each other.

"Thank you," I say, then clear my throat when the words come out a little rougher than I intended.

"My pleasure."

We both step back at the same time and he holds out his arm again. I put my hand in the crook of his elbow.

I could get used to this.

He's not even from the south and he acts like a perfect southern gentleman.

"Welcome, Mr. Winslow." The valet says as he opens the door for us.

So Wyatt Winslow comes to the lodge often enough to be recognized by name. Interesting.

Everything about Wyatt Winslow is interesting.

One look at him and my vow to myself to not date just shatters like a piece of glass into a million tiny unrecognizable shards.

CHAPTER
SEVENTEEN

Wyatt

IT DOESN'T TAKE LONG before I decide bringing Lilah to the lodge maybe wasn't the best idea in the world.

The lodge restaurant is nice. White tablecloths on the tables. Candles flickering on each one. Ambient lighting.

There's no doubt that it's a nice place to bring a date.

The downside is that everyone knows me here.

Still. I didn't want to drive down to Boulder. Spending over two hours driving isn't my idea of a way to spend a first date. This way I have more time to focus on her and not all my attention on driving.

I'm greeted by name by everyone starting with the valet. Then there's Zoe at the front desk as we pass by.

We pass Arabella as we walk across the grand lobby with the large four sided fireplace in the center with people taking advantage of the comfortable seating around it.

Lilah doesn't say anything about me being recognized by everyone and none of them linger long enough for me to introduce her. There will be plenty of time for me to introduce her to plenty of people as time goes by.

Right now I just want to get to a quiet table in the restaurant so I can be alone with Lilah. The hostess, a young lady I don't recognize, leads us, as I had requested, toward a table in the back right next to a fireplace with cozy gas flames.

I hold Lilah's chair while she sits down, then sit next to her.

A server, a young lady with her long hair pulled back in a ponytail high on her head, brings two crystal glasses and fills them with water from a matching pitcher. "What can I get you to drink?" she asks.

"What would you like, Lilah?" I ask.

"Water's good for me. Thanks."

"Water for me, too. Thanks." After the server walks away, I rest my elbows on the table. "I'm your designated driver if you'd like to take advantage of that."

"It's okay. It's bad form to drink on a first date."

"Really? When did they make that rule?"

She bites her lip and smiles. "I just made it up." She leans forward and lowers her voice. "I'm a lightweight."

"That's an interesting twist."

"A lightweight bartender. Not so rare as you would think."

"I actually never gave it any thought."

"So." She takes a sip of her water. "Tell me more about your flower shop."

"It's not really a thing. It's just something I thought of tonight when I went on a search for a flower for you."

"So I was your inspiration," she says with a little smile.

More than you will ever know. "I suggested it to John, the owner of the General Store. He's going to talk about it with his wife. But they should be thinking about retiring. Not starting their own business."

"A person's never too old to do what they want to do."

"Hm. But it was my idea. It wasn't something he would've thought about on his own."

She leans her arms on the table. "Then maybe you should do it."

I lean back in my chair, rubbing my chin. I know exactly where I'm headed with this conversation, but I don't want her to know that. Not yet.

"I would need someone who knows flowers."

She smiles. "You could learn."

"No." I say with mock seriousness. "I'm not that smart. I'd need help."

"I think you're smarter than you give yourself credit for."

I shrug. "Maybe. So far it's not working for me."

She picks up a menu. "I have a feeling you'll figure it out."

She knows good and well that I'm trying to get her to say she'll help me, but she's not falling for it.

Smart girl.

CHAPTER
EIGHTEEN

Lilah

AFTER DINNER, Wyatt is quiet on the drive back to Audrey's house. I point that out to him.

"You got quiet."

I wouldn't classify Wyatt as a quiet person by nature. We talked throughout dinner without any lulls in the conversation.

Our conversation shifted away from the flower shop he may or may not be serious about opening. I've never looked into it, but it sounds like an incredibly big endeavor.

I just finished one big endeavor (the bartending fiasco) and I'm not ready to start another one.

I want to paint. I'm an artist and I want to paint.

We talked about everything and nothing.

My trip up to Whiskey Springs. How the weather is so very different between here and Houston. His family's cabins and how they're always renovating one cabin or another.

He keeps his eyes on the road as we head up the mountainside—a road I'd rather not travel at night, but so far I was doing it anyway.

"I got an alert on one of the cameras we just installed," he says. "But when I checked the history, there was nothing there."

"The ones on the road?"

"No. The one behind the house. Down by the river."

"There was nothing there?"

"Just a deer. And a couple of birds. I may have to change the settings."

"Maybe. Isn't it better to get a false positive?"

"You're right," he says, slowing down as we reach the cliff.

"There's really got to be a better road than this."

"There used to be an old road that circled around. Came around and avoided the narrows."

"Why on earth would they change it?"

"I think this is a shortcut."

"Sometimes it's best not to take shortcuts," I say, keeping my eyes on the road as though that would help us avoid sliding off.

"Agreed."

"I'll ask Audrey to look into it. Maybe she can get the old road reopened."

"It would take a lot of money and influence to make that happen. I think someone bought that property."

"They bought the land where the old road is?"

"I think so."

"Well. She can just buy it back."

"Maybe. People tend to hold onto their land up here."

"You buy cabins all the time. How is that different?"

He parks the truck in front of the house. All the lights are out, even though it isn't all that late.

"I don't know. She can check it out. I've just noticed that people are more willing to sell land that has a house on it than straight up land. A house increases the taxes quite a bit."

"I see. I think everyone's asleep."

"They're like an old married couple," Wyatt says with amusement.

"They do seem to get along well, don't they?"

"I think Bradley is worried about rushing Audrey. It hasn't been all that long since she became a widow."

"He's got a good point. It hasn't been long. And I don't want to see her get hurt."

"Bradley won't hurt her. He likes her." He turns off the motor, leaving us in darkness.

"I hope so. She likes him, too."

"I'll come around. Help you out."

"Now I know what not to wear," I say as he opens my door.

"I like your dress. If you don't like me picking you up, I can help you slide out."

"It's okay." I hold out my arms. "We have it figured out now."

"Yes. We do. Don't we?"

He picks me up and lifts me right out of the truck. But this time, as he lowers me to the ground, he does it slowly, keeping me close.

For just a moment, my arms are around his shoulders and his arms around my waist.

He's taller than I thought he was. A full head taller.

The front porch light hums and pops on, bathing us in unexpected light.

"When did they do that?" he asks, pulling back.

"I don't know. I just got here."

"I know. Let me walk you inside. Make sure everything is okay."

"Those notes really have everyone spooked," I say as we walk toward the front porch, illuminated in bright lights. "Do you really think these lights will keep whoever it is away?"

"I hope so. I'm not sure what more we can do than these lights and the cameras."

Reaching the door, I unlock it with the key Audrey gave me.

Wyatt, it seems, is quite invested in this thing, too. But, of course he is. His brother is involved.

We step inside the quiet house. The fire is banked. The lights are out.

Biscuit, lying in front of the fireplace, stirs. Blackie is lying on the sectional, surprisingly not far from the dog.

"They've already gone up to bed," I whisper.

"I'm just going to go out back. Check things out real quick."

"Okay. I'll get us some water."

Wyatt, quiet as a mouse, steps outside while I get us a couple of bottles of water from the refrigerator.

His definition of real quick and my definition are different. He seems to be taking his time.

I sit on the sectional next to Blackie and scratch the cat's head. Blackie stretched as turns over.

The seconds tick by.

Wyatt should be back by now.

I said I wasn't sure if I was spooked about the notes, but now all the scary movies I've watched come back to haunt me. The ones where the guy goes outside to check on things only to be killed by the bad buy while the unsuspecting girl waits inside.

I'll give him another minute before I go check on him.

That minute passes quickly.

I pick up the poker next to the fireplace, take a moment to get used to its weight in my hand, then start toward the back door.

I'm honestly not sure if I should open it or lock it.
Unfortunately, I like Wyatt, so I can't just lock him out.
This is how the bad guys get us.

NINETEEN

Wyatt

I step out the back door and just stand there in the cool night air. The full moon is behind the clouds, so I'll have to wait until the clouds shift before I can see anything.

Even though I didn't see anything particularly unusual on the security cameras, the fact that an alert went off at all has me feeling unsettled.

This is the first time we've gotten an alert and yet I know it's not the first time there's been wildlife out here.

I wait patiently for the wind to shift. No surprising security lights out here just yet. I'll find out what Bradley needs help with and help him tomorrow.

We need to get all the systems in place to keep whoever is making these threats away from here.

Finally, after what seems like forever, the clouds shift, letting the light from the full moon shine through.

I walk to the edge of the back deck, carefully scan for anything that looks out of place, then turn around and study the house.

And then I see it.

A letter lying next to the back door.

"How are you doing this?" I ask under my breath.

I stride back to the door, pick up the letter, and slowly open the backdoor so as to not make any noise.

And there, right behind the door, is Lilah, standing there with a fireplace poker in her hands.

"What are you doing?" I ask.

"You didn't come back," she says, lowering the poker.

"I had to wait for the clouds to clear."

"You found something."

"Yes." I flip the backdoor lock and follow her back to the fireplace where she replaces the poker.

"What does it say?"

I sit down on the sectional and tug out the flap. She sits next to me.

I read aloud.

"You think there's safety in numbers. All you're doing is just putting more people at risk. This house doesn't belong to you. It doesn't belong to any of you. Don't ever forget that."

"Wow," she says. "I don't know what to say."

"It's bold."

"We need to give it the police."

"The police consists of a sheriff and he's an idiot."

"What other options are there?"

"I think the best option is catch whoever is doing it in the act."

"Wyatt. There are cameras at the back of the house. Cameras along the road. How could someone get past all the cameras?"

"I haven't figured that out yet. We will, though. We'll figure it out. There are four of us now and we'll figure it out."

I stare into the banked fireplace and wonder. I'm missing something. I have to be missing something. But I just don't know what it is.

"I'll leave this note on the kitchen island for them to see in the morning." I look over at Lilah. So beautiful. And there's a madman running around making threats. Distracting me from the simple act of appreciating her.

"Come on," I say. "I'm walking you up to your room."

"You don't have to do that."

"I'd feel better if you let me check your room. Then lock it behind you before I leave."

"I'm not afraid," she says, but the little shiver that runs through her says otherwise.

I take her hand and together we walk upstairs. My

brother's door is wide open. I can't but notice he's there sleeping in his bed.

Audrey's door is cracked, but not open all the way.

My brother is keeping his promise to stay here and protect her.

"This is my room," Lilah says. "Here at the end of the hallway. I have the best view."

We step inside and I see that she does, indeed, have a good view. Not that I can speak to the other views. I've never been up here before.

I check the bathroom. The closet. Even under the bed. While Lilah watches me with an expression I can't read.

"All clear," I say.

"Thank you."

I take her hands in mine. "You don't have to thank me."

"But I want to."

"Lilah," I say. "Call me anytime day or night. Anytime anything doesn't feel right."

"Okay." She nods. "But... I don't have your phone number."

I pull a business card out of my wallet. Hand it to her. "Promise me."

"I promise. But there are two other people here."

"They might not always be here."

"You're right." She shoves her hair back off her face with her hand. "Thank you for a lovely evening."

I cup her delicate chin in my hand.

She looks at me with green eyes that remind me of a mountain meadow. I just tumble right over into them.

Slowly lowering my face to hers, I pause as she tips her face up, her eyes fluttering closed, her lips parting.

It's enough.

I press my lips lightly against hers.

She leans into me, deepening the kiss.

Pulling back, she looks at me, her eyes wide, biting her lip. "Sorry," she says. "I'm sorry. I shouldn't have done that."

"Don't be," I say, pulling her into my arms and kissing her again.

I feel her yield to me and I deepen the kiss, kissing her bottom lip. Her top lip.

I don't want to let her go. But now isn't the time to get lost in her kisses. To get lost in her.

I kiss her on the forehead. "I'll see you tomorrow," I say.

"Okay." Her expression is soft. Vulnerable.

Beautiful.

I slide my hands down her arms and squeeze her hands.

"Lock your bedroom door behind me. I'll let myself out."

I walk away while I still can.

The only thing keeping me from turning right back around is knowing I'll see her tomorrow.

CHAPTER
TWENTY

Lilah

I STAND in the middle of my bedroom, watching Wyatt turn and walk away.

"Lock the door," he says over his shoulder before he closes it.

In a daze, I follow him to the door and lock it. It doesn't seem right, really, locking myself in when my sister is out there with her door open.

But she's got Bradley to watch after her.

Maybe Wyatt is right about me needing to stay in here and stay safe. Bradley can't be responsible for me when he's watching over my sister. Either way, I'm too exhausted to argue.

Not only exhausted, but I feel like I'm in a dream world.

I'd been wanting to kiss him since I'd first looked into his eyes, but now that I had, it was so much more than I expected.

My lips still tingle from the feel of his against mine.

Going into the bathroom, I look at myself in the mirror. My lips are pleasantly swollen from his kisses.

It's not just his kisses that has my lips curving into a little smile. It's the promise of more of them.

Unspoken promises of more to come. That's what he had given me.

I can live with unspoken promises.

As I change into my pajamas and wash my face, I replay the night.

Being around Wyatt has my blood racing through my veins and yet at the same time, I feel safe with him.

Safe.

Not exactly something I should be feeling right now.

I'd actually gone all evening without thinking about the possible lawsuit hanging over my head. Two years. I have two years to worry about that woman pressing charges against me.

Two years before I can completely let go of what happened with Trey and the damage that had done to me.

When I'm with Wyatt, all that stuff that happened to

me... Trey... Bernice... Natalie... seems like something that happened to someone else.

For a few short hours, I was able to put it aside and think about something else. To be someone else. To be the person I really am.

To be happy.

Wyatt makes me happy.

I didn't come out here to my sister's house to find someone who made me happy. I'd come out here to put my old life behind me.

And now that I'm here, I find out my sister needs me. Someone is leaving sinister and threatening notes for my sister.

There's even one she doesn't know about downstairs on the kitchen island.

Even after the guys had installed cameras, someone managed to get past them. But how?

It's almost like whoever left the notes is a ghost.

Why would someone want us gone from here? It has to have something to do with the inheritance. Someone else feels entitled to the inheritance.

The only person who comes to mind is Thomas's baby momma, but she's in Houston taking care of a child. She couldn't get up here to Whiskey Springs, much less leave notes on the doorstep. It's not her. I'm certain of it. That doesn't even add up. She got Thomas's insurance money and all the other money he had put away for the child.

Definitely not her.

Audrey mentioned something about the old man Albright having a brother.

Now that made sense.

I climb into bed and turn on the lamp.

I pick up Wyatt's business card and study it. Just his name, a phone number, and *Timber Ridge Cabins and Timber Co.*

No title.

I put his number in my phone and set it on the charger.

About two minutes later, I pick up my phone and send him a text.

Me: Just letting you know I have your number in my phone. This is Lilah. Good night.

My finger hovers over the send button. Playing with fire. That's what I'm doing.

There's plenty of fire where Wyatt is concerned.

I'm doing exactly what I'd said I wasn't going to do.

I've barely even arrived and already I'm getting close to another man.

Wyatt deserves better than someone who could be hauled off to jail at any minute.

I hit send.

I can't help myself.

He sends a message right back.

Wyatt: And now I have your number. Sweet dreams, Milady.

With a smile on my lips, I put my phone back on the charger.

Nope. I can't help myself.

Not even a little.

TWENTY-ONE

Wyatt

I GET BACK to Audrey's house just before nine the next morning.

Bradley leads me back to the breakfast table where he and Audrey are huddled over their morning coffee and from what I'm sensing, they've been in deep conversation.

"Thanks for the heads up," Bradley says.

"Sure thing." I sent Bradley a message about the note I'd found so he'd have it when he woke up this morning.

But, being the light sleeper that he is, and the responsible older brother who keeps his phone on all the time, he'd gotten the message right away.

I'd been on the phone with him when he walked down-stairs just before Midnight to read the note.

He had decided not to wake Audrey up to tell her. A very good idea and if I hadn't been afraid she would wake up first and find it, I wouldn't have messaged him as soon as I got home.

In hindsight, I could have taken the note with me or left it with Lilah, but it wasn't ours to decide.

Audrey looks well-rested despite the stress of finding a new note had been left for her.

"Good morning, Wyatt," she says. "Do you want coffee?"

"Sure. That would be great."

She slides out of her seat and gets to work making me coffee on her fancy coffee machine.

"I thought the cameras would have put a stop to all this," she says, handing me a mug of coffee and sitting back down.

"We all did," Bradley says.

"In a perfect world, it should have." I take the first sip of my second cup of coffee for the day. "Good coffee."

"Somehow they got past all our cameras."

"Did you go back and look?" I ask my brother. "See if you could find anything? Any gaps in time?"

"I did and I didn't see any time gaps. We both looked. We've been up since five o'clock."

"If they were trying to disrupt your life, they should be happy."

"Do you think whoever is leaving these notes is dangerous?" Audrey asks, running her fingers along her mug.

"We won't allow them to hurt you. Or Lilah," Bradley says.

"There has to be a way to at least find out who's doing it," I say.

"The sheriff ran the prints," Audrey says. "He's certain it's Claire. Her prints. But it can't be Claire. She's in jail. We should take this note in. Let him run it for prints."

"He's an ass hat," I say. "Even if Claire's prints are on it, doesn't mean she did it. She could have easily been set up."

"Or he could be lying about it," Bradley says.

"Exactly," I say.

At the sound of a door opening upstairs, I look toward the top of the stairs. Biscuit gets up from where he was sleeping in front of the fireplace. Shakes himself and races to the stairs.

Lilah stops.

"Biscuit," Bradley says. "Come here." Biscuit races over to Bradley. "Leave Lilah alone."

"Lilah's afraid of dogs," Audrey says.

"I'm not afraid," Lilah says, coming down the stairs.

Her gaze finds mine and holds. She looks a bit surprised to see me.

"Good morning," she says. Then shifts her gaze to her sister. "I'm just wary of dogs who look like small horses."

"She makes a good point," I say in her defense.

"Biased," Bradley says.

Lilah looks at me questioningly as she goes straight to the coffee machine.

"I told you I'd see you today."

"I know, but it's still so early."

I don't answer. Anything I can think to say involves pointing out that she's not only up, but showered, dressed, and her hair is freshly blow dried. She's even wearing light makeup.

"We're trying to figure out how to catch whoever is leaving these notes," I say in explanation for why I'm here.

"Cameras didn't stop him," she says.

"I'm not sure there's anything we can do," Audrey says, with a sigh.

"Don't give up," Bradley tells her. "We'll figure something out.

"Are the notes always left at night?" Lilah asks, bringing her cup of coffee over and sitting in the chair next to mine.

"Except for the one that was left in Audrey's book," Bradley says.

"And there's always some kind of noise, alerting you," she says.

"Except last night. Last night we didn't hear it."

"And I'd already taken Biscuit out for his walk," Bradley says.

"It's almost like he was watching and waiting."

"We should watch and wait for him," Lilah says.

"How?" we all ask at the same time, looking at her.

She sets her mug down.

"Like Wyatt said, there are four of us now. We set up a stakeout. Two of us watching the back and two watching the front. He might can get past cameras, but we should be able to see some sign of whoever's doing it."

"That's what we'll do," Bradley says. "We'll wait up for the son-of-a-bitch tonight."

"But not to confront. Just to take pictures," Audrey says.

I exchange a glance with Bradley and neither one of us says anything.

We can't guarantee we won't confront the ass hat who's doing this.

"I'm sure they'll be safe," Lilah tells Audrey. "whatever they do."

"I'm sure," Audrey murmurs behind her coffee mug.

Blackie jumps off the sectional and walks over to sit at Lilah's feet.

"Hey, little guy." She runs a hand over the cat's back, then looks at Audrey. "Has he eaten today?"

"Not yet."

Lilah scoops up the cat and puts him on the kitchen island. Fills a bowl with cat food. The cat gobbles it up like he hasn't eaten in days.

"You'll have to feed him up here," she says. "Someone will eat his food." She looks pointedly at Biscuit.

"He doesn't know any better," Bradley says in his dog's defense.

"So," I say. "Are we going to get those security lights installed in the back?"

"We'll do that this morning," Bradley says. "Then you'll be happy to know that the window shades came in."

"Great," I say with a groan. Window shades. Installing window shades are not my idea of fun. But they have to be done.

Anything to stop these insane threats.

TWENTY-TWO

Lilah

THE MEN DECIDE to divide and conquer.

Bradley gets started on installing the living room window shades with Audrey right there with him. The two of them work in a rhythm they apparently must have established fairly quickly. They act like they've known each other forever, even though in reality it's only been less than a month. I knew Audrey had done some things around her house in Katy, but I'd never actually seen her doing them.

It throws me off just a little. Seeing this side of my sister I haven't seen before.

Wyatt is the self-appointed electrical guy. He hauls three brand new motion sensor lights, still in the box, a ladder, and a drill out to the back of the house.

I put away the coffee mugs. Wipe off the table and counter with a damp cloth.

I don't need to get in Audrey and Bradley's way. They don't need my help. And I honestly don't care to be a third wheel.

After watching Wyatt out the window for a few minutes, I decide he doesn't need any help either.

With everyone working, I can't just gather up my paint supplies and head out, as much as I might want to.

Besides, I'd rather find an excuse to spend time with Wyatt.

Unfortunately, I know nothing about installing lights so I can't exactly genuinely offer to help him with installing the lights.

With nothing left to do but listen to Audrey and Bradley discussing their work as they go, I step out onto the back porch where Wyatt is perched on a ladder.

"Hey," Wyatt smiles. "I'm glad you're here."

"Yeah?" My heart skitters a bit.

"Would you hand me that cup of screws?"

"Sure." Not exactly what I was hoping for. But I can hand things up.

I grab the only cup of screws in sight and hand them up to him.

"Thanks," he says. "Keep me company?"

"Okay." I sit down on the nearest chair. "It's a beautiful day."

It's actually cool enough that I'm glad I have my sweat-shirt on, but the sun is bright and warms the air.

"A lovely day for painting," he says. "You should go paint."

"That would be bad form," I say.

"How do you figure?" Wyatt asks, deftly drilling into the wall.

"Everyone is working. I should be helping."

"You know anything about electrical?" I shake my head. "How about hanging window shades?"

"I don't know anything about that either. Should I be learning?"

"As long as you can keep me company and hand me things, you're good."

"I can do that." I bite my lip. This is a better arrange-ment than I expected.

"That was a good idea you had," he says, twisting two wires together.

"Which one?"

"The one about setting up a stakeout."

"Might be a little bit dangerous."

"I don't think so. We'll take the back of the house while Audrey and Bradley take the front."

"How do you think we're going to actually do it?"

He glances at me. Shrugs. "We'll set up at the windows. Anything moves, we'll see it."

I nod. "We can watch the cameras, too."

"We could. But the cameras are recording and so far they haven't given us anything. I think we try eyes on. If we see anything, we go back and look at the recordings."

"It might work."

"We're going to catch him," Wyatt says with all the confidence of a man who never fails at anything. "There's no way a person can keep dropping notes off and not get caught. We've got too many cameras. And with these motion sensor lights, we should most definitely catch him red-handed."

"Or frighten him away," I say.

"I'm thinking that would be okay, too."

I gaze toward the tree line, wondering how someone could be so bold as to walk right up to someone's door to drop off threatening notes.

"It has to be someone who knows the area and isn't afraid to walk around in the woods after dark," I say.

"I don't know where he parks. But finding a parked car is another way to go about it."

"He could park anywhere. How far is the walk between here and town?"

"It would be a hike," Bradley says. "But it could be done. There are a few cabins between here and there."

I pull my feet up under me and rest my chin on my

palm. "Any cabins that you're renting to someone? Within walking distance?"

Bradley stops. Looks at me. "Not sure. I'll have to check into that."

"Lots of possibilities."

"You've got a good head on your shoulders." He goes back to twisting wires together.

"It's all that time I spent exercising my brain learning to be a bartender."

"Just think how smart you could be if you'd learn about flowers."

I narrow my eyes at him. "Good try. But that sounds like a major endeavor."

"It would be. But I'd make it worth your while."

"And how exactly would you do that?"

"Haven't figured that out yet." He skins a wire and twists it to attach it to another one.

"Well," I say. "Let me know when you do."

"Thought you weren't interested."

"I was planning on coming out here to paint," I say, scanning the area, halfway expecting to see something or another move. Some kind of movement. Anything.

Wyatt leans his arms on the top of the ladder. "I'm getting the idea you're a lot like me."

"How so?"

"I'm getting the feeling you can't resist a challenge."

I smile up at him. "You are right about that."

But what I can't tell him is that I'm damaged goods.

One word from Bernice and I'll be summoned back to Houston to do my time in jail for assault.

Assault with wine. Whoever would have thought?

I can't tell him. It's too embarrassing. I can't even tell Audrey.

The only person who knows is Brianna.

And she's sworn to secrecy.

I guess I don't have anyone to blame but myself. I'd done it. I'd tossed the wine into Bernice's face. So I have to live with it.

It's what I get for being so sensitive about what happened with Trey. The whole thing left me feeling icky.

Rubbing my hands over my arms, I push the memories away. I'd like to shove them down into a deep dark hole, but things keep happening to bring them back to the surface.

I have a plan. My plan is to hide out here for two years and hope it goes away.

In the meantime, I can practice my art.

I sigh. Not thinking about whether or not painting is allowed in jail. Drawing. I can work on my drawing. All I have to do is commit everything I see to memory.

Making my living as an artist is my dream fantasy. In reality I know how unrealistic it is. At least for now. While I'm here, I have to do my part to pull my weight.

I'll figure something out.

The only thing I know for certain it won't be is bartending. That left a really bad taste in my mouth.

I glance up to find Wyatt watching me.

He winks at me and a whole bevy of butterflies lets loose in my stomach.

Maybe there's something about the fresh mountain air that affects us Sinclair girls.

Makes us lose our senses.

CHAPTER

TWENTY-THREE

Wyatt

THE DARKNESS of night brings thunderstorms and rain coming down in sheets, bringing a misty fog with it.

"I think we should postpone our stakeout," I say over ham sandwiches in the breakfast room. "No one is going to come out in this storm to drop off threatening notes on the doorstep."

"No," Bradley says. "I don't want to risk it."

Lilah and Audrey look at each other, exchanging some sisterly language only known to them.

"A person would have to be insane to be out in this weather."

"Let's think about that for minute," Bradley says. "Only an insane person would drop notes off to start with."

"Okay," I say, glancing at Lilah. "Good point."

I can think of worse ways to spend an evening than hanging out with Lilah, even if it does involve sitting upstairs in an unoccupied bedroom looking out over the backyard.

Audrey and Bradley will be in the attic watching the front porch area.

"It's dark," Audrey says. "He always leaves the notes after dark."

Despite the sheriff's insistence that Claire was the one who had been leaving the notes, the four of us agreed that it had to be a man. Only a man would come out in the woods at night to drop notes off at the door.

Two notes dropped off at the front door. One in a small jewelry-sized box. The other in an envelope. One note dropped off at the back door, also in an envelope.

Then there was the note in Audrey's book and the flowers with no note. Since the note in the book and the flowers left on the kitchen island required further explanation, we didn't include them in tonight's search parameters.

Lilah starts picking up empty plates.

"We'll clean up later," Audrey says.

"It won't take but a minute." Lilah already has the plates gathered up and is carrying them to the sink.

"I'll help you," I say. A rumble of thunder reminds us that we're in the middle of a thunderstorm. And I maintain my stance that a person would be crazy to be out here during this weather.

She was right. It only takes a minutes for us to have everything in the dishwasher.

Lilah even takes a cloth and wipes the table.

"Habit," she says.

"It's a habit you should consider picking up," Bradley says to me.

I shoot him a withering glance.

"Okay," Audrey says. "Bradley and I are going to be upstairs. Phones on silent. If you see something and can't call, text." She looks at Lilah. "Record everything that moves."

Lilah gives her a thumbs up. No one reminds her that we already have camera on every angle.

"I guess we're heading up to our location, too," I say.

Leaving Biscuit sleeping front of the fireplace and Blackie curled up on his end of the sectional, the four of us head upstairs, for all appearances, heading up to our respective bedrooms.

With the new shades pulled down over the windows, hiding the stunning views of the snow-capped mountains, a casual observer might even draw the conclusion that Lilah and I are hanging out in front of the fireplace. We'd left the television on to flicker along with the flames from the fireplace.

Audrey's nightstand reading light is on, just like it always is this time of night.

"Biscuit will bark before any of us see anything," Bradley says as he and Audrey veer off toward the attic stairs.

"I think he's down for the night," Lilah says.

"Never underestimate the power of a dog's hearing," I tell her as we enter the unoccupied bedroom.

Like the other bedrooms in the house, it's fully furnished with a king-sized bed. An inviting white comforter and pillows. A nightstand with a lamp. An unadorned dresser.

And most importantly at the moment...

Two windows. Two chairs.

She and I take our seats, just off to the side of either window, turned slightly to face each other.

We'd set the chairs up earlier, deciding this gave us the best view.

"It's hard to see anything in the darkness," Lilah says. "with the storm.

A flash of lightning punctuates her words.

"I think someone might have mentioned that," I say, but I keep my eyes fixed on the tree line. Each flash of lightning cuts through the darkness, revealing the branches thrashing in the wind.

"You did. But Bradley isn't wrong. Anyone crazy enough to do this to begin with, is probably crazy enough to not let a little bad weather stop them."

"We'll see."

We're both holding our phones. Both staring out the windows.

"I hope the motion lights don't scare him away," Lilah says. "I really want us to bust his ass."

"I couldn't have said it better myself," I say with obvious appreciation.

"Sorry." She winces.

"No need to apologize. I agree with you one hundred percent."

Rain slams into the windows and thunder crashes along with streaks of lightning.

I keep my opinion to myself. There's crazy. And then there's crazy.

Coming out in this kind of weather would take a whole different level of crazy.

TWENTY-FOUR

Lilah

I STARE through the window trying to see anything in the blinding rain until my eyes hurt.

What kind of person would come out in this rain to leave a threatening note?

The kind of person who would threaten someone to begin with.

I can't help but worry that the notes are just the first step for whoever is doing this.

Hopefully they're just idle threats.

The problem is there is more at stake than just the ownership of the house.

Wyatt, and not even Bradley know that the house is part of a package deal.

Whoever has possession of the house also receives a one million dollar annual stipend. The two go hand in hand.

A million dollars a year is a lot of money.

It's enough money that it's hard to say what lengths someone would go to in order to get Audrey, and now me by association, out of here.

A smart bad guy would go after me.

Putting me in danger would be one of the fastest ways to get Audrey to give up the house.

I really think Wyatt and Bradley should know that the stakes are higher than they know about.

"How far do you think someone would go?" I ask him. "to get Audrey out of the house?"

"I don't know. I guess it has something to do with how bad they want this place."

"Right. What if it's more than just the house?"

"Like what?"

I want to tell him about the money. I truly believe that the money is a big part of the whole thing. But it's not my place.

"Maybe it's about the Albright legacy," I tell him.

"I guess it could be," he agrees, but I can tell he doesn't think that has anything to do with it. "I don't understand the why of it. If someone has a right to it, why don't they contest it in court? We may never understand the why of it.

I just want to find out who's doing it so we can put a stop to it."

"Right," I say, distractedly. Was that a movement there at the tree line? I lean closer toward the window before I remember we're trying to stay out of sight.

"See something?" he asks.

"I don't know. I don't think so. Probably just the wind."

Wyatt picks up a pair of binoculars and aims them toward the tree line. "It's too dark."

I tighten my sweatshirt around me and stifle a yawn.

The grandfather clock in the foyer begins to chime the eleven o'clock hour.

Wyatt lowers the binoculars. "If you want to go ahead and go to bed, I'll keep watch here."

"No. It's okay."

"There's a bed right there. You can take a nap."

A bed I'm trying not to think about. About being alone in a bedroom with Wyatt. "I often work late. I should be used to staying up late."

"You're still adjusting to the time difference. And don't discount the higher elevation."

"The elevation," I say, feeling a distinct aha moment going off in my head.

"A lot of people stay sleepy until they adjust to the elevation."

"That makes perfect sense," I say, fighting back another yawn. "I have been sleepy since I got here. I thought I was just tired from...everything." Being fired. Driving for days. Having the threat of a lawsuit hanging over my head.

"Probably a combination," he says, picking up his binoculars again.

"Have you ever lived anywhere else?" I ask. "Besides Whiskey Springs?"

"No." He sets the binoculars aside. "I commuted to college in Boulder, but I never lived there."

"You live with your parents?"

"God. No. I have my own cabin. Actually a cabin I'm renovating for the family."

"So you don't actually own a place of your own."

"Not exactly."

"Huh."

Two birds fly together toward us and we lose track of them as they duck under the covered porch.

"I didn't know birds cold fly in the rain," I say.

"I guess birds can fly in any conditions. But yeah. Normally they don't."

"What was your major?" I ask. "In college."

"Business. Of course. But it didn't really interest me. Our brother, Caleb, is the one who likes to be in charge of finances and such."

"It takes a different kind of personality to like numbers."

"I agree."

"What's Caleb like?"

The birds fly out from the covered porch and head back toward the tree line, staying low.

"He's charming. He's probably the reason we have so many cabins right now. Anytime someone is thinking about selling their property, he can seal the deal. He's especially charming to little old ladies." He takes a breath. "I mean that in the best possible way."

"I'm sure you do. Wyatt?"

"Yes?" He pulls his gaze away from the window and looks at me.

I swallow. "Speaking of meaning things in the best possible way."

He waits for me to keep going. I do so in a rush of words spilling out.

"With it raining like it is and dark, I'd feel a lot better if you slept here." I nod toward the bed. "Instead of driving along those deadly cliffs."

"I thought you'd never ask."

I smile and bite my lip.

We sit quietly a few more minutes, our gazes focused on the area below. Both of us straining to see the tree line obscured by the sheets of falling rain.

The wind shifts sending the soft rain slamming against the windows.

We hear Audrey and Bradley coming down from the attic.

They stop at our door.

"I think we can turn in. Pick up again tomorrow night," Bradley says. "We can check the cameras in the morning."

"Sounds good to me." Wyatt stands up.

"Is it okay if Wyatt sleeps in here tonight?" I ask Audrey. "The weather is too dangerous for him to driving."

"I hope he does. I hope he doesn't try to drive down the mountain in this." She looks at Wyatt with that older sister look that means she's telling him he's staying here.

"Much appreciated," he says.

"We'll get up early," Bradley tells his brother. "Get to work on those shades."

"They're tedious, aren't they?" he asks.

"Very tedious," Audrey says, looking at me. "I think I just got fired."

"I think not," Bradley says, pulling her close. "I just think your time could be better spent doing something else."

"He should run for sheriff," Wyatt says.

"I agree," Audrey says. "He would be good at it."

"I don't know what I did to get you two on that kick," Bradley says. "I'm not interested in running for sheriff."

I smile and keep my thoughts to myself. I learned a long... long time ago not to say I wouldn't do something. I learned that that thing I said I wasn't going to do was the very thing I ended up doing.

Of course, Bradley might not have that problem. Maybe it's just me.

I do one thing for certain. I'm going to sleep a whole lot better tonight knowing that Wyatt is in the bedroom next to mine.

TWENTY-FIVE

Wyatt

"I'll go with you to walk Biscuit," I tell Bradley as we head downstairs.

"He's not going to like getting out in this."

Lilah and Audrey are already headed down the stairs in front of us to feed Blackie in his designated spot on the kitchen island. As an older cat, he has a little route he uses to get up there. Jumping from a chair to a barstool, then up onto the counter where he eats right in the center of the island, away from Biscuit's access.

Bradley and I grab jackets from pegs next to the back door and he grabs a towel for Biscuit.

"Biscuit. Come on. Out." Biscuit runs over as soon as Bradley opens the door, but seeing the rain outside, stops and looks up at him.

"I didn't do it," Bradley says. "Go on."

"Dog's too smart," I say, stepping outside behind my brother. Biscuit runs reluctantly out into the rain, but we stay underneath the covered part of the deck.

Biscuit's movements set off the motion sensor lights.

"Lights are working," he says.

"Of course."

"I think the rain is slacking off."

"Wishful thinking," I say. "I think it's settled in for the night."

Bradley puts his in hands in his jacket pockets. "Probably." He glances around like we all do now. "Didn't see anything?"

"Nah. Just a couple of birds."

"Yeah. We tracked an elk."

"The wildlife isn't used to this kind of weather," I say.

"A bit unusual. Global warming."

"Doesn't feel warm to me," I say, pulling my jacket tighter.

"How are things with your future wife?"

"Going good. Couldn't be happier."

"You're in what? Day two? Haven't changed your mind?"

"Not going to."

Tendrils of mist hover over the ground and white clouds with dark edges linger in the valley.

"Snowing up in the high country."

"Maybe."

Biscuit comes running back. Stops next to us and shakes before Bradley can get the towel over him, sending a spray of water over us.

"Payback," I say.

"The fastest he's ever done his business." Bradley tosses the towel over Biscuit and dries him off. "Hold still."

"At least we didn't get any threats tonight." I look around, even though I know there's nothing there. We've been watching.

"Just waiting for the other shoe to drop." Bradley opens the door and Biscuit shoots inside, heading right back to his spot on a rug in front of the fireplace.

"Anybody want a glass of wine?" Audrey asks.

"I'll take one," Bradley says.

"Just a sip," Lilah says. "to be sociable."

"What she said." I slide my jacket off, hang it up, and go stand next to Lilah.

"You got a little wet," she said.

"Biscuit gave Bradley payback for sending him outside in the rain. I just happened to be standing there."

The four of us take our glasses of wine to sit on the sectional in front of the fireplace.

Bradley kneels in front of it, gets the flames going again. Stacks firewood in, making a big fire.

"I think the stakeout was a good idea," Audrey says. "We should do it again tomorrow."

"I agree," Lilah says, holding her wine, but not drinking.

I'm more of a beer guy, but I can drink wine when I need to.

Bradley dusts his hands on his jeans and looks at me.

"You up for it?"

"I'm all yours."

Lilah looks at me with her brow furrowed. "You don't have any extra clothes, do you?"

"It's okay. I'm sure my brother has something I can steal."

"I'm sure I have something you can *borrow*," Bradley says, taking Audrey's hand.

I look over at Lilah sitting next to me. One day I'll be allowed to reach over and take her hand.

"I'll be okay," I say with a little smile.

And I'm not talking about having something wear. I'm talking about the rest of my life.

TWENTY-SIX

Lilah

FLAMES in the fireplace crackle as they devour the strategically laid stack of wood. Little sparks drift up the chimney as one log burns through and causes all the others to shift places.

Bradley gets up and, using a black iron poker, shoves them back into place, sending out more sparks in the process.

Outside, the rain continues to fall, slamming against the windows as the wind shifts. The rain brings cold air with it. Not unusual for this level of elevation, even if it is summer.

The heat from the fireplace warms the air all the way over to the sectional where I sit next to Wyatt. The old black cat curled up between us. I scratch his ears and he purrs. A really nice, soothing purr. I think he likes me because I'm the only here who doesn't smell like dog.

I take a sip of my wine. Dark cherries, blackberries, and the faintest whisper of vanilla beneath a hint of oak from its barrel. I hadn't seen the bottle, but I'm thinking it's a Cabernet Sauvignon.

I'm not a wine taster and I have absolutely no training in wine tasting. But I've studied it and I taught myself what to look for.

I've got all this knowledge about wine and drinks, but since I'm not much of a drinker, I'm not sure what I'm going to do with it.

Most of the wines I know about I haven't even tasted. This just happened to be one that I had. I actually think Audrey had this wine at her house once. Maybe last Thanksgiving. I was well into my study of wines at the time, so it stuck with me.

Our lives are so very different now than they were last fall, I can barely see the connections between them.

Just the tiniest of threads connecting who she and I used to be with who we are now.

Being close sisters, though, is one thing that won't change no matter not.

It's just she's a widow now. A rich widow living in a huge house in the mountains just on the outskirts of

Whiskey Springs, Colorado. She has a new boyfriend. Bradley Winslow. And Bradley comes with a giant horse dog.

From what I can figure, Bradley has moved in here. No one has told me officially, but it looks like he's moved in under the guise of protecting her from a stalker.

That's something else about her. She has an unidentified stalker who leaves threatening notes at the front and back doors.

And now the two of them, Audrey and Bradley are the stewards of a cat that belongs to the woman the sheriff believes is the one leaving the notes.

What a tangled web they weave.

Then there's me.

I was fired from my job as an upscale bartender/hostess at the Hobby Center after which I immediately quit my other bartending job.

So I'm jobless. Not only that, but I've been accused of assaulting a woman by throwing wine in her face. Of course I did it in my capacity as a hostess while on the job.

So... fired.

And the woman—all I know about her is her name— Bernice has two years to decide whether she wants to press charges against me for tossing the wine in her face.

It doesn't matter that she started it.

Isn't that how it goes? The person standing up to the bully is more often than not the one who gets in trouble.

So after getting fired from one job and quitting the

other, I pack everything up, turn in the keys to my apartment, and drive up here to Whiskey Springs.

And now I've met Audrey's boyfriend's brother. Wyatt.

I'd vowed to myself that I wasn't going to date again, at least not until I've gotten past the two years that I could be hauled back to a Houston jail for abovementioned assault with wine.

And yet I haven't even unpacked yet—not my fault— and I've already kissed Wyatt.

And, as it would be, I can't stop thinking about kissing him again.

Biscuit, the very large horse dog, stirs in his sleep. He's addicted to lying in front of the fireplace. I can't blame him. I like sitting in front of it, too.

The old solid black cat, aptly named Blackie, is sleeping next to me, snoring softly.

Audrey and Bradley have a few of the new window shades installed. Motorized, of course. Did I mention that Audrey is quietly wealthy?

She hasn't even told Bradley about the million-dollar— annual—stipend that comes with living in the house.

She will, though.

She assured me that she would tell him when the time is right. They might be old and gray when that time comes, but she'll tell him. Besides, he's eventually going to start to wonder where her money is coming from.

I hide a yawn behind the back of my hand.

"You should get some sleep, Sweetness," Wyatt says, leaning close to whisper.

"I think you might be right," I say, holding out my wine glass. His is empty. "Do you want this?"

"It's only a sip," he says.

"I know."

"You're not going to drink it?"

"Not right now."

"Do you want me to save it?" he asks skeptically.

I lean over and whisper back to him. "Just drink it."

With a look I can't decipher, he downs it in one swallow.

My life has so gone in a direction I hadn't thought possible.

One weak moment combined with a spontaneous decision along with one of those instant connections with a good-looking small-town man and here I go. Watching myself falling all over again.

TWENTY-SEVEN

Wyatt

A QUIET EVENING sitting at home. I confess that's unusual for me.

Not my home. My brother's girlfriend's home. Still. At technically at home.

If I'm at home, my home, by myself, I usually at least have the television on. Sitting, just sitting, in front of a cozy fire with the girl who has all my attention focused on her is a bit different.

It's late, nearly eleven o'clock, and I guess that's why our conversations have lagged into silence.

Outside, the storm continues to rage as it moves off into the distance, but it left a steady rain behind.

Tomorrow I'm supposed to help Bradley continue to hang the motorized window shades. It seems like a shame to cover up the spectacular views of the snow-capped mountains, but I see the reasoning behind it.

Right now, anyone could be standing outside looking in at us through the windows. In light of the recent threatening notes someone has been leaving on Audrey's doorstep, it's the logical thing to do. At night, anyway. I can see why she doesn't feel safe.

And now that I've claimed Lilah as my girl, in my head at any rate, I don't feel safe for her either.

So tomorrow Bradley and I will be doing the tedious job of hanging window shades. Not any easy job by any means, but with the two of us, and Audrey's help, we can knock it out.

Right now, though, it's time for me to get Lilah up to bed for some sleep.

Standing up, I hold out a hand.

"Can I escort you to your room, Milady?"

She blinks, telling me she's already halfway falling asleep and puts her hand in mine.

"Good night everyone," I say, linking my hand with Lilah's.

"Good night," Audrey and Bradley say together.

Biscuit stirs, but I don't think he's interested in going

back outside right now. One trip out in the rain is probably enough for him for one night.

I lead Lilah toward the stairs. She yawns.

"I think you missed your bedtime."

"I think so, too." She wipes at her eyes. "Sorry. It's not you."

"I know."

She smiles up at me sideways. "A bit self-confident?"

I grin, squeezing her hand. "I know you're still adjusting the elevation."

We reach the top of the stairs and turn down the hallway toward our rooms. My room is first. Hers is at the end of the hallway.

We pass mine and keep walking.

"Thank you," she says.

"For what?" I take both her hands and shift her so that I'm looking into her meadow green eyes.

She shrugs. "I don't know. For being here."

"You don't have to thank me." I pull her close against me, cupping the back of her head with my hand.

The last thing she needs to do is to thank me.

She's got me under her spell. Bewitched. From the first moment I saw her.

Shifted a bit so I can look into her eyes again, I put a hand lightly beneath her chin.

"There's something I can't stop thinking about," I say, my throat tight.

She bites her bottom lip. "What's that?"

I lower my head and press my lips against hers in a kiss.

"This," I murmur against her lips. "I can't stop thinking about this."

Pressing my lips against hers again, I practically devour her with kisses.

This. This is what life is all about.

CHAPTER
TWENTY-EIGHT

Lilah

THE NEXT MORNING dawns bright and sunny.

The air still has a slight dampness to it, but it won't last long. Unlike Houston, up here at this elevation, the air is dry. Even after a rain.

My first thought is Wyatt. Wyatt sleeping in the bedroom next door.

Somehow, even though it was supposed to just be Audrey living here alone, we've managed to fill up all four bedrooms of the house.

I stretch beneath the warm blankets, knowing that when I get up, the floors will be cold. I really, really like

Audrey's idea of installing heated floors. The best use of that million dollar stipend that I've heard so far. Slippers. I need to order some slippers that I can wear around the house. The ones I have are old and ragged and I tend to forget and leave them in the bathroom.

It won't be long before Bradley will be moving into Audrey's bedroom. That will free up one of the bedrooms.

And Wyatt won't be here except on rare occasions. Like last night. I couldn't bear the thought of him driving along the cliffs with no visibility. It had been a bad storm. One of the worst in recent memory according to Bradley.

Our stakeout had been a bust just as Wyatt had predicted.

I could see Bradley's point, though, about whoever is leaving the notes being crazy. And if he's crazy enough to do that, he's most likely crazy enough to get out in the storm.

Maybe our stalker, the best word I can think of that fits what he's doing, has enough sense to stay in out of the rain after all.

I don't mind having another stakeout tonight as long as it involves spending time with Wyatt.

I'm slowly learning a lot about him. I wouldn't have pegged him for having a degree in business. Something, sure. But not business.

Business is far too boring for a guy who can install electrical lights and from what I understand, just about anything else that needs to be done around a house.

Bradley has a degree in engineering and it seems like

Wyatt would have done the same. It would fit him better and he even admits that a career in business didn't fit him.

If I were at home, by myself, I would have hit the coffee machine in my pajamas and hair that looks like birds made a nest in it overnight.

But that's not going to happen. Not with Wyatt in the house.

I turn on the water and give the shower time to heat up while I dig out a pair of blue jeans and a long-sleeve shirt from my suitcase.

Audrey has some kind of thing about closets. She wants to design all of them from a blank slate. I must be a simple girl with simple needs. I just need a place to hang a few clothes, some shelves, and I'm good.

I find it interesting that my first thoughts this morning were not about Trey or Bernice or the possibility of being dragged off to jail in Houston—currently my biggest fear.

Instead, my first thoughts are about Wyatt.

I can't decide how I feel about that. I feel good about it, but I feel guilty about feeling good about it.

I can't get too close to him. It wouldn't be fair to him.

Too late.

I step out of the shower and towel off.

Having already kissed him is definitely too late to not get too close by anyone's definition.

It's bad, too, because I'm thinking I'm going to stay here. I don't know how long. I can't just freeload on my sister even if she is loaded.

I don't have to decide right now.

Right now I have some other things to do.

After I dry my hair, I'm going in search of coffee.

Then I'll see what's going on with everyone else. If everyone else is working, I'll need to chip in. If not, I'll get some painting in.

Either way, I have very little doubt that I'll be bumping into Wyatt.

And that has my blood thrumming through my veins with anticipation and has me taking a few extra minutes to straighten my hair.

I examine my appearance in the bathroom mirror and declare myself ready to go downstairs. In my humble opinion, I look rather cute in my blue jeans, long sleeve shirt layered beneath a plain gray t-shirt, and my lace-up boots.

Coming from Houston, I most definitely don't have the right clothes for the mountains.

I've only been here a few days and I'm seeing that.

My heart racing, my palms a little bit damp, I wipe them on my jeans and open the door.

The first sound I hear is the sound of a drill. They're installing the window shades. Good. That's very important to Audrey. Understandably.

And I'm happy about it because Wyatt agreed to help.

I head downstairs, turning right to go straight to the kitchen. I purposefully do not look to my left where everyone is working.

"Good morning, Sleepyhead," Audrey says.

"Hi." I pull a mug from the cabinet and get started making coffee in the fancy coffee machine.

"Did you sleep well?" she asks, coming over to join me.

"Actually. Yes. You know I love the sounds of a good rain storm."

"I know," she grins.

"How about you? Did you sleep well?"

"Yes," she says.

There's something she's not telling me. I glance over my shoulder just in time to catch Bradley whistling a happy little tune.

Things are most definitely moving along with those two. Just as I had predicted.

My coffee finished, I turn and lean against the counter.

Blackie uses his route to climb up on the chairs to the kitchen island, but instead of going for his food bowl, he comes right over to me. Holds one foot up and meows.

"Aw. Hi there." I go over and pet him, getting him going with that purr of his.

"He likes you," Audrey said.

"Where's Biscuit?" I ask, not seeing the horse dog in his place in front of the fireplace.

"Wyatt took him in to Boulder."

"Oh." Disappointment washes over me that Wyatt isn't here. "Why?"

"It's okay," she says, mistaking my disappointment that Wyatt isn't here to worry about something being wrong with the dog. "Some of our closet supplies came in and he went to get them. It was faster than having them shipped. Anyway, Biscuit likes to ride. And." She picks up a piece of toast. Takes a bite. "I think Wyatt wanted the company."

"That was good of him," I say. *I would have gone with him. I would have kept him company.*

"You weren't up yet," Audrey says with a smug expression. "And I asked him to pick up lunch on his way back."

"Lunch?"

"There's a seafood restaurant in Boulder that is supposed to have good seafood. That's one of the things I miss the most about Houston. The food."

I hide any comments I might have behind my coffee mug. If she had told me ahead of time, I could have gotten up to go with Wyatt.

Instead he took the dog.

Sometimes my sister is just clueless.

"Anyway," she says. "I thought you might want to get some painting done before lunch. After lunch, we're going to build closets. I thought you might want to help with that."

"Sure."

I'm rather glad she didn't put me in the position of choosing between painting and riding into Boulder with Wyatt.

As much as I love to paint, I have a very strong feeling that Wyatt would have won out this time.

TWENTY-NINE

Wyatt

EVEN THOUGH IT's a beautiful day for it, I had not planned on driving into Boulder today.

If I had planned on driving into Boulder today, I would asked Lilah to join me.

Most definitely a missed opportunity, but not by my choosing.

Audrey asked me to pick up the things she ordered for the closets and she asked me to pick up lunch on the way back. She even wrote down the lunch order for me.

I took one look at my brother, wearing his tool belt,

getting ready to climb up a ladder and install window shades to know I was getting the best deal.

I didn't even mind Biscuit coming along even if I did have to stop halfway into the city to take him for a walk.

After that particular stop, the dog and I had a conversation that led to an additional, unplanned stop at the pet store.

My brother might not like it, but this was between me and the dog.

Driving back toward Whiskey Springs, sipping a milk shake that I'd gotten at the seafood restaurant, I admire the wildflowers, mostly blue and white scattered about the meadow.

My first thought is that Lilah would like to paint them.

All that gets me thinking even more about the flower shop idea I had so blithely tossed out there to John at the General Store.

A flower shop really is a missing staple in the little town of Whiskey Springs. Besides the General Store, we've got just about everything else a town could want. A coffee shop. An ice cream shop. Even a bookstore.

But if you want fresh flowers you have to either make a drive, get someone to make the drive to bring in a delivery, or go into someone's backyard.

We *need* a flower shop in town.

The fact that I don't know anything about flowers normally would have put a damper on the idea.

But Lilah said something that I can't let go.

A person can learn about anything they want to.

So simple and I'm not even sure I believe it. But I don't *disbelieve* it. And therein lies the problem.

John showed some interest, but he and his wife should be retiring. Not taking on a new venture like that.

As hard as I try, I can't think of anyone who would want to take it on. There's the lodge. They could handle it and it's probably most logical for them to do it, but damn it, it was my idea and I want to explore it before I just give it away.

Being the youngest child in a family that came with a ready-made business wasn't easy. People always just assumed that I would work in the family business. Not own it or anything like that. That's Bradley's job as the oldest. But work in it. To just be part of the family business.

Lilah changed the way I'm thinking about it.

Lilah made me start thinking that maybe there's no reason why I can't be the one to start a flower shop in town.

To even entertain the idea, I have a LOT of research to do.

If I can get Lilah interested, she and I could do the research together.

I can actually see myself relying on her maybe a little bit too much.

That's a good enough reason for me to let it go.

If I can't do it on my own, then I don't need to even be thinking about it.

Unless... unless I were to make Lilah an equal partner.

As I turn off the highway onto the road leading up to

the Albright house, aka Audrey's house, Biscuit sits up and looks out the window.

"You know we're almost home, don't you?" I ask him.

He barks once in agreement.

"Home." What the hell is wrong with me? I'm not supposed to be thinking of Audrey's house as home.

I blame Lilah for that.

Lilah, the green-eyed goddess who's gotten under my skin.

THIRTY

Lilah

AUDREY ENCOURAGED me to take the morning for painting, but the ground is still damp from last night's storm. That's my story and I'm sticking with it.

It has nothing to do with wanting to be around when Wyatt gets back.

Besides, it's too cold outside for my paints.

I set up at the kitchen table with a sketch pad and pencils to sketch whatever catches my eye.

I start with the obvious. The rugged mountains in the distance. Capture their forever cap of snow draping down until it blends into the tree line. Aspen trees with their fluttering, musical leaves. Maple trees with their big, bold leaves. Spruce trees with their Christmas-tree like shapes.

With a sigh, I turn the page in my sketchbook and look around, closer in.

A blue bird sits perched on a pine tree limb at the edge of the deck. Knowing he won't sit there for very long, I slowly pick up my phone and snap a photo. Just as I expected, I'd no more than taken the photo when he flies off.

It's okay. I've got his photo. I zoom in on the photo and focus on sketching him.

Even over the sounds of Bradley and Audrey talking through their process of measuring and drilling as they hang the window shades, I hear Wyatt's truck coming down the road toward the house.

By the time he parks and I hear the car door slam, I have my sketching supplies tucked away.

While Audrey and Bradley go to meet him outside, to help him bring things in, I pull out my hair tie and let my hair sweep over my shoulders.

Even though my heart is pounding crazy in anticipation at seeing Wyatt again, I pull out four bottles of water and set them on the dining table along with napkins.

With that done, I wander toward the front door just in time to see Biscuit hop down from the passenger side of the truck.

"What have you done to my dog?" Bradley asks.

"Maybe you should talk to your dog about that," Wyatt says.

Biscuit is wearing a brand new harness and leash.

"What happened, Biscuit?" Audrey asks as the horse dog puts his front legs on Audrey's shoulders and licks her face. My sister, much to my surprise, just laughs and lets the dog lick her face.

Maybe she's not the same obsessive-compulsive Audrey I grew up with.

"He doesn't seem to mind wearing it," Bradley says.

"It was either start wearing a leash or start staying home. It was his choice."

"What did he do?" Audrey asks, taking the leash from Bradley so he can help Wyatt unload the truck.

"He'll tell you when he's ready. I'm not a snitch."

I hold the door open as they all come trooping inside.

"Hi." Wyatt smiles as he walks past, his arms loaded with wrapped up sets of long and short rods and poles and wire shelves and what must be a hundred smaller boxes of brackets and screws.

"Hi."

"Your sister put me to work," he says after he sets the armload down.

"She has a tendency to do that. It's her way."

"I'm getting that idea. Does she have you working, too?"

"She gave me the morning off with the catch that I'll be working on closets after lunch."

"Lunch smells great."

"It'll be a few minutes," Audrey says. "I'm going to put it in the oven to warm it up."

"Biscuit needs to take a walk," Wyatt says. "You want to come with?"

"Okay. Sure." I grab a jacket off one of the pegs by the back door and slide into it.

Wyatt opens the door and holds the leash tight as the dog dashes outside.

Instead of standing and watching Biscuit make his rounds, the leash requires us to walk with him.

"I feel better about him being out here with him on a leash," I say. "But what did he do?"

"It wasn't really his fault. Being from the country, he wouldn't know about traffic."

"He tried to run out in traffic?" I ask, horrified.

"Let's just say he was headed that way."

"I guess it's a good thing he had his uncle there to take care of him."

"Yeah. We had a talk. He understands."

It doesn't take long before Biscuit goes running back toward the house.

"And now he's hungry after his trip," I say.

"I didn't know I was going until your sister pushed me out the door."

"I know. She told me."

"Next time, we'll make a date of it."

"It's okay. Really." But my heart warms that he was

thinking the same thing I was thinking about how nice it would have been if I could have gone with him.

I don't want to think too much about what he and I are doing here.

I just want to enjoy it without overanalyzing it.

Thinking about it too much will take the sheen off.

Nobody said it would be easy.

CHAPTER

THIRTY-ONE

Wyatt

AFTER LUNCH, Audrey and Bradley unwrap all the rods and poles and shelves bound together with plastic that I'd picked up in Boulder.

Audrey sits in the middle of the living room floor surrounded by white shelves of all sizes and boxes of brackets. A measuring tape in her hands. A pad of graph paper next to her.

There are also lots of long metal bars and metal shelves. Apparently, it all goes together somehow like a puzzle.

"I'm not familiar with this particular system," I say. "Does it come with directions?"

"No," Audrey says, making a check on her list and pointing for Bradley to put a stack of metal shelves off to itself. "But Lilah knows how it works."

I look at Lilah sitting calmly on the sectional, the old black cat in her lap.

"Is this true? This makes sense to you?"

"It will," she says with a little shrug. "After Audrey gets it all organized."

"It took her forever to finalize these designs," Bradley says.

"Actually this is only my closet and Audrey's. I'll do the other two closets later."

"Everything has to be exact," Lilah says.

One of the logs in the fireplace burns through, sending sparks up the chimney and Biscuit stirs in his sleep.

"It's easier than it looks," Audrey says. "I promise." She gets on her knees, tears a sheet of paper from her pad and hands it to me. "This is for Lilah's closet. That stack goes with it." She points to her left.

"And the rest of it is for your closet?"

"Lilah wanted to keep hers simple."

I smile over at Lilah. She really is the girl of my dreams.

Lilah shrugs. "I guess I'm more into painting supplies than clothes."

"I'll be right back to get the shelves." I grab the longest of the bars and head upstairs with them.

"There are screws on the coffee table," Audrey says.

I am so thankful my brother got the complicated sister. Lilah is so not complicated. And I like everything about her.

I leave the bars in her bedroom floor and head back downstairs. I meet Bradley on the stairs, headed up, his arms full.

"Having fun?" I ask.

"Actually yes. You?"

"Should be interesting."

Lilah is waiting with my drill and a box of screws.

I pick up about half the shelves. They're heavier than they look.

Lilah walks upstairs with me. "Thanks for doing this," she says. "You don't have to."

"Wouldn't miss it," I say.

She gives me a look that suggests she doesn't believe me.

After I set down the shelves and she sets down the screws and drill, I close the distance between us.

I put both my hands on either side of her face and kiss her soft lips.

"Wouldn't miss it," I whisper against her lips.

"Me either." She bites her bottom lip and looks at me with those big meadow green eyes of hers.

I kiss her again, stopping only when we hear Bradley and Audrey are coming down the hallway.

"I guess we should get busy," I whisper. "on the closet."

"I guess so." She smiles at me, her eyes glazed.

Clearing my throat, I step back. "Where do we start?" I

ask, picking up a bracket. "Are you sure we're not going to accidentally build a spaceship?"

She laughs. "I think we would know that. The first step is to hang the top track."

"That's got to be this," I say, picking up the longest piece of metal.

"Yes. Now." She looks through the smaller boxes. "We need some of these long screws."

"Which way does it go?" I ask, turning it one way, then another. "The notches at the top?"

"No, Silly. The notches go at the bottom so you can slide in these other pieces."

Thinking how sexy she is when she's talking about sliding pieces into bottoms, I turn the track over and look at her. Her cheeks are a little pink and she keeps her gaze down.

"Let's do this," I say. "And hope your sister made good measurements.

"I'm sure she did. Audrey is a little bit OCD."

"I hadn't noticed," I say.

Actually I haven't noticed a whole lot of anything other than just how charming Lilah is.

If she wanted me to build a spaceship, I would figure out how to do it.

Fortunately, right now, it's a fancy closet system.

THIRTY-TWO

Lilah

THAT GRIN OF HIS—HALF trouble, half charm—spreads across Wyatt's face as he holds the level in place. "Fair warning. If I fall off this ladder, I'm blaming you."

I blink innocently. "I don't know what you're talking about."

"Right. Okay. Hand up that top rack thing."

I lift the top rack and hand up one end.

Together, we line it up with the pencil marks. Standing on a stool, I hold it steady it while he drills, the vibration humming through the wall. When the last screw goes in, I step back, a little breathless from holding it.

"That's one piece. The main piece," I say, brushing dust from my hands. "Only a hundred more to go."

"Then I hope this one is right," Wyatt says.

"Actually, we just finished the hard part. The rest of it is kind of fun."

"Good thing I'm in this for the long haul," Wyatt says, voice low as his gaze lingers on mine.

For a beat, the closet and the mess of rails and brackets don't matter at all.

My breath hitches.

In this instant, the fact that I've vowed not to get involved with anyone completely flees my head. My thinking is all focused on one thing and one thing only.

Wyatt.

He has that effect on me.

I can't help it. Couldn't help it if I wanted to.

And the thing about it is. I don't want to.

I show Wyatt how to hang the long bars and then how to attach the brackets and finally the shelves, snapping them easily in place.

"I think I've got the hang of it," he says, taking a step back to look at our handiwork.

"Yeah." I put my hands on my hips. "It looks good."

"If you sister ever needs a job, she can work as a closet designer."

"She could. That really is a thing." My brows crease. "In Houston. I don't know if there would be much demand for it here."

"People in Whiskey Springs need closets, too."

"Maybe."

"Want help hanging your clothes up?" he asks with a little grin.

"No. I... I think I'll do it later."

I think he flustered me on purpose.

I start gathering up the packaging, putting it in a big trash bag.

"We're a good team," he says.

"Yes. I agree. We can do your closet next."

He glances at me and the words hang there as I realize what I'd just said.

"Hey," Bradley comes to the door, looking slightly frantic. "Have you seen Biscuit?"

"No," we say.

"He was in front of the fireplace when I last saw him," I tell Bradley.

"Me too."

Bradley holds up the leash. "His leash is here, but... I can't find him."

"He has to be here," Wyatt says. "We've all been up here working. No one has been outside."

"Exactly."

"Let's check," I say, moving now. "Here's Blackie. On my bed."

That's a bit unusual. The cat doesn't normally venture upstairs.

Audrey is downstairs calling for Biscuit.

We check all the bedrooms upstairs. Just to be sure, then head down to check downstairs. Again.

I hadn't realized time had passed by so quickly. It's almost dark.

And Biscuit, large horse dog that he is, would be hard to miss.

He's not here.

THIRTY-THREE

Wyatt

BRADLEY and I grab our jackets from the pegs near the back door and flashlights before we step outside into the brisk cold air.

"How could he get outside?" I ask, knowing Bradley doesn't know any more than I do.

"Maybe the door was left cracked open."

"The cat didn't run out. The cat ran upstairs."

We look at each other. Somehow that seems significant, but I'm not sure how just yet.

"We didn't leave the doors open," I say. "We're all

hypervigilant about locking the doors, much less not leaving them open. Especially with pets."

"I know," Bradley says, running a hand through his hair. "I'm just trying to make sense of it all."

"I don't understand it either. I'm going to walk around. Check the trucks just in case."

"Okay." Bradley starts calling for his dog. Calling his name. Whistling. I can hear the strain in his voice.

I call out, too, for the dog as I walk around the side of the house, toward the trucks. I don't know how or even why Biscuit would get out to begin with, much less hop into one of our vehicles, but we're not leaving any stone unturned.

It doesn't take long for me to see that Biscuit isn't out here near the vehicles either. I walk down the road a ways, calling out, switching on my flashlight as I walk beneath the shade of the trees.

The sun is dropping behind the mountains quickly as it always does. It gets dark quick and early up here just by the nature of the position of the town and the mountains.

I walk down the dirt road, calling for Biscuit. Trying to figure out how the dog got out of the house to begin and end it all.

We were all upstairs, the four of us, working on closets. Biscuit was curled up asleep in front of the fireplace.

After the series of threatening notes that someone has been leaving at the house, I know the doors were locked.

Like I'd told Bradley, we're all careful about making sure the doors are locked. All the time.

The only explanation I can come up with chills me to the bone.

Someone let Biscuit outside.

The only tiny shred of hope I have is that he is now wearing a collar with his information on it. His name and Bradley's cell phone number.

If by chance he got out and if by chance someone finds him, they'll know who to call.

But we're so far away from any neighbors up here... that seems like an impossibility.

I shine my light out in the trees. So isolated.

Biscuit has never run off before. Before I put him on a leash... today... he always just ran around the perimeter of the yard. I don't think he's ever tried to run off. Not since Bradley got him.

Even today, when I'd pulled over at a park, he hadn't tried to run off. I was the one who had been nervous about thinking that he would. That nervousness that something would happen to him on my watch had me taking him to a pet store and outfitting him with a harness and leash and a new identification tag.

I'd thought I was helping to keep him safe.

And now this.

The wind howls through the trees, rustling the leaves on the trees. A wolf howls somewhere off in the distance.

If Biscuit is out here somewhere, I just hope he's safe.

And I hope he somehow finds his way home.

With that thought in mind, with a sudden idea, I turn around and head back to my truck. I'd heard that pets sometimes return to wherever they consider home to be.

I send my brother a quick message telling him where I'm going.

At this point, anything and everything is worth checking out.

THIRTY-FOUR

Lilah

AUDREY SITS on the sectional in front of the fireplace staring blankly into the flames.

I pace around the room, going from window to window. Door to door.

My mind racing.

When we'd come downstairs to start looking for Biscuit, the doors had not only been closed, but they had been locked.

"There's no way he could have gotten out," I say to myself for the tenth time.

"It's all my fault," Audrey says.

"How could it possibly be your fault?" I ask, walking over and sitting next to her.

She shakes her head.

"It's this thing. With the notes and the threats. Someone wants me out of here. They're using Biscuit to get to me."

"That's crazy. How could they get inside? You changed all the door locks."

"I know." Her voice is full of misery and guilt.

I put my arms around her. "It's not your fault."

"There's no other explanation. He didn't let himself outside. And he didn't vanish into thin air. Someone had to let him out."

"But where would he go?" A little chill runs down my spine. The horse dog would not run off. I haven't seen him try to run off not even once. But that doesn't mean that he wouldn't go with someone. "There has to be an explanation."

"I know. There has to be."

"They'll find him."

"Why would someone hurt an innocent dog?" Audrey asks.

I'm not sure how to comfort her. My sister has been through so much. It hasn't even been two months since her husband died in a plane crash.

She might look like she's coping well on the outside, but

she's still grieving. In her own way. She's still grieving in her own way.

Everyone is different. But this thing with the dog has her broken up.

"Audrey," I say with all the reassurance I can muster. "They're going to find him."

She nods and take a deep breath. "They have to."

The back door opens and Bradley comes inside. Alone.

"Nothing?" I ask over my sister's head. Audrey doesn't even look up.

"Not yet. Wyatt's driving down to my cabin to look around. Just in case he got out and headed back there."

"Good idea."

I get up so Bradley can sit next to my sister and busy myself with bringing them bottles of water.

It's dark outside now. I can't imagine Biscuit being out there. Not coming when Bradley and Wyatt call him.

I start pacing again.

"What can we do?" I ask, mostly to myself.

"We wait," Bradley says.

When I hear Wyatt's truck pulling up, I step outside onto the front porch and wait while he gets out. Alone.

"No sign of him?" I ask.

"Nothing."

I walk off the porch, around the side of the house, well aware that Wyatt is right behind me.

"What do we do?" I ask.

"We wait," Wyatt says. "Come on. Let's go inside. Figure out something to eat."

"Right. Audrey's not doing well. She's got some residual stuff she's dealing with."

"It's okay." He takes my hand. Leads me back inside. Locks the doors behind us. "We can make something. We all need to eat."

CHAPTER
THIRTY-FIVE

Wyatt

NOBODY ATE MUCH AT DINNER. Just sandwiches, but still. It's hard to get anything down when we're all worrying.

"We'll go out and start looking again in the morning," I say.

Just in case Biscuit did manage to get out, which he obviously did. And just in case he fell down the side of a cliff. We have to go look.

"I'm going to wait up," Bradley says, picking up Biscuit's leash.

"Okay."

"I'm going to wait up with him," Audrey says. Her expression looks drawn and sad.

At her core, she's still a grieving widow, even though Bradley makes her happy. She's still so vulnerable.

"I'm going to get some rest," Lilah says. "So I can get up at daybreak. Go out and help you look."

"It's the best we can do right now," I say.

I take Lilah's hand and we walk upstairs while Bradley and Audrey settle on the sectional. To wait for what, I don't know. Just to wait.

"How could this happen?" Lilah asks as we reach her room, out of earshot of Audrey and Bradley.

"I don't know," I say. "But if I find out who did this, there's going to be hell to pay."

"Too bad you don't have a decent sheriff in town to call."

"Even if we did, it wouldn't matter. Right now it's just a missing dog. Happens every day."

"But there are extenuating circumstances."

"You're right. But there's nothing we can do right now."

"I know. I just hate it."

"I do, too."

I kiss her on the forehead. "Good night, Sweetness. Try to get some sleep."

"I'll try."

"Lock your door tonight," I tell her.

She just nods, walks into her bedroom, but stops in the doorway. "Good night, Wyatt," she says, her eyes heavy.

I nod and wait and until I hear the click of the door lock.

With a sigh, I turn around and walk into my room next door.

Although I go through the routine of getting ready for bed, brush my teeth, put on my sleep pants and a t-shirt I'd borrowed from Bradley, I doubt I'm going to actually get any sleep.

It's hard to sleep when Biscuit is missing.

I feel like I should be doing something. But the truth of the matter is, there's nothing to do.

Desperate for something to do, despite knowing there isn't anything, I drag a chair over to the window and sit down. While I sit there, waiting for the motion lights to kick on, I review the camera footage from earlier.

In our panic, not one of us thought to do that.

We have cameras all around the house, but no one thought to look at the footage.

If Biscuit went out one of the doors, he'll be on record doing it.

I take my time, starting with the front of the house, looking for any sign of the dog leaving after I got back from Boulder and we unloaded the truck.

When I don't find anything at the front of the house, I move to the camera at the back of the house.

I see myself and Wyatt walking around calling out like idiots. But no sign of the dog.

Even though I take my time, watching carefully, I don't see any sign of the dog. None.

How is it possible that a dog vanished into thin air?

CHAPTER
THIRTY-SIX

Lilah

I GET READY FOR BED. Put on my pajamas. Climb into bed.

I crawl beneath the blankets and stare into the dark at the ceiling.

As usual, my window is cracked just enough to let a little bit of fresh air in.

A wolf howls in the distance.

I shiver, worrying about Biscuit being somewhere out there.

How did he get out without anyone seeing him?

Then it hits me.

We have cameras all over the place. Watching every door from more than one angle.

I open my phone to the security camera app and scroll back to where Wyatt and I had taken Biscuit for a walk out back.

From there, I watch the footage. If Biscuit went out, he'll be on camera.

I watch until my eyes get heavy.

I get up. Walk around. Then watch the footage until I see Wyatt and Bradley walking around looking and calling for Biscuit.

No sign of the big dog in between.

I switch over to the front of the house. Do the same thing.

I watch until my eyes hurt.

No sign of him getting out.

How is that possible?

It's not possible. Does that mean that the dog is somewhere in the house?

Getting up, I put on my shoes and walk downstairs.

The house is quiet. Too quiet.

Bradley and Audrey are curled up asleep on the sectional. Blackie asleep in the big comfortable chair.

I walk around. Checking doors first.

I honestly don't see any place that a big dog could hide. Not that he would. Biscuit is a social dog not prone to hiding. I can't see him hiding unless he were to get sick.

But we've looked everywhere.

The window shades are down. Comforting.

I walk to the front door. Look out.

Then walk to the back door and look out.

The only thing I see is a bird flying about.

Then I hear something scratching at the front door.

Hurrying to the door, I look out.

I see... a tail wagging.

A tail?

Then I hear a dog bark. A single familiar bark.

"Biscuit?"

I unlock the door.

Just as I unlock the door, I hear Wyatt bounding down the stairs.

"What are you doing?" Wyatt calls out, breathless.

I open the door and Biscuit rushes inside, wiggling all over.

Audrey and Bradley stir from their place on the sectional.

"It's Biscuit," I say, kneeling down to put my arms around the dog wiggling in ten different directions at once.

Biscuit licks my face and I let him. God help me, I let him.

I hadn't known just how attached I'd gotten to this big gangly dog.

Then Bradley and Audrey are there.

Audrey wraps her arms around the dog, tears dampening his fur.

Bradley checks him out. Looking him over from head to toe. No broken bones or scuffs or anything noticeable.

Wyatt steps out front to look for any sign of anyone who might have walked or driven up.

I follow. "He just wanders back up?" I ask.

"I don't know. He's doesn't look like he's been outside. His feet aren't muddy."

"What the heck?" I ask, looking at Wyatt.

He shakes his head.

Bradley sticks his head out the door. "Hey. You've got to see this."

There's a piece of paper, an envelope maybe, crudely taped onto his collar with packing tape.

After Bradley takes a photo of it, for evidence, Audrey cuts it off with scissors.

With trembling hands, she pulls the note folded up out of an also folded envelope and smooths it out.

"What does it say?" I ask.

After reading the note, Audrey hands the paper to Bradley who then hands it to Wyatt who finally hands it to me.

It's a handwritten note.

One line.

And it makes my blood run cold.

Are you sure you want to live here?

THIRTY-SEVEN

Wyatt

I'D ALWAYS figured Midnight was a good time to have a beer.

Tonight is no exception.

We offered Biscuit food, but he's not hungry. Whoever *borrowed* him must have fed him. Have I seen stranger things? Maybe. Maybe not.

I'm reserving that designation until I have more information.

All four of us, Bradley, Audrey, Lilah, and me, sit on the sectional in front of the fireplace. All of us watching Biscuit sleep. He's the only one of us who doesn't appear to be disturbed about being gone for several hours.

All of us, even Lilah, hold a bottle of cold beer in our hands.

The note lies on the coffee table like a harbinger. A vile harbinger that no one wants to touch now that we know what it is.

Audrey pulls her feet up under her and rests her head on Bradley's shoulder.

"How did he get past the cameras?" Lilah asks.

I reach over and take her hand in mine. "We missed something. That's all."

"And the driveway. We didn't get any alerts on the driveway. He had to have driven up here, took Biscuit, left with him. Then came back with him."

"Maybe he didn't drive," Bradley says.

We all just look at him. Too drained to process anything complicated.

"It's possible he dodged the cameras."

"He would have to know where they are." Lilah picks up her phone. Stares at the blank screen. "Where the blind spots are."

"I don't think we have any blind spots," Bradley says.

"There are always blind spots," I say, rubbing my thumb in little circles on Lilah's palm. "And I say that as the one who installed them. Making every endeavor to avoid blind spots."

"We missed it," Lilah says in my defense.

"We'll go back through all the footage. On all the cameras," Bradley says.

"Biscuit's sleeping in my room tonight," Audrey says, sleepily.

"Blackie, too," Lilah says, scratching the old cat's ears. He starts purring and turns over on his side, stretching out his paws.

I squeeze her hand.

"We go into hypervigilant mode," I say.

"No ladies or pets are to be left alone for any reason," Bradley declares.

I expect blowback from that statement, but we don't get any. All I can guess is that Lilah and Audrey are too tired or too shell-shocked from the whole night's ordeal to protest.

"Okay," Audrey murmurs.

"Yeah," Lilah says simply.

"When do you want to get started on going through the footage?" I ask Bradley.

"First thing in the morning. Need to get Audrey up to bed." Audrey lifts her head. "And I need to take Biscuit out for a quick walk."

"His definition of quick is different from everyone else's," I say. "I'll take him."

"Then I'm coming with you," Lilah says, looking at me with defiance. There's some of blowback I'd been expecting.

"I'll check the doors," Bradley says. "Drop the cat off in Lilah's room."

I stand up, pulling Lilah up with me. "Good plan." I pick up Biscuit's leash. "Come on, Boy. Looks like you're going to be wearing this thing permanently for awhile."

Biscuit stands up. Shakes off the sleep. I clip the leash onto his harness.

"Weird timing," Lilah says. "On the whole leash thing."

"A bit."

While Bradley heads upstairs with Blackie on one arm and Audrey on the other, we put on our coats and go outside, keeping Biscuit on a short leash.

We don't talk. I keep a firm grip on her hand as though someone might whisk her away if I so much as lose sight of her for less than an instant.

As we follow Biscuit around the perimeter, we both stay alert, looking around.

The reality of it is that whoever stole Biscuit is probably more than long gone.

It doesn't matter. The damage is done.

The full moon hangs low over the snow-capped mountains peaks, casting a glow over the white caps.

Biscuit doesn't seem to need his usual long length of time to do his business. It's almost as though he knows it's not his usual time to be outside. He scratches his back legs, throwing leaves into the air before heading toward the back door.

"I guess it's time for us to go back inside," I say.

"Not a minute too soon," Lilah says with one more glance around toward the darkness created by the tree line.

CHAPTER
THIRTY-EIGHT

Lilah

EVEN THOUGH BRADLEY already checked the doors, Wyatt checks them again before we go upstairs. Makes sure the fire is banked for the night.

Biscuit gallops up the stairs without protest. It almost seems like he knows he's not spending the rest of the night downstairs.

"He doesn't seem to mind," Wyatt says as we reach the top of the stairs and turn toward Audrey's bedroom.

"Maybe he knows she has a fireplace in her room."

"Does she?" he asks, surprised.

"She does. I can't wait until she gives in and installs heated floors."

"Bradley and I can install those," he says without a hitch.

"Well," I say. "That's handy."

"We do come in handy on occasion."

Bradley is waiting at Audrey's door for his dog.

"Here he is," Wyatt says. "All ready for the night."

Biscuit runs straight for the fireplace and lies down on the rug someone put there for him.

"That dog might be a little bit spoiled," I say after we tell them goodnight and walk down the hallway toward my room.

"I didn't hear you complaining when he was licking your face."

"You weren't supposed to see that," I say. "I can't stand the thought of someone hurting an animal."

I open my door and peek inside to see Blackie asleep on the foot of my bed.

"Do you have to go already? Or can you stay a little while?"

"I can stay."

"Good." I smile. I'm not ready to be alone.

He follows me into the bedroom and closes the door behind us.

"I wanted to talk to you anyway."

"Oh? What about?" I sit on the comfortable chair in the sitting area of my room.

"I'm worried about you being here."

"I'm not by myself."

"I know." He rubs the back of his neck. "As we saw tonight, that doesn't matter, does it?"

"I suppose not." Closing my eyes, I lean back in the chair. "I'm just relieved that Biscuit is okay."

"It's an offense to steal someone's dog. It's a felony here in Colorado. Class four. Up to six years prison time."

"I'm surprised you know that," I say, untying my boots and pulling my feet up under me.

"I have a fount of useless information in my head."

"Doesn't seem so useless to me. Now all we have to do is find out who did it."

"Harder than it seems."

"Is that what you wanted to tell me?" I ask, opening my eyes.

"No. I wanted to talk to you about staying with me at my cabin until this is resolved. Or if you don't want to do that, staying with my parents."

"Oh." I take a breath. That's not what I expected. Not that I had any expectations. "I can't leave my sister here alone."

"I had a feeling you were going to say that," he says, dropping onto the ottoman in front of the chair.

"You knew I would."

He takes my hand, clasps his fingers with mine. "In that case, I hope you don't mind me staying here."

"You've already got your own room," I say, trying to

keep the smile off my face. I like the idea of him staying here. "I don't mind."

"Good." He brushes a thumb over my knuckles. "Because I'm not letting you out of my sight until we get this sorted out."

"Then I guess we should spend some time tomorrow measuring and designing your closet."

"Looks like it." He looks at me with his blue eyes that remind me of a clear summer day.

He scoops me up and sits snuggled next to me in the comfortable chair.

I'm beginning to understand my sister a little better. How she's come up here and fallen in love in the high altitude with its clean air.

"So this is how it happens," I say, my voice muffled against his shoulder.

"What's that?"

"Nothing. Nothing at all."

I tilt my head up and he kisses me.

But it's not nothing, I realize.

It's everything.

CHAPTER
THIRTY-NINE

Wyatt

THE FOUR OF us spend the next morning going through all the recorded camera footage together. We put it on the television and sit on the sectional. Surely one of four sets of eyes will catch anything, however subtle.

Bradley and Audrey sitting side by side.

Lilah snuggled next to me.

Biscuit is in his place in front of the fireplace and Blackie is asleep on his end of the sectional.

As intent and methodical as we are in watching every minute of every camera, we don't see anything.

Just as we're finishing up, I get a call to go out to one of the cabins to fix a broken toilet.

Lilah walks me to the door.

"I know it sounds silly, but no one stays alone," I tell her. "Okay?"

"You don't have to worry about that. I'm on board."

"Good." He turns at the sound of a vehicle coming up the road. "The mail is here."

The mailman stops in front of the house and brings a box along with the mail to the door.

"Everything going good?" the mailman asks.

"As good as can be expected," I say.

"This one is mine," Lilah says, taking the box.

"What did you get?"

"Just some office supplies," she says with a little shrug.

The mailman gets back in his jeep and drives back down the road.

I watch him leave.

"You're wondering if he did it," she says.

"He wouldn't have any reason to do it."

"Not that we know of. I don't think we can rule anyone out right now."

"I'm missing something and I can't figure out what it is," I say.

"You'll think of it. Go. I'll be here when you get back."

"I'm counting on it."

I pull her into my arms and kiss her. I know she's not here alone. I know my brother is here and her sister.

But still. I don't like leaving her.

"We'll be okay," she says.

"I'm counting on it. Call me if you need me. If anything doesn't feel right. Anything at all."

"Don't worry." She smiles. You'll be right back."

As I walk to my truck, I realize that I will be right back.

And this is exactly where I want to be.

I want to be where Lilah is.

I'd known it all along. Since the moment I first saw her.

But this is different. This is a deeper feeling.

She stands there on the front porch, holding her box, watching me.

Before I back out, I lower my window. "Lock the door."

With a shrug, she opens the door and disappears inside.

I know exactly what she's thinking and I hate it that I'm thinking the same thing.

Locking the door doesn't change anything.

Someone is able to get inside anyway.

If I believed in ghosts, I would be thinking it was something ghostly.

I don't not believe in ghosts, but either way I don't believe ghosts are the ones leaving threatening notes and stealing a dog away for hours just to bring him back with, of course, a threatening note.

As I drive down the road, past the hidden security cameras, I can't shake the feeling that I'm missing something.

I'll figure it out.

One way or another, we're going to put a stop to this nonsense.

CHAPTER
FORTY

Lilah

WHILE AUDREY and Bradley install more of the motorized window shades, I make myself a mug of hot tea. So many windows. So many beautiful views. But at night, those beautiful windows give anyone outside a front row seat to whatever we're doing inside.

With my hot tea, I sit down at the kitchen table and sort through my new office supplies. It's not much. Just markers and index cards. Medium poster sized index cards and smaller index cards.

It's not much, but when I look at it, I see a world of possibilities before me.

Blackie comes over and, climbing up on the table, lays down to watch me work.

I reach over and scratch his head, then open my laptop and get started.

Despite the threats that loom over us at every turn, being here with my sister and her boyfriend feels cozy and comfortable.

I find myself wondering if our sister, Brianna, would like it here. I can't really picture her here, though. She's a city girl through and through.

And I wonder what she would think about the notes and the threats.

She'd probably have it figured out already.

Brianna is probably the smartest of the three of us. She's a paralegal and a personal assistant, and can do any office job put in front of her.

I think that's why she likes doing temp work. Not only does she like a challenge, but she would have trouble picking just what it is that she likes best.

"You look deep in thought," Audrey says, coming over for a drink of water.

"I'm taking Biscuit out for a walk," Bradley says. Then adds over his shoulder. "Don't go anywhere."

"We'll be right here," Audrey assures him, sitting down next to me. "I'm not even going to ask what it is you're doing," she say, glancing at my stacks of index cards.

"Good. Because I don't even know myself."

She narrows her eyes at me. "This reminds me of when

you started bartending." She holds up a hand and looks away. "But I'm not asking. I don't need to know."

I smile. It's nice to be understood without judgement. Something only a close sister can do.

I sit back in my chair and tap a marker on the table. "Do you think we'll figure out who's doing these things?"

"Yes," she says without hesitation. "With the four of us putting our heads together, we'll figure it out."

"I still think we need to tell the guys about the money. They need to know just how high the stakes are."

"You're right. I know you're right." She leans her elbows on the table and watches Bradley walking Biscuit out back. "Do you really think it would change anything?"

I wonder how she means it. "I don't think Bradley would see you any differently."

"I guess I worry that he'll think I'm just here for the money."

"Really? I hadn't considered it that way. Audrey. I said this all along and I still believe it. I think you'd be a fool to not at least give living here a try. And that's what you did." I follow her gaze out back. I understand her not wanting to upset things that are going well. "You do like it here, don't you?"

"I do. It's funny. I haven't gotten out much. Only been into town a handful of times. But I don't mind. It's peaceful here."

"Do you think you'll get cabin fever?" I ask. "Especially with winter coming up?"

"I guess we'll find out. But I don't think so."

I wonder how much of that has to do with Bradley. But I don't ask her. Not right now. That's a conversation for another day.

At the sound of a vehicle coming up the driveway, we both look at each other.

"Wyatt's back," I say. And my heart does funny little flip.

"Go let him in," Audrey says.

"Right. He doesn't have a key."

"Let me know if we need to fix that," Audrey says as I head toward the door.

I give her a look over my shoulder. But she knows.

She knows I like Wyatt.

I'm not sure I want her to know just how much.

Maybe I should start admitting that how much I like him to myself first.

FORTY-ONE

Wyatt

I PULL up to Audrey's house and park.

Before getting out, I grab the flower on the passenger seat. It wasn't a rose this time. Just a bright, happy yellow wildflower.

I hadn't bothered to go by the General Store and I hadn't wanted to stop by John's backyard, so I just stopped and cut a flower in a meadow on the side of the road. It was on our property, so no harm done.

Lilah appears at the front door.

I could get used to coming home and having my woman waiting for me.

"Hi," I say, leaning forward to give her a kiss.

"Hi." She smiles.

"I brought you something." I hold up the yellow wild-flower. "Nothing fancy. Just a wildflower."

Her face lights up. "It's a daisy." She twirls it in her hand and gives me a smug look. "Some people call it the old man of the mountain."

"That's odd."

"I can tell you more, but I'm not sure you want to know."

We step inside and lock the door behind us. Bradley is getting ready to go back up the ladder to continue installing the window shades. Biscuit is settling down in front of the fire-place. I assume they just got back inside from Biscuit's walk.

"Now you have to tell me."

"Well," she says, running a hand over the petals of the flower. "If I'm right. It takes 12-20 years to grow before it flowers just one time. Then it dies."

I feel the blood drain from my face. "Twenty years? That flower is twenty years old?"

"Maybe. I'll put it in some water."

"You're right. I didn't want to know that. I thought it was just a wildflower."

"It is. Now we get to enjoy it." She kisses me on the cheek before she places it in a vase full of water. "Thank you."

"No excitement while I was gone?" I ask, not wanting to

think about how I'd just randomly picked a flower that took twenty-years to bloom.

"No. It's been calm. Peaceful."

Blackie hops up onto the island and meows at her.

She opens a can of food and puts some on a plate for him.

I grab a bottle of water and go to the dining table where someone has been working.

Since Audrey and Bradley are doing their thing, I assume that person to be Lilah.

"What are you working on?" I ask, sitting down in front of the laptop computer where the screensaver is blocking her screen.

"Nothing," she says quickly. Too quickly.

While she pours some dry cat food in a bowl, I tap the keyboard, but the screen is locked.

Not my business anyway.

I pick up the top card from one of several stacks of index cards on the table.

"What's a pasque flower?" I ask.

She looks at me sideways, obviously debating on how to answer. "It's a member of the buttercup family. Also called the April Fool flower. It blooms in April, then usually gets snowed over and disappears."

"These flowers live a harsh and dangerous life."

I pick up another card. It has another flower name written on it.

With the card in my hand, I lean back in the chair and grin like a loon at her.

"You're studying flowers," I say.

She comes to stand next to me. Closes the lid on her computer.

"I was just playing around. I wanted to see just how much work you had ahead of you. In case you decided you wanted to go forward with your flower shop idea."

I pull her into my lap."

She laughs nervously, glancing toward her sister. I kiss her on the cheek.

"I see," I say. "Looks like you put in a lot of work while you were playing around."

"It kept me looking busy so I didn't have to help hang window shades."

"Smart girl. Want to help me cook pasta for dinner?"

"Okay. Sure."

And then she and I have some things to talk about. She's gone and done it now. I was on the fence about the whole flower shop thing. A lot of it hinged on her. I wasn't about to try doing it on my own. But with both of us working on it... that gives it a whole new life.

And, quite honestly, it gives me a whole new perspective on a lot of things, not the least of which is Lilah.

FORTY-TWO

Lilah

"Want to hear something funny about Bradley?" Wyatt asks as I boil water for the pasta.

"Always."

"He was convinced that if he could teach me and Caleb how to make spaghetti, we could use it to impress girls."

"That's kind of sweet."

"Yes, but..." Wyatt lowers his voice. "Our grandmother in Boston taught him how to cook it."

"What's wrong with that?" I turn on the heat under the pot of water.

"No spices. None. Blandest spaghetti ever."

The sound of Bradley's drill drowns out his words.

"I haven't heard Audrey complaining."

"She wouldn't. Besides, she doesn't count."

"She counts. She's from Houston. She knows good food."

"Don't doubt that. Still. She would like it because he made it. Anyway. I stopped by my cabin and cut some fresh basil and oregano. Makes all the difference."

"I'm looking forward to it. Are you making homemade sauce?" And the man grows his own herbs. This is getting more interesting by the moment.

"Of course. Even though I have to admit, when it's just me, I sometimes open a jar. Spice it up."

"Nothing wrong with opening a jar."

"I know, right? We'll do that next time."

"Okay." Every time he says something like *next time*, I get all giddy inside. Saying *next time* implies that we'll be doing something again. In the future.

I decide to push it a little. Just to see what he says.

"Maybe after all this threatening business is over with."

"Yes. After things settle down."

I go into the pantry and pull out a couple of cans of black olives.

"You put black olives in your spaghetti?" he asks.

"Of course. Don't you?"

"I guess I do now."

"It's not good without black olives," I say, finding a can opener in one of the drawers.

"Let me get that," he says, taking the can opener. "Do you chop these up or put them in whole?"

"I chop them."

"Okay." He gets out a cutting board and knife.

"So did it work?" I ask.

"Did what work?"

"Did it impress girls?"

"I don't know. I never tried it."

I stop and look at him. "I guess I'll let you know."

"I'm not sure this one counts. You added black olives to my recipe."

"Only to make it better," I say. "I think it counts."

"If you want it to count, it counts."

I smile. "You use fresh tomatoes?"

"Of course."

I stand with hands on the counter behind me, watching him slice tomatoes on a cutting board. He's handy. He can wield a kitchen knife as deftly as he can wield an axe. So many layers to this man. And I'd like to learn them all.

It wasn't a rose this time. Just a bright, happy yellow wildflower. But Wyatt had brought me a flower. And that means something in anyone's book.

It definitely means something in my book. It tells me I might not be alone in this growing affection that I'm feeling.

FORTY-THREE

Wyatt

LILAH TEARS LETTUCE for a salad as I chop tomatoes and black olives for the spaghetti sauce.

I smile when I catch her watching me and she looks away quickly.

She's complicated, this Lilah.

She can put together the pieces of a complicated closet without a hitch. She can paint a scene that makes a man think he's looking out a window. And she isn't the least bit afraid to learn anything.

She went from knowing nothing about alcohol to being

a bartender. And now she's going from knowing nothing about flowers to learning them.

She's impressive enough to take a man's breath away.

"So if Bradley didn't teach you how to make spaghetti sauce, how did you learn?" she asks.

"I took what he showed me and figured out how to make it better."

"So you're basically self-taught."

"I guess you could say that." I pick up a wooden spoon and stir the tomato sauce in the pot.

"We're a lot alike in that," she says. "Are you not close to your other brother?"

"Caleb? Yeah. We're all close. Caleb is just different. He travels a lot."

"I thought he took care of the family business."

"He does. But has other ventures, too. He likes Whiskey Springs, but I think it would stifle him if he had to stay here all the time."

"He sounds like our sister, Brianna. She can't stand to stay in the same job for too long. More than a couple of weeks and she gets antsy."

"How can she change jobs every ten weeks?" He looks at me in confusion. "Does she work for herself?"

"No. But she should. She does temp work for different agencies."

"Oh. What was it like growing up with two sisters?"

"We were two years apart, so we didn't have to compete. We had completely different social groups."

"Yeah. You don't really get that privilege in a small town. Everybody knows everybody and we were all right there together even though we were in different grades."

"I can't imagine. Can I have one of your tomatoes for the salad?"

"Sure. Catch." He holds up the tomato and makes as though he's going to toss it to me like a football.

"Oh no." She holds up a hand. "You do not want to do that. I'm not good at sports." She glances over her shoulder. "Audrey will kill me for making a mess."

I step over and gently place the tomato in her hand. "Have I stumbled upon something you're not good at?"

"Maybe," she says, setting the tomato on her own cutting board.

"Hard to believe. So if you didn't play sports growing up, what did you do?"

"Guess. What do you think I did?"

"Hmm." I put a hand on my chin and study her. "Something in the spotlight, but not too much. Not a cheerleader."

She watches me with amusement.

"Majorette," I say. "That's definitely it."

"Close enough. I actually did a couple of majorette parade things, but color guard."

"Color guard? The flags?"

"That's right. I can twirl a flag like you wouldn't believe."

"It suits you," I say. "With the colors and the movement."

"You think so?"

"Yes. You're not flashy. You're artistic. And you're too pretty to be hidden in a band uniform."

"Audrey was in the band. Don't tell her that."

"I won't. So your other sister, let me guess. Cheerleader."

"How did you know that?" she asks, looking truly baffled. "You haven't even met Brianna."

"Just from what you've said about her."

"Very little," she says, her brows knitted.

"Would you believe I played football?" I ask to distract her away from my uncanny ability to figure out what people are good at.

Now she's studying me. "You don't look like a football player."

I put a hand over my heart. "Now you've wounded me."

She laughs. "I meant that as a compliment."

"You do know I'm a guy, right?"

"I am well aware. Quarterback?"

"What gave me away?"

She shrugs prettily. "I can't tell you that."

Lilah Sinclair has tested my resolve since the moment I first saw her.

"I—"

Bradley walks by, interrupting whatever I was going to say. "We're taking Biscuit out for a quick walk," he says.

I notice that Biscuit is on his leash.

"No hurry," I say. "It'll be awhile before dinner is ready."

After Audrey and Bradley are outside, I pick Lilah up by the waist and set her on the island counter.

"You're driving me crazy with wanting to kiss you," I say just before I place my lips on hers.

We kiss until we hear my brother and Audrey coming back to the door, talking to each other. I slide her off the counter and we both, for all appearances, go back to what we were doing.

Lilah has somehow placed a spell on me.

I simply can't get enough of her.

FORTY-FOUR

Lilah

"It's a pretty night," Bradley says after dinner, while we're still sitting at the table.

"It doesn't seem as cold tonight," I say.

"Want to go outside? Sit on the porch swing?"

"Is that allowed?" I glance over at my sister.

"We agreed that no one would be left alone," she says. "We didn't agree that we'd be prisoners in our own home."

"Good point," I murmur. "Okay. Sure."

"You two cooked," Bradley says. "We'll clean up. Go on."

We put on our jackets and step outside, the motion light

clicking on. It might not be as cold, but it's definitely cooler than what I'm used to back in Houston.

We sit on the swing and wait for the motion light to cycle off.

"It feels like we're doing something dangerous," I say.

"We probably are."

I look over sharply at Wyatt, but he doesn't look the least bit concerned. He looks relaxed.

I pull my jacket tighter.

"Cold?" he asks.

"A little."

He scoots closer and puts an arm around me. We sit still. Waiting for the light to click off.

I can't help wondering if we're being watched. Wondering when the next note will appear somewhere.

The light clicks off, leaving us in darkness. It takes a minute for my eyes to adjust.

"It's peaceful out here," Wyatt says.

"I guess so."

"Close your eyes. Listen."

I close my eyes. I hear the river rumbling in the distance. The eerie sound of a wolf somewhere hopefully far away. The television playing inside the house.

"It is peaceful," I admit. "I just hate that someone is trying to take that away."

"We won't let him." He kisses the top of my head. "I wanted to talk to you."

"What every girl wants to hear."

"Not like that. This is a good thing. Hopefully. I hope you'll like it."

I can't help holding my breath. He'd said he would stay here until the stalker is stopped. I don't want him to move out. His being here is one of the things I like most about living here.

"I've been thinking about the flower shop."

"Oh." I should have known that was what he wanted to talk about. "What are you thinking?"

"Do you think it's something you'd like to take on? With me?"

"I can help you get started. I've already started learning basic flower things. I know there's a ton more. Soil. And light. And how to water. And what's popular."

"I know. But not like that. I mean a partnership. We go in 50-50."

Again. Not what I was expecting.

"Why?" I ask.

He doesn't answer right away.

The wind rustles in the aspen leaves and an owl makes his presence known with loud hoots.

"I have several reasons," he says.

"Like?"

"First of all, I think you'd be good at it. I've got the capital and you've got the brains."

This comes as a surprise to me. I know that his family

owns their own business but that doesn't always mean they have working capital for other things."

"I don't have any money," I say.

"Like I said. I've got the money." He takes my hand and laces his fingers with mine.

"Who would run it?" I ask.

"We would."

"You've got your family business."

"I can do both. Actually my part is pretty small."

"Where?" I ask.

"That's the part I don't have figured out yet. There's a vacant building in town. We could check that out. See if there's room behind that building for a greenhouse."

"What's the other option?"

"We'd have to talk to Audrey, but we could put it here."

"Here? Where?"

"I'm thinking somewhere walking distance of the house."

"Do you think people would drive up here? For flowers?"

"I do think so. It's not that far. But. We'd build a website so most of our work would be deliveries."

"Or special events. Like weddings."

"Yes. And the lodge is always having some kind of function. We could market to them. Save them from having to drive in to Boulder to pick up flowers. They might even use more flowers if they have somewhere local to shop."

"You've really thought a lot about this."

"I guess I have."

"I thought the idea just occurred to you. What? A couple of days ago?"

He looks into my eyes. "When I figure something out, I don't like to waste time."

I wonder if we're still talking about the flower shop now.

"I was hoping to get some painting done," I say, but I have a sinking feeling that my painting just took another back seat.

"You can do both. I'm not asking you to give up anything." He looks away. "Maybe it was a bad idea."

"No," I say. "It's a good idea. And if we can do it here, it's an even better idea."

"Think about it then," he says. "Take your time. There's no need to rush into it."

"Maybe we should talk to Audrey and Bradley. See what they think."

"I think we should. You're freezing. Let's go inside."

"Good idea." I'm up before he is and the motion light clicks on.

He's right behind me and seconds later, we're back inside the warm house.

I'm not sure if I'll ever get used to the cold weather. Not completely anyway.

But I'm pretty sure I'm getting used to being with Wyatt.

Now I have to figure out if I can take a commitment as

big as helping him open a flower shop when I could be summoned back to Houston at any time.

I already know I can't put him off for two years while I wait to see what my future holds.

Wyatt isn't the kind of man who waits for anything.

FORTY-FIVE

Wyatt

I GET up before daylight the next morning to find my brother already up making coffee.

"Morning," I say. "What are you doing up so early?"

"Biscuit needed a walk." He hands me a mug of coffee, then makes another one for himself.

"Good reason. I guess."

"He thought so."

"Did we make it through the night without incident?"

"It appears so."

"Any new ideas on how to put a stop to it?"

"We can do the stakeout again."

"We can." Something occurs to me. "Trent."

"What?"

I've got a friend in Boulder. His name is Trent. I can drive down. See what he thinks about the videos. See if we're missing something."

"Okay." He sits at the table. Notices Lilah's index cards. "What's all this?"

"Just a project Lilah and I are playing around with."

"Flowers?"

"There's no flower shop in town."

"Needs to be."

"I know." Somehow hearing my brother validate my crazy idea makes me feel less crazy.

"Thinking you'd put one in town?"

"Maybe. Or up here."

"Hmm. Might be a challenge in winter. Getting deliveries into town."

"At least we'd be here when the weather gets bad. Instead of being obligated to drive in to town. And to keep an eye on things."

"Yeah. I guess you could use one of those drones to deliver them down to town."

"A drone. Sometimes you're brilliant."

"I was just kidding."

"Right. But it's not a bad idea. I don't know how it would work. But it has possibilities."

"You think on it, Bro. Let me know when you're going in to Boulder to talk to your friend."

"I will," I say.

"The flower shop's a good idea. Especially with Lilah helping. Audrey says Lilah's memory is crazy good."

"We'd be partners," I say.

"I would expect so. That's how it usually works when you're married."

I don't say anything.

"Getting cold feet yet?" he asks, taunting me.

"Not going to. Wondering why you're dragging yours though."

"I don't move as fast as you do."

"You like her, right?"

"You know I like her."

"Okay. You'll figure it out."

We both sit quietly sipping our coffee.

"Is it weird us living here together?" I ask.

"Not to me. Now if Caleb lived here, too, that would be weird."

I laugh. "I have to agree with you."

"I'm going to take Audrey coffee in bed."

"That's a sweet gesture."

"I'm a sweet guy."

"Who needs to figure out his next move."

"My next move is taking Audrey coffee." He gets up and starts making coffee.

"Good God, Man. You move slow."

"Shut up."

I grin. Things are going well. It's early, but I go ahead

and text my friend. See if he has time to look at the videos on my phone apps today.

He answers immediately.

"Don't have to go in to Boulder. He can log in and look at our camera footage remotely."

"It's the world we live in, Bro."

"Yes. It is."

"I'll see you in a bit," he says. "Try to stay out of trouble."

Laughing, I take a sip of coffee, then give Trent a call so he can help me figure out how to get him into our cameras.

I'm good at installing them in the right places, but I'm missing something. If anybody can figure it out, it's my buddy Trent.

FORTY-SIX

Lilah

WHEN I GET DOWNSTAIRS, the next morning, Wyatt is sitting at the kitchen table, with the iPad we use for the security cameras.

He's talking to someone on the phone.

"Good morning," he says, looking up.

"Good morning."

"Call me if you figure anything out. I've got to go make breakfast for my girl."

I stop, almost to the kitchen. Blackie winds around my legs and I absently pick him up, running my hands through his fur.

For just a second, there's a hitch in my thoughts. I wonder who he's going to make breakfast for.

Then I realize he's talking about me.

"Want a bacon, egg, and cheese sandwich?" he asks.

"Sure." *My girl.* He told someone on the phone that I'm his girl.

While he's pulling everything out of the refrigerator, eggs, bacon, cheese, I fill Blackie's food bowl.

"Everything okay?" I ask, my hands shaking a little bit.

"Yes." He cracks an egg into a bowl and looks at me. "I made an executive decision. I hope you're okay with it."

"Me?"

"Yeah. Maybe I should have asked Audrey. Either way." He goes back to the refrigerator for milk.

"What kind of decision?" I slide onto a barstool.

"I have a buddy in Boulder. We went to college together. He's a genius when it comes to technology."

"Okay."

"I gave him the password to your security cameras."

"Why?" I ask slowly, trying to figure out what he's thinking.

He whips the egg and milk together in the bowl while he watches me.

"Because I'm missing something and I can't figure out what it is. If anybody can figure it out, Trent can."

"Okay," I say with a shrug.

He smiles.

"I trust you Wyatt. I don't think you'd do anything to put us in any kind of danger."

He dumps the egg mixture in the skillet. Adds some spices. "I'm doing everything I can to keep you safe."

"I know. So what did he say?"

"He's going to need a little time to take a look. He's got to work today, so it might be this weekend before he gets to it. But knowing Trent, he won't be able to resist working on it."

"You told him what's going on?"

"More or less. That someone is getting past the cameras." He puts bacon in a skillet on the stove.

"It's really strange, isn't it?" Then. "Where is everybody?"

"They're upstairs planning Bradley's closet."

"I see."

"Yeah. I don't think it's really for Bradley though."

"How long do you think they'll pretend that it's his room?"

Wyatt laughs. "My brother is a little slow sometimes."

"He's not slow," I say. "He's being respectful of Audrey's newly widowed state."

"Right. You're right." He turns the bacon. Stirs the eggs.

Resting my chin on my hands, I think back over my conversation with Audrey. About how she needs to tell the guys about her inheritance. It's relevant. It would let them know just how high the stakes are. A motivation for someone wanting us out of the house.

Maybe I need to be open with Wyatt. Maybe I need to tell him why I shouldn't get too close to him.

"I need to tell you something," I say.

"Okay," he says, buttering four pieces of bread.

But I don't want to tell him. I REALLY don't want to tell him. I don't want him to think less of me. I don't want him to know that I'm anything other than who he thinks I am.

Not someone who could be going to jail.

He deserves better than that.

"What do you want to tell me?"

"The reason I'm here," I say. I'll start off slow. Start with the easy stuff, then work up to the harder stuff.

He puts a sandwich on a plate. Slides it over to me.

Then comes around with his own.

"Coffee," he says. "I forgot your coffee."

"No." I put a hand on his arm. "I'll get some orange juice, then drink coffee after I eat."

"I'll get it." He's up, getting me a glass of orange juice.

"Be careful," I say. "I could get used to this."

"That's my plan."

I smile, but on the inside, I'm groaning. I can't do it. I can't tell him. Not right now.

Maybe I'll tell him later.

I love the way he looks at me. I don't want to do anything to jeopardize that.

Not yet.

I can't let him think I'm some kind of person who could

go to jail. Even if it wasn't really my fault. Even if I was provoked.

The conversation shifts back to Audrey and Bradley and my statement about telling him why I'm here falls aside, lost in the air waves.

I left it drift away. Another day.

I'll bring it up again another time.

Maybe after this whole stalking thing is sorted out. Right now there's just too much going on to complicate things.

Guys don't like things that are too complicated and I don't want to run him off.

I want to keep him.

"This is good," I say. "Why do guys always know how to make eggs."

"Didn't you know? They teach that in *How to Treat a Girl Right 101.*" He says it with such a straight face, a laugh bubbles up before I can stop it.

FORTY-SEVEN

Wyatt

While Lilah researches flowers and makes index cards, stopping to go back over them now and them. Telling me little things about them, I research greenhouses.

"It's like learning a foreign language," she says. "Just linking things together. Like this daisy. It's called the old man of the mountain because the petals look sort of like beards. So I picture a daisy with a beard."

I glance at the yellow daisy on the table in front of us. "I'll never look at daisies the same way again."

"Don't think about it like that. Just be silly with it. The sillier the better."

When the doorbell rings, Lilah nearly jumps out of her skin and I'm not much better off.

Before we even have time to react, Audrey and Bradley are coming down the stairs.

"Who's at the door?" Audrey asks.

"I don't know," Lilah say.

"I'll get it," Bradley says.

"I don't think our guy is going to come up and ring the doorbell," Wyatt says.

"I agree," Lilah says. "That's a good point."

Bradley opens the door and Claire is standing there.

"Claire. Come in."

Claire steps inside. "I hope I'm not intruding. It smells so good in here. Like a coffee shop." She glances over at us, wringing her hands nervously. "The sheriff told me you were keeping Blackie and I—"

Blackie jumps down from where he'd been sitting on the sectional and runs over to her.

"There you are," she say, scooping him up.

I can hear him purring all the way over here.

"She's going to take him home," Lilah says. "I'll gather up his things." She proceeds to start gathering up all Blackie's food and putting it in a tote bag.

"How are you, Claire?" Audrey asks, putting a hand on Claire's arm. "You've been through so much."

"You probably don't want me here," Claire says. "I hope you believe me when I say I'm not the one who left notes at your door."

"I know that," Audrey says. "I'm so sorry you got accused like that."

"Well. It's water under the bridge now," Claire says with a nervous smile.

"Are you okay?" I ask Lilah, speaking softly so only she can hear.

"Yes. I just got kind of attached to Blackie. I get attached to animals."

"It's okay. You can visit him."

"You're right," she says with a forced smile.

"I know. It's not the same. Let me take this bag." I take the bag of food and carry it toward the door.

"Come on in," Audrey tells Claire. "Have a seat."

"I don't want to impose."

"Please. I want to talk to you anyway."

"I have his food," I say. "I'll take it out when you're ready." I put the bag of food by the door and go back to Lilah.

After Claire sits down on the sectional, Lilah sits down next to her and I sit next to Lilah.

Audrey introduces them.

Blackie leaves Claire's arms and walks over to sit in Lilah's lap.

Lilah's face lights up and she hugs him.

"Oh. He likes you," Claire says. "I'm so glad he made a friend."

"We're best of friends," Lilah says.

"So. Claire," Audrey says. "I'm hoping you're planning

to come back to work for us."

"Oh," Claire says nervously. "I don't know if Mr. Fields will allow it."

"Give me his number," Audrey says. "I'll call him and make a personal request."

"I'll do that," Claire says. "If you're sure you don't mind."

"It's settled then," Audrey says. "Be thinking about when you can come back."

"I can come back whenever you need me," Claire says. "Do you need me to do something right now?"

"No. Of course not. You've got to get home and get settled back in. Come back in a day or two."

"I'll be here tomorrow," Claire says.

"We'll be pleased to see you," Bradley says.

We all look at him.

"What? None of us have exactly taken the time to do any cleaning."

"You've got us spoiled, Claire," Audrey clarifies, elbowing Bradley. "It's a good thing."

Lilah, her eyes wide and moist, her face pressed against Blackie's fur, looks over at Claire. "Do you think maybe you could bring Blackie when you come to work?"

"Of course I can," Claire says, smiling. "I think he would like that. He hates being left alone all day."

"So would I," Lilah says, smiling over at me.

"I'll get out some of the food. Just enough so you don't have to pack it back over here."

"Wyatt's a good man," Claire says, looking at Lilah. "You're a lucky girl."

Lilah looks at Claire in confusion.

"Actually I'm the lucky one," I say, bending over to give Lilah a kiss on the cheek.

Claire clasps her hands together beneath her chin. "This is so romantic. I'm so happy for you all and I'm so lucky to work here."

I go over to take a few cans of cat food out of the tote bag and the almost empty bag of dry cat food.

I am definitely the lucky one. No doubt about that.

CHAPTER
FORTY-EIGHT

Lilah

The house seems empty after Claire leaves, taking Blackie with her.

I sit at the table, researching roses, but my heart isn't in it.

"It'll be okay," Wyatt says. "She'll be back and she'll bring Blackie with her."

"I know. I just got used to Blackie sleeping on my bed."

He reaches over and puts a hand over mine. "Let's go into town tonight. Have pizza."

"Leave Audrey and Bradley?" I ask.

"They can come if they want to, but I don't think they'll have any complaints about being left alone."

"Okay," I say with a little smile. "You're right."

His phone rings. "It's Trent," he says.

"About the cameras."

"Yeah. He must have something. I'll put him on speaker."

"Hey Trent. You're on speaker with Lilah here."

"Hi Lilah," Trent says.

"Hi Trent."

"You must have something," Trent says.

"I do have something and it's not what I expected."

"That can't be good."

"Well. It's something I personally haven't seen before. I had to consult with my boss."

"What was it?" I scoot my chair closer to Bradley's, keeping my gaze locked on his.

"Well. Let me see if I can explain it."

"We're listening."

He takes a breath. "Take me off speaker."

"Okay." Wyatt takes him off speaks and holds the phone up between us so can both hear.

"You've got some time gaps."

Wyatt looks at me. "Gaps? When someone came in and took the dog."

"Yes. My best guess. Someone put a scrambler on your Internet."

"Wait. What?" Wyatt holds the phone out, staring at it.

"It's quite sophisticated," Trent explains. "They just flip a switch and your Internet goes off. Everything stops recording. Then it comes back on and you don't even know it happens."

I feel heat rising in my cheeks. It's the same feeling I had just before I tossed the glass of wine in Bernice's face. Only this time there's no target. No one to throw anything at.

"How?" Wyatt asks. "How would he get past the cameras to begin with?"

"I'm thinking he's doing it remotely. Probably has the scrambler installed somewhere in the house. Just flips a switch and walks in the door."

"He doesn't have the code," I murmur, knowing it's a detail that doesn't matter.

"She means the door lock code to get inside the house."

"Digitized codes are so easy to override. If you're going to get anything other than an actual key, get the fingerprint ones."

"Now he tells us," I say.

"So, Trent," Wyatt says. "Are you telling us that someone pla—"

"Wyatt," Trent says. "Assume your walls have ears."

"Okay. Just walked right in without being detected?"

"Yes. That's what it looks like."

"Wait." I press my fingers against my brow. "But we're here. It's not like we're not home when he does it. We're right here."

"Any ideas, Trent?" Wyatt asks.

"Again. This is my best guess. Not being there to see for myself. But he probably has cameras of his own."

A chill runs down my spine. "What do you mean?"

"Cameras are so small now. They used to call them nanny cams, but now they're everywhere. He could have cameras anywhere. A power outlet. A digital clock. A smoke detector. Even an air vent."

With goosebumps on my skin, I look at Wyatt. "How do we find out?"

"You need someone with the right equipment to find out."

"When can you be here?" Wyatt asks.

FORTY-NINE

Wyatt

A FEW HOURS LATER, we sit in the pizza shop.

Lilah next to me. Audrey and Bradley across from us.

Blue checkered faux leather table cloths on the tables. Worn blue leather booths. Eighties music streaming from a jukebox in the background.

It's crowded as always. Touted as the best pizza in Whiskey Springs. Probably goes along with being the only pizza in Whiskey Springs. Still. It's good. Better than anything I ever found in Boulder as a college student dedicated to finding the best pizza, even if I did commute.

Commuting didn't mean I didn't stay over at friend's houses on a frequent basis.

Biscuit, on his leash, sits beneath the booth.

We get a few looks about that, but when the owner says it's okay, it's okay.

There's no way we were going to leave the dog alone at home or even in the truck.

"So please explain," Bradley says, "why we couldn't talk at the house or in the truck."

I lean forward, my elbows on the table. A quick glance at Lilah's drawn face.

"I talked to my friend Trent in Boulder."

"Right," Bradley says. "You told me about him."

"I gave him access to our cameras." I glance at Audrey. "Apologies for not asking your permission first."

Audrey shakes her head. "No need. We're all in this together."

I take Lilah's hand and lace my fingers with hers.

"He thinks he has an explanation for what's been happening. Not all of it, but an explanation for how someone got in the house without us knowing it and walking out with Biscuit."

"How?" Bradley asks. "We were all home."

"We were. But we were upstairs."

"He probably has cameras on us," Lilah says.

Audrey looks at her sister. "Cameras in our house? Watching us?"

"Yes. Tiny spy cameras."

"That would explain a lot," Audrey says, rubbing her arms. Bradley puts an arm around her and pulls her close.

"So he's spying on us. But that doesn't explain how we couldn't see him on our cameras."

"Trent thinks he has a scrambler somewhere in the house. He can turn it on and off remotely."

"A scrambler," Bradley says. "Son of a bitch."

"What does that mean?" Audrey asks.

"It means he can turn off our Internet anytime he wants to," Lilah says with a hint of venom in her voice.

I squeeze her hand. "It leaves time gaps on our cameras. Time gaps we don't notice."

"Why?" Bradley asks. "Why go to so much trouble?"

"He wants us out," Audrey says flatly.

"I don't understand." Bradley says with heat. "Why not just offer to buy the house? Or something. Anything. Anything that's legal. Not all this stealing the dog crap and sneaking around leaving notes at the door."

Lilah and Audrey exchange a look. Lilah nods, but Audrey shakes her head.

"They need to understand," Lilah says to her.

"It won't matter," Audrey says.

"It could matter," Lilah insists. "It matters."

"What are you not telling us?" Bradley asks.

Audrey sighs. "I don't see why it matters."

"How can it not matter?" Lilah asks. "Tell them. Just tell them and you'll see."

"Audrey," Bradley says, kissing her on the top of her

head. "If you know something that could help us solve this thing, maybe you should consider telling us."

Lilah crosses her arms. "It matters."

Our conversation comes to a halt as the server comes and takes our order. Takes her time pouring water into our glasses.

"Can I get you anything else while you wait?" she asks. "Some breadsticks?"

"We're good, Maribelle. Thank you," Bradley says.

"You know her?" I ask, looking over my shoulder at the girl, not more than eighteen, walking away.

"He knows everybody," Audrey says.

"I know. It's just... You should really run for sheriff."

"Audrey gets money for living in the house," Lilah blurts.

We all look at her.

"How much money?" Bradley asks, looking at Audrey.

"A lot," Lilah answers for her.

"No," Audrey says. "I told you not to tell anyone. I need to get out. Bradley. Please let me out of the booth."

Bradley stands up while Audrey takes off toward the bathroom.

"I should go," Lilah says.

"Before you go," I say. "Tell us how much money we're talking."

"She doesn't want me to tell anyone. It's her inheritance. I overstepped."

"Wait," I say. "You're right. This could mean something.

This could mean whoever is doing this wants the inheritance money for himself."

"Exactly," Lilah says.

"How much money?" Bradley asks, keeping one eye on the bathroom door, watching out for Audrey.

"It's an annual stipend for as long as she lives in the house."

Bradley nods his head. "She told me she has to live in the house. Didn't really say why."

"Her husband left everything else to a child he has with someone else," Lilah says. "She didn't know about this child until after Thomas's crash. She lost everything. Even the house they lived in. This house is the only inheritance she got."

"How much money?" Bradley asks again.

"It's not our business," I say. "What matters is someone wants her out. Someone who thinks they have a claim to the house."

"It would have to be someone related to Albright in some way," Bradley says.

"Seemingly." I agree. "Why else would they think they have a claim?"

"Could be related to Thomas. Could be the child."

"Can't be," Lilah says. "The child is maybe three-years-old. At most. There's no way the mother could get up here to do this."

"Someone related somehow," I say.

"I need to go check on Audrey," Lilah says.

I stand up to let her out of the booth.

"She's coming back," Bradley says with obvious relief.

I figure there's going to be hell to pay, but Audrey climbs back in the booth, her expression blank. Her eyes are a little red, but that's it.

She looks from Lilah to me to Bradley.

"A million dollars," she says, keeping her gaze on Bradley's. "A million dollars goes into my account every year."

No one says anything.

Lilah was right. Lilah was so right. This changes everything.

A whole lot of people would go to a whole lot of trouble to get their hands on a million dollars every year. It would have nothing to do with living in the house. Nothing at all. Most people would live in a hovel for a million dollars a year.

The stakes just got a whole lot higher.

Along with the stakes getting higher, so does my resolve to keep Lilah safe.

No matter what it takes.

FIFTY

Lilah

"Thank you," I mouth to my sister.

"So now you know," Audrey says, keeping her gaze down.

"Thank you for telling us," Bradley says.

"It doesn't change how I feel about the house." Audrey looks back up at Bradley, searching his eyes. "Or you."

"I know," he says. "Why would you even think that?"

"Because..." Audrey says. "I just don't want you to think the worst of me.

Hearing Audrey say that out loud, I realize that particular fear must be something that runs in my family. It's how I feel about telling Wyatt that I could be arrested for throwing wine in Bernice's face.

I feel ill just thinking about it.

Maybe it's not that big a deal. The guys are looking at Audrey like they don't understand how she could be worried about them thinking badly about her for this.

But it's nothing she did.

She inherited the money.

I *did* what I did.

It's all on me.

"Lilah," Wyatt asks. "Are you okay?"

"Yes." I force a smile and hope it comes out less wobbly than it feels.

"The pizza's here," he says.

"Okay. I was just lost in thought."

He puts an arm around me. "It's going to be okay. "Whatever it is. We can handle it."

"I know." I catch Audrey looking at me questioningly. I haven't even told her, but she knows something's up. She knows there's something I haven't told her.

"Trent's coming up in the morning," Wyatt tell them as we eat our pizza.

"He's a good guy," Bradley says. "But. We still won't know who's doing it."

"We'll do the stakeout again," Wyatt says. "It didn't work last time, but I think it can."

I listen to them talk while I eat a slice of cheesy pizza.

Things were supposed to be less complicated here than in Houston.

But instead of peacefulness, I get a different kind of trouble.

As we're finishing up, Biscuit comes out from under the table.

"Come on Audrey," Bradley says. "Let's take Biscuit outside."

"I'll take care of the check, then we'll join you outside," Wyatt says. "You think Audrey's going to be okay?" he asks me after they're out of earshot.

"I think so. She'll be cross with me for a while. But I still think you needed to know just how much is at stake."

"I agree. It changes things to my way of thinking."

"Mine too. I don't think it's something we can minimize."

"I never minimized it, but this takes it to a whole other level. Kidnapping Biscuit showed me just what a dangerous game he's playing."

"You're worried that he'll escalate."

"I am," he says, looking into my eyes. "I'm not letting you out of my sight until the son-of-a-bitch is behind bars."

He makes me feel safe. No doubt about that.

But the way he says it, tells me he doesn't tolerate anyone who doesn't uphold the law.

If he knew what I'd done. If he knew that I almost got arrested, he might not look at me the same way.

I can't tell him.

I can't tell him and I can't not tell him.

CHAPTER
FIFTY-ONE

Wyatt

WHILE THE LADIES are downstairs sitting on the sectional with Biscuit, Bradley and I search the house from top to bottom.

It's creepy knowing that someone is probably watching our every move, but I'm with Audrey. We're not giving him the satisfaction of running us out of here.

Some ass hat has decided that he can run us off and claim the house and the stipend for himself.

I need to talk to Audrey. See if she can contact her attorney. Find out what the contingency plan is in the event she no longer lives here.

There has to be one. No one sets something up like that without a contingency plan. What if she hadn't come? What would happen to the house and money then? There has to be a chain for what happens next.

Finished going through the house, Bradley and I join the ladies downstairs.

I lean close to Lilah, recognizing that the walls have eyes and ears, so only she can hear me.

"He probably knew we were watching for him when we were doing our stakeout."

She nods. "That's how he knows when to show up."

"I guess we should wait until after Trent comes and finds the cameras tomorrow."

"And the scrambler."

"Is that a car?" Audrey asks as headlights shine through the window shades.

No one says anything as we listen for the car. Wait for them to realize they took a wrong turn, circle around, and head back the way they came. It happens sometimes. People out sightseeing drive up here, not realizing it's a private driveway.

But the car doesn't circle around and turn around. It stops. Whoever is driving turns off the motor.

Biscuit sits up and a low growl rumbles deep in his throat. Audrey puts a hand on his harness.

"Who would be coming here this time of night?" Lilah asks.

"Stay here," Bradley says as he and I get up to go to the door.

We wait while someone gets out of a car and walks toward front stairs.

"We should have a weapon with us," Bradley says.

"I have one," I say. "It's upstairs."

Bradley scowls at me. "Might be a good time to have it on you."

"Maybe."

We wait until the person knocks.

I hang back out of sight while Bradley opens the door to a man who at first glance is obviously from the city. He's got a slick haircut. Khaki slacks. A white button-down shirt.

I immediately don't like his looks. He looks like one of those guys who thinks he's better than everyone else because he lives in the city.

"You get turned around?" Bradley asks, looking deceptively friendly, but I see the coiled tension running through him just below the surface. He's in protective mode. We both are.

"No," the man says. "I think I'm in the right place. I'm looking for Lilah Sinclair."

I step forward. "What's your business with her?"

"I'm her boyfriend."

CHAPTER
FIFTY-TWO

Lilah

Sitting next to Audrey while the guys answer the door, I barely breathe. I have a really bad feeling about someone driving up this time of night.

Has whoever's been leaving the notes finally just decided to drive up here and threaten us out in the open?

Whatever it is, it can't be good.

But then I hear *his* voice. The man I've tried so hard to forget. The one who caused me so much upheaval in my life.

Trey.

If it weren't for the cloud hanging over my head about

what Beatrice might or might not do, I'd be grateful to him. Grateful for shaking me out of my comfort zone and getting me here.

Hearing his voice, everything inside me just freezes.

I slowly stand up.

"Lilah," Audrey says. I ignore her and take a step forward.

Wyatt turns to face me and I see the disappointment on his face.

I shake my head, but the damage is done.

Bradley is the one who steps in.

"Lilah," he says. "Is this true?"

"No," I say.

"Just let me talk to her," Trey says. "We had a misunderstanding."

I don't move. Instead my gaze strays back to Wyatt. I try to plead with him with my eyes, but he looks away.

Audrey steps in front of me and addresses Trey. "You can talk to her in the kitchen. For ten minutes."

I look at Audrey.

"Brianna told me what he did," she says to me. "If you don't want to talk to him, we'll send him away."

I look from her to Bradley to Wyatt.

Wyatt seems to be the only one who doesn't know the whole story.

He looks confused now. But he hasn't moved. He still stands between me and Trey, even if he is off to the side a bit.

"I'll talk to him," I say.

"Come outside with me," Trey says. "So we can talk in private."

"I'm not going outside with you. I'll talk to you in the kitchen. Or you can go."

Trey hesitates. I mostly hope he just turns around and leaves. I hadn't planned on ever talking to him again.

But instead he steps inside the door.

With a sigh, I turn and go into the kitchen, not caring if he follows or not.

More than halfway hoping he doesn't.

But he does. He follows me.

I notice that he doesn't take off his coat and unlike the cocky expression he'd worn when he first came to the door, he looks a little uncertain now.

He's surrounded by people who are obviously looking out for me and from the looks of Bradley and Wyatt, they are more than ready to toss him out on his ear.

I found Wyatt handsome from the first time I saw him, but now looking at Trey, I realize that one of the things that attracted me to Wyatt is that he doesn't have that polished, metro look that Trey has.

"Why are you here?" I ask.

Trey glances over his shoulder. I just raise an eyebrow at him.

"Beatrice told me what she did."

"Why would you say those things to her?" I ask, my voice low and measured.

I feel calm, not heated like I'd felt when Beatrice had baited me.

It comes as a surprise to me that I'm calm because I don't care what Trey has to say.

"I never said anything but good things about you."

I cross my arms. "Why should I believe you, Trey?"

"Because Beatrice has been chasing me for years. She wants me for herself."

"Then. Go." I wave a hand. "Be with her. There's nothing stopping you or her."

"She's with someone now. But she can't stand the thought of me being with anyone else."

"Why are you here?" I ask again, hearing the weariness in my voice. "How did you even find me?"

"It wasn't easy to find you. I'm here to bring you home."

A movement behind him catches my attention. Bradley is sitting next to Audrey, their heads bent together in a private conversation.

Wyatt is leaning against the back of the sectional, his arms crossed, watching us.

"No." I shake my head. "This is my home now."

"You can't live here," he scoffs. "Why would you even want to?"

"You can go now." I raise my chin.

"Seriously? This is how you're going to play it?" He takes a step toward me. I don't move.

But Wyatt does. He steps forward. "The lady asked you to leave."

"Lady," Trey scoffs again.

"Don't make me ask you twice."

"Fine. Stay here." Trey turns around, but before he does, he has one more comment for me. "You'll be hearing from Beatrice's attorney."

"You don't scare me Trey," I say.

But after Wyatt follows Trey to the door and locks it behind him, I collapse on the nearest chair, my knees feeling too weak to hold me up any longer.

Audrey is there. Handing me a glass of water.

"I'm so proud of you," she says.

I take the glass, my hands trembling.

I glance around, but I don't see Wyatt. Or Bradley.

"Brianna told you what happened."

"She did."

"You didn't tell me."

"She made me promise."

"Yeah. And I made her promise not to tell you." I put the glass to my lips.

"It's one of those things I needed to know about."

I put a hand over my face and close my eyes.

I hear Trey's car motor turn over. Hear his wheels on the gravel driveway. Listen as he drives off.

He's gone. Trey was here, but he's gone now.

"How did find me?" I ask.

"I don't know. But it's going to be okay."

"It's not. Beatrice is going to have me..." I lower my voice. "arrested."

"We won't let that happen."

"You can't stop it." I set the glass on the table. "I'm going to be sick."

"No. You're not. Take a deep breath."

I shake my head. Then I'm up, rushing to the powder room. I make it just in time.

As I kneel in front of the toilet, throwing my guts up, I vaguely realize that someone is holding my hair back.

Someone hands me a wash cloth for my face.

I sit back on my heels and let hot tears run down my cheeks.

"Lilah." It's Wyatt. Wyatt was here. Wyatt is the one holding my hair back. Wyatt is the one holding me close while I cry.

It's Wyatt. Wyatt is the one.

FIFTY-THREE

Wyatt

"I'VE GOT YOU," I say, holding Lilah close, rubbing little circles on her back, soothing her.

"I'm sorry. I'm so sorry he came here."

"You didn't know," I say. "You didn't have anything to do with him coming here."

She lifts her head and I look into her beautiful green eyes, so full of sadness.

"Don't be sad, Sweetness."

"I—"

Audrey and Bradley walk by, interrupting.

"We're going to take Biscuit out for his walk," Bradley says. "Then go upstairs."

"Watch your back," I say.

"We'll be okay. Take care of Lilah."

After the door closes behind them, Lilah searches my eyes.

"I need to tell you something."

"You can tell me anything."

"I need to, but I don't think I can."

"Oh Sweetie." I kiss the top of her head. "There's nothing you can tell me that would change my mind about you."

She takes a deep breath. Lets it out slowly.

"You deserve better," she murmurs.

"Whatever it is, you can tell me when you're ready."

"What if I did something very bad? Something I'm ashamed of?"

"We all do those things."

She shakes her head. "I got fired."

"Okay."

"There was a guest where I worked. It was at a theatre in Houston. A black tie event. I was serving champagne. This woman. Her name is Bernice." She stops. Takes a deep breath.

"The one Trey was talking about?"

"Yes. She... taunted me. Called me names. Told me that Trey said bad things about me."

"What Trey said doesn't mean anything."

"Well. I sort of lost it."

"What did you do?" I ask, curious about why she could possibly have done that she believes is so bad.

"I tossed a glass of wine in her face."

I look at her a moment, trying to picture that scene.

Then I laugh.

"It's not funny." But a smile tugs at the corners of her lips.

I run a hand over my mouth. "It sounds like she got what she deserved."

"I'm not denying that, but I got fired over it."

"I'm actually rather thankful that you did. It got you here."

She looks away. "Did you know that in Texas, tossing wine at someone is considered assault?"

"I can't say I did."

"It's an offense with a two-year statute of limitations."

"I see."

"So. You see my problem."

"Yes. She's going to hold this over your head."

"And Trey can get her to move on it."

"I guess he can try."

Right about now, I'm wondering if I'm too late to catch that son-of-a-bitch and give him a bloody nose. Among other things. Give him a reason to think twice about threatening my girl.

It won't happen again. I can guarantee that much.

FIFTY-FOUR

Lilah

I'M FEELING SICK AGAIN.

I told Wyatt the truth. I told him the worst thing I've ever done and just how much trouble I've gotten myself into.

And right now he won't even look at me.

Audrey and Bradley come back inside and head upstairs. Laughing about something Biscuit did.

If only life were that simple again.

Someone told me once. *Wherever you go, you take yourself with you.*

It couldn't be more true.

I've come up here to a brand new place, a beautiful place, and I brought my old self with me. The old self that did something so embarrassing.

"I understand if you don't want to talk to me anymore," I whisper past the lump in my throat.

He puts a finger gently beneath my chin.

"Bernice or whatever her name was got what she deserved. Don't worry. If anyone tries to take you away from me. For whatever reason. I'll fight them tooth and nail. You don't ever have to worry about that."

"But... Two years. For two years I have to worry about them taking me back to Houston."

"They won't try it but one time."

I look at him. At the fierceness in his expression.

"But Wyatt. You're so law abiding. I don't want to be an embarrassment to you."

"Did I tell you about the time Caleb and I got arrested for climbing the water tower?"

I look at him with disbelief. "You? You got arrested?"

"And then there was the time Bradley and I got in a bar fight. Like I said. We all do things in the heat of the moment. It doesn't define who we are now."

"It really doesn't bother you? What I did?"

"It bothers me that the ass hat would threaten you. Do you love him?"

"No. I don't love him." I shake my head.

"Then the next time he comes around here, he'll leave with a broken nose. He won't try it more than once."

A warmth spreads through me.

I'd feared the worst about telling him. I'd feared that he wouldn't want to talk to me again. But now he's threatening to do bodily harm to Trey if Trey comes back around here.

"Thank you," I say.

He pulls me close against him. "For what?"

"For not judging."

"I'm proud of you, love."

A tear slides down my cheek. I think I've found the person I'm supposed to be with. A person who understands me.

Someone who stands behind me no matter what I might do.

"Now I have something to talk to you about," he says.

"What's that?"

"How would you feel if I moved in with you and Audrey and Bradley?"

"Move in? Like live here?"

"I'm already living here. I'd just bring the rest of my clothes. Make it official. We got an offer on the cabin I'm living in. They want to buy it and fix it up themselves. That leaves me free."

"I think I would like that very much. But. It's Audrey's house. We'd have to ask her."

"I know. But I wanted to ask you first."

"Yes," I say, biting my lip to keep from grinning. "Let's ask her."

The thought of Wyatt not being here is not something I want to think about.

He kisses the tears away from my eyelids. Then presses his lips against mine.

This is where I belong and this is who I belong with.

I feel like a huge weight has been lifted off of me.

Then there's a sound at the front door.

We both freeze.

"Something is out there," I say, my heart pounding dangerously.

"Stay here. I'll go see what it is."

"We should get Bradley."

"I'll be right back."

I pick up my phone and send Audrey a quick text.

Me: Someone is outside.

FIFTY-FIVE

Wyatt

I REACH the front of the house and look out the window, moving the window shade just an inch. There's no time to check the cameras and even if there was, they probably aren't recording at the moment.

I don't see anything. Just the wind tree limbs rustling in the wind.

Nothing unusual.

Then Bradley is behind me.

"Where did you come from?" I whisper.

"We have a network," he says.

"I guess we do," I say, glancing back at where Lilah and

Audrey stand together. They'd left Biscuit upstairs, but I guess no one can get to him up there. Surely not.

"What did you hear?" Bradley asks.

"Not sure."

"There's something out there," he says, looking out the other window.

"Where?"

"On the ground."

"I don't see it."

Bradley unlocks the door and opens it. I follow him outside into the cold air.

The motion light clicks on, lighting our way.

Without hesitation, he walks down the steps to pick up an envelope camouflaged by the rocks and dirt.

So he struck again. But how? No cars. No sign of anyone walking up.

"How did he get past the motion light?" I ask, mostly to myself.

"Maybe the sensitivity is too low."

"I'll change it in the morning."

We go back inside, Bradley handing me the envelope while he locks the door behind us.

"Do the honors," he says.

"Right." I walk over to the fireplace, the others behind me and carefully open the unsealed flap, like all the other notes, and pull out a folded sheet of paper.

I read the note by firelight.

There once were four little Indians. Then there were three. Which one will be first to go?

"That's enough," I say, thrusting the paper in Bradley's hands and striding toward the front door.

I throw open the locks and step outside.

"Come out you coward," I shout toward the trees. "Come out and show yourself. Be a man."

"Wyatt," Bradley says, coming out to stand next to me. "He's long gone."

"How?" I ask. "How is he long gone?"

"I don't know. Let's go check the recordings. Maybe there's something there."

"Right." I follow him back inside, but I already know there won't be anything on the recordings.

The coward has it figured out. He's figured out a way to leave us notes without showing himself. And now he's threatening us.

It has to stop.

Tomorrow Trent will be here and we'll have another piece of the puzzle.

We'll get this figured out and whatever son-of-a-bitch is doing this is going to find himself in jail.

Or the infirmary. Infirmary first, I vow to myself. Then jail.

FIFTY-SIX

Lilah

I WAKE in the middle of the night to find Wyatt sleeping in the chair.

He'd promised me he would stay a little while, then he'd go to his own room.

He can't possibly be comfortable sleeping in that chair like that.

I contemplate waking him up. But if I do, he'll go across the hall to his own room.

I selfishly don't want him to go. Even if he is uncomfortable.

Lying very still and quiet, I listen to the river rushing in the distance. To the sound of a wolf howling in the distance.

No cars. No trains. No distant roar of civilization.

We're isolated out here. I know civilization isn't too far away, but it's too far away for us to hear any signs of it out here.

I haven't even heard a siren since I got here. Not even one.

So now, after tonight, Wyatt knows everything.

He knows that Audrey is getting a million dollars a year to live here in this cabin.

He knows that I could go to jail anytime in the next two years for assaulting someone with a glass of wine. Just the liquid. Not the glass. Unfortunately it doesn't seem to matter that it was just liquid. It still counts as assault.

And yet none of that seems to matter to him. He's still here.

In fact, he wants to move in.

I don't think Audrey will mind. As long as I'm happy, she'll be okay with it.

Wyatt and Bradley are close so there won't be any animosity between the two of them.

Wyatt didn't say how long he'd live here. Just that he needs a place to live at the moment.

It's good enough for now.

I wouldn't blame him for doing the opposite. For getting out of here. There's so much going on. With the threatening notes at the door. With my ex-boyfriend, using that word loosely, showing up unannounced at the door. With me living under the threat of being arrested.

Why would anyone subject themselves to this on purpose?

Me? Sure. Audrey is my sister. It's what family does for each other.

But Bradley and Wyatt aren't family.

I don't really see why either one of them would put themselves through this willingly.

I'm falling hard for Wyatt.

One glance at him and my heart skitters.

His nonjudgmental attitude toward me makes me feel even more for him.

Maybe it's time I stop trying to hold him at bay and start letting him know how I feel about him.

If my past doesn't bother him, maybe it's nothing I should worry about either.

"How long have you been awake?" he asks, startling me.

"Not long," I say. "How did you know?"

"You're being too quiet."

"Are you saying I'm a noisy sleeper?"

"Not at all." He shifts, sitting up in the chair.

"I know I don't snore," I say. "My sisters would have delighted in telling me."

"You don't snore," he says. "But when you're awake, I can't even hear you breathing."

"Well," I say. "You don't snore either."

"That's good to know."

"I'm sure someone would have told you," I say.

"Don't know who it would be. It's been a long time since I slept in the same room with anyone."

I can't help but wonder if I should believe him or if he's just saving my feelings.

"You can't possibly be comfortable in that chair," I say.

"Can't say it's much of a bed. Why aren't you sleeping?"

"I don't know. Edgy, I guess."

"There's a lot going on." He sits up. "Want me to come over there? Keep you company?"

"Why would you do that when you have a comfortable bed?"

"Solidarity?"

"You have a kind heart, Lilah Sinclair. Why don't I come over there and keep you company?"

I pat the bed. "I would have asked, but I didn't want to be too forward."

He laughs and gets into the bed on the other side.

"Come here," he says, pulling me into his arms. "You're safe."

I snuggle into his arms, pressing my cheek against his chest.

"I know."

If I don't know anything else, I know I'm safe with Wyatt.

FIFTY-SEVEN

Wyatt

IT'S MID-MORNING. A bright sunshiny summer day in the mountains.

Trent started in the kitchen. By the time he finishes scanning the downstairs area, he's found four tiny spy cameras. All hidden away in places we would never look. He leaves them in place on the outside chance that we're being watched at the moment.

As far as anyone can tell at an easy glance, everything is normal. He's wearing what looks like an exterminator uniform. Carrying an exterminator canister on his back. But his wand is actually a bug and spy camera detector.

Lilah sits at the kitchen table working on her flash cards. Audrey is sitting on the sectional in front of the fireplace drawing lines on a pad of graph paper. Closet designs.

Bradley is out back chopping some kindling.

"He had this place well covered," Trent says, keeping his voice low. "We'll check upstairs, then we'll check outside and your cars."

"Headed upstairs," I say so the girls can hear.

"Okay," Audrey says easily. "Do what you need to do."

"Yes ma'am," Trent says. "We'll have these pests out of here in no time."

I smile over at Lilah as we start upstairs.

Trent's wand lights up in every bedroom and he takes a photograph of each camera.

The hallway, though, is clear.

"Where do we look for the scrambler?" I ask him.

"Is there an attic?"

"Has to be," I say, looking behind us down the hallway. "Looks like access might be there." I point to a square in the ceiling.

Standing beneath it, Trent points his wand at it. The light goes off. "Found it," he says. "Got a ladder? We can disable it."

"I'll be right back."

Three minutes later I'm back with a ladder.

Trent scurries up like he's done this a thousand times.

"Pretty sophisticated equipment," he says.

"Can you disable it?"

"Yep. He won't even know it."

"Now that's the way to do it."

"You betcha."

Two seconds later, he's coming down the ladder. "You need something else?" I ask.

"No man. It's done. The scrambler is scrambled."

"Impressive."

"Ready to head outside? Check around. See what's he's got in your vehicles."

"Sure."

"I'm going to send you a file with the location and images of all the cams."

"What about our cameras? You think he's watching them?"

"I doubt it. He's got his own system. Doesn't need yours."

"What do you recommend we do now? With this information?"

"I think you'll figure it out."

"What would you do?"

"Business as usual. Watch your own cameras. With his scrambler off, he's going to slip up. Won't be long."

He finds bugs and trackers in our trucks and the girls' cars. A couple of outside cameras.

We walk down to the river and look back up at the house.

"Whatever this guy is up to, he's serious about it." Trent shifts his canister.

"He had the cameras in place before Audrey moved in?"

"I'd say yes. But they're definitely the latest technology."

"I don't know how to thank you."

"As you can see by the disguise, I've done this before. It's not unusual."

"How much do I owe you?"

"You don't owe me anything. Buy me lunch next time you're in Boulder."

"I'll buy you lunch right now."

"And I'd take you up on it, but I've got to get back. Raincheck."

We walk around the house to his truck where he loads up his equipment. He really does legitimately look like an exterminator.

We clasp each other on the shoulder. "Thanks, Man."

"You betcha. Don't forget to let me know when you're in town."

I watch him drive away.

Now. Now we're going to find out who the son-of-a-bitch is that's been leaving these notes and kidnapping our dog.

FIFTY-EIGHT

Lilah

TAKING BISCUIT WITH US, the four of us walk down to the rushing river where Wyatt explains what Trent found.

"He really did have a scrambler in the house," Bradley says, running hand through his hair.

"He really did. And he's watching everything we do. Listening to everything we say."

"What do we do now?" I ask, feeling the need to do something, anything, running through my veins.

"We wait. The next time he comes to the door to leave something, we'll know it. Our cameras will be working."

"It's hard to be patient," I say watching Biscuit sniffing along the edge of the riverbank.

"Lilah has very little patience," Audrey says.

"They're a good match," Bradley says and we all look at him. "What? Wyatt doesn't have a lot of patience either."

I look at Wyatt. "I haven't noticed."

"You will," Bradley says, earning a jab from Audrey's elbow.

"They're like an old married couple," Wyatt says, looking pointedly at his brother. "Thinking they have everything all figured out."

Bradley crosses his arms with a smug expression.

"Wyatt's moving in," I say, deciding this is as good a time as any to let them know.

"I thought he already had," Audrey says.

Wyatt and I exchange a look. "I guess that means she's okay with it," I say.

"I guess so."

"While we're exchanging news," Audrey says, looking up at Bradley.

"I thought we were going to wait," Bradley says.

"You just want to torture your brother," Audrey says.

Bradley winces. "Audrey and I are getting married."

"What?" I look at my sister for confirmation.

"Not yet. We have to go get a ring and we're going to wait. Maybe until... I don't know."

"Maybe the holidays," Bradley says. "When your family can be here."

"Our family can come anytime," I say.

"We want this... mess to be behind us before we start planning," Audrey says.

"I'm so happy for you." I give my sister a hug. "Congratulations to both of you."

Biscuit runs to us from the riverbank, wrapping us all together in a circle with his leash.

Wyatt takes my hand. "I think Biscuit just gave his approval."

"We're all one family now."

Bradley goes about unwrapping us and Biscuit charges back toward the house, tugging him along with him.

"I guess we're going back inside now," Audrey says.

"I guess so," I say, walking along behind them, holding Wyatt's hand. "It's such a beautiful day."

"Do you feel like painting?" he asks.

"I should.... But not really. I don't want to be away from the house right now."

"I'll come out with you."

"I'm kind of on a roll with my flower project right now."

"Did you talk to Audrey about it yet?" Wyatt asks.

Audrey looks back at us over her shoulder. "Audrey says you can put it wherever you want to. It's your house, too."

"Did she just refer to herself in the third person?" Wyatt asks me.

"She means well," I say. "You'll see. She's going to be your sister."

Does that mean Wyatt is going to be my brother?

No. Absolutely not.

I look at him sideways. Not Wyatt. Bradley. Bradley will be my brother.

"You're thinking too much," he says.

I don't even question how he knows that.

It doesn't matter. He's right.

FIFTY-NINE

Wyatt

THE FOUR OF us stay close together the rest of the day.

We work on our own projects. Make homemade pizza. Then settle down on the sectional to watch a movie.

I have the iPad open, watching the cameras. Knowing someone has been randomly turning our cameras off is unsettling. But knowing that won't be happening again is empowering.

Now if someone comes up to the door, we'll know it. We'll see it on the cameras.

Lilah sits snuggled up beside me while the movie plays. It's a comedy, something we all need.

Something on the cameras catches my attention.

Just a bird. Flying the length of the front porch before heading back to the trees.

"See something?" Lilah asks.

"Just a bird," I say. I'd turned the sensors up all the way, but it still wasn't enough for the bird to kick on the exterior motion lights. It's almost like it flies just under the detection range.

A few minutes later, a bird flies around by the back door. Same bird? Surely not. Again. The light doesn't click on.

I decide it's the angle. Maybe I'll add another light to cover any direction someone could use, including coming up from the side of the house.

When the movie's over, Biscuit stands up and barks once.

"I know. I know. You want to go outside," Bradley says, disentangling himself from where he'd been curled up with Audrey. He tells Biscuit. "Go put your leash on. Uncle Wyatt did a good thing getting that leash."

"I have uncanny timing," I say.

Lilah looks at me sideways. "Is that so?"

"Sometimes. Sometimes I do." I kiss her on the cheek.

Audrey goes to the door to keep an eye on her fiancé while he secures the leash on the dog and takes him outside.

"We need to order new door locks," I whisper to Lilah.

"I think Audrey and Bradley are working on that."

"Good."

Bradley comes back inside a few minutes later with dog in tow.

"Anybody recognize this?" he asks.

"What now?" Lilah asks with a groan.

"What is it?" Audrey asks, looking at what is in Bradley's hand, but not touching.

"It's a flower. A daisy. Like the one on the dining room table."

"The one I gave Lilah. Which is still there." I glance in that direction to be sure.

"But this one has a ribbon around it," Audrey says, looking at us.

"I didn't do it," I say, standing up and walking over to get a better look. "Where was it?"

"On the back porch. Just to the left of the door."

"Son-of-a-bitch," I say. "How? How did he—?" I stop myself. I know how. "There's a blind spot someone can use if they come up along the side of the house."

"How did you figure that out?" Bradley asks.

"By accident. Watching a bird's flight path."

"He must have walked up through the woods," Audrey says.

"Is there a note?" Lilah asks.

"No note this time," Bradley says.

"He didn't need one," Lilah says. "His meaning is pretty clear." She looks at me.

"You're right." I know she's right even though I don't

know what that meaning is. Whatever it is, it has some-thing to do with me and her.

Maybe he knows I'm moving in. Maybe he knows I gave her a flower like this. A whole lot of maybes.

Whatever it is, it needs to stop.

"I'm going into town tomorrow," I say. "Get some more motion lights."

"I can order them," Lilah says. "Have them here in a day or two."

"Let's look," I say. Now that I think about it, I don't think anyone needs to be left alone here right now. And I don't think we need to all leave the house either. Not when someone obviously has access.

No one and nothing is safe right now.

Like Lilah, I'm feeling edgy. I'm worried that the son-of-a-bitch is going to do something stupid. Something to try to hurt Lilah.

I think that's what the flower means. I think it, but I don't say anything. Not yet. I'm not an alarmist. But I'm a cautious man and I'm not leaving Lilah alone tonight.

If I'm lucky she won't let me sleep in the chair.

Lilah

"You can sleep in my room, but you can't sleep in the chair."

"Where would you have me sleep?" Wyatt asks.

We're alone in my bedroom with the door locked.

Audrey and Bradley are in Audrey's bedroom with Biscuit, their door locked, too. This is no way to live.

It's a little hard to complain though. Being locked in my bedroom with a handsome man.

Definitely hard to complain and no one will hear me doing it. Not with any seriousness anyway.

"You can sleep in the bed," I say, deciding which pajamas to pull out of my dresser.

"Milady is very kind."

I smile, biting my lip. "As long as your intentions are honorable."

"Nothing else." He sits down to take off his boots. "Do you think we should let our siblings have their wedding first or would you like to have a double wedding?"

I freeze. Slowly closing the drawer, my favorite pajamas in my right hand.

"I think maybe I heard you wrong." Turning around, I lean back against the dresser, my heart pounding frantically in my chest.

He walks toward me, slowly, his gaze intently locked onto mine.

He stops inches in front of me. His expression unreadable. Intense.

"Lilah," he says. "I've known I wanted to marry you since the moment I first saw you across the meadow."

I swallow. My breath coming in little gasps.

I keep one hand on the dresser behind me to keep myself steady.

"What took you so long to tell me?" I ask, my voice barely more than a whisper.

He wraps his arms around me and kisses me until I'm weak in the knees.

Then, as though he can sense how weak he makes me, he picks me up bridal style and carries me to the chair.

"Lilah," he says, kneeling in front of me. "Will you marry me?"

"Are you sure you want to marry me? I could be arrested at any time."

"If you are, I'll be right there with you, every step of the way."

"You deserve better," I say, my gaze searching his.

"There is no one better," he says. "There's no one better for me. You're it."

"I feel the same way."

He grins. "Then... Yes? You'll marry me?"

"Yes," I say, biting my lip. "I'll marry you."

He kisses me again, pulling me into his lap, making me breathless.

A limb bumps against the window, making me jump.

"What about the stalker?" I ask.

"We'll figure out who's doing it. I know where the blind spots are now." He kisses my forehead. "Whatever happens, we're in this together."

I nod. "You don't think it's weird? Your brother and my sister?"

"I think it's efficient."

"Efficient. That's a good way of looking at it."

He kisses me again.

"Wait?" I put a hand on his chest. "Am I just a convenience for you?"

"Lilah Sinclair. You're everything to me."

"And you're everything to me. Should we keep it a secret? Let Bradley and Audrey have their moment?"

"We can if you want to, but Bradley always knows."

"How does Bradley know?"

"I told him that day I met you. I told him you're the girl I'm going to marry."

"You did not."

"Scout's honor. You can ask him."

"I'll take your word for it." I'd much prefer to take his word for it than to get anyone else involved, even Bradley or Audrey. This is between me and him.

Just us.

There are so many things we don't have figured out. So many things still unresolved.

But together he and I can get past all those things.

We can get past those things and we'll have our own happily-ever-after.

EPILOGUE

Lilah
Two Weeks Later

I'm standing in the middle of an area measured off with little stakes of wood stuck in the ground adorned with orange plastic streamers.

"The concrete truck is on the way," Wyatt says walking toward me.

"We're really doing this." I look toward the house, several yards away. Our flower shop, as yet unnamed, is within walking distance just as we'd planned, but it's hidden from the house by a grove of trees.

"That's right." He wraps me in his arms. "We're doing it. You and me."

"Aren't you a little bit afraid?" I ask.

"I'm not afraid. You and me. We can do anything."

Once things started moving, they started moving quickly. Wyatt, I'm learning does not waste time when he decides to do something.

"Winter's coming," I say, looking toward the mountains where clouds hover over the peaks. It's so strange that it's still summer in most of the country, but not here. Here it's about to be winter.

"You just skipping right over fall?" he asks.

"Right. You said fall is the prettiest season."

"It is. When the leaves turn colors. You're going to love it."

"I guess I'm just wondering how we're going to get flowers down the mountainside in the bad weather. Once the roads are closed."

"Drones. Bradley's idea about the drones is the best one I've heard."

"You really think drones can carry bouquets of live flowers?"

"I do. I don't think you understand how far drones have come. Other companies are doing it. We can do it, too."

"Show me," I say, pulling my jacket closer. It might still be summer, but the wind up here is perpetually cold.

"Okay." Wyatt unlocks his phone and begins typing. "Here."

He holds up his phone, showing me photos of drones.

I expected to see ugly metal drones, but instead the page he's holding up has drones that look like birds.

"Wyatt," I say quietly. "These drones look like birds."

"Birds?" He shifts so he can see the photos with me. "Birds."

Neither one of us says anything. We just stand there looking at the page of bird drones on his phone.

"Oh. My. God." I put a hand over my mouth.

"Birds," Wyatt says. "That's how he did it. He delivered the notes with a drone. A bird drone."

We just look at each other while he slowly lowers his phone.

"Let me see," I take his phone and scroll down the page. "There. This one. This is the bird we kept seeing. But it wasn't a bird."

The concrete truck rumbles up the road, coming up the curving mountainside road toward us.

"Now we know *how* he did it," Wyatt says. "All we have to do now is figure out *who*."

For the first time, I feel confident that we're going to figure out who's been leaving notes at our door.

We know he was turning off our WI-FI when he kidnapped Biscuit. That's why the cameras didn't record.

But we haven't been able to figure out how he was leaving the notes.

We've been seeing a whole lot of birds flying around though.

"So smart," Wyatt says. "So smart we couldn't figure it out."

"But we did," I say. "We did figure it out."

He takes my hand and kisses me.

"You and me," he says. "We can do anything."

I'm starting to believe him.

"Right now we're about to lay the concrete foundation for our flower shop," I say.

"I can't wait to tell Bradley and Audrey what we figured out."

"What are we going to do about it?"

Wyatt grins. "Bradley and I are going hunting. Starting tonight. We're going to shoot ourselves a bird drone."

And then we'll know. Then we'll know who's been threatening us.

And we can get on with the business of living our lives.

Together.

"I love you," he says, giving me a kiss on the lips. "Everything about you. I always have and I always will."

And that's all I need to know.

The End.

AUTHOR OF JUST SURFACE
KATHRYN KALEIGH
Just
MELT
THE GRAVITY OF US SERIES

"So," I say, determined to change the subject. "How long are you planning on staying?"

"Oh." She sweeps her hair out of her face. "I don't think I'm going back to Houston."

"Ever?"

"No. My parents are in Atlanta and my sisters are here. I'm thinking I'll find a place of my own in Whiskey Springs."

"It's a whole lot different from Houston," I say. "It might take you a minute to get used to the small town."

"My sisters like it. I think I'll be okay."

And then there were three.

That's all I can think.

Somehow all three Sinclair sisters have found their way to Whiskey Springs.

I refuse to be like my brothers.

I refuse to fall for one of the Sinclair sisters.

No matter how hot she happens to be.

ONE

Brianna Sinclair
Houston, Texas

I DECLARE A DATING moratorium on the Friday evening after Thanksgiving.

The weather is unseasonably cold for November in Houston.

So cold, in fact, that I'm wearing black tights beneath my beaded little black dress.

Never mix work with pleasure.

Even knowing that, I fell prey to the allure of an older man, an attorney I've been working for for all of a week when he asks me to meet him for drinks after work.

He had such a nice smile. In his thirties, at least ten years older than me, I decide it can't hurt anything.

After all, I spent Thanksgiving alone. By myself. I've never spent Thanksgiving alone.

But my parents are in Atlanta and both my sisters are living in Colorado.

I was invited, of course. Invited to Atlanta and invited to Colorado.

But... work.

I'm sitting in a restaurant I can't afford on my salary as a temp worker, wearing a dress I never should have cut the tags off of. Never cut the tags off a dress that comes with a warning. *No returns once tags are removed.*

There are no qualifications on the tags. No exceptions. Nothing that says you can return the dress if your date doesn't show up. Even if your date asked you to a really expensive restaurant and you went out and bought this really expensive dress to wear to the really expensive restaurant with the handsome, charming boss man who didn't show up.

And there was once an old lady who lived in a shoe.

I glance at the time on my phone. I've been waiting for forty-five minutes.

Forty-five minutes.

Now I have to go. Even if he showed up now, I would look desperate for waiting this long.

The restaurant is crowded with couples and a groups of people coming out for dinner after a day with family.

The tables are covered with crisp white table clothes. Real candles. Live flowers in vases on each table.

Waiters in formal black tuxedos dart silently and efficiently between the tables, seeing to their customers' needs, often before the customers even realize they need anything. Refilling drinks. Sweeping away empty plates. No one notices them. They're simply moving furniture.

Conversations are hushed. No one speaks too loudly or laughs too loud. Not here. Not in this too expensive for working people like me restaurant.

I envy them. Not the formality of it all, but the friends and families. I envy them even though I had chosen not to be with my own family this holiday.

Just like I chose not to be with my family, I'm choosing not to date again.

I've worked in the business world long enough to know that a moratorium needs to have a specified time limit.

Well. I don't have a time limit on my moratorium.

I declare my moratorium to be until further notice. It's my moratorium and if I want it to be until further notice, then it can be until further notice.

I pull a twenty out of my handbag to cover the glass of wine I barely touched and lay it on the table.

No one notices when I get up and slip out of the restaurant.

It's almost like everyone knows I don't belong here. They don't care if I leave. Why would they?

I broke my own rule. I agreed to a date with an employer.

As I wait for the valet to bring my car around. Hand him another twenty I can't afford to spend. I get an email from the temp company that employs me.

With nothing else to do while I wait for my car, I open the email.

Another mistake in a long line of mistakes that are the building blocks of this day.

Dear Ms. Sinclair,

We regret to inform you that we no longer need your services effective immediately.

As you know, we have a zero tolerance policy against employees fraternizing with employers.

My car arrives and I don't even bother to read the rest of the email.

Last time I checked, fraternizing would involve two people. If they think I'm fraternizing, they need to check their sources.

No one showed up.

The man who asked me out must have set me up.

What a champ.

I could respond to the email. Insist that he never showed up. But that is an admission of intent. I have no defense.

Not worth the fight.

Couldn't pay me to talk to him again or to set foot in his office ever again.

Something good comes out of everything.

After I'm in my car, the valet closes my door and I take off.

This is the last Thanksgiving holiday I'll ever spend alone.

In fact, as I drive along the festively decorated streets of Houston, it occurs to me that I no longer have ties to Houston.

My parents are in Atlanta. My sisters in Colorado.

Both of my sisters are engaged to local men, so they won't be moving back to Houston.

It's like adding insult to injury after a long day of disappointments to realize that I no longer belong here.

I've overstayed my welcome.

Without giving myself time to second think myself, I dial my sister Audrey's phone.

CHAPTER
TWO

Caleb Winslow

"I'm out," I say, folding my cards and placing them face down on the table.

We're sitting at the dining room table at the widow Audrey's house. Correction. Audrey, my brother's fiancé.

The wind is howling outside. The wind always howls at nine thousand feet in elevation in the Colorado Rockies just outside of Whiskey Springs where both my brothers now live. With the widow Audrey and her sister Lilah.

"Seriously?" Bradley says. "You're letting Wyatt win again?" Bradley is the oldest of us three brothers and he's the one marrying the widow.

"I can't help it if I always win," Wyatt says. Wyatt is the youngest of us and he's marrying Audrey's sister, Lilah.

It's all one big sloppy mess, if you ask me. But they didn't ask me.

Two brothers engaged to two sisters.

Audrey and Lilah Sinclair. Both nice ladies. No doubt about that. And my brothers are happy. No doubt about that either.

Just not for me.

Audrey comes and sits down in Bradley lap. "Guess what?" she asks, putting her arms around him in an overt display of affection.

"Please tell me it's something good."

"It is." She grins. "Brianna is coming."

"To visit? Finally." Bradley looks at me. "Brianna is their sister."

"That's great news," I say. "I look forward to meeting the elusive third sister."

"We haven't seen her in months," Audrey says.

"What's happened?" Lilah says, pulling off her headset and looking over the back of the oversized sectional.

The first floor of what some call the Albright cabin, others call it the Albright estate due to its large two-story size. The first floor is open with the kitchen, dining room, and living room all spaciously arranged. The second floor has four bedrooms, each with ensuite bathrooms and walk-in closets. Audrey's room has its own spa-like bathroom, two walk-in closets, and a sitting room.

"Brianna is coming," Audrey says.

"Really? When?"

"She's flying up…" Audrey glances at her phone. "Monday."

"Monday," Wyatt looks at me. "Don't you have to be in Denver on Monday for a meeting?"

"I think so." I know so, but I can already sense where this is going.

"You can pick Brianna up at the airport. Save her having to drive up here."

"Yes," Audrey says. "That would be great. Brianna's not the best driver."

"And she always manages to get lost whenever she goes anywhere new," Lilah adds.

Great. Just great. I can already see I'm not getting out of this one.

"I don't know her. I don't even know what she looks like." It's a feeble attempt to get out of it and I know it.

Audrey and Lilah look at each other. "She looks like me with dark hair," Lilah says getting a nod of agreement from Audrey.

"It's time," Bradley says, glancing at the clock on the mantle.

"Yes. We better get going," Wyatt says, pushing back his chair.

"Where are we going?" I ask. Anywhere is better than here with them making plans for me.

"We're going hunting," Wyatt says.

"Oh." I hold up a hand. "I don't think so."

"Come on, Bro," Bradley says. "You don't have to shoot anything. You can do the spotting."

"Gave that up years ago," I say.

"I'll get the guns," Wyatt says, heading to the back door where we keep the guns.

He comes back with two shotguns.

"You're serious," I say. "What am I missing here?"

"It's just bird shot," Wyatt says, handing Audrey a small gun, the size of a pistol, but a type of gun I've never seen before. "But this is for the kill shot."

"You people are starting to scare me," I say.

I grew up around guns. I can shoot. I'm a good shot, actually. Really good. But as an adult, I choose not to hunt.

"This is a VSKP03. An anti-done gun," Audrey says. "We have to use both."

"Wait a minute. You're shooting down someone's drone?"

"If we're lucky."

I glance over at Lilah, sitting with the big dog, a black lab, in front of the fireplace. She is apparently the only one of the bunch who has any sense.

All four of them look at me, then look at each other.

"Yes," Bradley says. "And you are now sworn to secrecy by default."

"Come on Lilah," Audrey says. "You and Wyatt are at the back of the house."

Lilah gets up and follows Wyatt toward the back door.

We all put our coats and scarves on before heading outside.

"Why doesn't Lilah have a gun?" I ask, going with Bradley and Audrey.

"We only have one of these," Audrey says. "And she doesn't like to shoot."

"Well, we have that much in common."

"Stay close to the wall," Bradley says as the three of us step out the front door and line up against the wall.

"I'm really hoping for an explanation."

"You'll get one," Bradley says.

"How do you know there will be a drone?" I ask, my hands in my pockets.

I know it's been awhile since I spent any quality time with my siblings, but this is ridiculous.

Maybe they're just messing with me.

I'm about to call it a night. Just get in my truck and head home.

But then I hear the distinct sound of a bird flapping its wings.

Both Bradley and Audrey lift their respective guns.

"Stay back against the wall," Bradley warns.

The sound of the bird is getting closer. It doesn't sound like any bird I've heard before. It's... louder. With a whirring sound.

Just as the bird sweeps beneath the overhang, Lilah lifts her gun and points it toward the bird. The whirring stops, but the bird keeps going.

That's when Bradley aims and shoots.

The sound of the gun echoes through the night.

I immediately hear the back door slam, then Lilah and Wyatt burst breathlessly out the front door.

The motion lights click on.

"Did you get it?" Wyatt asks.

"Of course."

The bird lies on the ground, just on the other of the porch.

"You said drone," I say, my ears still ringing from the shotgun.

"Bird drone," Wyatt says, stepping out to pick it up.

"Why are we killing bird drones?" I ask. "Please tell me you have a good reason for this."

"Do you remember us talking about someone leaving threatening notes at the door?" Wyatt asks.

"You took care of that."

"It stopped for awhile, but then it started up again." Wyatt takes the bird drone inside and we follow him.

Bradley locks the door behind us, throwing two dead bolts.

Wyatt drops the bird drone on the floor and peels an envelope from its little talons.

"It comes bearing tidings tonight," he says, handing me the note.

"I don't want it."

"Read it."

Giving up on avoiding whatever this is, I take the envelope and pull out a sheet of paper.

"What does it say?" Lilah asks.

"It says *Enjoy your last holiday here. Your days are numbered.*"

"As are his drones," Lilah says with a little scoff.

"Wait a minute. How many of these things have you shot down?"

"This makes four."

"Four drones. Do you know how expensive these things are?"

"Do you know of anyone who would be using them to drop off notes like that?" Bradley asks.

"No. I do not. Isn't this a job for the sheriff?"

"He's an ass hat," Wyatt says.

"It's his job."

"Try telling him that."

Audrey kneels down, digging through the feathers. "Wyatt's friend is tracking down the serial numbers. He'll eventually find out who these things belong to."

"Trent," Wyatt says clarifies. "Trent is helping us."

I rub a hand over my eyes. What the hell has my brothers gotten into now?

"Does Brianna know what she's getting into?" I ask. Do they even understand how serious this could be? Someone is buying expensive drones for what looks like the sole purpose of trying to threaten Audrey and Lilah and possibly now my brothers away.

"No," Audrey says. "We don't want her to worry. We'll explain it when she gets here."

That's got to be a huge mistake. She needs to know. But it's not my decision.

"Okay," I say. "You've gotten me into this. I think you need to back up and tell me the whole story."

Whatever is going on sounds far more serious than they're letting on.

I don't want to be involved, but in a moment of weakness I came up here to spend an evening with my brothers who will no long go anywhere without their women and their dog.

And this where it gets me.

"I need to know everything."

CHAPTER
THREE

Brianna

In retrospect, I've been preparing for this move for longer than I realized.

I hadn't renewed my lease. Instead, I've been paying month to month and I've been living a minimalistic lifestyle. My condo was furnished, so the furniture isn't even mine to begin with.

It's almost like I've been planning my getaway.

That what it feels like anyway as I board the commercial jet that will take me from Houston to Denver.

I spent the weekend boxing up all my belongings.

Everything that doesn't fit in my two oversized suitcases, got dropped off at the UPS store on the way to the airport.

Done and done.

God help me, I'm putting Houston in my rearview mirror. Didn't think I would ever do that. But these past few months of living here with no family have been just plain lonely.

It was bad enough when my older sister got married and moved out to Katy. It was one of those sudden marriages that made no sense to me. But the guy looked good on paper and the background check I secretly ran on him came out clean.

Turned out, though, that the background check missed some rather important details.

Like the baby he had with another woman before he married my sister.

This probably never would have even come out except that he, Thomas, crashed his private jet and died. All his insurance money went to the baby and the baby's mother. Even the house he'd been living in with my sister was sold out from under her and that money, too went to the child.

But Thomas's grandfather had left a house just outside of a small town in Colorado. Whiskey Springs. He left it specifically to Thomas's wife who just so happened to be Audrey.

The only stipulation was that Audrey live in the house. She doesn't own the house, but she'll live there free and clear, all expenses paid as long as she wants to.

With a one million dollar stipend deposited in her account every year.

I'd been skeptical about the whole thing when it went down, but Audrey had been determined that she had no choice but to go.

She really didn't have a choice. Who wouldn't go? She had to at least try.

Lilah and I tried to go with her, but Audrey wanted to do it on her own. Said she needed to do it herself as part of the process of learning to be single again. That didn't last long.

She'd no more than gotten to the house, not even settled in, when she met Bradley Winslow. They're engaged now.

And not long after that, my other sister, Lilah, got herself in some trouble and went up to live with Audrey in the big house.

Lilah is now engaged to marry Wyatt Winslow.

So my sisters are engaged to brothers.

"Excuse me," I say to a teenage boy with earphones on. "That's my seat."

He stands up and I crawl over into my window seat.

There's a reason I don't fly. It's self-imposed misery. The reason I haven't been to visit my sisters in the six months or so that they've lived in Colorado.

That and driving is out of the question. I rarely even take a day off. How could I possibly drive up there and back? Why would I drive up there and back?

I settle into my seat and watch the baggage handlers toss our luggage from the luggage cart into the cargo hold of the airplane.

It's raining now, so our luggage is getting wet in the process. The only saving grace is that my luggage is hard-sided.

I feel sorry for those people with cloth luggage.

I check my phone. No messages.

Send a quick message to Audrey letting her know I'm on the airplane.

Apparently Bradley and Wyatt have a third brother named Caleb who is supposed to pick me up from the airport and drive me up to Whiskey Springs.

I would have said absolutely no thank you, but I always get lost when I go somewhere new. And from what I'm told, the mountain roads are treacherous, especially since it'll be dark by the time I would be driving up to Audrey's house.

I suppose it's Lilah's house, too, since they're all living there. All four of them. My sisters and their fiancés.

I give myself a few days, maybe a week, and I'll be looking for a place of my own. Need to find myself a job first though. I'm thinking with my experience I can find a job easy enough. Give me a computer and I can do just about anything.

That's the beauty of doing temp work. I learned how to do everything. I can work in any kind of office.

"Fasten your seatbelts, folks, and prepare for takeoff.

We're going to be pushing away shortly and should have you in Denver earlier than expected."

I lean my head back against the seat and close my eyes.

I just want to be there already.

Maybe it's a good thing Caleb is picking me up. No telling where I would end up if left to my own devices. Probably end up in Wyoming or New Mexico.

The airplane starts backing out of its spot and we start driving. I'm beginning to wonder if we're going to drive all the way to Denver when the plane starts racing down the runway and we leave the ground.

Maybe driving, like Lilah had done, wouldn't have been such a bad idea, I decide as I grip the edge of the seat.

For the next few hours, it's just me and my teenage seatmate lost in his own world, headphones over his ears.

Maybe he has the right idea.

Me? I keep reminding myself.

Life changes come with strife.

If life changes were easy, everybody would do it.

CHAPTER
FOUR

Caleb

As instructed, I get to the Denver airport, park, and find my way to the luggage carousels.

I'm on time. A little bit early, actually, but the plane, it seems, must have arrived earlier than scheduled.

Passengers are frantically grabbing their luggage, as they always do at airports, and heading out of the terminal, meeting me head on. I dodge them. A lot of families traveling together this time of year. A few businesspeople wearing their business suits.

I fit in with the businesspeople. I look like just another businessman wearing a business suit, except I'm going the wrong direction and I'm not here for myself. I'm just here to pick someone up.

The things we do for family.

Speaking of family, my brothers have gotten themselves tangled up in some kind of mess revolving around the widow Audrey.

From what I was told, she inherited the house from her late husband's grandfather, the only stipulation being that she has to live in the house. She can't not live there and she can't sell it.

Oh. And every year she gets a million dollars deposited in her account.

Not a bad deal.

And apparently someone else knows about this arrangement. Someone who wants her out.

Someone wants her out so they can move in.

So far their tactics have been leaving threatening notes at the door. Messages, they learned after some time, left by bird drones.

One of their tactics, however, was not harmless. They kidnapped Bradley's dog, Biscuit.

As far as I'm concerned, that was taking it too far.

Biscuit was unharmed, returned unscathed a few hours after he was taken from their house, right while everyone was upstairs working on installing shelving in the closets.

Whoever was able to get into the house to get the dog, without being recorded on their cameras, had installed their own scrambler *inside* the house.

Since no more incidents like kidnapping the dog have occurred, whoever did it must know that his scrambler has been disabled. Very likely since he had cameras planted inside Audrey's house.

Cameras that they pulled down and stored out in the tool shed.

Me? I would have pulled them out and put them down the garbage disposal or tossed them in the river. But they're keeping them for evidence even though they won't go to the sheriff with this thing.

Bradley went to the sheriff when it started, but the sheriff blew him off. Now they've decided to take things into their own hands by shooting down the guy's drones.

It seems like a dangerous game to me.

I'm not sure they see the danger.

If someone will mess with a pet, he'll mess with a person.

Something needs to be done. I don't know what it is, but I know there has to be something.

A young lady who absolutely does look like Lilah with long dark hair grabs at a black hard sided suitcase from the conveyor belt. She wobbles on high heels and the suitcase continues its path on the belt.

She's wearing a charcoal gray pencil skirt and matching jacket with an emerald green blouse peeking out beneath it.

I instantly know she's Brianna Sinclair. There is no mistaking her resemblance to Audrey and Lilah.

I cover the distance in three long strides and, stepping to her right, drag the suitcase off the belt.

"This one, too?" I ask, nodding toward the matching one coming along behind it.

"Yes," she says, watching with dismay as it rolls past her.

I grab it, too, dragging it off the moving conveyor belt.

"Thank you so much," she says, pushing her hair back. "I missed them the first time around."

"I can see why. They weigh a ton."

She looks at me with a little bemused smile.

She looks like her sisters, but she's so much prettier. At first I think it's her bow-shaped plush lips with the little smile. But, no, it's something in her eyes. So deep and such an unusual shade of teal green. Looking into her eyes, I see so much wisdom. This is not a shallow girl. This is a woman with depth. The kind of woman a man could hold a deep philosophical conversation with.

"I'm Caleb Winslow," I say.

"Brianna." She holds out a hand. Even with three-inch heels, the top of her head only comes to my shoulder.

My gaze never leaving hers, I put my hand in hers.

A connection shoots through me and for a moment I forget where we are. I forget why I'm here. Hell, I'm not even sure I remember my own name.

"I guess you're my ride then," she says.

"I guess I am." I reluctantly let go of her hand and take the two handles of her suitcases.

She moves to pick up the leather computer bag sitting at her feet.

"Let me get that," I say.

She smiles. "I'm so glad you're here," she says. "I don't know how I would have gotten this out to the rental car place."

"Your flight must have been early," I say, noticing that there are only a couple of other people at the luggage conveyor belt.

"It was. The pilot was no nonsense."

"Did you fly first class?" I ask as we make our way along the concourse.

"What? No. But it wasn't bad. The teenager sitting next to me just sat quietly and listened to music the whole time."

"Good. You never know what you're going to get on these commercial flights."

She looks at me with questions she doesn't ask.

"You hungry?" I ask.

"A little. Yes."

"Me too. If you're not in a hurry, we should stop for food before we head up into the mountains."

"Okay." We step outside and she pauses.

"What's wrong?"

"Nothing. It's just. Cooler than I expected."

"Your sisters didn't warn you about the weather?"

"They did. It's just. I don't even own a coat."

"How do you not own a coat?" I ask.

"Houston." She shrugs.

Houston. A quick reminder that she's only here to visit. And she's practically related to me with both my brothers engaged to her sisters.

I pull myself together.

It's not like I haven't seen pretty girls before.

CHAPTER
FIVE

Brianna

CALEB WINSLOW IS MUCH MORE handsome in person than he was in the photo Audrey sent me. And no one warned me that he's a gentleman.

It's such a relief to have someone to help with my luggage. I honestly hadn't given much thought to how I was going to handle it when I'd packed.

All I'd been thinking about was just how much I wanted to get out of Houston.

One slip up and it was like I suddenly had a vile taste in my mouth for the city.

Honestly, though, I think it had been building up.

Maybe I'd sort of self-sabotaged myself. That or I had simply gotten so lonely so I just wanted to spend one evening with an interesting man who found me attractive.

Caleb is nothing like what I expected.

The photos my sisters had sent me of Wyatt and Bradley always were with them wearing flannel shirts and work boots. So that's what I had expected of Caleb.

After all, he lives in the same small town and runs their family business.

But instead of a flannel shirt, he's wearing a business suit. Since I'd worn office work clothes by habit, he and I actually look like we could be colleagues. I hardly even know how to wear anything else.

His car also surprises me. He drives a new Lexus SUV. I had expected him to drive a truck. Somebody, Lilah maybe, had mentioned that the brothers all drive trucks. Maybe that's just for work. And since this isn't work...

After loading my luggage in the back, he opens the passenger door and holds it while I climb inside.

Then he goes around and climbs into the driver's seat.

"I hope this wasn't too far out of your way," I say.

"Not at all," he says, turning on the heater. "I was in Denver for a business meeting today."

"Right. Well. I appreciate the ride."

"I don't mind. It's no trouble. Besides, we can't have you getting lost up in the mountains."

"My sisters told you I get lost easily." I look out the

window at the mountains in the distance. "Is that where's we're heading?" I ask.

"It is. We have a bit of a drive. There's a sandwich shop I usually stop at. Sound okay?"

"It sounds good to me. Anything is fine."

"That's what we'll do then."

His definition of a sandwich shop is slightly different from mine.

My definition of a sandwich shop is literally grabbing a sandwich and chips to go.

Caleb's idea of a sandwich shop is what I call a pizza place. A sit down restaurant.

If he doesn't mind taking the time to eat, then I don't mind either. It's not like I'm in any hurry now that I'm here and on my way to Whiskey Springs.

We order our food and find a table near the window to wait.

"Do you come into Denver for business often?" I ask.

"About once a week or so. Not for the family cabin and timber business though. I have some... what most people would call side hustles... of my own."

"Side hustles. I'm a fan of side hustles."

"Oh? You have one?"

"No. Not at the moment. But I've given it a lot of thought."

"Somebody told me you do temp work."

"That's right. I'm actually a paralegal, but I like learning different things. You can put me in any office anywhere and I can do the job."

"That's impressive."

I can almost see him thinking. Wondering if I'd be a good fit working for him.

"But what I want to do is to translate that into working for myself," I say before he can get any ideas.

"It's the only way to be successful. To be really successful."

"Are you really successful?" I ask.

"I'm getting there."

"How do you do it? How do you run your family business and do your side hustle at the same time?"

"My two brothers do all the hard work. I just make sure the work gets done. And our mother is the office manager."

"That's efficient."

"It is actually."

One of the servers brings out our sandwiches.

"This is good," I say after one bite of the cheesy sandwich.

"Stick with me, Kid," he says. "I won't steer you wrong."

Something about the way he says it has a delicious little shiver running along my spine.

I believe him.

There's something about Caleb that garners my confidence.

As I eat, I study him beneath my lashes.

Clean-shaven. A strong jaw. A metro haircut. He looks

like he could be from Houston. A businessman from Houston. Easily.

But then there's something different about him, too.

Mesmerizing blue eyes. Eyes the color of a stormy sea.

Those stormy eyes go well with the passion I sense coiling just below his serene surface. So calm on the exterior, but there's more to this man than meets the eye.

He's not the typical businessman I work with. And there's something about the way he looks at me that has my blood thrumming through my veins.

It's going to be a long ride up to Whiskey Springs.

CHAPTER
SIX

Caleb

WE'VE NO MORE than gotten back in my SUV and headed out of the city when I get a call from Bradley.

The Denver highways, as always, are crowded. There is no time of day when Denver highways have a lull that make it easy to get around. The city outgrew its structure years ago.

"And I thought Houston traffic was bad," Brianna says. "Is it always like this?"

"Pretty much. My brother is calling." I push the answer button on my steering wheel. "Hey Bradley. You're on speaker with Brianna."

"Hi Brianna."

"Hi Bradley."

"Something up?" I glance over at Brianna. The poor girl is walking into a mess and she has no idea about what she's getting into. None.

"Yeah. Something's happened." He hesitates and I almost take him off speaker. "We just got a call. Claire's house is on fire."

"Wait. What?"

Claire is Audrey's housekeeper. She's been taking care of the Albright house, now Audrey's house, for as long as I can remember.

"Is she okay?"

"Yeah. She just so happened to be here today. And she brought her cat with her."

"Thank God."

"Yeah. We're all going to pile in the trucks and drive over there. See if anything can be salvaged."

"Taking the dog?" I ask, knowing they can't leave him home by himself. Not after what someone kidnapped the dog.

I want to warn him that this could be a ploy to get them out of the house, but I can't say too much without having to explain it Brianna. She doesn't know yet and it's not my place to be the one to tell her.

"Of course. "We're taking the dog and the cat."

"Good deal. So I've got Brianna. If I get there before you get back, I'll..." I glance over at her.

"Just drop me off at the house," Brianna says. "Audrey can send me the code."

"Okay," I say. "I'll do that."

And I'm counting on them being back. I'd rather not leave Brianna there at the house alone.

We end the call.

"From what I've heard, Claire's had a really hard time lately," Brianna says.

"I guess she has," I say. Still not committing to much because I don't know what Brianna knows about Claire.

"She was in the hospital, right?"

"Right. I think she slipped down."

"That's what Lilah told me. She didn't say much else about it."

"So," I say, determined to change the subject. "How long are you planning on staying?"

"Oh." She sweeps her hair out of her face. "I don't think I'm going back to Houston."

"Ever?"

"No. My parents are in Atlanta and my sisters are here. I'm thinking I'll find a place of my own in Whiskey Springs."

"It's a whole lot different from Houston," I say. "It might take you a minute to get used to the small town."

"My sisters like it. I think I'll be okay."

And then there were three.

That's all I can think.

Somehow all three Sinclair sisters have found their way to Whiskey Springs.

I refuse to be like my brothers.

I refuse to fall for one of the Sinclair sisters.

No matter how hot she happens to be.

CHAPTER
SEVEN

Brianna

THE RIDE from the restaurant up to Whiskey Springs isn't nearly as bad as I had imagined it would be when I agreed to riding with a stranger.

Caleb is pleasant and entertaining. He tells me trivia about the area as we drive into the mountains. Tells me about the "Great Flood of '2010" that closed the roads to Whiskey Springs for six months while they rebuilt them. How he had been devastated because he missed out on summer camp.

"I never had the opportunity to go to summer camp," I tell him.

"Seriously? Going to summer camp every year played a significant role in making me who I am today."

"I did some summer college classes between my junior and senior years of high school. That was about it."

"What did you do all summer?"

"We spent some time with our grandparents. Went swimming. Watched television. Played games."

"A life of leisure."

"Surely you had some free time during the summers."

"We did. Our Grandpa took us boys hunting, but never together. Said it was too dangerous to keep up with three boys all carrying guns at the same time."

"Sounds like a very smart man." I look out the window as we cross a bridge over a mountain stream full of rocks and boulders. Nothing in any way like the rivers back home.

"In case you're wondering," he says. "Hunting did not stick with me. I haven't been hunting since I was sixteen."

"Why not?" I shift my attention over to look at him. He doesn't look like the kind of guy who would hunt. But still. He is from the small town.

"I don't know. I guess I couldn't see the point of killing for sport."

"I don't either. That's what stores are for."

"Exactly. And they could leave kitchens out of houses, too."

"That's what restaurants are for," I say.

"Exactly."

"It's like washing your own car."

"Or doing your own taxes."

In that moment, I feel a connection with Caleb. A real connection. One I haven't felt in a really long time.

Over something so simple as a shared understanding that people really don't need kitchens in their houses.

No one else in my family ever understood that concept. They believed in making homecooked meals. But me? To me cooking at home was right up there with trying to sew your own clothes.

In Caleb I've met a kindred spirit.

It's getting dark now and he concentrates on driving. The roads are more narrow now. The curves shorter. And we're climbing higher into the hills.

In the darkness I can't see much. But I can see enough to know that we're moving into what is not only beautiful, but dangerous country.

A little like Caleb himself.

Beautiful but dangerous.

CHAPTER
EIGHT

Caleb

WE STOP for a short restroom break on the east side of Whiskey Springs, giving Brianna her first look at the small town.

"Is everything decorated?" she asks once we're back in the car and I drive slowly along Main Street.

"Pretty much. They have a saying around here. 'If Christmas was a town, it would be Whiskey Springs.'"

"That's a good saying. And it fits."

"We take pride in our Christmas festivities. Every Christmas Eve, there's a masquerade ball at the Whiskey Springs Lodge."

"There's a lodge," she says.

"A very nice one." I almost tell her I'll take her there, but I catch myself. "I'm not even sure your sisters have been. You should all go."

"I'll ask them about it," she says.

I turn off the main highway and start the climb up toward the widow... toward the Sinclair house. Might was well start thinking about the house as the Sinclair house and not the Albright house. And while I'm at it, I should think of Audrey as Audrey. Not the widow.

"The road up near the house is treacherous," I tell her. "Very narrow with steep cliffs. Nothing between the car and the edge of the cliff. If the weather is bad or even just foggy, I suggest you avoid it at all costs."

"Thanks for the heads up. Has anyone ever gone over the side?"

"There have been tales."

She shivers. "But not anyone you know personally?"

"The old man Albright is the only man who lived there for years and he was mostly a recluse."

I have to give her credit for not looking afraid as we drive across what I call the narrows. The area I spoke of with the severe drop off. She merely looks curious.

"The house is right up ahead," I say. "They must be home." There are lights on in the house.

But as I pull up in front of the house, I see that there may be lights on, but their trucks aren't there. Claire's car is parked there and so is the sheriff's truck.

"What's the police doing here?" Brianna asks.

"I don't know."

I pull up in front of the house and put the SUV in park, leaving the motor running.

Sheriff Morgan is sitting in his truck.

"Wait here," I say. "I'll find out what he's doing."

"Okay."

The sheriff rolls down his window as I walk up to his truck.

"Sheriff," I say.

"Evening Caleb."

"Something wrong?"

"Just checking things out. Making sure there are no problems."

"What kind of problems?"

"With Claire's house burning down and all."

I put my hands on my hips and look back over at the big house, lit up now with motion sensor lights. "Not seeing the connection."

"I'm sure you heard they had some trouble out here," the sheriff explains.

"That was a long time ago," I say. "In the summer."

"Just doing my job."

"See anything suspicious?" I ask, keeping my voice calm, but I'm feel tension coiling beneath the surface.

"Everything looks okay."

"Well then. I'm going to get Brianna settled inside."

I swear the man's eyebrows lift off his head. I've never

seen much reaction from the sheriff, but he has a visible reaction to Brianna's name.

"So the other sister finally made it up here," he says.

I'm wishing I hadn't told him Brianna's name. Not much I can do about it now.

"I think we've got this," I say.

"Going to just sit here and make a phone call before I head out," he says, picking up his phone.

"Alright then," I say. Not much I can do if the sheriff wants to sit outside the house and make a phone call.

I go around to the passenger side and open Brianna's door. "You have the code, right?" I ask.

"Yes. What does he want?"

"Nothing. Just wants to sit there."

I walk around to the back of the SUV and pull out her luggage.

"Strange?" she asks.

"A little. But he's the sheriff."

"Okay," she says. "I guess I should feel safe with him sitting outside." She glances over at his truck.

"I'll stay with you until they get back."

"You don't have to do that. They'll be back soon and you've done far more than you signed up for."

I grab her computer bag from the back seat, toss it over my shoulder, and heft her luggage up onto the porch.

I watch behind her, looking toward the sheriff's truck, thinking about the bird drone they'd shot down a few days ago, while Brianna keys in the code to the door lock.

It shouldn't be unsettling having the sheriff in front of the house. It seems like it should be comforting, all things being equal.

Wyatt called the guy an ass hat. Maybe I should have explored that a bit more with my brother. To find out if there's something specific he doesn't like about Sheriff Morgan or if it's just a general dislike. I never had much (any) dealings with the sheriff myself. I'm a law-abiding citizen and keep my nose clean.

The door opens right up for Brianna and she steps inside the dark house. I automatically reach for the light switch on the wall, taking in a quick scan of the room, before I roll her two suitcases inside.

I leave her leather computer bag on the kitchen island next to a vase with white roses.

The vase of roses wasn't there last Friday night when I'd been here.

Lilah and Wyatt are building a flower shop and greenhouse here on the property not far from the house, but it's taking them longer than they expected to get it off the ground.

As such, I'm curious where they got the flowers, but not my business.

"I can just wait here until they get back," I say again.

She runs a hand through her hair. "I'm just going to change clothes, wash my face, then sit here." She sweeps a hand behind her toward the sectional. "Maybe take a little nap before they get back."

"Okay," I say. I can't very well insist that I stay here when she's telling me to leave.

Audrey doesn't want Brianna to know about the stalker until she tells her.

And besides, the sheriff is right outside.

What can possibly go wrong?

"Thanks again for giving me a ride up," she says with a little smile that I find endearing.

"I enjoyed the company," I say. "Well. You have my number, right?"

"Yes. Lilah sent it to me."

"If you need anything at all... if you get frightened up here... just call me. I'll come right back."

"I'm not afraid," she says. "I'm sure, everything considered, I'll see you soon."

I smile. "Yes. I have no doubt about that."

"Walk me out," I say. "And lock the door behind me. I think there are deadbolts."

"I'm okay," she says. "The police is right outside. I don't think anyone is going to break in."

"You're right. It's just... it's a new place." I should so tell her to be wary.

But my phone chimes with a text from Bradley letting me know they've left Claire's house and are on their way back.

"They're on their way back," I tell Brianna. "So I'll say goodnight."

"Goodnight."

She follows me to the door and I stand on the porch and wait, listening until she clicks all the deadbolts into place.

My hands in my pockets, I walk over to my car, ignoring the sheriff and climb inside.

I think my brother Wyatt is onto something. Something doesn't sit right with me about Sheriff Morgan. I can't put my finger on it, but it's there. Maybe he's just, like Wyatt said, an ass hat.

Thinking about that as I put the car in drive and head down the mountainside makes me smile to myself.

Or maybe it's not really thinking about the sheriff being an ass hat.

Maybe it's thinking about Brianna.

What is it about these Sinclair women that us Winslow boys find so damned attractive anyway?

Brianna

I TAKE a minute to look around the first floor of the house, but with the FaceTime calls I've shared with my sisters, I feel like I know the house well enough.

What I didn't know, however, from the videos was just how clean it smells. Claire, the housekeeper, was there today and she left the house smelling like outdoors, specifically like the fresh scent of spruce trees.

Not even trying to haul my suitcases upstairs, I open one of them up, rummage around for some sweatpants and a sweatshirt, some sneakers, and head upstairs to the empty bedroom.

Four bedrooms and only one of them is unoccupied. I'm a little surprised that Wyatt hasn't moved in with Lilah, but right now he has his own bedroom.

I get changed, hanging my business clothes in the empty closet, newly designed by Audrey, and empty hangers waiting. Then I wash my face, pull my hair back, and head downstairs with a book in hand.

I curl up on the sectional in front of the banked fireplace and wonder if I can figure out how to start a fire.

I'd just decided that I need to leave it alone for now when someone knocks on the door. I hadn't heard anyone drive up and I hadn't seen any headlights coming through the closed window shades.

It's not my sisters because it's their house. They wouldn't knock.

Annoyed more than anything else at being disturbed, I get up and walk over to the door.

"Who is it?" I ask. This might be a remote cabin outside a small town, but I'm from the city. I don't just open the door because someone knocks.

"Sheriff Morgan."

Of course. I hesitate. There's probably some kind of penalty for not opening the door to the sheriff. If television is any indication, he might just knock the door down and come inside anyway.

I unlock the top deadbolt first. Then the second one.

Then I unlock the door itself and pull it open.

The sheriff is standing there, in his full uniform, thumbs

in his belt loops, sunglasses, at night no less, and he's chewing gum.

I don't like to make quick judgements on people, but I have an instant inexplicable dislike for him. I honestly attribute the dislike to the sunglasses. Not a big fan to begin with. But a law officer shouldn't come to someone's door at night wearing sunglasses. It's just creepy.

"Everything okay in here?" he asks.

"Everything is great. What do you need?" I realize, a little too late, that I should probably curb my tongue before I make an enemy of the small town sheriff before I'm even introduced, but he just smiles.

"I've heard a lot about you and I wanted to introduce myself."

I lean against the door. "I'm Brianna Sinclair," I say, hoping that will satisfy him. "Audrey and Lilah's sister."

"Uh huh." Chewing gun. Creeping me out with the sunglasses.

"So," I say. "They aren't home. Maybe you can come back when they're home."

"If you don't mind, I'd like to come in and take a look around."

"Why?" I give up on trying to keep the annoyance out of my voice.

"There was a report."

"Of what?"

"Step aside, ma'am. I'll be out of your way in no time."

I have no choice. Not knowing what this police officer

will do if I don't comply, I'm not inclined to find out. I step away from the door, letting him saunter inside.

"I've always liked this place," he says.

I step back, watching him. Not saying anything.

He walks over to the kitchen, leans over and sniffs one of the flowers.

"What kind of report?" I ask.

"Excuse me?" he turns and looks at me. He seems to have completely forgotten why he's here.

"You said there was a report."

"Right," he says. "Probably just kids." He slides his sunglasses off then and I immediately change my mind about not liking them.

I liked him better with sunglasses. As he peers at me with piercing brown eyes. I cross my arms and take a step back.

"How long are you planning on staying?" he asks, with a quick glance over at my luggage standing at the bottom of the stairs.

"I haven't decided yet." Not his business if I have.

"Well. The winters around here are what most call unforgiving."

"What are you saying?"

"I'm saying that a city girl like you isn't likely to enjoy being up here in the mountains in the winter. Summer maybe. But not winter. It's much too... unpredictable."

"I'm sure I'll be fine." How dare he warn me away like this?

He takes another step toward me and I'm feeling decid-edly uncomfortable now.

I don't know this man and I don't know what he'll do.

I move over to the couch and pick up my cell phone. Hold it front of me like a shield. I don't know what I'm going to do with it. I don't know who I'm going to call, but I feel better with it in my hand.

I don't know how far out from here my sisters are. It probably doesn't make any sense to call them.

But Caleb can't be too far away. He did tell me to call if I need anything.

Then I see headlights shining through the window shades.

Relief washes through me.

My sisters are home and they'll have their boyfriends with them.

This sheriff can take up whatever bug is up his ass up with them. I want nothing to do with him.

Narrowing his eyes, he looks toward the door.

I give him a little smirk.

He points his sunglasses at me. "You've got an attitude." There is no humor in his tone.

I shrug.

Someone knocks on the door.

"Come in," I call out, leaving no uncertainty that I want whoever is here to come inside. Please. Anyone.

Caleb pushes the door open and take in the room, looking at me, then the sheriff.

"What's going on?" he asks me, but he's looking at the sheriff.

I shake my head.

"There was a report," the sheriff says.

Caleb looks at me. "Did you make a report?"

"No," I say, shaking my head again.

"Sheriff Morgan." Caleb crosses his arms across his chest. "What can we do for you?"

"Just paying a friendly visit," he says. "Following up on a disturbance report."

"Who made a report?" Caleb asks.

"Came in anonymous," he says. "Probably just kids."

"Probably," Caleb says. "We'll call you if we need anything."

"I'll leave you to it then." Sheriff Morgan slides his sunglasses back on his face and heads to the door.

Caleb looks at me, then follows the sheriff.

As soon as the sheriff is outside, Caleb locks the door.

I drop onto the sectional.

"What was he doing here?" Caleb asks.

"I don't know. He just showed up at the door. Insisted on coming inside. I had to let him in, right? He's a policeman."

"I guess," Caleb says.

"How did you know to come back?"

"I pulled over at the cabin just down the way to wait for him. When he didn't leave, I came back."

"I'm glad you did. He sort of creeped me out."

We listen as the sheriff drives off and just as he's leaving two more sets of headlights come this way.

"That's Wyatt and Bradley," Caleb says.

"I hope so," I say, leaning back on the sofa, more than content to let Caleb take over from here.

Audrey steps in through the door first, along with Biscuit pulling on his leash, Bradley right behind her.

"What's going on?" she asks. "We just passed the sheriff leaving."

I get up and meet Audrey halfway across the room, sweeping her into a big hug.

"It's so good to see you," I say. "Let me look at you."

Lilah comes inside, rushing straight over to give me a hug, too.

"I missed you so much," Lilah says.

My eyes are misting over with happiness at seeing my sisters for the first time in months.

Wyatt comes in next, an older woman with him, and lets the door slam closed behind him.

"What was that ass hat doing up here?" Wyatt asks.

Caleb and I look at each other.

"I was hoping you would know," Caleb tells Wyatt.

"Where did those flowers come from?" Lilah asks, seeing the vase of white roses on the kitchen island.

Audrey walks slowly toward them, then stops. Looks at me. "Did you bring these?" she asks.

"There were there when we got here," I say.

"I think you need to tell her," Caleb says.

"Tell me what?"

"Everything," Audrey says, turning back to me.

I sit down again. I have a bad feeling about this.

"I'll just be upstairs, settling in," the older woman says.

"Brianna, this is Claire," Bradley says. "She's going to be staying with us for awhile.

"Hello Claire," I say. "I'm so sorry about your house." The damage must be bad enough that she needs to stay here.

"It's okay." She holds the pet carrier close to her. "I have what's important. The rest doesn't matter."

CHAPTER
TEN

Caleb

I SIT down next to Brianna and listen while Audrey and Lilah go through the story about how someone has been threatening them since Audrey arrived here at the house last summer.

I hadn't known about the flowers that had appeared in the house shortly after Audrey arrived. They still didn't have an explanation for how they had gotten inside the house.

As for the vase of white roses on the counter, Wyatt takes it out the back door and leaves them there.

"They could have bugs," he says, seeing us all looking at him when he gets back inside.

"Bugs?" Brianna asks.

"Wyatt's friend swept the house for bugs... cameras... and found nearly a dozen."

"What's going on here?" Brianna asks. "You should have told me."

"We didn't want you to worry," Lilah says.

"You should be worried. Have you reported this to the police?"

"That was the police," Caleb says. "The man who just left."

I make a face. I don't know what to say about that.

"He's an ass hat," Wyatt says, sitting down next to Lilah.

"Surely there's someone else to report this to," Brianna says.

"We decided to figure out who's doing it on our own," Bradley says.

"I'm not sure that's a good idea," Brianna says.

"Agreed," I say. My brothers just look at me. "What? I do. I don't think shooting down someone's drones is the answer."

Brianna looks at me. "Drones?"

"They've been shooting down someone's bird drones," I tell her.

"What's a bird drone?" Brianna asks me.

"It's a drone disguised as a bird. Someone has been

dropping threatening notes off with the drone. It took them a long time to figure out how someone was dropping notes off at the door without getting caught."

"Who would have thought to notice a bird flying past?" Audrey adds. "It was quite ingenious."

"How did you figure it out?" Brianna asks.

"Wyatt and Lilah figured it out," Bradley says.

"Actually it was Wyatt," Lilah says.

He takes her hand. "I share the credit."

Brianna and I exchange a glance. It seems like our siblings aren't taking this nearly as seriously as it warrants.

Maybe they've been part of it for so long that they can't see it anymore.

"I need to go up and help Claire move my things to Lilah's room," Wyatt says.

"Not to change the subject, but what's the status of Claire's house?" I ask.

"Burned to the ground," Wyatt says softly as he stands up. "Audrey and Lilah decided she should live with us for the time being."

Just like Bradley and then Wyatt moved in temporarily.

"Seems like you're going to need to add on some extra rooms," I say.

Audrey and Bradley look at each other and I can see from their expressions that I just inadvertently provided them with the solution to a problem they'd been working on.

"Well," Wyatt says. "In the meantime I'm going to be sleeping on the chair in Lilah's room."

Right. I admire him for protecting Lilah's reputation, but we're all family here. There's no need to pretend.

"Can I talk to you for a minute?" Bradley asks me.

"Sure."

"Let's just get our coats and take Biscuit for his walk."

"My coat's in the car," I tell him. "I can get it."

"We're got extras. Come on."

Biscuit, hearing his name, gets up and does a full body shake, then barks once.

As we're heading out, a black cat comes down the stairs and jumps up on the kitchen island like he knows right where he's going.

The Sinclair house or whatever name they decide it goes by, is getting more than a little crowded.

CHAPTER
ELEVEN

Brianna

Sitting on the sectional, I watch all the activity around me.

This is nothing like what I expected to be walking into.

Wyatt is upstairs, moving his things into Lilah's room so the housekeeper can have a room of her own. They don't seem to mind making him moving into her bedroom official. But it's not for me to say.

Lilah has been through a lot herself. When she moved up here to Whiskey Springs, she'd been getting as far away from an ex-boyfriend as she could.

After an altercation that involved her tossing the contents of a glass of wine into a woman's face at the

Hobby Center where she was working as a hostess, she was fired. It didn't matter that the woman, Beatrice, had started it. That she had been taunting Lilah. Lilah was the one who had tossed the wine.

I'd been with Lilah the night all that had happened. I'd seen just how devastated she was. She vowed that she was giving up bartending, a promise to herself she had stuck to. She'd also vowed that she wasn't going to date again. That promise to herself didn't seem to have stuck.

A lot of what she'd been afraid of was the two-year statute of limitations for the woman, Beatrice, to file charges against her for tossing wine in her face.

But either way, Lilah looks happy now. Wyatt knows what happened. I might have been a long way away in miles, but the three of us are close and we share most of what happens.

I guess that's why I'm surprised they didn't tell me about the bird drones and how the stalker is still leaving threatening notes.

Lilah is feeding the cat on the kitchen island and Audrey is acting like it's the most normal thing in the world.

With Bradley and Caleb outside, Wyatt upstairs, it's just me and Audrey sitting on the sectional.

"How are you?" I ask.

"I'm good," Audrey says. She looks good. I don't see any signs of the strain that were there a few months ago after her husband had died in a plane crash. Like Lilah, she looks happy.

"And you?" she asks. "What do you think about our guys?"

"I've hardly had time to get to know them, but my first impressions are good. You two certainly look happy."

"What about Caleb?" she asks.

"What about him?"

She shrugs. "Just curious to know what you think about him. He doesn't come around very often, so Lilah and I don't know him very well. You probably spent longer with him driving up here than we've spent with him altogether."

"Well. He seems like a nice guy. Likeable." He definitely won points with me when he came back to rescue me from Sheriff Morgan. I hope what I felt from the sheriff was my imagination, but it certainly hadn't felt like it at the time.

"Have you met Sheriff Morgan?" I ask.

"Yes." Audrey scrunches up her face in distaste. "Unfortunately."

"Then it wasn't just me."

"What? You met him?"

"Oh yes. He came inside the house. He totally creeped me out. Caleb came back and the guy finally left."

"What did he do?" Audrey pulls a throw pillow into her lap and holds it there.

"It's hard to explain. It's like he was looking around. And he was asking me personal questions like how long I'm planning on staying here. And telling me how I won't like the winters up here."

"Wyatt calls him an ass hat."

"I know. It's rather fitting, isn't it?"

"He's actually the one who came and told us about Claire's house. And he came back here?"

"I guess so. He was here when we drove up."

Lilah, finished feeding the cat, comes over and flops down on the sofa.

"You know what would be funny," she says. "If you started dating Caleb and we all lived here together."

"Lilah," Audrey says with a warning in her tone.

"No," I say. "That would not be funny, Lilah."

"He is kind of cute, right Audrey. And he's a businessperson, like you, Brianna."

I sweep a hand down my sweatpants. "Not such a businessperson right now, am I?"

"Whatever. You know what I mean."

"I'm going to forget you said that," I say, glancing toward the back door where Caleb is out there right now with Bradley.

And even though I said I was going to forget she said it, I know perfectly well that *actually* forgetting about it isn't going to be nearly so easy to do.

Because she's right. Caleb is a handsome man. And, yes, I noticed his stormy sea blue eyes. But. No. Not interested.

Definitely not interested in getting caught up in whatever it is my sisters have going on here.

CHAPTER
TWELVE

Caleb

After I put on an old coat Bradley tosses in my direction at the back door, we follow Biscuit around while he makes his rounds about the back yard. Apparently he has a very specific route he follows and he never goes past the shadows of the trees.

"You always keep him on a leash now?" I ask. "Doesn't look like he wants to run off."

"Absolutely. He doesn't get any alone time either. Not since he was dognapped."

"Yeah. Somebody crossed a line when they did that."

"You can say that again. You don't want to be around when I find out who took my dog."

"Actually I kind of do. I want to see you kick that person's ass. Because if you don't, then I'll have to do it."

"Have to get in line behind Wyatt and the girls."

I look back toward the house. All the lights are on, but all the shades are also down. Bradley and Audrey had installed motorized shades on all the windows so that no one could stand outside after dark and watch them inside the house.

The motion light at the back door clicks off, but there's plenty of moonlight to guide our way. Not that Biscuit needs light at all. He knows his route by heart.

"This old house is filling up," I say.

"You've got that right. Not what I expected to happen. But having Lilah here makes Audrey happy."

"You don't mind it then? Not really? And now the housekeeper lives with you."

"That's just temporary."

"Right. Just like you were going to live here temporarily."

"That's different," he says.

Biscuit finds the place that suits him and throws leaves everywhere like he's frantically digging for treasure.

"What did you want to talk to me about?"

"Just wondered what you thought about Brianna. We're all just meeting her."

"She's smart," I say. "I get the impression she can do anything she sets her mind to."

"Sounds like the other sisters."

"And she's fiercely independent. More so than either Lilah or Audrey."

"I get that vibe from her, too."

"I don't think you have to worry about her living here in the house for long," I say. "I think as soon as she finds a place of her own, she'll be moving out. As soon as she finds a job."

"Huh. Not really what I was asking. If having here making Audrey happy, then I'll deal with it. Biscuit's finally ready to head back inside."

The dog takes off at a run toward the house. Bradley gives him full rein, but the dog stops just before he reaches the point that it snaps back.

"How does he do that?" I ask. The motion light clicks on as Biscuit hits its range.

"I don't know. I'm surrounded by people who are smarter than me."

I scoff. "First of all that's decidedly not true. And second, Biscuit is not people."

"Try telling that to him." The dog is sitting at the back door, waiting for us to come along and open it for him.

"I wouldn't mind knowing what's up with that sheriff," I say before we reach the door.

"What do you mean?" He opens the door and lets

Biscuit run inside by himself, leaving the two of us alone on the back porch.

"He was hanging around outside when we got here. So after I left Brianna here, I stopped at your old cabin just down the way and waited for him to drive past. When he didn't, I came back. He was inside the house. Standing there looking at Brianna."

"Looking at her how?"

"I don't know, but Wyatt's right. There is something seriously wrong with that guy."

"I thought it was just me. That's why we don't tell him anything."

"You think he knows who's doing it?"

"I don't know what he knows," Bradley says. "But I do know that I don't like him being around here."

"Agreed."

"It's freezing out here," he says. "Let's get back inside. Get a fire going in the fireplace."

"Thought you'd never say that."

"Here," he says, stepping toward the stack of cut firewood. "Make yourself useful."

He proceeds to pile firewood in my arms. Not the least bit concerned that I happen to be wearing a designer suit beneath this old coat.

CHAPTER
THIRTEEN

Brianna

BISCUIT RUNS in the back door, by himself, still wearing his leash, and lays down in front of the fireplace.

"Three went out. One comes back. Should we be concerned?" I ask.

"Nah. They're just outside. Talking."

As though on cue, the back door opens and Caleb walks in behind Bradley. Both of them have their arms loaded down with firewood.

Bradley carrying firewood looks perfectly natural.

But seeing Caleb carrying an armload of firewood, especially while he's wearing what I know to be a designer suit beneath the old coat, makes it hard for me to look away.

It just says so much to me about him. Here's a man who basically has his own business in addition to running his family business, wearing designer suits, and looks like a Houstonian. But at the moment, he's wearing an old coat that obviously doesn't belong to him and he's carrying an armload of firewood.

Those two things together exemplify everything I know about him so far. He's successful and yet he puts his family first. That's what I'm seeing from watching him stand there while Bradley unloads the firewood from his arms.

He must sense me looking at him because he looks over and smiles.

I look away quickly, feeling like I've been busted studying the man who's been nothing but kind to me.

My face feels a bit heated as I look down at my phone, pretending to be suddenly engrossed in its blank screen.

"Want a beer?" Bradley asks, dusting his hands on his jeans after unloading all the firewood.

"Sure," Caleb says.

"Anybody else?" Bradley asks.

My sisters and I shake our heads.

Wyatt comes back down the stairs. "All done," he says. "Anybody want a beer?"

"Great minds," Caleb says, sitting down beside me.

I try not to read too much into him sitting next to me. Where else would he sit? He knows that Bradley is going to sit next to Audrey and Wyatt is going to sit next to Lilah. Unless he sits on the hearth or on the chair off to itself, next to me is that only place left.

Bradley and Wyatt come back with beers, handing one to Caleb. He just holds it, not drinking it.

I pick up my bottle of water and drink, trying not to look at him.

"Is Claire okay?" I ask Wyatt.

"She's settling into her room. We stopped at the General Store on the way back and bought her some basics to get her through the next couple of days. She's a very strong woman. Very resilient. Insists that as long as she has her cat, nothing else matters."

"I can't even imagine going through something like that," Audrey says. "And not being upset about it."

"She's upset," Lilah says. "She has to be. But she's been through so much lately. It's probably just one more thing to have to deal with on top of everything else."

The black cat, Claire's cat, hops onto the back of the sectional and climbs into Lilah's lap. "Why aren't you up there with your mother?" Lilah asks, but she buries her face in his fur.

"What's a typical day like around here?" I ask during the moment of silence while Bradley gets a fire going. "Shooting down bird drones. Houses burning down. Creepy sheriffs coming into the house?"

They all just look at me for a moment. Audrey and Lilah. Caleb. Wyatt. And Bradley.

Then they all laugh.

"Welcome to Whiskey Springs," Audrey says. "Where there's never a dull moment."

Great. Walking into a hornet's nest is exactly what I wanted to do.

But for them, it seems to be their new normal.

"Bad timing on my part," I says. "Showing up on the same day that Claire needs a place to stay. I could have shared a room with Lilah."

"It's okay," Lilah says, squeezing Wyatt's hand. "Wyatt's been sleeping in the chair in my room anyway." She looks more serious than she has since I got here. "After what happened with Biscuit, we sleep in our rooms with our doors locked. Just to be safe."

I look at Caleb then. I don't know why. I guess I just wonder what he thinks about all this. Like me, he's not really a part of it.

And somehow that makes me feel like he and I are kindred spirits.

I hadn't realized just how much I needed that feeling of connection with someone.

And it just so happens that he's the one I'm getting that feeling from.

Not my fault.

CHAPTER
FOURTEEN

Caleb

WITH THE FIRE crackling in the fireplace, Biscuit snoring softly, and the cat, aptly named Blackie, I listen to the conversations flowing around me.

Two conversations at once, sometimes connecting, sometimes not.

Audrey and Bradley talking about the possibility of adding onto the house.

Lilah wondering if there's any kind of stipulation in the trust about that.

Lilah and Wyatt talking about the greenhouse and flower shop they're trying to get off the ground. Apparently they had some kind of setback that kept them from moving as quickly as they had hoped.

Audrey suggesting they wait until spring, which neither one of them want to do.

"It's going to start snowing any day now," Bradley says. "And you'll be forced to wait whether you want to or not."

"That's why we need the greenhouse up and running so we can have flowers growing over the winter."

"If you're not ready to start selling, won't they just be lost?" I ask.

"Well, yes," Lilah says. "But they'll be practice flowers. This is all new to us."

"I guess that makes sense," I say, taking a sip of the beer I'm not going to drink. Not when I have to drive down the mountainside. In the dark.

"It can't hurt," Wyatt says. "We have to learn how to put together arrangements."

"That," I say. "Would be so far over my head, I can't even begin to imagine."

"Anybody can learn anything they want to learn," Lilah says.

I lift my beer to her. "I like your optimism," I say.

"If anybody can do it," Brianna says. "Lilah can." She looks at her sister. "Have you been getting any painting done? I haven't heard you say anything about it lately."

"A little. When the weather's warm enough, Wyatt and I walk down to the river's edge and I paint. I'm also doing some sketching."

"I'd like to see," Brianna says.

"Okay. I'll show you tomorrow."

I'm getting the impression that Brianna is highly protective of her siblings, especially Lilah, the youngest.

"I didn't know you painted," I say to Lilah.

"She's very good," Wyatt says. "And I'm not just saying that because I like her."

Lilah shoves at Wyatt, but he just wraps his arms around her, holding her close.

Brianna obviously knows that Lilah is artistic and wants to encourage her.

"I'd like to see some of your work, too," I say. "It's nice to have someone artistic in the family."

Lilah looks up at Wyatt with questions. He just shakes his head.

There's something they aren't telling us. Audrey and Bradley are officially engaged, but I'm getting the sense that Wyatt and Lilah have talked about getting married, too. Privately.

"Well, I've got to drive home," I say. "And I've got to go to work tomorrow. So I'm going to say goodnight."

"Give me that beer," Wyatt says. "And I'll walk you out."

After I hand the beer over to Wyatt, I glance over at Brianna who's studying me again with those intense teal green eyes of hers. Eyes that seem to see everything. Even things people don't necessarily want her to see.

"I'll be seeing you soon," I say in what sounds like a general statement, but I know it's directed at Brianna.

I love my brothers, but Brianna is the one here that I find interesting.

And as much as I do not want to get involved in whatever they have going on here... this Sinclair-Winslow connection, I already know that I want to see her again.

No getting around that.

Maybe I'm just curious about her.

She and I have a lot in common and I'm curious about what she thinks about all this chaos surrounding our family and I'm curious about what she's going to do now that she's here.

Wyatt follows me as I step outside onto the porch. Pulls the door closed.

"Tomorrow we're all going out to search for a Christmas tree to chop down. You in?"

My plans for tomorrow flash through my head. After spending today in Denver and then tonight here, I have lots of catch up on and I don't have a lot of flexibility in my day.

I can't keep getting behind.

"Sure," I say. "What time?"

"Lunch."

"Is it a surprise?"

"Just didn't want to put you on the spot."

"On the spot?"

"You know. With Brianna. Don't want to make any assumptions."

"Okay. I see." I clasp him on the shoulder. "Thanks for

inviting me. Trying to be more involved in family things. So. I'll be here."

As I head to my car, I wonder just how much more it is than that.

Doesn't matter though. Not really.

I was planning on being involved more with my family anyway.

And now that I know about all the threats they're getting, they could use my presence.

It has nothing to do with Brianna.

Not one single thing.

I smile to myself as I climb into my truck.

CHAPTER
FIFTEEN

Brianna

SHORTLY AFTER CALEB LEAVES, I head up to my room.

I ignore, as best I can, the odd sense of loss I feel as he drives off. It's not like me to feel that way.

Bradley carries my luggage upstairs, but I don't unpack yet. There's plenty of time for that.

Instead I change into my pajamas and wonder what it is about Caleb that I find so intriguing.

I've avoided dating for a very long time because I work all the time and work is the only place I ever meet people.

Since my company has...had... no longer my company... a very strict policy against dating those we work with...

even if the guy doesn't even show up for the date... I just avoided dating.

If I had met Caleb under different circumstances, I might have allowed myself to look at him with the possibility of dating him.

Even though my family doesn't a policy against dating people in the family (obviously), I could date him if I wanted to.

But. It's just too weird.

Too interconnected.

And I'm too well-schooled in not mixing things. Dating Caleb would be too much like mixing family with... well... family.

I'm too tired to try to understand it right now. I just need to get some sleep and everything will look better in the morning.

After getting changed into my pajamas, I walk over to the door and throw the lock.

Something has to be done about living this way.

Living in house where we don't feel safe doesn't seem like a very good way to live.

I understand Audrey being determined to stay here in the house.

This house is the only thing she inherited from her late husband. The house and the million dollar annual stipend that she gets along with it.

That's nothing to sneeze at. And, yes, I'm pretty sure I'd fight to stay here, too.

And on top of that, she's got Bradley behind her.

From what I've gathered through various conversations, the Winslows have money of their own so the money isn't their motivation for wanting to weather all this to be with my sisters.

They seem to genuinely care about my sisters and my sisters are definitely smitten with their men.

I stand at the window and look outside. I have to raise the window shade to look out, but I refuse to hide behind it.

With the lights out, it's not like anyone can see inside anyway.

I stand there and look across the meadow, across the valley, at the tall, rugged mountain peaks capped with forever-snow glowing in the moonlight.

It's beautiful here. And if I raise the window just a fraction, I smell the fresh scent of the spruce trees outside. It's so refreshing and so clean, it almost hurts to breathe it in.

Despite all the chaos going on, with the threatening notes and the bird drones and the creepy ass sheriff, I can see the beauty of this place. It's the kind of place a person could get used to.

Our parents raised us girls in Houston, only moving back to Atlanta after we were grown and out of the house to care for their elderly parents, so I've always been a city girl.

Is it so easy, then, with just one day, to turn a city girl into a small-town mountain girl?

I have plenty of time to figure all that out. Plenty of time of experience the small town. The winter that I've been told I won't survive.

Thinking back over that conversation with the sheriff, makes me bristle and makes me feel all the more determined to stay here at least through the winter. Just to prove the ass hat wrong.

He doesn't know me. He's just trying to frighten me away.

The thought makes me pause.

But why? Why would the sheriff care who lives in Audrey's house? What stake could he possibly have in our lives?

I shake off the notion and turn away from the window. I leave the shade up just out of spite.

Just to show whoever might be out there watching my window that I'm not going to cower behind window coverings. If someone wants to watch me sleep, if they find a way to see into my second-floor window, then more power to them. Let them be bored out of their minds.

I have nothing to hide.

I climb into bed, click on my reading light, and open up my book.

I've barely read more than two short paragraphs when I find my attention wandering back to Caleb. Wondering what he's doing tonight. Wondering how he spends his time when he's not working.

I shake my head.

Not my business.

I should not be thinking about him. My thoughts are being very bad for distracting me into thinking about Caleb Winslow.

Not for me.

Definitely not for me.

I'm not in the market.

This Winslow-Sinclair thing is far too complex.

CHAPTER
SIXTEEN

Caleb

THE NEXT MORNING I get as much work done as I can. I'd prioritized everything in my head last night, so I take care of what has to be done first. The rest can wait.

There has to be some kind of perk to owning my own business even if it is getting spend time with my family.

About eleven o'clock, I drive home from the office and change into blue jeans and a sweatshirt layered over a t-shirt. I put on my hiking boots.

It's been a while since I went out in the woods for any reason and going out to hunt down a Christmas tree seems like a good excuse to get myself outside again.

I'm enjoying getting to know my brothers' girlfriends.

And maybe I'm looking forward to seeing Brianna again.

It's not such a bad thing. She's going to be part of my family now anyway.

Since it's a dreary day and looks like snow, even though it's not in the forecast, I take my truck.

I mostly drive my truck around Whiskey Springs and take the car when I'm driving into Denver.

I toss an axe into the truck bed just in case, even though I'm certain my brothers will have everything they need for chopping down a tree.

Even though Wyatt is the designated lumberjack of the family, we're all proficient at using an axe and a chainsaw. About half our business is trees and firewood and the other half is cabin rentals.

It all goes hand in hand and we can all do whatever needs to be done in any part of the business, having learning everything from the ground up as children. A rite of passage. Our after school activities consisted of chopping wood and following our father out on maintenance calls.

I pull up to Audrey's house and feel a twinge of unexpected nostalgia at the sight of smoke drifting out of the chimney.

My brothers have something I don't have. They have a home life.

As they should.

They deserve to be happy.

I could have a home life if I wanted to.

I just never found the person I wanted to commit to spending the rest of my life with.

And that includes sporadically looking with intention—if dating apps are included in that definition.

I can safely say that I have had no luck in my romantic search endeavors whether by accident or intent.

Sure. I could have settled. There are plenty of women in Whiskey Springs who consider any one of the Winslow boys a good catch.

Maybe that's why I refused to date anyone who knows my family.

Being someone's good catch is not my idea of dating. To me that's sort of like going hunting by baiting elk.

As I step out of my truck and walk up to the front door, I find myself looking around for anything suspicious.

I hate that. I hate it for my brothers and their girl-friends. Having to be on edge all the time is no way to live.

I'll do whatever I can to make that go away.

Bradley opens the door as I step up onto the front porch.

"Just in time," he says. "We're about to have lunch."

"Good." I step inside the warmth of the living room and take off my coat.

I look around. Claire is there, doing something in the kitchen along with Audrey. Lilah is sitting at the computer at the kitchen table, stacks of different colored index cards all around her. Wyatt is banking the fire in the hearth in preparation for leaving the house.

But I don't see Brianna.

Maybe she's decided she doesn't want to go with us.

Wyatt had given me a heads up in case I didn't want to feel like I was being set up with her. Maybe someone had done the same thing for Brianna and she had chosen to stay home.

I'm rather surprised that they will let her stay home alone while everyone else is out hunting for a tree, but then maybe Claire is staying behind, too.

Deciding that makes sense, however disappointing it might be, I sit down at the kitchen table.

"Can I help you with anything?" I ask Lilah.

"No. I'm just adding a few flowers to my list."

"So this is how you do it?" I ask.

"Pretty much," she says with a little shrug.

I'd like to know more. I'm intrigued that she can learn anything she sets her mind to, but before I can ask her anything else, a movement at the top of the stairs catches my attention.

It's Brianna. Anything I was thinking about involving index cards and flowers and learning vanishes out of my head.

All I can see is Brianna.

CHAPTER
SEVENTEEN

Brianna

WHILE AUDREY and Claire make lunch, I dash upstairs to grab a cashmere scarf I remembered packing in one of my suitcases.

I'm getting the feeling that Audrey likes having Claire here. I have to admit it's not bad having a live-in house-keeper. We certainly didn't have that growing up, but things change.

I'm also getting the impression that Audrey likes having a house full of family. That part rather reminds me of when we were growing up, but this is better because we're the adults now and for my sisters, at least, they have their boyfriends.

They're happy. I can see it all over their faces.

And today we're going out in the woods to chop down a Christmas tree.

A new tradition, Audrey is calling it.

We had a fake tree growing up. It was nice. Festive and elegant all rolled into one, but it wasn't real. I had a boyfriend who always had a real tree in their home and I envied him. Their house always smelled like Christmas. It was a scent I never forgot and it could take me back to my teenage years in a heartbeat.

Even after I moved out on my own and could have gotten a real tree, I didn't, because well... it was just me and I didn't see the point.

But now with all of us together, it seems like the perfect thing to do.

The only thing missing is a boyfriend for me.

Of course, since I don't have a boyfriend, it's a little difficult to imagine how that piece might fit into the puzzle.

But... I can't help but think about Caleb. Maybe it's because I'd spent so many hours with him yesterday. It was quite honestly the closest thing to a date I've had in a very long time. At least the closest thing to a date where the guy actually showed up.

But it's not something I should be thinking about.

I'm sure he has better things to do than traipse about in the woods with us looking for a Christmas tree. How many people does it take to find and chop down a Christmas tree anyway?

Halfway down the stairs, I stop, my boot clad feet frozen to the wooden step, one hand on the railing.

Sitting at the kitchen table, looking right at me with stormy sea blue eyes is Caleb.

I was just thinking about him and here he is. Looking at me with a slightly amused expression.

My heart slams into my throat.

It's almost like I conjured him up by thinking about him.

It takes me a second before I realize I'm grinning.

Pulling my gaze away and looking straight ahead, I wipe the grin off my face as best I can, not very well, I'm sure, and continue my way down the stairs.

I walk over to the dining table where he's sitting. It would be rude to do otherwise and put my hands on the back of the nearest chair.

"Hi."

"Hi." He smiles at me with something in his eyes that has drunken butterflies flying about in my stomach.

"I didn't expect you to be here today," I say.

"I could hardly turn down the chance to find the perfect Christmas tree to bring home."

Home. I bite my lip.

I sense Lilah watching me out of the corner of my eye, but right now I don't care.

"They say it's a new tradition," I say.

"I guess what's old is new."

I look at him, my head tilted sideways. So going out to chop a Christmas tree is nothing new to Caleb.

And yet... he's here.

"Okay," Audrey says, bringing a platter piled high with sandwiches over to the table. Bradley behind her with two bags of potato chips. "Sandwiches and chips for everyone. Lilah, Dear, can we borrow your table?"

"Sure," Lilah says, closing her computer and putting it on the counter behind her.

I notice that no one touches her index cards or even offers to. Apparently it hadn't taken long for everyone to learn that Lilah doesn't like her things messed with.

She has a system that works for her and works well.

No one questions that.

"Have a seat," Caleb says, pulling out the heavy chair I'm standing behind.

I sit down next to him.

As everyone takes a seat and the platter of sandwiches makes its way around, I wonder just why no one bothered to tell me that Caleb was coming today.

Maybe they hadn't known.

Or maybe they hadn't thought it was worth mentioning.

The fact that I think it was worth mentioning tells me something. I need to be careful.

This Sinclair-Winslow connection thing just might be contagious.

CHAPTER
EIGHTEEN

Caleb

COMING today had been a good idea.

A very good idea.

One look at Brianna across the room, her standing on the stairs, her eyes locked onto mine, and I know I'd made the right decision.

She was caught off-guard. I have no doubt about that. No one had told her I was coming. I like that. I like having the element of surprise on my side.

Brianna Sinclair is a vexed brunette elfin princess.

As beautiful as she is, she always wears a slightly vexed

expression. As though she's thinking and thinking thoughts that only she can think.

I get the sense that her thoughts are so more complex than anyone else, they don't even begin to compare.

I don't know much about her sisters to compare her to them, but I do know that Lilah is a genius at learning things.

Audrey, I don't know what her super power is yet.

But Brianna. Brianna is just plain brilliant.

Nothing gets past her.

I listen to the conversation swirling around us.

Bradley is trying to tell Audrey which trees make the best Christmas trees.

"Definitely the blue spruce," he says.

"According to what I researched," Lilah says, jumping into the conversation. "The Douglas and Frasier fir trees are actually best. The Douglas fir is one of the top-selling Christmas tree varieties. It has soft, sweet scented needles and a full form. The Frasier fir is durable and has a strong scent."

"Her mind is like an encyclopedia," Bradley says.

"Tell her something once and she'll remember it forever," Wyatt says affectionately.

"Scary, isn't it?" Audrey says.

Even as the conversation swirls, I'm focused on Brianna. She smells like a mix of lavender and vanilla.

She watches the others while she eats, not saying anything.

She's like a guardian, watching over her sisters. Waiting for someone to make a misstep. I would not want to be the one who made the mistake of stepping out of bounds with one of her siblings.

"What kind of tree do you think is best?" she asks, turning to me.

"The blue spruce," I say, then add a nod toward Lilah. "No offense. But it's what we sell."

"Your tree farm," Brianna says.

"Yes. People flock from the whole state to buy our trees."

"The whole state?" she asks with one eyebrow raised in amusement.

"Maybe not the whole state. But definitely all around."

"It could be the whole state," she says.

"What do you mean?"

"With the right marketing, you could go national."

No one says anything for a few minutes. I get the vague impression that everyone is watching us with interest.

"I think your father tried that once, didn't he?" Claire asks.

"That was before our time," Bradley says. "Things were different then. It might be worth checking into."

"We would just need a good website," Audrey says.

"Oh," Lilah says, leaning forward. "We could do guided virtual tours and people could pick out their own trees."

"Then you just have to figure out the logistics of shipping," Brianna says.

My brothers and I all three lean back in our chairs and look at each other.

We don't have to say a word to know what we're all thinking.

These Sinclair women are freaking amazing.

They're amazing individually, but together, they're unstoppable.

It's an amazing thing to witness.

As I sit there eating my sandwich, I realize it's already too late for me.

I'm hooked.

CHAPTER
NINETEEN

Brianna

After lunch, we all meet up at the back door to put on our coats.

Since I don't have a coat, I'm instructed to just choose one from the rack of half a dozen coats left over after everyone grabs theirs.

It appears to me that all the coats are men's coats and are much too big.

"Try this one," Caleb says, pulling a red faded coat from the rack.

He holds up what looks like a well-worn wool coat. A lady's coat.

"Okay. It's smaller than the other ones," I say.

"I don't know how it ended up here. No idea at all, but it looks like the coat my grandmother used to wear."

"Really?" I slide my arms into the sleeves while he holds the coat. "How did that happen?"

"I guess one of my brothers must have brought some coats from our parents' house." He begins buttoning me into the coat. "I have a feeling you're not the only southern girl who arrived without a coat."

I can't say why, but him buttoning my coat is truly one of the sweetest things anyone has ever done for me.

"A perfect fit," he says after I'm all buttoned in.

I look up at him as he adjusts my scarf around my hair.

His gaze snags on mine and I practically forget to breathe.

His stormy blue eyes look into mine with such an intensity that I can't quite wrap my head around.

"Alright," Bradley says. "Everybody bundled up? It's going to be cold out there."

"I think we're all good," Caleb says just before he slides a wool cap onto my head, down over my ears.

I scowl at him, knowing this can't possibly be a flattering look for me.

He just shrugs and a quick glance around tells me that everyone else is wearing similar wool hats. Definitely not flattering. But apparently a necessary evil.

"Are you sure you're going to be okay here by yourself?" Wyatt asks Claire.

"I'll be okay," Claire says, patting the phone in her pocket. "One cross vibe and I'll have you on the phone."

"I feel better about leaving the house with you here," Audrey says, giving the older woman a quick hug.

"Go have fun," Claire says. "I'll have everything ready for the tree when you get back. Just like we talked about."

With Biscuit leading the way, we all head out, wind slapping the cold air into our faces the minute we're outside. Now I see why Caleb tucked my hair beneath the scarf. Otherwise it would have been all in my face.

Bradley holds a chain saw in one hand at his side and Wyatt carries an axe easily across one shoulder. Caleb, unlike his brothers who look like they mean business, has no weapon. He looks like he's just out for a stroll.

Audrey and Bradley, hand in hand, lead the way, urging Biscuit out of his usual route and heading along a path that leads into the trees.

Lilah and Wyatt, also walking hand in hand, follow along after them. Lilah gazes at everything, doubtless with her artist's eyes.

Caleb and I are left to bring up the rear. Unlike the others, we are not walking hand in hand.

In fact, it seems so strange and strikingly obvious to me, that I shove my hands in the pockets of my coat... Caleb's grandmother's coat.

We follow along a trail that takes us alongside the rushing river, so loud it's almost impossible to hear each other talking.

As we veer away from the river, I glance over at Caleb.

"Do we have a particular destination in mind?" I ask.

"I'm sure Bradley already scoped out some trees."

"If you have a tree farm, why don't we just go there and find one?"

"Because that would be too easy," Caleb says. "This way, you all get the whole experience."

"I see. So it's about the experience. But I don't see how it's different from going to your tree farm for the whole experience."

"Has anyone ever told you that you're too smart for your own good?" he asks.

I smile over at him. "I might have heard variations of that before, but never as a compliment."

"It's definitely a compliment," he says. "Do you need me to kick anyone's ass for you?"

"Sounds like you're just itching for a fight."

"Maybe you bring out the knight-in-shining armor in me."

"In that case, I'll let you know," I say.

As we follow the trail, leading downhill, it becomes less easy to walk. A bit more rugged and, for me, as a city girl, more treacherous.

My boot slips on a loose rock and before I can do more than put up a hand to catch my balance, Caleb is there grabbing hold of my arm to keep me steady.

"Be careful there, City Girl," he says.

I look over at him sideways. He just smiles and takes my hand, squeezing it palm to palm.

Something. A new awareness. Shimmers through me.

With the cold hitting me from the outside and the warmth flooding me from within, I'm overwhelmed with feeling.

A bluebird flies across the trail in front of us and the sun comes out, casting a glittery glow to the air.

I feel a lightness in my step that I can't remember feeling since... well... since forever.

In this moment, fleeting though it may be, all is right with my world.

TWENTY

Caleb

WE REACH A MEADOW FULL OF, imagine it, blue spruce trees.

Now that I have Brianna's hand in mine, I don't want to let go. Ever.

It's an odd sensation, watching her wearing my grandmother's wool coat.

Even though it felt like we'd walked downhill, we've reached a meadow with a light layer of snow on the ground.

The high country.

Brianna stops and looks around. "It's beautiful here," she says with obvious awe.

"It is, isn't it?" I follow her gaze.

"Have you been up here before?"

"I'm sure I have. My brothers and I have been all over these mountains at one point or another."

"You were just free to roam?"

"Pretty much."

"It seems treacherous beneath its beauty. Making it deceptive."

"It'd say that's accurate."

"Are we supposed to be looking for a tree?" she asks, lightly touching one of the

"Yes." I'm looking at a blue spruce tree off to our right. Doing a mental height gauge. Decide it's too tall for inside the house.

Brianna steps around the tree I'm looking at, and since I'm still holding her hand, I follow.

We walk around a tree not more than five feet tall.

"Nice tree," I say.

She looks at me with her teal green eyes. "Are we allowed to cut here? Who's land is this?"

"It's Audrey's land," I say, a little impressed that she would ask that question. "She can cut whatever tree she wants to cut."

She looks at me with a perplexed expression, like she doesn't quite believe me, but Lilah calls out, interrupting whatever she was thinking.

"Come look," Lilah says. "We found the perfect tree."

Brianna takes one last longing look at the tree in front of us. "I guess the search is over," she says.

"Go ahead," I say, letting go of her hand. "I'll be right there."

As she walks off, I pull a red streamer out of my coat pocket and tie it around one of the limbs of the tree.

Then I catch up to her just as she reaches the others.

"You don't think it's too tall?" I ask her.

"Not if we cut off the bottom," Wyatt says.

I nod my approval. Not at the tree. I couldn't care less about which tree they decide on. But he has my approval at supporting his girl's choice.

I already know that Brianna will get behind whatever Lilah chooses.

"Is this the one we're getting?" Bradley asks Audrey.

"Looks like it," Audrey says.

"Okay, Kids, stand back. This could get messy."

I herd the ladies, along with Biscuit, back away, out of range of the tree, while Wyatt stays next to Bradley, holding the trunk of the tree, getting ready to make sure it falls in the direction they want it to.

It's a big enough tree that it's going to easily reach the ceiling of the house.

The chain saw echoes through the air, disrupting what was a serene vista. Biscuit paws at the ground and barks, tugging at his leash, not liking the disruptive noise.

I wonder how long it's been since a chain saw has been heard out here. If ever.

The tree crashes to the ground with a loud thud, landing in exactly the spot it was supposed to.

Bradley turns off the chainsaw and the quietness returns leaving just the memory of its loudness lingering on the air.

Now it's time for us to wrap the tree up to protect its limbs and carry it back to the house.

"Time for me to go to work," I tell Brianna before I leave her with her sisters to help my brothers.

The fun part of the trip is over.

Brianna

WE WALK AHEAD of the guys on the trip back to the house.

The guys walk behind us, the three of them carrying the tree.

Personally, I think it's going to be too tall for the house, but Lilah picked it out and as the youngest sister, she pretty much gets what she wants.

If it was me, I would have picked out the little tree I'd found. It was the perfect height with perfectly formed limbs. I console myself with the knowledge my perfect tree gets to live another year. Maybe next year. Maybe next year, it'll be my turn to pick out the tree.

"This was fun, wasn't it?" Lilah asked as we make our way back toward the house.

"It was," Audrey says. "Our new tradition."

"It just seems so normal," Lilah says. "We don't get a lot of normal around here."

I see now why Caleb asked if he needed to kick someone's ass. I feel like asking that very question right now.

Not that I would or could if I wanted to. I've never been in a fight my whole life. The closest any one of us has ever been to being in a fight was when Lilah tossed the contents of a wine glass into someone's face.

We're a pretty tame bunch, all in all.

I get the sense that the Winslow brothers can't say the same thing about themselves.

They're good guys, but no one is going to mess with them. Especially not when they're together.

They make a formidable team, the three of them.

Formidable and handsome. My sisters have done well for themselves and I'm maybe a tad bit envious. My sisters chatter about nothing and everything as we walk back toward the house. Their noses are red from the cold, but they're both smiling.

Secure and happy in their relationships.

As we round a curve in the path, I look back over my shoulder toward the guys following close behind us. They, too, are talking animatedly among themselves. I can't hear their words, but they sound happy, too.

Caleb catches me looking back and grins at me. I grin back before I catch myself. Grinning back at him is like a spontaneous reaction. I can't control it. Even if I wanted to.

Looking forward again, my heart skitters with lightness.

I can almost imagine what it might be like if Caleb and I were together.

Maybe it wouldn't be so bad. Three sisters and three brothers.

Rather old-fashioned.

People in Houston would probably have a field day about the whole thing.

I can hear them now.

She couldn't go and find a man of her own.

She just hooked up with the brother of her sisters' boyfriends.

It's like one of those old black and white westerns.

Caleb laughs at something someone says.

Who cares what other people think.

If they met the Winslow brothers... if they met Caleb, they would understand.

And even if they don't understand, it's not their business.

"We should go on a sleigh ride," Audrey says.

"A sleigh ride?"

"Yeah. You know. With horses. It could be another one of our traditions."

Maybe my imaginary acquaintances in Houston aren't

so very wrong. Maybe being up here in Colorado is like being in a different world. Maybe even a different century.

Looking over at Lilah, I shrug. I guess we'll be finding some horses. And a sleigh.

As long as Caleb is part of this activity, I won't mind. In fact, it might be a little bit fun.

TWENTY-TWO

Caleb

"I told you this tree was going to be too tall," I say as we lower the tree down on its side to assess whether to cut some more off the bottom or maybe off the top.

"If we cut some more off the bottom," Wyatt says. "We'll have to cut off some of the bottom limbs, too."

Bradley stands back with his hands behind his head. "That would work. It would still be proportional that way."

"Let's take it outside. Again." Wyatt puts his coat back on.

Bradley and I do the same.

The girls are sitting in front of the fireplace with a fire that looks dangerously high for the fireplace, but no one seems to be worried about it.

With the tree back outside, we lay it extended out across the steps and Bradley picks up the chainsaw.

Wyatt and I hold the tree steady while he cuts off a good six inches, then some of the lower branches.

"Lilah wants to keep these branches," Wyatt says, stacking them up on the porch.

"What for?" Bradley asks, taking a broom and sweeping the saw dust off the trunk of the tree.

"I think she wants to use them to make garland or something," Wyatt says.

"Good idea," Bradley says.

I watch my brothers with amusement. The both of them are so far domesticatedly gone, it's just funny. Two grown men stacking tree limbs and sweeping off the trunk of a Christmas tree before they take it back inside.

"What are you smirking about?" Wyatt asks.

I hold up my hands. "I didn't say a word."

"Didn't have to," Wyatt says. "I can see it written all over your face."

"I don't know what you're talking about. I think it's cute. The two of you living in domesticated bliss."

"Jealous," Bradley says.

"Yep."

"Just give him a minute. He'll catch up."

"I can just go," I say. "If you two want to continue this conversation without me. Since you seem to have forgotten that I'm standing right here."

"You're not going anywhere," Bradley says.

"Once you fall under the spell of a Sinclair woman, there's nothing you can do but ride it out," Wyatt says.

"From what I hear," I say. "You fell under that spell in about two seconds."

"I don't think it was that long," Bradley says, looking at Wyatt. "Do you think it was that long?"

"Nah," Wyatt says. "It was more like instantaneous combustion."

"At least he admits it," Bradley says. "Most men wouldn't have the nerve."

"Let's get this tree back inside," Wyatt says. "It's going to be a perfect fit this time."

We carry the tree back inside, wrangle it back into the tree stand, then get it standing up again. And, as predicted, this time it fits perfectly. Just enough room at the top to put whatever decoration the girls decide they want up there.

"We're having hot chocolate," Audrey says walked past us toward the kitchen. "Anybody want any?"

Bradley and Wyatt do, of course. When I don't say anything, they look at me.

"Sure," I say. "Why not?"

I glance over toward the sectional where Brianna and Lilah are sitting to find Brianna looking right at me.

Her eyes widen and I smile.

She looks away, but not before she smiles back.

I might be protesting this whole domesticated thing, but Brianna is making it difficult to do so.

All she has to do is look at me with those big teal green eyes and I forget whatever it is I'm protesting.

TWENTY-THREE

Brianna

I'M SITTING with Audrey in front of the fireplace, flames burning entirely too high, sorting through stacks of decorations. She has multi-colored lights. Clear lights. Big old-fashioned lights, that oddly enough, are brand new in the box.

"Did you get a little carried away with the lights?" I ask.

"I couldn't decide which ones would look good on the tree."

Lilah holds up a strand of the big old-fashioned looking lights. "These," she says. "Definitely these."

"I agree," I say. "You can wrap the smaller twinkly ones along the banister."

"And around the fireplace with some of those tree branches they're cutting off," Lilah adds.

"We should have hot chocolate," Audrey decides as the men come back inside after making another adjustment to the height of the tree. "Want hot chocolate?"

"Sure," Lilah and I both say.

Audrey heads over to the kitchen to heat water.

"You two are really in the festive spirit," I say.

Lilah reaches over and puts a hand on my arm. "Don't look so vexed. It's good to see Audrey so happy."

"Yes. It is. And you, too."

Lilah smiles and wraps her arms around herself. "I keep hoping I don't wake up just to find out that it's a dream."

"It's not a dream, Lilah. It's a life you're making for yourself."

"I'm so glad you're here."

My gaze strays toward Caleb. He looks so at ease with his brothers. "Me too," I say.

Lilah leans forward and whispers.

"You think he's cute," she says.

"We're not twelve," I say, wiping the grin off my face and replacing it with my usual vexed expression.

"Too bad," she says. "I think he likes you."

"How do you know that?" I ask, my gaze straying involuntarily straying back to Caleb.

Lilah rolls her eyes. "I can tell. Anyone can see it."

"You're imagining things," I say.

"Why would I do that?" Lilah asks, looking vexed herself now. "That would take entirely too much effort and there would be no point."

I look over at her.

"I didn't mean it like that," I say.

"I know. But Caleb is a nice guy. You should give him a chance."

I bite my tongue. If she weren't my sister, I would have so many retorts to that statement.

Like... who said I was looking for a guy to begin with. And... just because he's here and he's kind of cute doesn't mean I'm obligated to give him a chance at anything.

"Are you planning to use all these decorations?" I ask. "Or just pick out some of them?"

"That's Audrey's department. But I vote we pick out a theme and stick with it."

"Good idea."

"Hot chocolate is ready," Audrey says. "Caleb, would you take this over to Brianna?"

Both my sisters are conspiring against me.

Caleb brings over two mugs of hot chocolate. Hands one to me. Then he sits down next to me.

Maybe it's not just my sisters who are conspiring against me.

Maybe it's Caleb, too.

Caleb and my own treacherous heart.

"I haven't see those big old-fashioned bulbs like that

since my grandparents used to put them on their tree. They'll look good on the blue spruce."

I sigh.

"What?" he asks. "What's that about?"

"Nothing. Just nothing. When in Rome..."

"You can't fight it," he says. "Besides, is it really so very bad?"

I look around at my sisters sitting with their boyfriends, all holding mugs of hot chocolate. The scent of the chocolate swirls with the scent of the blue spruce tree and the pleasant scent of the wood smoke from the fireplace.

And I have to swallow a lump in my throat.

The scene is so innocent and serene. Tears sting the back of my eyelids at being part of it. I acknowledge the feelings. What else am I going to do?

But I never ever would have imagined being here in a place like this with my sisters. Not in a million years.

TWENTY-FOUR

Caleb

APPARENTLY AUDREY WORKED out a deal with Claire. In exchange for room and board, Claire will not only do the cleaning she's getting paid for through the trust, but she also will do most of the cooking.

While Claire cooks lasagna, the rest of us work on decorating the tree.

With Bradley on a ladder, Audrey and Bradley string the lights, the big old-fashioned ones that they really had no choice but to use. They're perfect for the big tree.

Wyatt and Lilah work on tying together some of the tree limbs and arranging them along the banisters. Wyatt talked her out of putting tree limbs on the mantle due to the possibility of a fire hazard. Very astute if you ask me.

Audrey has a tendency to keep a blazing fire going and Bradley aids and abets that particular tendency.

Brianna and I are left with the task of sorting decorations.

"It looks like someone went to three different stores and bought one of every possible decoration."

"That's exactly what they did," Brianna says.

"You know this for a fact?" I ask, looking as Brianna as she makes three stacks of decorations. Modern. Farmhouse. And whimsical.

"There's no other explanation," she says, sweeping a hand around the stacks.

"True," I say.

Biscuit stands up from his place in front of the fireplace, shakes, and barks once.

"What's he telling us?" I ask.

"He needs to go outside," Brianna says.

"We can do that," I say. "Want to take a walk in the moonlight?"

"Okay," she says, uncurling her feet from beneath her and standing up.

"We're going to take Biscuit outside for a walk," I say to no one in particular.

"Have fun."

I hold the red coat that I now consider to be Brianna's coat while she slides her arms into it. What was my grandmother's is now hers. It seems fitting somehow. After putting on my own coat, I clip the leash onto the dog's collar.

When she doesn't make any move to button the coat, I hand Brianna the leash and begin buttoning her up.

"Think we'll be outside that long?" she asks.

"You have obviously never accompanied Biscuit on his evening outing."

She smiles and looks into my eyes as I button the buttons on her coat.

There are some things in life that could so easily become one of those habits that a man cherishes and this happens to be one of them.

The simple act of buttoning up Brianna's coat. I can't even remember ever buttoning another girl's coat for her, but with Brianna it just seems like the natural thing to do.

Biscuit barks again, reminding me that I might be lingering a bit too long over those buttons.

I zip up my own coat, then take the leash from Brianna. "I don't trust him not to bolt out of here and pull you down."

"Lilah calls him a horse dog."

"Lilah has a keen sense of observation."

"It's because she sees everything with an artist's eye," Brianna says as we step outside and the sting of the cold wind slams against our skin like a million little needles. The air is colder than I expected it to be. So cold it almost hurts to breath it in.

Brianna takes her gloves out of her pockets and slides them on. I do the same.

"Do you think it's going to snow?" Brianna asks as we follow Biscuit as he makes his way around his route that takes us along the edge of the trees. Not into the trees. Never into the extra darkness of the trees, but away from the light of the motion sensor lights and around the perimeter of the yard.

"I think so," I say. "But not tonight. Tonight it's too cold to snow."

"Too cold to snow. Is that really a thing?"

"Absolutely. The temperature has to be just right."

"Huh." She looks up toward the sky. "Stars," she says. "We don't usually see stars in Houston."

"Now that's a travesty."

"I know." She lowers her gaze back to me, then stops walking.

"What's wrong?" I ask.

"I saw something," she whispers.

"Where?" I keep a firm hold on the dog, reeling him slowly back toward us.

"There," she says. "Near that big maple tree."

"What was it?" I ask.

"I don't know."

Biscuit emits a low growl from deep in his throat, also looking toward the big maple tree.

"An animal or a person?" I ask.

"It's too dark," she says. "I couldn't tell."

"Enough of this," I say. "I'm going over there. Wait here."

I put Biscuit's leash in her hand and take two steps forward toward where she saw something move, toward the large maple tree, my boots crunching on fallen leaves.

"I don't think so," she says, following along after me.

Reaching back, I take her gloved hand. If she's coming with me into the darkness, I won't have her disappearing.

Biscuit moves forward slowly, his ears forward, a low growl in his throat.

CHAPTER
TWENTY-FIVE

Brianna

THE GLOW of the moonlight and the bright stars of night light our way as we follow Biscuit along his route in the backyard.

I know the moment the motion sensor light clicks off, leaving us with nothing but the glow of natural light behind us.

I saw something move beneath the trees. I know I did. I just don't know what it was. It was there and then just as quickly, it was gone.

Whatever it was, it sends chills up and down my spine.

The moment I realize Caleb is walking toward the big maple tree where I'd seen the movement, everything inside me protests.

He's not leaving me out here by myself while he walks into the darkness.

Even with the dog to protect me, I'm not letting him leave me out here by myself.

Too many scary movies where the damsel gets left alone after the well-meaning hero gets himself killed by trying to be brave.

As I reach him, he takes my gloved hand firmly in his own gloved hand.

We reach the maple tree, circle it, but find nothing there other than leaves softly fluttering in the breeze.

Caleb pulls out his phone and turns on the flashlight. The light, though, is feeble and doesn't allow us to see anything beyond where we're standing.

"Maybe it was nothing," I say. "Just the wind blowing in the trees."

"Maybe," he says, not moving, straining like I am to see any sign of anything that doesn't belong.

Biscuit is quiet now, just standing here like we are, as though waiting to see what we're going to do.

I shiver.

"They're going to wonder where we are," he says after what seems like a few minutes of standing there, but was probably only a few moments.

"Rightly so."

Just as he goes to turn off the flashlight and put his phone away, I see something shiny reflecting on the ground.

"Wait." I put a hand on his arm.

"What is it?"

"What's that?" I ask. "There. On the ground."

"I don't see anything," he says.

"Shine your light. There. By the tree."

Letting go of his hand, I squat down and study the shiny thing on the ground.

"Don't touch it," he says.

Ignoring him, I reach down and pick it up by the corner.

"What is it?" he asks, holding the light so we can see what's in my hand.

"It's a gum wrapper," I say.

"A gum wrapper? Out here?" He looks out into the trees as though expecting to see whoever dropped the gum wrapper still lurking about.

But there's only the wind brushing through the spruce leaves.

"Are there any more?" he asks, turning back, focusing the light on the ground, moving it around methodically, searching.

"I don't see anything."

He holds out a gloved hand for me to put the gum wrapper in.

"Let's get this inside," he says.

"Okay."

I have a feeling this could be important.

I don't even know anyone who chews gum anymore. Certainly not my sisters. And for a wrapper to be left out here makes no sense. Probably just blown in by the wind.

It could have come from anywhere.

TWENTY-SIX

Caleb

Brianna and I walk straight back to the house, no protest from Biscuit, and don't even stop to take off our coats once we're inside.

I do pause to lock the door behind us.

Brianna unclips Biscuit's leash and he runs straight to his favorite spot in front of the fireplace, turns around three times, and lies down.

As we walk straight and purposeful to the kitchen counter, everyone stops what they're doing to watch us.

"What's up?" Bradley asks.

"Something happened," Wyatt says.

I drop the shiny gum wrapper on the counter and everyone gathers around to look at it.

"Where did you get this?" Audrey asks.

It's rather odd that no one points out how it's strange that we're making a big deal out of a piece of trash we found on the ground. Under normal circumstances... well... nothing is normal here at the moment.

"There's a big maple tree not far into the trees. Due west."

"I know the one," Wyatt says.

We all look at him.

He shrugs. "Biscuit always stops there and sniffs the air."

I look at Wyatt and we all seem to realize the same thing at the same time.

This was not just a piece of trash that the wind randomly blew up to the maple tree. This is something else.

"Can we get prints off of it?" Lilah asks.

"I'm not sure Whiskey Springs has a lab," Brianna says distractedly.

"What about Trent?" Bradley asks Wyatt. "Does he have access to fingerprinting?"

"I can ask him," Wyatt pulls out his phone and walks away to call his friend.

"Why not just give it to the sheriff?" Brianna asks, but I hear the hesitation in her voice. "Never mind. We don't trust him."

"I thought it was just me," Claire says.

"You don't trust him either?" Brianna asks.

"No." Claire shakes her head. "He arrested me. For no reason."

"Right." Brianna narrows her eyes and walks off toward the fireplace.

She stands there a moment, staring into the flames.

"Is she okay?" I ask.

"Thinking," Lilah says.

Wyatt comes back. "Trent knows a guy. We just have to take it into Boulder."

"I can drive it down tomorrow," I say.

"We need to put it in a plastic bag," Audrey says.

Claire goes to the pantry and comes back with one. Hands it to Audrey.

Brianna, still wearing the worn red wool coat, turns around and looks at us, her gaze locking on mine.

"The sheriff chews gum," she says.

"That's right," Claire says. "He does. He's always chewing gum."

"That doesn't necessarily mean anything," Bradley says. "As much as I don't like the guy."

"It doesn't necessarily not mean anything," Wyatt says.

"It means something," I say. "Brianna saw someone..." I glance at her. "Something... near the tree."

"He was out there," Lilah says. "Watching us."

"We can't jump to conclusions," Audrey says.

"The prints won't lie," Brianna says. "If he was out

there, we'll know it. But someone was definitely out there. Biscuit knew it, too."

CHAPTER
TWENTY-SEVEN

Brianna

AFTER DINNER, some fine lasagna made by Claire, the six of us sit in front of the fireplace. Claire goes upstairs, taking Blackie with her.

"I told you the sheriff's an ass hat," Wyatt says, tapping the beer bottle in his hand.

"You can't just assume he did it because he's an ass," Audrey says.

"Maybe not, but it definitely makes it seem more likely, doesn't it?" Lilah asks.

"There's definitely something creepy about the guy," I

say, suppressing a little shiver as I remember the way he's stood right here in this room and looked at me.

I don't even want to think about what could have happened if Caleb hadn't shown up when he did.

Probably nothing, but in the moment, I was most definitely creeped out.

"We have to remember that he's dangerous," Audrey says. "He took Biscuit."

There are several murmurs of agreement. The fact that someone kidnapped the dog is certainly something serious enough to keep front and center in our minds.

"And don't forget," Bradley says. "The sheriff arrested Claire AFTER she got out of the hospital."

"Yeah," Audrey agrees. "That never made any sense."

"You're certain she didn't have anything to do with the notes?" I ask.

"She didn't do it," Audrey says. "She couldn't have. She was in the hospital."

"Why did he arrest her?" I ask, staring into the flames.

I'm sitting close enough that my shoulder rests against Caleb's.

Bradley and Wyatt are drinking a beer, but the rest of us are just drinking water.

"I have an idea about that," Bradley says. "I think he wanted to make us think she did it. To plant the possibility that she did it. To distract us."

"That makes a lot of sense," I say. "Except did he not think we'd figure out she couldn't have done it?"

"He was probably just hoping," Lilah says, covering her mouth to hide a yawn.

"I don't trust him," Wyatt says. "That's just the be all and end all of it."

"Do you think he saw us?" I ask Caleb, circling back around to the maple tree where we'd found the gum wrapper.

"I have no reason to think he didn't."

"Then that means he knows we know," I say.

"Maybe. It was dark. It depends on whether he hid or if he ran. If he ran, he might not have seen us looking. Might not have seen us find the gum wrapper."

"But if he stayed and hid. To watch us..." I say, letting the idea linger.

"Then he might know we know something. But he won't know for sure that we put it all together."

"Unless he bugged the house again," Wyatt says.

We all look at him.

"Claire's house fire. We were all over there while he was here."

"That's right," I say. "He was here. Sitting outside. Doesn't mean he hadn't been inside the house."

"He probably has cameras along the road and knew we were on our way to the house," Caleb says.

"We can't do anything about it tonight," Wyatt says, kissing Lilah on the top of the head. "I need to get this one up to bed."

"We all need to get some rest," Audrey says.

"Do you have a long drive?" I ask, looking into Caleb's stormy blue eyes.

"Not so long," he says. "Just down the mountain."

I cringe, remembering the steep drop off on the side of the road. I pull out my phone to see what the weather says. It was clear earlier, but that doesn't mean it's still clear.

"Caleb," Audrey says. "There's no need for you to drive this late. Sleep here on the sofa."

"We need to set up that guest room like we talked about," Bradley says.

"Where would we set up a guest room?" Lilah asks.

"We're thinking about building a maid's quarters behind the kitchen. Claire could live there. We haven't talked to her about it yet. We're just thinking about it."

"It's a good idea," I say. "You need to keep a guest room available."

Wyatt stands up, pulling Lilah up with him. To my surprise, he picks her up, bridal style, and carries her off up the stairs. "Good night," he says over his shoulder.

"Well," I say.

"You don't have to carry me," Audrey says with amusement.

"Don't worry, Love. I was planning on making you walk."

"Good night," Audrey says after rolling her eyes at Bradley. "There are blankets and a pillow tucked in that ottoman."

"I'll think about it," Caleb says. "Thank you."

"She's right, you know," I say as my sister and her fiancé walk upstairs. "It's safer if you stay here."

"You just trying to get me to spend the night?"

"No," I say. "I'm just thinking about those steep roads. But you can go if you want to."

"I'm thinking maybe I'll just sleep here."

"Okay," I say with a shrug as though it doesn't matter to me one way or the other.

And, of course, it doesn't matter.

"I have to be careful, though," he says.

"Why is that?"

"That's what happened to my brothers."

"What happened?"

"Sleeping over one night for one reason or another. Then... here they are."

"I think they had other reasons for staying over than a late night with possible fog on the road."

"They stayed to make sure the girls were safe. You're right."

"You'd be staying to make sure *you're* safe."

He narrows his eyes at me. "And just what makes you so sure about that?"

I feel a bit of heat rise to my cheeks as I look into his eyes. "It's what we said." I make an effort to swallow the lump in my throat.

"We say a lot of things."

A log falls, sending embers scattering up the chimney.

"They left their dog down here," I say. "Either they forgot him or they're planning on you staying."

"I don't think they forgot him."

"No." I shake my head. "They wouldn't forget him."

"I guess that settles it then," he says.

"How so?"

"I guess I'm staying. Can't leave the dog down here by himself."

I smirk at him, then drop onto the floor to slide open the ottoman. Just as Audrey said, there's a blanket, two actually, and a pillow tucked inside.

I stack them on the sofa behind me. "Do you need anything else?" I ask.

Biscuit snores softly in his sleep and turns over.

When Caleb doesn't answer, I turn around to face him.

He's focused on me with those stormy blue eyes.

I lift an eyebrow.

His gaze dips ever so briefly down to my lips and a bevy of drunken butterflies scatter in my stomach.

"Stay with me for a bit," he says.

Since I can't think of anything I'd like more, I sit down next to him, pulling my stockinged feet up under me.

He unfolds one of the blankets and wraps it over us.

When he puts his arm around me, I rest my head against his shoulder.

There are things a girl can fight and things maybe a girl should fight.

Then there are things that just quite simply should be allowed to run their course.

TWENTY-EIGHT

Caleb

"WANT TO WATCH A MOVIE?" I ask after Brianna rests her cheek on my shoulder.

"Okay," she says, but doesn't move.

I hear people walking around upstairs. My brothers and her sisters are upstairs getting ready for bed, leaving us alone down here with their dog.

The shades are all down, which is rather a shame, considering that they're blocking what could be a wonderful view of the mountains in the moonlight.

The reasons for the shades are sound. Anyone, perhaps

even the sheriff, could be standing outside watching us through the windows.

"I left my window shade up last night," Brianna murmurs against my shoulder.

"You're quite the rebel aren't you?"

She smells good. Like lavender with a hint of spruce from being outside today and messing around with the tree limbs.

The tree in the corner looks good there. So far it only has lights on. Big oversized lights that harken from another era. Blue. Green. Red. Yellow. They don't even blink, but they don't need to.

Tomorrow it'll have decorations on it. I don't which theme they'll go with, but it won't matter. Whatever they go with, the tree will still look old-fashioned. In a good way. With those oversized lights, it has no other choice than to look old-fashioned. Like bringing the past and present together.

Like the well-worn red wool coat that Brianna wears. The one that belonged to my grandmother.

I like it that she wears it. Not only does it suit her, but I like the idea that Brianna is wearing something that belonged to someone I loved.

It feels like a natural continuity.

When I kiss her on the top of her head, she sighs.

"I told myself I wasn't going to do this," she murmurs.

"Do what? Sit in front of the fireplace on a cold winter

evening? With an oversized blue spruce Christmas tree taking up half the living room?"

She smiles, but doesn't lift her gaze. "Something like that."

"If it's any consolation, I told myself the same thing."

"Did you now?" She tilts her head up to look into my eyes.

"I did. I refused to risk following my brothers' footsteps."

"And yet here you are."

"Yes," I say with a little smile. "Here I am."

"And here I am."

"In my defense," I say. "No one warned me."

"No one warned you that spending time with your family could be hazardous?"

"Are you a hazard now?"

"I've been called worse." She lowers her head, snuggling her cheek against my shoulder.

"I'm going to have to kick someone's ass yet. I can see it coming."

She puts a hand on my arm and closes her eyes.

"Warned you about what?" she asks.

"Oh. Let's see. That the Sinclair women have some kind of spell they weave around the Winslow men. Or that the mysterious sister is a beautiful goddess in disguise as a mere mortal to most men."

"You have a very active imagination," she says.

"You have no idea."
I already know that I'm lost to her.
Kissing her would be a very bad idea.
Kissing her would only make things worse.
A very bad idea.

TWENTY-NINE

Brianna

MAYBE I SHOULD HAVE KNOWN all along what I was missing.

Maybe if I hadn't had my head stuck in the proverbial sand of city life, I would have realized that there was a good reason both of my sisters came up here to Whiskey Springs and stayed. They just stayed.

For a lot of reasons, obviously. But taking away the inheritance and its stipend, it's easy to see why they wanted to stay.

Even with the danger of someone threatening them, trying to get them to leave, it's easy to see why.

Maybe it's the Winslow men.

Or maybe that's just a part of it.

It's definitely part of it.

Sitting here in front of the warm fire would be cozy in and of itself, but sitting here in front of the warm fire wouldn't be nearly so alluring if I wasn't in the arms of the handsome Caleb Winslow.

I'm doing exactly what I said I wasn't going to do.

I'm falling for the brother of my sisters' boyfriends.

I'm not even sure what I'm going to do with my life now that I've been fired from my job and moved away from Houston, leaving everything I knew.

But this place has a charm I hadn't expected. Sure. I saw the videos my sisters sent. I spent time on the phone with them. Hearing the roar of the river and the chirping of the birds in the background.

But there are things I had no way of understanding without actually being here.

The way the cold mountain air is so clean it almost burns the lungs. The scent of the blue spruce trees that smell better than any of the candles we burned at Christmastime.

The way the fire crackles in the fireplace, sending little fireworks of embers up through the chimney.

I understand now why they won't let anyone run them off.

Between the inheritance and the Winslow men and the cozy fireplace. The danger just seems to pale in comparison.

Not that something doesn't need to be done about the

danger. It does. And finding that gum wrapper just put it all together for me. I know I just got here and I don't expect to be the one to just swoop in and solve everything, but I think I'm onto something.

The question, of course, is why. Why would the sheriff care who lives here? Why would he go to all the trouble of buying bird drones and dropping off threatening notes? Why would he kidnap the dog just to frighten everyone?

It makes no sense.

There has to be something we're missing.

"I can feel you thinking," Caleb says.

"You do not."

"Convince me you're not thinking too much right now."

I lift my head from his shoulder and look into his stormy blue eyes. Eyes that seem to be so calm right now.

"I..." I forget what I was going to say as he lowers his face to mine and his breath mingles with mine.

Knowing he's going to kiss me makes my whole system overheat and come undone.

Everything else disappears into the background, leaving only us.

The sound of my sisters and their boyfriends walking around upstairs as they get ready for bed. The fire crackling the fireplace. Biscuit whimpering softly as he has puppy dreams.

The whole world comes down to just Caleb and me. Nothing else matters. Nothing else exists.

He gently puts a hand on my cheek and my eyes flutter closed.

When his lips touch mine, it feels like everything fits together, everything in my life up to this point fits together like the scattered pieces of a puzzle that suddenly make sense.

With a little sigh, I yield to the feel of his lips against mine.

So right.

Nothing has ever felt so right.

CHAPTER
THIRTY

Caleb

Kissing Brianna is my new favorite bad idea.

What I'd tried to convince myself was a bad idea is now the best idea I think I've ever had.

Her lips are so soft and sweet beneath mine. So yielding.

Now that I've kissed her, I don't think I ever want to stop. I don't think I could stop if I wanted to.

But, truly, why would I want to?

I shift her a bit so that her legs are across mine and I have better access to that mouth of hers.

So smart. She's one of the smartest people I've ever met. And the most beautiful.

And now kissing her is like the best thing I've ever done.

I don't know how much time passes. When I do notice things around us, I know that the house is quiet. That the fire has burned down to a normal glow.

"There's a problem," I say, replacing my lips with my fingertip.

"No problem," she says, making me smile.

"I don't ever want to stop kissing you."

"Good problem," she says, turning so that she kisses the palm of my hand. "to have."

"Agreed," I murmur, putting my lips back on hers.

I lean her back on the couch, exploring her wonderful, delicious mouth. My tongue caressing hers. Touching the roof of her mouth, making her gasp a little.

When the clock chimes Midnight, I know we have to stop.

At least for now.

"I should walk you to your room," I say.

"Okay," she murmurs against my lips.

"You're not making this easy."

"No," she says.

"Is it possible to get drunk on kissing?" I ask.

"Yes."

"Alright." I give her little kisses on the edge of her lips. On her cheeks. On her eyelids. "You're going to hate me tomorrow if I don't let you get some sleep."

"Sleep is overrated."

"So says the woman drunk on kissing."

I manage to disentangle us and get us both to our feet.

"Shall I carry you up the stairs to your room?"

She looks over her shoulder toward the stairs. "That will take some practice. I don't think you're ready."

"Okay." I take her hand firmly in mine. "Another time then."

"Yes. Another time."

We walk through the shadowed room to the stairs, then start up.

"Has anyone ever told you you're a bad influence?" I ask.

"If you say that, you might have to kick your own ass."

"You might be right." We reach the top of the stairs. "You going to ride into Boulder with me tomorrow?" I ask, knowing I don't have to explain why.

"Wild horses," she says.

"Does that mean yes?"

"Yes, but…" We stop in front of her room. "I think I need a goodnight kiss first."

"I think you've had enough kissing for one night," I tell her.

She pouts prettily and opens her door.

I pull her back against me. "Don't say I didn't warn you."

The clock is striking one o'clock before I find the fortitude and discipline or whatever it is that's required to finally tell her goodnight.

My head is so full of Brianna as I leave her room and

make my way back downstairs, that I don't hear the back door open.

THIRTY-ONE

Brianna

"It's gone."

"What's gone?" I ask, sleepily, heading for the coffee machine.

"The gum wrapper," Audrey says.

"What do you mean it's gone? Did someone throw it out?" I obviously did not get enough sleep last night to be dealing with whatever crisis Audrey has going on this morning.

Audrey leans her hands on the kitchen island and looks right at me. "Brianna. The gum wrapper is gone."

Something in her voice has me turning around and facing her.

"Where did you hide it?" I have no doubt that Audrey hid it somewhere.

She opens the cabinet where she keeps the coffee mugs. "Here," she says. "Behind the mugs."

"No one took it," I say, pulling the coffee mugs out of the cabinet, one by one, looking inside each one. Determined to prove that it's just misplaced. "Is anyone else up?"

"No. We're the first ones."

"Huh." Not surprising for me. I get up early every morning to get ready to go to work. It's not a habit that I'm going to break anytime soon. But Audrey. "Why are you up?"

"Sometimes I just wake up."

"Is Bradley up?"

"He's in the shower. He hasn't been down yet."

I look over toward the sectional. "When did Caleb leave?"

"He was gone when I got up. I don't know."

I nod. Thinking. Putting the coffee mugs back on the shelf and going to the next shelf above it.

"It's not here," Audrey says.

"Is Claire up yet?" I whisper.

"I haven't seen anyone else." Audrey pushes her hair back off her face. "You were the last one to leave down here last night. You and Caleb."

"You hid it. So no one else knew where it was. Caleb is

supposed to take it in to Boulder today, but I'm supposed to go with him."

"Maybe he got up, made coffee, found it, and left with it."

I run a hand over my still swollen lips. "He wouldn't do that."

Audrey studies me a moment. Then turns her eyes toward the ceiling with a sigh. Not quite an eye roll. Almost.

"Who else?" Audrey asks.

"Claire," I say. "As much as I don't like the sheriff, maybe he knows something we don't."

Audrey shakes her head. "Claire wouldn't do it."

"Did she see where you hid it?" I choose a mug and start making my coffee.

"I'm sure she did. She sort of just blends into the background."

Audrey and I stop talking as someone starts down the stairs.

"Good morning," Claire says, coming into the kitchen. "Can I make breakfast?"

"That would be nice," Audrey says. "If you feel up to it."

"I don't mind a bit." She goes to the refrigerator and starts pulling out eggs and bacon and butter.

Audrey and I look at each other.

"Claire," Audrey says. "We can't find the gum wrapper."

"What?" Claire asks, setting the eggs carefully on the counter. "You put up there. Behind the coffee mugs."

"It's not there."

"Let me see." She starts pulling the mugs out of the cabinet just as I had.

Audrey and I stand back and let her look. I finish making my coffee and take a sip.

"Have you had coffee?" I ask Audrey.

"No."

I shove my mug into her hands. "Take this one." I grab another mug and make another cup for myself.

"I don't understand," Claire says. "Maybe Mr. Caleb took it in to Boulder already."

"He didn't," I say. "I'm supposed to go with him."

"Oh." Claire looks at me. Then Audrey. "You think I did it."

"No," Audrey says, putting a hand on her arm. "I don't think you took it."

"You have every right to think so. I'll pack my things and get out of here." She turns around, her gaze landing on the carton of eggs. "But I'll make breakfast first."

"No," Audrey says. "Claire. We don't think you took it. We just need you to help us figure out what happened to it."

"I haven't seen any rats around here," she says.

I hide a smile behind my coffee mug. This is going to be interesting.

I walk to the window overlooking the backyard. The shades are already up—apparently they're on some kind of timer. And the view out over the meadow past the trees, looking over toward the forever snow-capped peaks, is nothing short of spectacular. With the way the early morning sunshine glitters on the dewy ground, everything just sparkles.

Audrey was gifted one of the most beautiful places I've ever seen.

No one is going to run her away from here. No one.

And I just might include myself in that. No one is going to run me away from here either.

I've hardly even seen the little town of Whiskey Springs, other than the drive up here, but I don't need to.

This is one of those places a person could call home.

THIRTY-TWO

Caleb

Since I hadn't brought any extra clothes with me yesterday, and I woke up early, I just dashed home for a shower and a change of clothes.

I can be back before anyone even realizes I'm gone.

While I'm there, I toss a couple of changes of clothes in a duffle bag and throw it into the backseat of my truck.

Presumptuous? Maybe. I prefer to think of myself as prepared. Knowing I've got to drive into Boulder today to take the gum wrapper, I don't know what time I'll be back. Especially so since I'm going to be taking Brianna.

The thought makes me smile to myself.

I don't even care that I was wrong.

I had been wrong for thinking that I would absolutely positively not be interested in the third Sinclair sister.

Talk about saving the best for last.

They saved the best for last.

Brianna is beautiful and kind and smarter than anybody I know.

Not to mention the way she kisses.

She looks like a goddess and kisses like a siren.

Maybe I have my metaphors mixed up, but I don't care.

I drive over the narrows, secretly hoping I'm on the side of the Sinclair house when the roads close. And they will. One good snowfall and this road won't be passable.

I can still get there, though. I can put on some snow-shoes and hike in and out.

After parking in front of the house, I knock on the door.

Claire answers the door.

I was not prepared for the activity level going on inside the house.

So much for slipping back inside unnoticed.

"I'm so glad you're back," Claire says.

"Why? What's going on?"

"They'll tell you," she says and leaves me standing there. "I've got bacon cooking."

Bradley, Audrey sitting next to him, is sitting on the sectional, his eyes glued to the iPad. A closer look tells me he's looking at the security cameras.

My stomach twists.

"What happened?" I ask.

Wyatt and Lilah are at the dining table having breakfast.

But I don't see Brianna.

Bradley doesn't answer. I don't think he heard me.

I walk to the dining table and ask Wyatt.

"What happened?" I ask again.

"The gum wrapper is missing."

"Missing? How does a gum wrapper go missing? Where's Brianna?"

"Upstairs getting dressed," Lilah says.

Relief floods through me.

I guess I'd been worried that something had happened to her.

"Sit down," Claire says. "Have some breakfast."

I sit down. "I'll wait for Brianna," I say.

"Brianna already ate," Claire says as she puts a plate with eggs and bacon in front of me. "Eat up."

As I scoop up a forkful of scrambled eggs, it occurs to me that Wyatt and Lilah wouldn't be calmly having break-fast if something had happened to Brianna.

Maybe it's my brain that's gotten scrambled.

"How did the gum wrapper go missing?" I ask. "Did someone throw it away?"

Lilah looks at me and shrugs.

If I ever wanted a role model for being unconcerned about things, it would have to be Lilah. I don't know what she's feeling on the inside, but on the outside, she presents as calm, cool, and collected.

Then I hear Brianna coming down the stairs and my attention is focused completely on her.

Just seeing her coming down the stairs makes the whole room light up.

THIRTY-THREE

Brianna

SHOWERED, hair blow dried, and maybe straightened a little more than necessary—I tell myself it's a habit honed from years of getting ready for work. Nothing to do with my planned trip into Boulder today with Caleb and certainly nothing to do with simply seeing Caleb.

Without the gum wrapper, there is no longer a reason for driving into Boulder.

Instead, everyone is doing what they can to figure out what happened.

Bradley is going over the security camera footage, looking for any sign of anyone coming in the house.

My question is how in the world would whoever came into the house know where to look for the gum wrapper.

Wyatt has already called his friend Trent and Trent is trying to get away to come up here to see what he can see.

No one has called the police.

Hello. We'd like to report a crime. We found an empty gum wrapper outside and now it's missing.

Ah. No. We are truly on our own on this one. And now I'm seeing more clearly why Audrey and Bradley are trying to solve this by themselves.

Especially with the town's sheriff being their primary suspect now, they certainly can't report it. Not to him.

I reach the top of the stairs and do one of those automatic scans of the room.

My gaze stops when I see Caleb, looking right at me, sitting at the dining table.

He smiles and my heart does summersaults.

After hours of kissing last night, he's been pretty much all I've thought about.

I'm disappointed, a little, that he and I won't be going into Boulder. But. He's here. And as long as he's here, I don't mind staying home.

And I don't mind that I'm thinking about my sister's house as home.

I even unpacked some of my clothes already, hanging them in the closet. That seemed to do it. Home is where your clothes are hanging.

I reach the dining room table and sit down next to Caleb.

"I guess they told you," I say.

"Someone stole the gum wrapper."

"Yes. I guess that means someone got into the house again."

"That's why they take the pets upstairs with them at night and lock the doors."

"You were down here," I say. "By yourself. You didn't hear anything."

"I heard nothing. Either I was sleeping or upstairs."

"I don't understand why the cameras didn't catch him."

"He probably put another scrambler on the house," Wyatt says. "Trent can tell us that."

"So whoever took the gum wrapper is most likely the guilty party," I say.

"If anyone heard us talking about gum wrappers like this, they'd think we'd lost our minds," Caleb says.

"What people think is irrelevant," I say, looking at Lilah.

She gives me a little nod of agreement.

"I guess we won't be going into Boulder," I say.

"I've already been recruited to help decorate the tree."

"Really? Is that something you have experience in?" I ask.

"Not even a little. I'm counting on having someone teach me the ropes."

"I decorated a tree once," I say, picking up a slice of bacon off his plate and biting into it.

"The blind leading the blind," he says. "Always a good sign."

"Might as well have fun with it," I say, going over to the coffee machine to make myself a second cup of coffee.

THIRTY-FOUR

Caleb

AFTER BREAKFAST, I head outside with Wyatt to chop some firewood.

"One thing about being with the Sinclair girls," Wyatt says, balancing a piece of wood on a stump. "It takes a lot of firewood."

"I noticed," I say. I'm also noticing that my brother is tutoring me on the Sinclair girls. Seems to me like he's making some assumptions. I tell him so.

"You're assuming I need to know these things."

Wyatt brings the axe down, deftly dropping two pieces of wood on either side of the stump.

"The signs are all there, Bro."

"I don't know about signs."

Wyatt picks up the two logs and puts them back on the stump to make another chop for kindling.

"You're a lot more like Bradley than you are me."

"I can't tell if that's an insult."

He brings the axe down. "Just an observation. He resisted admitting how he feels about Audrey."

"I just met Brianna two days ago," I say.

"Spontaneous combustion." He hauls the axe back and lets it down easy, making little splices for kindling.

"And if I admit I like her?"

"You don't have to tell me. I already know it." He gathers up the little pieces of kindling and puts them in a stack out of the way.

I adjust my coat. Gaze out toward the trees around the perimeter of the yard, then up toward the snow-capped mountain peaks that almost look like they're close enough to reach out and touch. Maybe just a short little hike. Of course, it's so very much further and treacherous.

I shake my head. Looks are deceiving.

What is it about his whole gum wrapper thing that we're missing?

Maybe we aren't missing anything. Maybe whoever is doing it is just covering his tracks. He knows we found the gum wrapper and he retrieved it. Evidence. He retrieved the evidence.

"You really think the sheriff has something to do with all this?"

"If I was a betting man, I'd put money on it."

"What makes you so sure?" I ask.

"It all adds up," he says, dropping the axe through the middle of a piece of wood, letting it crash to the sides onto the ground.

"Okay." I tilt my collar up to cover my ears. "Let's say you figure out that it is him. What are you going to do about it? He's the law around here."

"I guess we'll have to take it to the county authorities."

"The sheriff is closer to Bradley's age. What? A couple of years older? What does he think?"

"He definitely thinks it's the sheriff."

"You could confront him," I say.

"That won't help. We need evidence."

"The cameras. But he keeps sabotaging the cameras."

Wyatt adds more kindling for his stack.

"I think you're just avoiding talking about your crush on Brianna."

"Is that why you wanted me to come out here with you? To talk about my crush on Brianna?"

"No," he says. "I need you to hand me that log behind you."

I hand him the log.

"You want to take a swing?" he asks. "See if you can still split a log?

"Nah. I'm good."

"It'll make you feel better."

"I feel fine."

He slams the axe down again. "I was thinking."

"Never a good sign."

"This house is plenty big for all of us. You could work from here."

"Not enough room for all of us to work from here."

"Sure it is. Lilah and I are building the greenhouse and flower shop. You could build an separate office if you need your own space."

"Does Audrey know you're building a whole community up here?"

"It was her idea."

I scowl at my brother. "Which part?"

"All of it. She asked me to talk to you."

CHAPTER
THIRTY-FIVE

Brianna

"WHAT ARE YOU DOING?" Lilah asks as I type on my phone.

I feel like I could ask her the same thing. Lilah has a box of live flowers that cost God knows how much money to have shipped here, arranging them in a vase, using a YouTube video as a guide.

"Filling out an application." My gaze flicks past her to where Wyatt is chopping firewood and Caleb is standing nearby. "What are they talking about?"

"I don't know," Lilah says with a little shrug. "Guy talk. What kind of application?"

"I'm trying to find a job."

"In Whiskey Springs?"

"Yes." I go back to filling in my experience which is vast.

"Brianna," Lilah says, leaning toward me. "Where's your car?"

"My car?" My fingers hesitate on the screen.

"Yes. Your car. Where's your car?"

"I left it at a used car lot. They're trying to sell it for me."

Lilah puts her palm against her forehead. "Are you serious?"

"Yes. I did some work for the owner and he was willing to help me out."

"So how do you plan to get to work?"

"I'll take your car," I say, mostly just to annoy her.

"My car isn't winterized." I look at her blankly and she explains. "It needs new windshield wipers. Winter tires. An emergency kit."

"What's an emergency kit?"

"Blankets. Candles. Food and water."

"It's not that far into town," I say, feeling a bit queasy at her implication that blankets and food and water are required to get a car ready to just drive into town.

"Maybe. But it's far enough that you could be less than a mile away and snowed in for days."

"I have a cell phone. I'd call you."

Lilah huffs out a breath. "We wouldn't be able to get to you. I'm trying to make a point."

"And your point is?"

"My point is you shouldn't be applying for jobs. You should work here."

"Doing what?" I ask, sitting back in my chair.

"I don't know, but you have enough experience doing a million different things, surely there's something you could do from home."

"I don't know what it would be. So. I thought you were coming up here to draw and paint."

"I am drawing and painting. But this is fun, too."

I narrow my eyes at her. "You just like having something to do with Wyatt."

"Is that so wrong? To have a project to do with someone you love?" She pulls the flowers out of the vase and starts the video over.

There. She said it.

"So Bradley and Audrey are engaged. Are you and Wyatt...?"

She smiles broadly, but keeps her voice low. "Yes. But we're giving Audrey a minute in the spotlight before we announce it."

"Audrey's not blind," I say.

Lilah pauses her video. "Maybe we'll have a double wedding. Or a triple wedding."

"What? Is Claire getting married, too?" I know she's not talking about Claire, but I can't resist being purposely obtuse.

"Not Claire." Lilah rolls her eyes and starts her video back up. "You."

"Something's wrong with you."

"Maybe it's not me that something's wrong with."

"It would be too weird. Three brothers and three sisters. It's not natural."

"Okay. So you'd rather swipe left and swipe right hoping to find someone you like who happens to live close enough to have a relationship with than just pick the one who's standing in front of you. Just because he happens to be the brother of you sisters' husbands?"

I don't answer her.

I don't answer because I don't have anything to say in defense of that.

THIRTY-SIX

Caleb

"I THOUGHT you said you didn't have any experience in tree decorating."

I'm standing on a ladder while Brianna hands me little bird decorations to attach to the upper tree limbs.

"I think I might have said I have limited experience. There might be a difference."

"Maybe it's a case of birds of a feather flock together." I'm referring to the way I'd grouped the birds close together.

"Maybe," she says. "Come down."

"What? You're firing me already?"

"No. I'm going to demonstrate by doing."

"A lady shouldn't climb ladders," I say as I climb down.

"It's okay. It's the twenty-first century."

"You're putting a lot of trust in this old wooden ladder," I say as she starts up and the ladder wobbles.

"I'm actually putting my trust in you."

Her trust is not misplaced. I'd throw myself beneath the ladder before I'd let her fall to the ground.

She moves one of the birds two inches to the right.

"There," she says. "Does that look better from down there?"

"I can't tell any difference. I think you moved that bird over two inches though."

She gives me a vexed look that only makes me smile.

I've ever known anyone who looks so beautiful when she's vexed.

She moves one of the other birds over a little bit, too. "Would you hand me another one?"

"Another bird? Yes. And maybe one of those little pinecones."

I hand her the bird first. Then the pinecone.

"Somebody is here," I say. Someone driving a truck pulls up to the front of the house.

"Probably Trent."

"Probably. This should be interesting."

"I think the sheriff put up another scrambler while everyone was over at Claire's house," she says, taking one step down.

"Do you think he burned Claire's house on purpose?"

"Yes. Want to help me down? I want to hear what he has to say."

I turn back to her just in time to see the ladder wobble and tilt back.

In one single instant, I realize that she's going to fall. And I only have a second, tops, to prevent it.

Putting out my arms, one hand under her knees, one under her shoulders, I catch her and swing her out of the way of the ladder just before it clatters to the ground.

Her arms around me, she looks at me with her teal blue eyes.

"You saved me," she says with an amused expression.

If I didn't know better, I would think she orchestrated this just so she could end up in my arms.

"Everything okay?" Lilah rushes over in time to see the ladder lying on the floor.

She looks from the ladder to us. Raises an eyebrow and continues her way toward the door.

Brianna looks at me and shrugs.

"What was that about?" I ask her.

"I have no idea."

With her being this close, I have no choice but to kiss her.

She closes her eyes as I lower my lips to hers, giving her a chaste kiss, suitable for public display.

"Wyatt thinks I should move in," I say.

"So does Lilah."

"He said it was Audrey's idea."

"You know how it is with people in relationships. They're always trying to fix people up."

"I've noticed that." I lower her gently to her feet as Trent comes inside the house.

He takes one look at the ladder on the floor.

"Everything okay?" he asks.

"We're going to need a new ladder," I say.

THIRTY-SEVEN

Brianna

WHILE TRENT SWEEPS the house for bugs, I help Audrey and Lilah make sandwiches. Claire had to drive into town to take care of some paperwork regarding her house fire.

"Do you really think Claire's okay?" I ask, slicing a tomato.

"I think so," Audrey says. "She's really tough. And I think she rather likes living here."

"Maybe she didn't feel safe living by herself."

"I can see why," Audrey says, taking a stack of plates out of the cabinet. "She was arrested for something she couldn't have done."

"I don't think she has it in her to be threatening," Lilah says. "She's a very kind person."

"Are you really going to build her a maid's quarters?" I ask, keeping any thoughts to the contrary about Claire to myself.

"I'm thinking yes. If not for her, then for somebody."

"You like having somebody to cook and clean," I say.

"Don't you?" Audrey asks.

"Don't be defensive. I'm just asking. We never had anyone to help out when we were growing up. So. It's different. I'm just asking."

"I know," Audrey says with a sigh. "I shouldn't feel guilty about it. But yes. I do like someone to keep the house clean and to do the heavy cooking."

"Nothing wrong with that," Lilah says. "I always thought I'd have a big house and a housekeeper when I grew up. I sort of thought everybody did."

We both look blankly at her.

"I can't help what I thought. I just assumed that I'd have it someday."

"Even though we didn't," I say.

"You're questioning the logic of a child."

"Well," Audrey says. "I guess as long as you stay here, you'll have that. It's in the trust."

"That remind me," I say. "I don't remember reading in the paperwork about what happens to the house if you decided you didn't want to live here anymore."

"I don't remember seeing that either," Lilah says, putting pickles on a plate. "It should have been there though." She looks at me. "You spent the most time going through it. There wasn't anything?"

"No." I open a loaf of bread and pull out a half a dozen slices. Then I do a quick count in my head and pull out six more.

"That won't be enough," Audrey says. "Guys eat more than we do."

"I know," I say. "It's just weird how much food it takes to feed everyone."

"I don't mind though," Lilah says. "I thought it might be weird, but it's not. It's kind of nice having everyone here."

"I agree," Audrey says. "I thought I wanted some time to myself. but I'm glad we're all here together now."

"I'm glad, too," I say. "I think it would be a good idea to call your attorney and find out the answer to what happens in the event someone did convince you to leave. You have his number, right? Andrew Harrington."

"Of course I have his number." She looks toward the stairs where the men are going through the house.

"Last time he was here, he wore a disguise," Audrey says. "Not this time. If the house if bugged, he'll know we know."

"There are more of us here now," Lilah says.

"We already know he's bold," Audrey says.

"I don't think anyone is *that* bold," Lilah says.

"I think I'm going to take a walk down to the river while they finish up," I say. "I'll take Biscuit."

I just need to clear my head. To have a few minutes alone with my own thoughts.

"Sure," Audrey says. "I'll call you if they get finished before you come back."

"Thanks, Audrey," I say.

All I have to do is grab Biscuit's leash and he's up racing toward the back door, ready to go outside.

The horse dog, as Lilah calls him, is ready to go outside. Lilah has warmed up to Biscuit, but she still seems to prefer the company of the cat over the dog. Not surprising. We never had a dog growing up. A cat, but not a dog.

I step outside into the cool air and warm sunshine, an odd juxtaposition that still surprises me.

I follow the dog who knows the way and seems to know that we're heading to the river.

Reaching the river bank, the rushing water blocks out all other sounds behind me.

I sit down on a sun-warmed boulder and watch the water swirl around the rocks. Biscuit sits down next to me.

When an elk walks up to the bank across from us, I put an arm around the dog to keep him from reacting, but Biscuit doesn't seem to either notice or care about the elk.

I like it here. A lot. That surprises me.

I also like Caleb Winslow. That surprises me even more.

And it surprises me that I don't want to change that. It's

not that I want to have what my sisters have. I'm my own person.

I just like Caleb. I'd like him in Houston and I like him here.

He's kind and sweet and makes me smile.

Maybe I'm at a different place in my life than I've ever been before. Not so focused on work. That could have something to do with it. Whatever it is, I'm okay with it.

As for work, I don't know what I'm going to do.

I guess I don't have to figure anything out right now. I have some savings. And Audrey has the house. As long as I'm here, I don't have to worry about paying rent. So my savings will last that much longer. Until I figure out what I'm going to do.

Trent should be finished sweeping the house by now and I really want to hear what he has to say.

Standing up, I stretch and turn around. Biscuit stands up, too, and shakes.

We have to walk through a grove of spruce trees to get back to the house. It's cooler in the shade and I put my hands in the pockets of my red wool coat.

Someone steps out from behind one of the trees, blocking my way.

"What are you doing here?" I ask. Biscuit barks twice. "We were just talking about you."

Andrew Harrington, wearing jeans and a heavy coat, stands in front of me. I almost don't even recognize him.

Then Biscuit's leash slips out of my hand as someone grabs me from behind.

"Run, Biscuit," I say, but someone has me by the throat and the words come out as a whisper.

"Get out of here, you mutt," the man holding me says.

My blood chills. I recognize that voice.

THIRTY-EIGHT

Caleb

I FOLLOW BRADLEY, Wyatt, and Trent back downstairs.

Trent is holding a scrambler he pulled out of the attic. Apparently whoever left the first scrambler there replaced the old one that Trent had disabled. Must have thought the old one had gone bad.

"I'm just glad you didn't find any more cameras," Bradley says.

"I guess he decided it wasn't a good route to go," Wyatt says. "Since we obviously caught onto that particular scheme."

"Right," Trent says. "Anybody can buy little bug detectors now."

"Where's Biscuit?" Bradley asks, reaching the first floor.

"Brianna took him for a walk," Lilah says. "I'll call her."

"By herself?" I ask, my heart slamming into my throat. I thought we'd decided that no one would go anywhere alone.

"She just wanted a minute to herself," Audrey says.

Lilah bites her bottom lip. "It has been a little while. She should be back by now."

I'm already putting on my coat. As I throw open the back door, I see Biscuit racing toward me, his leash dragging behind him.

"Something's happened to Brianna," I shout just before I take off running toward the direction the dog had come from.

I vaguely hear footsteps behind me, a little delayed.

Instinctively, I run toward the river, hitting the trail running through the trees, directly toward the river.

What I see as I round a curve in the trail, chills me to the bone. My breath coming in gasps, I stop and take a step back to give me time to assess the situation.

I see Brianna, wearing her faded red wool coat, in a choke hold.

The sheriff. The sheriff has her in a choke hold. There's another man in front of her, a man I don't recognize.

"I told you I don't want this to be violent," the unrecognized man says.

"Sometimes violence is necessary," Sheriff Morgan says.

"No. I won't go to prison because you were stupid."

"I'm the sheriff. I say who goes to prison."

Bradley and Wyatt come up behind me. I hold up a hand behind me to stop them.

They stand quietly, also taking in the situation.

I hear the women coming up behind them. We're all here now.

It's time for me to put a stop to whatever is going on.

"I'm going in," I say to whoever is listening.

"You don't have a weapon," Bradley says.

"Doesn't need one," Wyatt says. "He's got us."

As I step forward, they fall in at my sides like shadows.

"Let her go," I demand, my words cutting through the charged air.

"We're just having a conversation," the unidentified man says.

"Doesn't look like much of a conversation," I say easily. "Seeing as how Brianna can't get a word out."

"We're just sending a message," the unidentified man says.

"Message sent and received," I say. "Now let her go."

Sheriff Morgan shifts, but doesn't let go.

Brianna's teal green eyes lock onto mine and I see the fear in them. Wide and filled with fear. But also with trust.

And that's all I need.

Audrey steps out of the shadows. "Andrew Harrington,"

she says with a scolding tone to the unidentified man. "Attorney Harrington. What are you doing?"

"Just taking what's ours," he says.

"Yours?" Audrey asks.

While Sheriff Morgan is distracted with Audrey, I move in, my brothers right there with me.

Morgan tries to use Brianna as a shield, but Bradley slips around behind him,

With a sharp yank on Morgan's shoulder, Bradley wrenches him backward, breaking his grip on Brianna.

Brianna stumbles free, falling into my arms, while Wyatt steps in to pin Morgan down.

"Told you. You should be sheriff," Wyatt tells Bradley.

"Assaulting a police officer," Morgan says. "Smart move. You're all going down."

"I don't think so," Lilah says. "I've got it all on video."

Sure enough, Lilah is holding her phone up, videotaping everything.

"Smart move," Brianna says, rubbing her neck.

"It worked against me. It'll work against him."

"You okay?" I ask Brianna.

"I am now."

Audrey, hands on her hips, is standing in front of Andrew Harrington.

"Explain yourself," she says.

Andrew blows out a breath. "It was a bad idea. I knew it was."

"Why?" Audrey persists. "Why are you doing this?"

"The house. It should go to my nephew."

"Wait," Audrey says, looking a little pale. "Your nephew?"

"That's right. My sister wouldn't do anything about it, so her brothers had to do it."

"Brothers?" Lilah asks, looking from the sheriff to the attorney. "You two?"

"That's right. This house rightfully belongs to our sister and her son. You may have been married to him, but the boy is his legacy."

"Didn't she get enough? She got everything else." Brianna finds her voice.

"She might not want it now, but she'll want it later," Andrew persists.

"Enough of this," I say. "Where's Trent?"

"I'm right here," Trent says, stepping around the curve in the trail, two state policemen right behind him. "I made some calls."

Wyatt releases the sheriff and steps aside.

"Sheriff Morgan," one of the state troopers says. "We've had our eyes on you for some time now. Looks like you finally tipped your hand."

"It's over, Morgan," the other trooper says as he slaps handcuffs on Morgan and proceeds to read him his rights.

"Thanks for your help in all this, Wyatt," the first trooper says.

"The pleasure was all mine."

As the state troopers haul Morgan and Harrison off, Bradley and I look at Wyatt.

"What was that about?" I ask. "What did you do?"

"I've been giving them copies of all the notes. Keeping them in the loop."

"You didn't say anything," Lilah says.

"I couldn't," Wyatt says. "I was working undercover."

"Undercover?" Bradley wraps his arms around Audrey.

"We're going to be needing a new sheriff," Wyatt says.

I take Brianna's hand and we all start walking back toward the house.

"Guess you've got the job," Bradley says.

"Nope. It's all you, Bro," Wyatt wraps his arms around Lilah. "All my plans revolve around this one."

"What kind of plans?" Bradley asks.

"You know. Marriage. Babies. The usual."

"Told you," Audrey says to Bradley.

"You want to get in on that?" I ask Brianna.

She elbows me. "I think you need to work on your delivery."

I grin. "All I need is a little incentive."

She stops right there, stands on her toes, and kisses me on the lips. "Consider yourself incentivized."

She looks at me with her teal blue eyes and I am indeed incentivized.

THIRTY-NINE

Brianna

AFTER A LATE DINNER, we sit in front of the fireplace with its dangerously high flames.

Audrey snuggled up next to Bradley. Lilah lying with her head on Wyatt's lap.

Me sitting pressed up next to Caleb, his arm around me.

"Are you sure you're okay?" he asks, kissing me on the top of my head.

"I'm sure. I knew you'd be there to rescue me."

"Twice in one day," I say. "I'm on a roll."

"I can't wrap my head around an attorney in Houston

and a sheriff in Whiskey Springs being brothers," Audrey says.

"I just assumed Morgan was his last name," Lilah says.

Bradley says. "I think they might be half-brothers. I never knew Morgan to have a brother."

"You would have known," Audrey says. "Since he's from here."

"You're right, my love, I would have known."

"And since you never met Audrey's attorney," I say. "You couldn't have put it together."

"I guess they'll come back tomorrow to take our statements," Lilah says, hiding a yawn behind the back of her hand.

"You can't be sleepy," I say. "With all this excitement."

"Missed her nap, didn't you, Little One?" Wyatt holds her close.

"Yes. I did."

"Creative people need their naps," Wyatt says.

Lilah looks up at him. I can see the love in her eyes. Wyatt gets her. He really gets her.

As an older sister, that makes me so happy for her.

"It's dark outside," Caleb points out.

We all look toward the windows with closed window shades.

"Do you think we'll ever feel safe enough to sit in here with them open at night again?" Audrey asks.

"I sleep with my window shades up," I say.

"You're quite the rebel."

"Just one of the many things you like about me," I say, looking up at Caleb.

"That and your brilliant mind."

"I can't figure out why they targeted Brianna," Audrey says. "I'm the one they want out of here."

"Opportunity for one," Wyatt says. "And also they know that the most efficient way to get you out of here is to threaten your family."

"What were they going to do with her?"

"I don't know."

"Nothing," I say. "I was getting ready to fight back. I just had to wait for the right moment."

They all look blankly at me. I shrug. "That and I knew someone would come looking for me. Especially with Biscuit running to the house."

"I'm getting really fond of that horse dog," Lilah says sleepily.

"He's a good dog," Bradley says.

"I'm going to get this one up to bed before she falls asleep right here," Wyatt says.

"You ready for bed?" Bradley asks Audrey.

"Yes." She whispers something to Bradley and he glances toward us.

"Good point."

They all head up to bed, leaving Caleb and me alone in front of the fire, down to a normal level now.

"It seems a shame to waste such a good fire," he says.

"You angling for a reason to stay the night again?" I ask.

"I'm getting used to sleeping here. Besides, I brought extra clothes this time."

She smiles. "Well then. I guess that settles it."

"But that's not really a good reason, is it?"

"It is if you're looking for one."

"I've got all the reason I need right here," he says, pressing his lips against mine.

I sigh and sink into the kiss.

"We're getting into dangerous territory here, you know," he murmurs against my lips.

"How so?"

"This is how it happens."

I arch forward, my lips back on his again. Even a moment apart from him is too much time away.

"I don't know what you mean."

He shifts me so that I'm leaning back against his arm.

"Boy meets girl. Boy rescues girl."

Another light kiss.

"Boy falls in love with girl."

My heart skitters and I know I'm already more than halfway in love with the boy.

"You know I'm a rebel," I say.

"Yes. You are a rebel. And yes. That's just one of the many things I love about you.

The End.

AUTHOR OF JUST BREATHE
KATHRYN KALEIGH
SHE RAN FROM DANGER
HE MADE HER BELIEVE IN FOREVER
Out of
ASHES
A NOVEL

OUT OF ASHES
PREVIEW

Chapter 1
McKenna Monroe

Everything went sideways on a temperate spring Friday night in Houston.

The Houston skyline at night has always has always had a magical quality to it.

Standing on the twenty-first floor of my condo balcony, I'm surrounded by tall buildings. Most of them far taller than my building, but a few smaller buildings scattered here and there.

It's like standing in a forest of buildings instead of trees.

Brightly lit windows. Corporate buildings with people inside still working. Apartments and condos with people relaxing after a day of work. Hotels with people enjoying the city vibes.

I bend down and pull off my high heels, the cold concrete of the balcony beneath my feet. It's worth it to have my feet flat after a long day.

Holding my heels by the straps, I lean over the railing, allowing me to catch a glimpse of the swimming pool several floors below.

Half a dozen people sit around it, no one in the water. Their voices drift upwards, blending with music coming from the concert pianist two floors down who plays beautiful classical music every evening. Tonight is no exception.

I close my eyes and let the music drift through me. Who needs to go to the symphony when there's music like that just outside my door.

The wind flutters the verdant green leaves of the potted ivy sitting on a little table next to my outdoor sofa. It's my only plant. A memento of my grandmother's funeral. I'm not normally a plant person, but I've somehow managed to keep it alive since the funeral going on three years ago.

A firetruck is heading this way now, its siren not out of place, oddly enough.

In the small Texas town where I grew up, the sirens of a firetruck were a big deal. Either something was on fire and the phone lines burned up with gossip about what that something was or maybe there was a parade. Either way, people took note.

Here in Houston, no one pays them much mind.

Firetrucks are routinely called out for just about any emergency. A car wreck. A stuck elevator. A person stabbed on the street.

Living in the city is not for the faint of heart. There are emergencies and incidences constantly. It's just part of everyday life.

When the wind shifts just right, I can smell pizza from the little pizzeria on the street below. Otherwise, the air up here smells like a blend of exhaust, the pungent scent of refineries in the distance, and Texas wind.

Sometimes I catch the scent of the neighbor's two cocker spaniels or the neighbor on the next floor up who cooks a lot of Indian food.

Tonight I don't care.

Tonight I'm happy to be a Houstonian, even if I wasn't born and bred here.

Houston is my city.

And today was a good day at work. Today I did my part to put an arsonist behind bars.

As a criminal prosecutor, I almost always have the public on my side and that's a good feeling.

It's a satisfying job, but it's not my end goal. I want to be a judge. I want to be the person who makes that final decision. The one who weighs all the evidence. Who makes sure the attorneys are playing fair. Who watches out for the juries.

I make a difference now, as an attorney, but it's on a

smaller scale. I hope to make a difference on a larger scale. Later, of course. After I've paid my dues.

Maybe soon if I work hard and keep up my reputation as a good prosecutor. I never say no to a case and I've only lost three cases in my career. It's a really good record.

I won't lie. It's a lot of pressure to keep up that kind of record and a lot of people consider me the one to beat.

When the doorbell rings, I hurry back inside and throw open the door to my best friend. Jennie.

"You're here!" I lock Jennie in a fierce hug. "Come in," I say, grabbing her suitcase and rolling it inside. Lock the door behind us.

"I'm so sorry I'm late. I know we had dinner plans."

I wave her off. "Your flight was late. It's not your fault. How are you?"

"A little tired, but I'm okay." Jennie is a petite blonde with a pretty smile. When she walks into a room, men notice.

I've never been jealous of Jennie. We've been best friends since first grade. She's like a sister to me. I can't think of a single big event in my life where Jennie hasn't been a part of in some way. Good and bad.

Even when I went to law school and she went to architect school, we were there for each other's graduations.

"Want a glass of wine?" I ask. "Or a beer?"

"Wine," she says. "Do you even have beer?"

"I had a six-pack of beer delivered in honor of your visit."

"Then I suppose I'll have a beer then, won't I?"

"Settle in," I say. "I'll get our beer."

"Do I still get the guest room?" she asks.

"I don't even call it the guest room. I call it Jennie's room."

"I'll be right back then. You're still wearing your work clothes."

"I just got home." I wiggle my freshly manicured red-painted toes.

"How do you have time for a pedicures?" she asks. "I swear I'm so busy I don't even think about it."

I open two beer bottles and we go outside to sit on the balcony. Friday night traffic is loud. Teenagers driving along the streets, music spilling from their open windows.

The concert pianist has stopped playing for the night. Too bad.

"It's not like I'm not working when I'm sitting in the salon. You know that."

"Sure. The successful prosecutor has to keep up her image."

"It's not like you sit in a dungeon and work all day."

Jennie winces. "Sometimes it feels like maybe I do."

"How do you like Dubai?" I ask. "What's it like?"

"It's pretty. Clean. But honestly? It's... lonely. People don't socialize like they do here. Or at least not the people I work with. They do their work and they go home."

"How dare they?"

"I know. And most of them are young, too. The

company is strict. We're not allowed to date anyone at work."

"That's probably smart on their part."

"I know." Jennie pulls her shoes off. "It's just there's this guy on my team. Single. And so hot."

"Is he straight?"

"I hope so. Not that it matters. Can't date him. So I barely even talk to him."

"You don't trust yourself around him."

"No. Counselor. I do not. Again. Smoking hot."

"So you're not seeing anyone?"

"Nope." She sweeps a hand down her torso. Like me, she's wearing business attire. A pencil skirt and matching blazer. "All this is just going unappreciated."

I laugh. "Not for long, I'm sure."

"I'm only here for two months tops. Hardly time to meet someone much less get into a relationship."

"Who said anything about a relationship?"

"I missed you so much," Jennie says.

"Me too. You want to have pizza sent up from downstairs?"

"Maybe," she says, sipping her beer. "Actually. You know what I really want to do? Let's go down there and eat. Is that little bar still open?"

"I think it is. We can get pizza, but I don't know about going to the bar."

"Why not? We have to celebrate my being here."

"We do. But with Trevor not being here, it doesn't seem right. For me."

"Where is Trevor Miles these days?"

"He's in Kenya. Working on clean water initiatives in rural communities."

"When you put it like that, it sounds like such important work." She gets up and walks to stand at the railing, looking down over the activity below.

"It is important," I say. "I admire him for what he does."

Turning, she leans against the railing and studies me a moment. "Do you really think he's spending his Friday nights sitting home alone?"

"Well. Yes. Of course." But even as I say the words, I have a sinking feeling in the pit of my stomach. Because do I? Do I really believe that?

Trevor is good-looking. Charming. Outgoing.

Not the kind of guy to sit home alone on a Friday night.

As much as I don't want to admit it, Jennie is right.

Trevor would not be sitting home alone on any night, Friday or otherwise.

Why would he? We haven't seen each other in six months.

Six months.

He calls every week.

We laugh. We talk. We have wonderful conversations about everything and nothing.

But then... nothing from him for the rest of the week.

"I'm busy," I say. "He's busy."

"You're right," Jennie says, but there's a little pout on her lips. "I'm sure you're right."

"Okay," I say. "I'll go out. With you. But not to meet anyone. Not for me."

Jennie's expression brightens.

"Are we going like this? Or putting on go-out clothes?"

"Go out clothes," I say. "If we're going out, let's do it right."

I would rather stay home. I've got some work I could be doing. But it's just one night.

What could it hurt?

OUT OF ASHES

PREVIEW

Chapter 2
McKenna

AFTER SHARING A PIZZA, Jennie and I walk next door to the little local bar.

That's one of the things I love about living downtown. Everything is right here within walking distance.

My own little rendition of New York City. My second choice of a place to live, after Houston, would be New York. I love the idea of not needing a car.

Houston is a driving city and I have a car for running errands and such, but the best days are those days when I just walk to work and back home again. I actually bought my condo downtown for the very reason that it was close to my work.

Jennie and I look good, if I do have to say so myself. We're both wearing solid black sequined cocktail dresses with sweetheart necklines.

But with her blonde hair and blue eyes, she's the one who turns men's heads.

We step into the little bar and find one seat left at the bar.

The music is loud. The conversations are louder.

Not only are all the seats taken, but there are a few people, like me, standing around. Unlike me, they're all holding drinks. Doing the Friday night thing.

What I call the mating ritual. They come here and even though they say they aren't looking for someone to hook up with, almost all of them are. Being an exception myself, I know there are others. There just aren't that many of us.

Jennie walks right up to that empty bar stool and sits down. Does a little flip thing with her hair. I stand back, waiting for a seat to open up.

The next thing I know, the man to her right is up, waving me over to sit on his stool.

"I'm okay, really," I say, walking close enough for him to hear me. "You don't have to get up."

"Anything for my new friend," the man says.

I look at Jennie. She just shrugs with a little smile.

I shake my head.

"What can I get you?" the bartender asks as he slides a cosmopolitan over in front of Jennie.

"Just water with lemon," I say. "How did you get that so fast?" I ask her.

"I have skills."

"Yes. You do. Impressive skills, too."

"Well. You already knew that."

Jennie is in her element. I had forgotten just how much being out like this was her element.

She takes a sip of her pretty pink drink. "You sure you don't want anything?"

"I had that beer."

"Which you barely even touched."

"I have lots of work to do tomorrow. I need a clear head."

"All work and no play…" she says.

"Hush now," I say. "I'm here, aren't I?"

"You are here," she agrees. "Reluctantly as it may be."

"What about your friend?" I ask, looking over my shoulder for the guy who gave up his seat for me. "Shouldn't you be talking to him?"

"Oh." She waves a hand. "I told him I'd find him later."

"I don't see how you do it," I say, picking up my glass of water and taking a sip. "I can see why you're not digging Dubai."

"I know, right?"

"You don't go out by yourself?"

She makes a face. "Not my style. It reeks of desperation."

"You are most certainly not a desperate woman."

"Nope," she says, flipping her hair back. "I'm just a girl who likes to have fun. After working hard, of course."

"Of course. So tell me how you really ended up back here?" I ask.

"Dubai was temporary."

"Oh." I shift on the bar stool, leaning away from a young man who squeezes in on my other side to place a drink order. "I thought you're heading back there. In what? Two months?"

"I don't think it'll be Dubai."

"Where then? And how did you get so lucky to get to travel the world?"

"Berlin maybe. At least that's what they're saying. And not so sure just how lucky I am. If you were with me, it would be different. But I'm not really into traveling the world by myself."

"I get it." I glance around at the people in the bar. People I've never seen before, despite living right above this place. "But this where I belong."

"I know." She puts a hand on my wrist. "I would never ask you to give up your dream of being a judge."

I shift a little uncomfortably. She's the only person who knows that being a judge is my dream. Jennie is the only person who knows a lot of things about me.

Even though we grew up together and shared every single thought with each other, I'm not really that person anymore. I'm creating a new life for myself.

A life where I'm a serious prosecutor not a giggling girl who shares everything with her best friend.

"Of course," I say. "I'm just going to find the restroom. Don't run off with anyone, okay?"

"I promise I will be right here when you get back. And I'll save your seat."

"Don't make promises you can't keep," I say before I start the process of weaving my way through the bar toward the restroom.

Once inside the restroom, I take a breath.

The noise level is several decibels lower in here than it was in the main part of the bar.

I can actually hear myself think.

Sitting on a stool in front of a gilded mirror, I refresh my lip gloss.

Two girls, giggling and obviously a little drunk walk around me like I'm not even there.

Bars have never really been my scene. Anytime I went, it was because Jennie wanted to go.

It was often entertaining. Mostly watching her talk to men. Get their hopes up. Then leave with me. Not saying she didn't get more than a few numbers and I'm pretty sure she even called a few of them.

I got a few numbers myself, but I never called them. I prefer to meet my guys the safe way. On the Internet. That way I have time to vet them properly before spending any actual time getting to know them.

It's worked well so far.

Just because my current boyfriend is halfway across the world has nothing to do with it.

I rather like it that way. It gives me more time to focus on my career.

I always feel like my life will be better if I can just get to the next level of my career.

I'm not even sure where I got that from. I didn't get it from my mother. She was content to stay home take care of the house. I didn't get it from my father. He was content to just work. Earn his pay and go home.

And they're doing what all successfully retired parents do. They're traveling.

I'm the only person in my life who isn't traveling.

I don't even like traveling.

There are airline schedules. Hotels. Rental cars.

In my experience, there is nothing fun about spending the night in a strange place. Worrying about checkout times. Where to get coffee and breakfast.

Where to get anything.

I like my routine. My home. My schedule.

I like knowing what I'm going to do and where I'm going to be from one day to the next.

It's okay to not like travel.

Just because everyone else is doing it doesn't mean I have to do it.

I glance at the time on my phone and wonder how much longer before I can convince Jennie that it's time to go home.

Heading back toward our seats at the bar, a sense of panic sweeps over me.

Jennie isn't where I left here. Two other people are sitting in our seats. I wasn't gone THAT long. She promised she wouldn't leave without me.

Headlines flash through my head.

Young lady last seen at bar. Never seen again.

Then I see her on the dance floor with her new friend along with a dozen other people crowded into the little dance area.

Relief washes through me.

I'm such an overprotective friend. But then in my work, my focus is on sending people who hurt people like Jennie to prison.

It's just my everyday world.

It's like the firetrucks that no one notices.

But I notice.

It's my world.

OUT OF ASHES
PREVIEW

Chapter 3
McKenna

I'm good at making the best of wherever I am.

I wrangle my way up to the bar and order myself a fresh sparkling water with lime.

Then I find an empty chair to sit in while I wait for Jennie to close the place down.

As much as I'm ready to go home, I know how she is. She'll close the place down. And being the good friend that I am, I won't leave her alone. Too many things could go awry.

She's still dancing with the same guy. That's not so unusual.

As I sit there, with the loud music spilling over me, I reflect on my day.

It was a good day.

I put another person behind bars.

The girl sitting next to me gets up and a minute later, a man sits down next to me.

"Hi," he says. "What's a girl like you doing sitting here by herself?"

"Just waiting for my friend," I say.

"Doesn't sound like a good way to spend a Friday night. Just waiting."

"I have a boyfriend," I say.

"It's okay," he says, holding up his hands. "Just looking for some conversation."

I take a second to study him. He looks like a nice enough guy. The kind of guy I work with. He could even be an attorney. But fortunately I don't recognize him. I don't care to be spotted hanging out in a bar, even if I am just drinking sparkling water.

I've got my reputation to protect. The one my future judge-seeking self will appreciate one day.

"Okay," I say. "Tell me about you."

"I'm Adam and I'm in a band."

I look at him again and try to keep a straight face.

"You don't look like the kind of guy who's in a band," I say.

"It's my night off."

I think about the concert pianist. I've never known him

to miss a night. Unless he's in a concert. Musicians don't take days off.

But I decide not to confront him.

At least not directly.

"Okay Adam. What's your day job?"

He looks crestfallen. Like I've just seen straight through his game.

"I'm an accountant," he says.

I nod. "You look like an accountant."

"Well then," he says. "I'll have to work on that, won't I?"

"Yes—" I glance in Jennie's direction. My job, after all, is to make sure she doesn't become one of those girls who goes missing and is never seen again.

But it's not Jennie that catches my attention. It's the man sitting alone behind her.

In just that one instant, recognition slides along my spine and somehow settles like a bur in the back of my throat.

I know that man.

I spent days looking at his face across a courtroom. And that was after days of looking at his face in a case file in preparation for that trial.

He wasn't supposed to ever see the outside of a prison.

And what's more. He's watching me. With his bottomless black eyes. I may not can see them across the room, but I spent enough time looking into them that I'll never forget them.

In that instant, I realize that not only did I spend days looking at him, he spent those same days looking at me.

"I'm sorry," I murmur to the man sitting next to me as I pull out my phone. "I have to…"

I stare at the message on my screen.

MILES

You should know. He's out.

There's more to the message, but I don't need to read it. I'll read it later.

I know exactly who he's talking about. He's talking about Silas Crowe.

My most difficult and heaviest case. Silas Crowe killed his girlfriend.

The evidence was irrefutable and I convinced a jury of that. They put him away for life.

Or so it was supposed to be.

But things happen. They happen all the time.

People get out of prison for all sorts of reasons.

Reasons I can't even think about right now. There are too many to name.

As I fist my hands together in my lap, keeping my face expressionless, I force myself to do the math.

Silas Crowe has been in prison for four years. Some days I don't even think about him, at least not much more than in passing.

He'd made my reputation. No one thought it could be done.

But I'd been young and determined. Fearless.

I hadn't thought about the possibility that he might get out of prison.

That he might be sitting across a bar not far from my home, looking at me.

Cold. Calculating.

Even across the room, I see those cold, calculating snake eyes watching me. He looks the way he'd looked in the photos I'd studied. Before the trial. Bearded. Scraggly.

He doesn't belong here. His clothes are wrong, but no one pays him any mind. He's wearing tan pants with a blue shirt. Some kind of uniform. I can't make out the words stitched on his pocket.

How can no one notice that he doesn't belong here? They walk around him like he's a piece of furniture. Old furniture. He's in his mid-thirties, but could easily pass for fifty years old.

There's nothing in his hands. No drink. He's so obviously here for the sole reason of finding me.

He's gotten out and he's tracked me down.

Other than my hands fisting around my phone, I don't move a muscle.

Adam is saying something, but I don't hear him.

I turn to look at him, force a smile onto my face.

"Adam," I say. "How would you like to do a good deed tonight?"

"I'm always up for a good deed," he drawls. "What's in it for me?"

"Knowing you saved a life."

A little dramatic perhaps, but I need his help.

Jennie is between me and Silas Crowe. Approaching Jennie means getting far too close to Silas.

"What's the favor?" Adam asks, still hoping there's something in it for him, no doubt.

"See that girl on the dance floor? The pretty blonde wearing the black dress?"

"I see her."

"Walk up to her. Say *there's an emergency and McKenna needs to leave.*"

"That's it?"

"That's it. Say it back."

"There's an emergency and McKenna needs to leave."

"Now. If she resists, add *now.*"

"You do look kind of pale."

I turn and look in Adam's brown eyes. "Because there's an emergency. This is urgent, Adam. Life or death. Will you help me?"

"Sure. Sure. I'll do it."

"Good. Do it now."

"I got this," Adam says.

Under other circumstances, I might find this amusing. But there is nothing amusing about it right now.

I keep my gaze on Silas Crowe as Adam makes his way over to Jennie.

Adam looks back at me just before he taps Jennie on the shoulder and delivers the message.

Jennie's gaze lands on mine.

Maybe she sees the shock on my face.

She won't know what's wrong, but she doesn't need to know right now.

All she needs to know is that we need to get out of here. Now.

She says something to her friend and dance partner.

He doesn't want to let go of her hand. To her credit, Jennie pulls loose and follows Adam back in my direction.

It occurs to me then that I can't let Silas Crowe see me talking to Jennie.

The thought crashes into my head that I might be too late.

Refusing to accept the possibility, I stand up and whirl around heading back to the restroom. Jennie will know to follow me.

She'll know.

Inside the restroom, after checking to make sure I'm alone, I lean against the wall and wait for Jennie to join me.

"What's wrong?" she asks, coming through the door.

"You don't know me," I say, turning the door lock. "Okay? From here on out, you do not know me."

"Okay." Her brow creases in concern. "What happened?"

Panic gathers in my throat.

"McKenna. Sit down."

I drop onto the vanity chair where I sat earlier.

"There was a case. About four years ago. My first big case. You might remember it. A man killed his girlfriend."

"Of course I remember. It's all you talked about for months."

"It's all I thought about for months." I shove at my hair. Breathe in. Breathe out.

Jennie leans on the counter. Puts a hand on my shoulder. Waits.

Someone tries the doorknob. When it doesn't open, they knock.

"Just a minute," Jennie says.

"He's here," I say, my voice barely more than a whisper.

"Here. Where?"

"Out there. In the bar. Silas Crowe. He... he saw me."

"But how? Didn't he get the death penalty?"

"Yes. I don't know how. I just know he's out there."

Jennie pales and drops onto the edge of the chair next to me.

"Are you sure?"

I hold up my phone where the text message is still front and center.

"You think he found you?"

"Yes." I don't want to think it. I want to think it's random. But it can't be random. It's too much to be random.

I have a very vivid memory of the words Silas Crowe spoke to me as they carried him away after the verdict.

He'd been wearing a light gray suit that was too big for

him. A gaunt man, wasting away in jail. His face clean-shaven, too clean-shaven. So different from his photos. Hollowed out cheeks. Thin lips. Eyes full of hate and evil that he could turn on and off at will.

With the full extent of that evil turn on, he looked right into my eyes as he walked past, hands safely cuffed behind his back. "You'll pay for this." He hissed the words through gapped teeth, spitting them at me like a venomous snake.

I'd felt safe. Stupidly safe. And I'd been so stupidly proud of myself in that moment. Ignoring the chills that he gave me. I'd held me head high and I hadn't looked away.

I'd won.

I'd sent the bad guy away.

But now the bad guy was out of prison and he was here. He'd found me.

"We have to get out of here," I say, hugging my stomach that threatened to roil with the shock of it all.

"Okay. He'll see us leave."

"There will be no us," I say. "He can't see us together."

"What then?"

I have to think. I have to figure this out.

"You leave first. Go straight to my condo. Take your new guy friend if you can."

"Okay."

"I'll call an Uber." My hands shake as I unlock my phone. "Drive around for a minute, then meet you at home."

"It's so cloak and dagger," Jennie says.

"Jennie." I grab her hand. "He's dangerous. He's a dangerous man. Do you understand?"

"Yes. I understand." She stands up. "I'll see you at your condo."

I stand up and hug her. "I love you."

"Love you, too. Now. Let's get out of here."

"Wait." I put a hand on her arm. Keep her there while I call the concierge. Explain that Jennie will be heading up before me. To let her in. Only her.

I've never had a problem with security. My building is secure. No one gets in without clearance. But I have to make sure they let Jennie up to my condo.

I press my door key into her hand.

"Don't look at him," I say.

"How could I? I don't know what he looks like."

"Good. All the better. Now go."

I unlock the bathroom door, letting the line of women spill in.

They look at me, full of questions and irritation at holding up the bathroom. I don't care.

I stand against the wall. Waiting. Biding my time. Giving Jennie a head start.

I check the time on my phone. Five minutes. It's only been five minutes since I ducked in here, but it feels like an eternity.

It could easily take her five minutes to convince her new friend that she needs him to walk her home. She needs a good reason. I should have helped her with a reason. But she's smart. She'll think of something.

The women leave the restroom and more come in. I ignore them.

I'm just a girl hiding out in the restroom. It happens. For all they know, I'm hiding from an abusive boyfriend.

Doesn't matter.

I check the time again.

It's been ten minutes now.

I've been in here too long. Silas Crowe is going to wonder why I'm in here.

I quickly schedule an Uber. Two minutes out.

It'll take me two minutes to get out of here and meet the Uber outside.

If he followed me here, he already knows where I live.

Can't think about that right now. Anyway, I'm not walking outside by myself.

Leaving the restroom, I see him still sitting there in his out-of-place clothes. A girl with a ponytail is talking to him.

What's wrong with people? I may never go to a bar again.

It's too dangerous. Anyone could be lurking about. We joke about accidentally meeting serial killers at places like this. But it really does happen.

There really are killers among us and no one realizes it.

I feel obligated to warn her away from him.

But that obligation is overridden by my own survival instincts.

I step outside into the night air, still warm from the day's sunshine just as my Uber pulls up to the curb.

"The Galleria?" he asks.

"Yes." I sit back. Bide my time. Watch out the back window to see if anyone follows. They don't. Silas Crowe would not expect me to get into a car.

Patience is not easy in this situation.

I send Jennie a text.

Are you home?

JENNIE
Yes. Just got inside. Where
are you?

Lock the door.

"Something's come up," I tell my driver. Can you take me back downtown?"

OUT OF ASHES

PREVIEW

Chapter 4

McKenna

Safely back in my condo, I crash onto the sofa and close my eyes.

"I'm so sorry about that," I tell Jennie who's texting her new friend. "What's his name?"

"James."

"What did you tell him?" I open my eyes and look at her.

"Just that something came up and my friend needed me."

"Vague enough."

"Don't worry about that." She sets her phone aside. "What are you going to do about that Silas guy?"

"I don't know yet. I'll talk to Miles tomorrow."

"Miles?"

"My boss. He'll know what to do. Not that there's anything we can do. But at least we'll have more information."

"I'm glad I'm staying here with you while I'm stateside."

"Me too. I'm going to get some sleep."

"Good idea." Jennie is texting again. She'll probably be up all night texting the guy. James. But I'm too exhausted to care. Besides, it's her business.

I'm the one with the serial killer tracking me down.

Jennie is just a girl doing her thing.

I go to the balcony door, lock it, and look out on the city that just hours ago had made me so happy. Now all I can think about is Silas Crowe being out there somewhere.

He's supposed to be behind bars.

"Do you really think he tracked you down?" Jennie asks. "Or do you think he just ended up here?"

"What are the odds of him just randomly showing up in bar below my condo?"

"Good point. I wonder how he got out of prison."

"I'll find out tomorrow. He won't be out long. He'll do something stupid and get himself thrown back in."

"I just hope he doesn't hurt anyone again."

"We have to be careful," I say.

"You might have to move. At least for awhile."

"I won't let him run me out of my home."

"Do what you have to do, McKenna. To stay alive." She sweeps a hand around my little condo. "It's just a place. I know it's yours and I know you're attached to it, but in the end, it's just a place."

"How did you get so wise?" I ask.

"I'm not wise," Jennie says. "You can remind me I said that when I finally have a place of my own."

"Don't worry. I'll remind you."

"Don't worry," Jennie says. "Whatever happens, everything will be okay."

"I know. You're the best."

I try not to think about how if Jennie hadn't wanted to go out, I wouldn't have seen Silas Crowe tonight.

It's not her fault. If he tracked me down, he would have found me somewhere else.

Maybe it's better that he found me in a public place instead finding me alone on a street.

Everything happens for a reason.

I just hate it that what had been such a good day had to end on a such a negative note.

But tomorrow will be another day.

Everything will look better tomorrow.

Keep Reading Out of Ashes...

Secrets and Second Chances

Honeymoon with a Stranger

Not Our Wedding

(SILVER PINES)

The Way Back to You

Back to Where We Began

When We Were Us

(ONCE UPON FOREVER)

My Forever Guy

Our Forever Love

Forever Vows

Finding Forever

Accidentally Forever

(TRUE NORTH)

Borrowed Until Monday

Still Mine

The Moon and the Stars at Christmas

Perfectly Mismatched

On the Way to Forever

A Merry Little Christmas

On the Way Home to Christmas

It was Always You

(UNBREAK MY HEART)

Begin Again

Love Again

Falling Again

(FOR THE LOVE OF THE FLIGHT)

Just Stay

Just Chance

Just Believe

Just Us

Just Once

Just Happened

Just Maybe

Just Pretend

Just Because

(MAGNETIC NORTH)

Second Chance Kisses

Second Chance Secrets

First Time Charm

Three Broken Rules

Second Chance Destiny

Unexpected Vows

(FALLING FOR CHRISTMAS)

The Heart of Christmas

The Magic of Christmas

In a One Horse Open Sleigh

A Secret Royal Christmas

An Old Fashioned Christmas

(CITY SKYLINE BILLIONAIRES)

Billionaire's Unexpected Landing

Billionaire's Accidental Girlfriend

Billionaire's Fallen Angel

Billionaire's Secret Crush

Billionaire's Barefoot Bride

(TRULY, MADLY, DEEPLY)

The Lady in the Red Dress

On the Edge of Chance

Sealed with a Kiss

Kiss Me at Midnight

The Heart Knows

(STOLEN ECHOES)

When Cupid's Arrow Strikes

Chasing Fireflies

A Chance Encounter

(EDGE OF THE HORIZON)

The Forever Equation

Pretend Boyfriend

All our Tomorrows

Kissing for Keeps

Out of the Blue

The Princess and the Playboy

(RED LIPSTICK KISSES)

Red Lipstick Kisses and Small Town Wishes

Stolen Dances and Big City Chances

Chance Connections and Upside Down Plans

A Christmas Kiss on the Twenty-Fifth

Believe in the Magic of Christmas

Vows of Inheritance Series

(Reading Order)

Vow to Protect

Vow to Redeem

ROMANTASY

(IN THE SPIRIT OF LOVE)

Spirits of the Heart

Out of Dreams and Ashes

Etched Upon the Heart

WESTERN ROMANCE

(LONE STAR HEARTS)

Wanted by a Texas Ranger

Saved by a Texas Ranger

(WHISKEY SPRINGS)

Finding Natalie

Promising Samantha

Falling for Allyson

Saving Savannah

Claiming Charlie

Rescuing Keira

Protecting Gabriella

Courting Isabella

TIME TRAVEL

(INTO THE MIST)

Written in the Wind

Scripted in the Stars

Destined in the Twilight

Promised in the Mist

Trapped in the Melody

(DRAGON'S BLOOD)

Dragon's Blood

Lavender Blue

Champagne Silver

Twilight Frost

Mountbatten Pink

(WHEN HEARTSTRINGS BECKON)

Rescued in Time

Meet me in 1879

(WHEN HEARTSTRINGS ECHO)

Messages Across Time

Falling Through to Forever

Once Upon a Winter's Spell

(BECKONED)

Before the Storm

Twist of Fate

When the Stars Align

Once Upon a Christmas

Once in a Blue Moon

A Wish Upon a Star

(BEGUILED)

When Lightning Strikes

Storm of Time

Midnight Storm

When the Moon Falls

Stormborn Angel

(SPELLED)

Time Tempest

The Heart Remembers

A Moment in Time

Moonlight Shadows

HISTORICAL

(TAPESTRY OF BLUE AND GRAY)

Shadows Beneath Magnolia Blooms

Secrets Among Southern Roses

(IT HAPPENED BY ACCIDENT)

Accidentally Alluring

Accidentally Married

(SOUTHERN BELLE CIVIL WAR)

Beyond Enemy Lines

Love Always

Hearts Under Siege

Hearts Under Fire

Away Down South in Dixie

The Reluctant Bride

Stay with Me

Jasmine Kisses

Magnolia Kisses

Gardenia Kisses

(THE QUINNS)

Wait for Me

Take Me Home

Keep Me Safe

FATED MATES

Riley's Mate

Aiden's Mate

Brayden's Mate

STANDALONE SUSPENSE

Lost and Found

All I Want for Christmas

Serenity

Courting Alley Cat

All of the books in each Series are standalone and can be read out of order. However, some books have characters from the previous stories in them.

Sign up for my NEWSLETTER to get all my romance releases, sales, Kickstarter announcements, and a **FREE** romance, SEALED WITH A KISS